DANCING IN A
DISTANT PLACE

DANCING IN A DISTANT PLACE

Isla Dewar

review

First published in 2003
by HEADLINE BOOK PUBLISHING

A REVIEW softback

10 9 8 7 6 5 4 3 2 1

ISBN 0 7553 0079 3

Typeset in Cochin by Avon DataSet Ltd,
Bidford-on-Avon, Warwickshire

Printed and bound in Great Britain by
Clays Ltd, St Ives plc

HEADLINE BOOK PUBLISHING
A division of Hodder Headline
338 Euston Road
London NW1 3BH

www.reviewbooks.co.uk
www.hodderheadline.com

For Bob

I have many people to thank for their help with this book. Sibyl and Gordon, for their warmth and generosity, hot soup, scones, wine, laughter, and willingness to dip into and share their knowledge of country school life. Bob, my husband, for his endless encouragement and enthusiasm, and for being there every evening, ready to listen to my writing day.

I am also indebted to my editor, Marion Donaldson, and my agent, Jo Frank, for their suggestions and advice, but mostly I'd like to thank them for caring.

The Missie

A crowded bar in Glasgow, a shiny place, chrome and glass and very noisy, a constant thrum and babble, conversations and laughter. Too noisy for Iris, really, though she loves the city, the movement, the bustle. It's raining outside, a thin soaking drizzle, streaming endlessly. Cars hiss past on the road. She watches the world through the window, slightly steamed, and glowing reflections. She can see herself, though tries not to. Her face always surprises her these days. How did that happen to it? Not the lines and wrinkles, she knows how they got there. Time and worry have done that. Like they have to all the familiar faces round the table tonight. No, it's the slightly mournful look that seeps into her eyes, a deepening sadness. She remembers times past, and always, always she thinks, I could have done better. She is hard on herself. All her life she has found it difficult to forgive herself her mistakes, or thinks, when considering a past situation or problem, that she could have done more, pushed herself further.

'Bloody weather,' she says. Everyone agrees.

But there is something lovely about the rain. Especially when you are looking at it from the warmth inside. Rivers of water run down the pane, lights gleam, reflected in pools on the pavement. An alluring glimmer.

A chill November night. Iris sits with her friends, and her daughter, Sophy. She drinks champagne, though she claims she does not like it. 'It's fizzy. And proper drink isn't fizzy.' She laughs. Her laughter is a song, loud, rhythmic. Her face wreathes into mirth. Tonight she wears a purple silk ankle-length skirt, a matching purple shirt, black velvet jacket. Round her neck, to cover time's cruelties, a pink silk scarf. In her small crowd, all well dressed but

1

more sombrely, she sticks out. In fact, she sticks out in the whole room. Eyes wander over to her. And it isn't just the clothes, it's the face – small, lively – and the extravagant, easy laughter. Iris loves that. Basks in those sidelong furtive stares.

They have come to the theatre. It was originally only going to be Iris and Chas, but then Sophy and her husband asked to come along. Then the Vernons, Stella and John, who she has known for more years than she likes to think she's known anybody. And Morag who she's known for longer even than the Vernons. But that doesn't matter because she has always known Morag. Only Scott is missing. He is an anthropologist based in Toronto.

Isn't it often the way? Iris thinks, looking round the table. It starts with just the two of you, then, turn around, blink your eyes, and there's a crowd. She notices a young man watching her, and smiles openly at him. She can do that now, she is old enough for it not to matter. This smile is just a smile. There is no secret sexual inference in it. No playing, no other meaning than a friendly upturn of the lips.

A drink first. A meal after the play. Then home. Iris will sleep with her head on Chas's shoulder. There are of course many, many more friends, but these, tonight, are her special people. She is seventy-four. Doesn't look it. Her face is smooth, just a few wrinkles round her eyes, and lips. 'But,' she says, 'I've earned those wrinkles. They're mine. Battle scars from a life of work and angst.' Her hair, once fair, the colour of corn stubble, is grey, but still with unruly curls that sneak across her cheeks. She notices the bottle has been moved.

'Oh, look at that. You put it out of my reach. You don't want me to drink too much and embarrass you.'

'Iris,' says Chas, 'you always embarrass us. You don't need drink to be embarrassing.'

She grins.

They have been together for over thirty years, not married. Iris won't marry, though Chas has asked her often. 'I'm not doing *that* again. Once is enough.'

She reaches for the bottle, refills her glass. 'Just a drop.'

Chas makes a face.

'You're cramping my style,' she says to him.

'I have never cramped your style. You were messy and loud-mouthed when I met you, and you're still messy and loud-mouthed.'

'You tell her,' says Sophy. 'I don't know how you put up with her.'

'He's madly in love with me,' says Iris. 'You have to admit he's got terrible taste in women.' And laughs.

'Laughing at your own jokes,' says Chas.

'Well, they're funnier than yours.'

'That's true. I'll give you that.' He loves her.

Not that she doesn't love him back. The sight of him across a crowded room, that beloved face, still moves her. Sometimes, even yet, when she sees him coming towards her she feels herself melt. He always made her smile, like she had done all those years ago when he'd turned up at her door with a basket piled high with vegetables. Over a hundred miles he'd driven with them, and all he said was, 'I brought your veg. I said I would. It was our deal.'

That was what had done it. He was someone who always kept their word. At the time, she'd needed that. Though, at the time, love was the last thing she'd been thinking of.

'Love,' she'd said to Morag. 'Don't want it. Don't need it.'

Morag had said, 'Oh, yeah?'

But love was a kind of sickness. It ruined your judgment. It made you vulnerable, fearful lest you weren't loved back. It made you worry that something might happen to the loved one. It hurt. No, she'd decided, she wasn't up for any of that.

'Love,' Iris said, 'I think the world would be an easier place if we didn't have any of it.'

'I think I'm hearing someone who is scared to commit,' said Morag. Thinking, She's fallen for Chas.

'Love,' said Iris, 'gets in the way of things. It stops you thinking. It makes you nervous. It halts you in your tracks, disrupts the flow of things. You're always on edge. What if the one you love goes away from you one way or another? No, I think the whole universe would tick along fine if everybody in the world just liked each other.'

She had thought she would settle for liking Chas a lot. But liking was not enough for Iris. She needed love, and how could she not love Chas? He fixed things. Everything. Not just blocked sinks, leaking roofs, errant vacuums, but people, situations. With a look, a smile, just by putting his hand on someone's arm, or saying something that stilled the room. Something shocking, but not insulting. There would be a moment's quiet as his words sank in, then the outrageousness of what he'd said would make them smile. And everything would be all right.

The young man across the room is still staring. He looks at Iris quizzically. He smiles. She tries to place him. The face is familiar, but only vaguely. But, for sure, he will be one of hers.

He comes over, stands before her. He wears jeans, suede boots that were probably very expensive, Iris doesn't know. She has long lost touch with such things. His jersey is soft, grey and expensive too, she thinks. His glasses are small, wire-framed, chic.

'Remember me?' he asks.

Iris considers him. He's lovely. She'll flirt. At her age she can flirt with anybody and get away with it. 'Give me a minute,' she says.

'Colin,' he tells her, leaning down slightly.

'Colin!' says Iris. 'My God, Colin!'

The whole group responds in the same way. 'Colin!' they say.

It hovers on Iris's lips to remind him that he used to be small and fat, and wore lumpen woolly jumpers his gran knitted for him. But she decides against it. No, she won't say that. Besides, looking at this man, she knows he has left that small, tubby, insecure boy far behind him. Some people you meet still have the disturbed, misunderstood child they were inside them, waiting to come out weeping and tell the world their woes. But Colin seems well, balanced, happy even. How do people manage that? It's a mystery, Iris thinks. 'So, what are you doing now?' she asks.

'I'm a journalist.'

'A journalist?' She's delighted. 'It's all my good teaching. Good grammar will get you everywhere.'

'I remember,' says Colin. 'You and your grammar.' He nods. For a moment he's eight again, and Iris is before him, talking about singulars and plurals and apostrophes. And he's wrestling with it all, working with a stubby pencil, chewed at the end.

'The grammar these days,' expounds Iris. 'I don't know. You see it in the papers, hear it on the radio. It's appalling. Of course they don't teach it the way I did nowadays. Teaching's changed. You can't even touch your pupils these days. Some of the little ones need the odd cuddle. Mind you, it's a good thing teachers don't have to do some of the things I had to do. Still, folk do not know what to do with an apostrophe.'

There is a stiffness round the table, people expecting a lecture on the correct way to commit collective ownership on to a page. Where to put the apostrophe? Before or after the s?

Grammar is one of Iris's passions, along with the Amazonian rain forest, the plight of whales and dolphins, oil pollution, the imminent extinction of many birds and animals, including tigers, which are her favourite. The recent demise in the population of sparrows, larks. The profusion of rhododendrons that is slowly, slowly squeezing out native blooms. Starvation anywhere it turns up. Oh, the list of Iris's causes is long, as is the list of people she writes to. Most world leaders, every newspaper in the land, MPs, the Chancellor of the Exchequer (she takes great exception to the effect the price of petrol has on rural communities) have all received a missive from Iris. Only last month she wrote to the President of the United States complaining about the mutilation of manatees by high-speed boats in the seas round Florida. So far, though, no reply. She plans to drop him another note reminding him of the manatees and pointing out how rude it is not to answer when people get in touch.

Colin looks across at a woman who is waiting for him. 'I must go. But I had to come over and say hello.'

'Well, hello,' says Iris. 'And sorry I didn't recognise you. You're so grown-up and sophisticated.' Then she remembers. 'I thought you were going to grow up and marry me? You said you would.'

'No,' says Colin. 'You said you would never marry me because I couldn't tie my laces.'

'Ah, well, as I've got older I've lowered my standards. You can marry me now.'

'I don't think my wife would like it.' He takes her hand, her small one in both of his. 'I've always wanted to thank you for, you know . . .' He's suddenly shy, searching for the right word. 'Caring.'

'How could I not have cared about you, Colin?' she says. You were such a soul, such a poor little soul. She doesn't say that, for it would surely embarrass him. The little soul he was is gone. Left long ago in a tiny village with a phone box, a sparse little shop, and a road running through it.

'And how's Ella?' says Iris.

'Still going strong. Past eighty now. Plays a mean game of whist. Buys a Lottery ticket every Saturday. Bakes for the WRI. She's expecting her first great-grandchild in six months, she's knitting already.'

'Congratulations,' says Iris, for the baby will have to be Colin's. He was the only grandchild. 'Your gran was always a knitter.' And they smile, remembering the dire garments she produced.

'I have to go,' he says. 'My wife is waiting.' He squeezes her hand. 'Take care.'

'Taking care cramps my style,' says Iris.

He moves back across the room to an elegant woman waiting for him at the door.

But Iris never can resist a bit of gentle mockery. 'Hey, Colin,' she says, loud enough for everyone in the bar to hear, 'have you still got my plate?'

He smiles, puts his hand to his face in shame, remembering one of those humbling moments that sneak up when the mind idles. He nods. 'As a matter of fact, I have. Do you want it back?'

She shakes her head.

At the door to the bar, Colin looks back. Gives Iris a swift wave.

'Who is that?' asks his wife.

'That's the Missie.'

His wife stares. A look. So that's her.

'Oh, I know that look,' says Sophy. 'She's putting a face to all the stories she's heard. She'll know all about you.' And so, she thinks, will hundreds of wives and husbands of people who sat in Iris's classrooms. She was one of those teachers. Ask any of them who was their favourite teacher, who made a difference to their life, and they'd all say, 'Mrs Chisholm.' Though Sophy could tell other stories. About Iris the mother, for instance.

Iris watches. Notices the curve of Colin's cheek as he leans into his wife, and sees, for a moment, the boy he was. The silent, watchful child. She thinks of a line from Robert Burns: '. . . *a cheild's amang you takin' notes*'. That was Colin, observing the world, drinking it in, taking notes.

Sometimes that's all it takes, a little thing – a song on the radio, the sound of a blackbird making his five o'clock claim to the garden, the smell of chrysanthemums on the kitchen table, the sound of bells on a Sunday morning, children's laughter, chalk, notebooks, a lawn mower in the distance, a dog barking, all sorts of things, different things – to set her reminiscing. And she's back there, in that tiny place, all those years ago.

A distant place she lived in, danced in. She always remembers the dancing in the schoolroom when the light outside was fading and music inside hurtled into a wild stomp. She remembers mornings, standing, small in the school doorway, clanging her bell, and the children coming running.

Isn't it Strange How You Know?

Tuesday morning, eleven o'clock, February 1968. There were rumblings of trouble in Czechoslovakia, the Beatles were in the charts, Iris's girl pupils all wore skirts that stopped three inches short of their knees and most of them were in love with Paul McCartney. The boys favoured George Best. And her life was about to change.

Iris can remember every detail of the moment. She was talking to her class about Christopher Columbus. 'What year did Columbus set sail, Myra?'

'Fourteen hundred and ninety-two, miss.' The reply came as a chant.

'Excellent. And what was the name of his ship?'

'The *Santa Maria*.'

'Very good. And what else do we know about him, John?'

'He was deaf in one ear, miss.'

'Was he? I don't think so.'

'Yes, miss. And when someone said something to him that he didn't want to know about, he listened with his deaf ear so he wouldn't hear it.'

'I think we are getting Columbus mixed up with Nelson who was blind in one eye,' said Iris, wearily. We? Why did she always say 'we'? She was not involved in this misconception. She walked to the window. Back turned to the class, she said, 'George, what is that you are eating?'

'Nothing, miss.'

It was February. A chill and cloudy day, the frost hadn't melted on the grass in the park across the road. The trees were bare. The roads icy. A bird floated in the air, level with her second-floor window. Behind her the class moved, and sighed. She heard rustlings and whispers. 'Who gave Columbus the money for his voyage?' The soft sound of arms being raised. A police car moved out of the flow of traffic and into the school grounds. It stopped at the front door, and two policemen got out. They spoke across the roof of their car, breath spanning out as it hit the bitter air. Iris watched, and knew they were coming for her. She didn't crystallise this knowledge into thought. It was just there, a certainty, a tremor in her stomach.

'King Ferdinand and his wife Isabella funded the trip. And on the third of August Columbus set sail in the *Santa Maria*. Two other ships accompanied him, the *Pinta* and the *Nina*. There were one hundred and twenty men in all. And where did they go, George?'

'Australia, miss.'

'That was Cook. Today, in case you haven't noticed, we're talking about Columbus,' Iris said.

Miss Moffat's face appeared in the glass panel of the classroom door, creased with anxiety. She signalled Iris out into the corridor. Iris felt her own face freeze into an ashen look of foreboding.

'There's two policemen to see you, dear. In my room. I'll take your class,' said the headmistress.

The 'dear' came out softly. Miss Moffat touched Iris's arm, nodded, and let her lips slip into the gentlest of smiles. Iris knew something awful had happened. Fear spread through her, prickled across her scalp.

The policemen filled Miss Moffat's room. Two huge people, smelling of cold that clung to their uniforms. A good room, Iris always thought. Dark wallpaper, a fire in the grate, the comforting sound of flames pushing through coals. There was a green velvet-covered sofa by the window. Plants lined the window sill. Books on the wall opposite Miss Moffat's polished and tidy desk.

'Iris Chisholm?' asked the older policeman.

She nodded, and sank on to the sofa. She no longer trusted her legs to keep her upright.

'Your husband is Henry Chisholm?'

'Yes.'

'He drives a red Volvo estate car, registration number . . .'

'Please,' said Iris, 'what has happened?'

Sounds. A car's tyres humming on the road outside. The movement of heavy material, the black coats the policemen wore. A teacher shouting, 'Don't run in the corridor.' A blackbird in the park across the road clacking alarm. The air in the room was stiff with shock, hurt, pain.

'Your husband was driving along Maybury Road at nine o'clock this morning. He moved out to overtake a Renault in front of him, lost control on the ice and hit a lamppost.'

'Is he all right?' Iris asked. She hoped. But she knew Harry was not all right.

'I'm afraid he's dead,' said the policeman.

Iris could see he was wrestling with this. He'd considered other ways to put it, gentler ways. But in the end, there it was. He had to tell her. She felt momentarily sorry for him. But the horror of the news stilled her heart. 'Dead? Harry?'

This couldn't be. Only this morning, in the midst of the routine, everyday bustle – cheery DJ on the radio playing the Kinks' 'Waterloo Sunset', Scott playing Canned Heat upstairs, Sophy doing her French homework at the kitchen table, toast singeing under the grill – they'd had a small tiff about his grey coat, which Iris had taken to the cleaner's without telling him.

'It was grubby,' she said.

'I like that coat. It's my only warm coat.'

'You'll be in the car,' said Iris. 'Then in the office. You won't be wearing a coat in there.' He'd given a disgruntled, 'Hmm,' and gone upstairs to get his raincoat. 'No warmth in this at all,' he told her.

'I hate that grey coat,' said Sophy. 'It's an old man's coat. You look like Winston Churchill in it.'

'How do you know what Winston Churchill looked like in a grey coat?' Harry said.

Iris shrugged. 'Sorry. I thought you'd be pleased. I'll pick it up tomorrow.'

Harry made a thick, unhappy, nasal sound; kissed her cheek, lightly. A small placatory peck. Made for the door. 'There's nothing

11

wrong with looking like Winston Churchill,' he told Sophy. And left.

'What was he doing on the Maybury Road? That's nowhere near his work.'

The policeman didn't know.

'Only he'd said he was to be in the office all day. He didn't have his warm coat.'

There, that was it. It couldn't be Harry. He didn't have the right coat with him. It was some other man, possibly a man who'd had the right coat, who had died.

'The victim was wearing a light beige raincoat,' said the policeman. He looked at Iris, a soft, steady gaze, and saw her torment. He'd been in the force for twenty years, and knew about moments like this. The strange things people said. The turmoil that took over their minds. He knew about clutching at straws.

Iris identified Harry's body. The look on his face, which would remain etched into her memory for the rest of her life, was not, as she had hoped, contented or beatific. It was tortured, the horror of that fleeting moment when he knew what was about to happen clearly reflected.

'That's Harry,' she said, and stood looking at him. Poor Harry. It was the end of him. And she would go on, breathing, moving through the world they'd once inhabited together – alone. She could not help thinking that if he'd had on his grey coat he'd have been warmer when the end came. He must have been cold when he died. Maybe if he'd had on the right coat he wouldn't have gone to Maybury Road. Guilt descended. It was all her fault.

She collected Sophy and Scott from school, took them home. Sat them at the kitchen table and told them their father was dead. She was wringing her hands as she spoke and, unable to find a suitably tactful, soothing way to let them know of their loss, blurted it out. They said nothing. Scott stared at the matching salt and pepper set. Sophy twirled a strand of her hair round her fingers.

'He ran into a lamppost,' said Iris.

Scott snorted.

'Was it sore?' said Sophy.

'I think he died before he felt any pain,' Iris told her. 'I think it was all so sudden he didn't feel anything.'

Scott snorted again. And Iris shot him a look. Let her believe. The news seemed to pin them to their chairs. Sophy started to cry, a whimper that grew into a howl.

Iris put her arms round her. 'You cry. Go on, cry. It's all right.'

Scott put his hand on Iris's shoulder. She turned to look at him. 'We'll be OK,' he said.

Scott's hand, long, bony, young and slightly cold. He's a nice boy, Iris thought. That must be Harry's influence. It couldn't be mine. She was coming to think that she had no right to be alive when her husband wasn't.

Iris phoned Ruby, Harry's mother, and gave her the news. She arrived soon after, grieving, and ready to bustle. To whisper, fuss and watch Iris, and make tea. To do anything that would keep her hands busy, and stop her from thinking about what had happened.

'She hasn't cried once,' said Ruby to her neighbour next day. 'Not a tear.'

'She will,' said the neighbour. 'It's all in there. She's holding it back. And once the floodgates open, well . . .' She shook her head, knowing the volume of tears to come.

'You never think your own are going to go before you,' sighed Ruby.

'It must be hard,' said the neighbour.

Ruby nodded. It was hard. But she was used to hard, expected it. 'Aye,' she'd say, lips tightening. 'It's as well we don't know what's coming. We'd probably do away with ourselves.'

And if Iris hadn't shed a tear for her son, Ruby had shed many. She cried for the child he'd been, the chubby blue-eyed baby, hair the colour of sand who was lost to her. And the boy in his sailor suit who'd held her hand every Sunday morning when she'd taken him to Sunday School to learn stories from the Bible. And the teenager who'd left school at fifteen to work in Leith docks, cycling off into the morning, trousers tucked into his socks, whistling. And the young man who'd joined the Air Force when the Second World War broke out, hoping to fly, but was too short-sighted to become a pilot and had ended up a sergeant, always on the ground, a mechanic fixing planes. And how glad Ruby had been at that. Her Harry was safe. How grand he'd looked in his uniform, though. She had a framed photograph of him on the dresser in the living room. Smiling, but only slightly, a thin moustache on his upper lip making him look like David Niven. In 1946, he'd left the Air Force and come home to his old job. Something to do with warehouses in the docks. He'd married five years later when he was thirty-six. A small ceremony at Leith Register Office. Ruby had been beginning to despair of his ever finding someone. There had been a certain shame in having such a grown-up son still living at home. But he'd fallen for Iris and soon she'd presented him with two children of his own. Ruby was a grandmother, and happy to be one. And she'd had little baby grandchildren at a time when her friends all had teenagers coming round for Sunday lunch. She was the envy of them all.

Then, suddenly, surprisingly, Harry had got old. Sometimes Ruby thought he was older than her. He'd always been thin but he became positively sparse. His skin was grey, and a dense scattering of worry lines appeared round his eyes, at the corners of his mouth. In the last few years he'd taken to dropping by to see her in the middle of the afternoon.

'Shouldn't you be at work?' Ruby would say.

'What's the point of being the boss if you can't sneak an hour or two off to come visit your old mum?' he'd reply.

'But you're not the boss. You've got people above you. That Tom Oliver, isn't he the boss? He'll be noticing this, you skipping off in the middle of the day.'

'I'm boss enough to take an hour or two to come for a cup of tea.'

And she would smile at that, tell him to sit himself down by the fire while she fetched him a cup of tea. He would sink into the armchair and stare into the flickering grate. He'd never been tall, about five foot ten, but these days looked smaller. Tired. His pale hair, once sandy, turning grey, as was the David Niven moustache. Sometimes Ruby would return to the room, the promised cup of tea on a tray with a selection of biscuits and fruit cake, and Harry would be sound asleep. She'd let him be, watching him, thinking how thin he was. At four o'clock she would gently shake him awake and tell him she'd made him a bite to eat, a steak pie or bacon and eggs. 'I doubt that Iris is feeding you,' she'd say reproachfully.

He would smile and say Iris was feeding him well enough. But he always ate what he was offered. Several times, after he'd visited, Ruby had noticed money missing from her purse. At first she convinced herself she was mistaken. Must have miscounted the amount she'd had. But at last she admitted to herself that Harry must have taken it. Well, she thought, he must need it. Maybe the kids were asking for things he couldn't afford. Or maybe Iris wasn't managing their money very well. Young ones these days, she thought, it's all spend, spend, spend. She herself managed money well, and had thousands in the bank that Harry would tease her about. 'How much have you got salted away?' he'd ask.

'Enough,' Ruby would say briskly.

'Enough for what?' he wanted to know.

'Enough so you won't ever have to bother about keeping me when I'm old, or burying me when I'm gone,' she'd say. Though in fact she had a good deal more than enough for either of those things. She had enough to seriously impress her friends when she died and her estate was published in the local paper, a column she and everyone she knew read with fascination every week. Ruby knew that when she died and her house was sold and the sum it raised was added to the amount in her savings account, she had enough to cause small whistles of awe and envy.

They had never got along, Ruby and Iris. Ruby thought Iris too young for Harry who'd needed someone more his own age, not a young college thing. Iris had been halfway through her degree when they married. He'd been fifteen years older than she was.

Ruby was small but wide, all hips and bustling movement. She couldn't sit still, didn't know the comfort of silence. She liked to talk and seemed rarely to think about what she was saying. Words flooded out of her – thoughts, emotions, opinions – that often left other people breathless and weakened in their wake. 'Oh,' Iris would say if Sophy or Scott were offended by Ruby's outpourings, 'it's only your grandmother. You know what she's like. She means well.'

Her children were unconvinced by Iris's excuses for Ruby. But then Iris was unconvinced by her excuses for Ruby. She, too, was often hurt by Ruby's thoughtless tongue. She wished Ruby was more like her own mother, Janice, who Iris thought wonderful. Perhaps, though, wanting two Janices was greedy.

Janice was a scarves and lipstick woman. Prone to smiling, even when smiling wasn't called for. Iris had rarely seen her angry. Life seemed to flow over her. It wasn't any kind of resigned acceptance of her fate, it was just how the woman was. She'd died when Iris was twenty-five.

'Don't you ever get angry?' Iris used to ask her.

'Can't be bothered,' Janice would answer. 'Life's too short.' And she'd smile.

Iris had loved her mother with an intensity that often surprised her. She'd still remember things Janice had done, and smile fondly. After William, Iris's father, had died suddenly when she was fifteen, Janice had taken a part-time job in the local library to supplement the family income. 'God, I hate working,' she'd said. 'It cuts into your day.' Janice had happy days. She read, listened to music, went to recitals, saw friends, cooked a little, cleaned only when she had to. 'When the dirt becomes noticeable, then it has to go.' The day Iris left home, Janice quit work. She celebrated by sliding down the wide banisters of the county building. 'I've always wanted to do that.' She'd been fifty-eight.

Iris was embarrassed when her mother told her. 'You're too old to do things like that.'

'Nonsense! It was wonderful. Now I'm just a library member, not a library worker, I'm going to do it all the time.'

'Lord help us,' said Iris.

Janice got a bike and went on long runs into the countryside. She took picnics. Once she stole apples from an orchard she was passing. 'Didn't take many, just enough for a nice pie.' She would spend whole days reading, give no thought to cleaning up.

'Don't you ever feel guilty?' Iris asked her.

Janice, eating a lump of chocolate at the time, shook her head.

'God,' said Iris, 'I feel guilty constantly about everything. The children, my work, the house, the food I eat, my body, not reading enough, not seeing films I ought to see, not knowing what's new out there music-wise, not following the news, not . . .'

Janice interrupted her. 'You've got to cut that out.'

But Iris didn't know how. And six months after that her mother had died.

The guilt, the gnawing anxiety, the self-castigation, were always worse when Ruby was around. They irritated one another, Iris and Ruby. That they were never quite honest with one another did not help their prickly relationship. Each put up with the other. Always polite, always moving away from any confrontation. And both aware that a good flaming row might clear the air, clear up the misunderstandings and misinterpreted looks.

Their trouble was they stereotyped each other. Ruby saw Iris as a typical modern mother, working when she should be home looking after her children, whom Iris molly-coddled and spoilt when she was with them.

Iris thought Ruby old-fashioned, strait-laced and severe. A few weeks before Harry died, Ruby had come to stay for Christmas, and she and Iris had taken the dog for a walk. It was Boxing Day, the park was frosted white, children were out displaying their Yuletide gains – roller skates, bikes. A little boy dressed in a Batman suit was running across the grass, arms spread.

'He'll catch his death, weather like this,' Ruby said.

'He's too busy saving the planet to get chilled,' said Iris.

Ruby tutted. She always thought Iris too soft with her children. When they'd been born, she had turned up to help. She wasn't needed, she was sure, but it was a grandmother's duty. Every time the baby cried, Iris would rush to the cot to lift the sobbing one, hold it to her, kiss the little head, croon.

'You're spoiling that child,' Ruby would say. 'Leave him to cry. It's good for his lungs. He mustn't think you'll come running at every little whimper.'

17

But Iris loved to pick up her infant, loved to hold him to her, feel the tiny body against hers. She loved the smell of his head, and to feel the soft fine fuzz of baby hair on her cheek. She'd hush him to sleep and let him lie pressed to her till his hot cheek started to sweat and stuck to her chest. Ruby tutted. Children needed to be left alone in their cots so their backs would grow straight and strong, and they'd learn not to be demanding. Iris was a fool to herself.

In the park Ruby had seen a young couple walking entwined, stopping every few steps to kiss. She watched the girl put her lips to the boy's cheek, and he'd put his hand on her head and his lips on her hair. They couldn't get close enough. She followed them with her eyes, her lips moving, and sighed. Iris mistook the slow exhalation for a snort of disapproval.

'It's love,' she said. 'It's the sixties. Love is everywhere.'

Ruby said snippily that she knew that. She was hurt that Iris should think her strait-laced. She hadn't been disapproving at all. What she'd been feeling was envy. Thirty years a widow, it had been years since she'd been touched. She wanted someone to kiss her like that. She missed it. Lips on hers, a tongue slipping into her mouth. Hands on her body, on her breasts. Someone to turn to in bed. To love.

On the day her son died, Ruby sat on the sofa in Iris's living room. Two fat knees, thought Iris, looking at them. Ruby spoke of death and mourning, she knew what lay ahead for Iris.

At four in the afternoon, Iris thought to phone Harry's office. They'd be wondering what had happened to him. She dialled the number and asked to be put through to Tom Oliver, Harry's boss, a friend they once saw socially. But no longer, not for a couple of years now. Tom was out, so Iris spoke to his secretary.

'I'm phoning about Harry Chisholm,' she said. 'I expect you're wondering what's happened to him.'

'Who?' said the secretary.

'Harry,' said Iris. 'Harry Chisholm. He had an accident this morning.' She swallowed. She'd better get used to saying this. 'I'm afraid he was killed. I wonder if you could please tell Tom when he gets back in?'

'Harry Chisholm,' said the secretary. Slowly, writing it down. 'Yes, I'll tell Mr Oliver.' She rang off.

Iris thought it strange the secretary hadn't heard of Harry, but decided she must be new, and probably hadn't met all the staff yet. 'People are always chopping and changing jobs these days,' she said to Ruby.

It became a time of whispers. Hushed voices. Sympathetic looks. Hands. Iris always remembered the hands. They touched her back, ushering her into rooms. They held her hands. And there was tea. She drank a lot of it, offered it to callers, accepted more cups than she wanted. There was constantly the distant sound of dishes clattering, and kettles boiling. It gave sorrowers, who did not know what to say, something to do – make a pot of tea.

Iris had discovered that bad news grows wings and flies through communities, and Harry's swift and spectacular ending made a good story to pass on in supermarket queues and pubs. She was receiving phone calls of sympathy from people she didn't know, and didn't know Harry knew. Johnny Briggs, Frank Walters, Gordon Wilson – all new names to her. She received a card that read, '*In deepest sympathy, from Marsha and James Hunter*'. Who? she thought, turning it over in her hand, examining the writing. Next day another card arrived from '*All the gang at the Dog and Duck*', where Harry had apparently been the life and soul of the party. Harry? The Dog and Duck? Iris was bewildered. The life and soul of the party? She didn't think so. He had been a quiet man, witty, yes, but with a dry, gentle humour. Not the stuff of belly laughs, and hardly the sort of wisecracking that would make him the life and soul of anything. Party? Harry hated parties. So much, in fact, Iris often went to them alone. She loved parties.

The crematorium was crowded. Iris, Sophy and Scott were last to enter, and as they walked to the front pew, Iris saw rows of faces that were strange to her.

'Who are these people?' said Sophy.

Iris whispered that she did not know.

After the service she stood in the foyer shaking hands, thanking people who'd come to share her grief, and to say farewell to Harry.

Strangers came up to her, pressed their palms to hers, gripped her shoulder and told her what a fine man Harry had been, and how much he would be missed. They were a mix of people, some obviously rich with their expensive suits, manicured nails, slight fragrance of cologne. Some were more down-at-heel in worn sports jackets, shirt collars fraying; a woman overly made up and smelling of sherry. It was all so odd, bizarre, Iris was caught undecided between breaking down into uncontrollable weeping and bursting into hysterical laughter. Maybe there was a mix-up, maybe some other Harry Chisholm had died on the same day. Maybe all the people who should have been at Harry's funeral, some of the people he'd worked with, for instance, who were unaccountably absent, had gone there and the other Harry's people had come here.

They came, these strangers, to the house afterwards. Their cars lined the street. They ate the sandwiches and cake Ruby had prepared. They drank the whisky and sherry Iris offered. They mingled, but only with one another, laughing and making remarks like, 'Sad day, this.' And, 'Sorry to see old Harry go. Nobody like him.' And, 'Never knew when to stop.' Iris and the few close friends who had turned up huddled in a corner, watching.

Morag, a long-time chum, took Iris's hand. 'Are you all right?'

She said, 'No, I am not all right. I want to be alone, to sit and mourn Harry, and think about him and cry. I want to cry and cry. But, to tell the truth, right now I'm too confused to cry.'

Next day she wrote to her husband's boss, Tom Oliver. She said that she was sorry he hadn't made it to the funeral, but understood the pressures of work. The real reason for this letter, however, was that now Harry was gone (she wasn't ready to say dead) she would have to sort out her affairs. She couldn't afford to pay the mortgage and all her other expenses on her teaching income, and would need Harry's pension. He had been contributing to the firm's fund for almost thirty years and it must be worth quite a bit now. If Tom could hurry up whatever procedure was necessary before payment could be made, she would be grateful.

She received a letter by return from the firm's accountant telling her that her husband had been made redundant more than three years ago, and that the pension had been paid to him then, along with generous redundancy.

Iris read and re-read the letter. She put it down, made a cup of tea and returned to it. What? If the pension and redundancy had been paid, where was the money now? In Harry's bank account? She searched for his statements, but couldn't find any. They had never shared a bank account. Harry had been old-fashioned about money. Iris put her earnings into a separate account and paid for the groceries and all the household bills, the telephone, electricity and gas. Harry had paid the mortgage and had run the car. He also dealt with the various insurance policies they had.

Morag always told her that Harry was a bit patriarchal. 'Only financially. Otherwise he's a sweetie. But definitely a bit funny when it comes to money, which should be mutual.'

Iris had agreed. Then shrugged. 'I know. Other people have joint accounts. But we do what we do. It works for us. I always have money for clothes and nights out. I can't complain.'

She wrote to the car insurers telling them of the accident and asking for a claim form. The answering letter told her that, as the motor insurance had lapsed several months ago, there could be no claim.

She wrote to Harry's life insurers. Got a letter back saying his policy had been cashed in over a year ago. She was due nothing.

She wrote to the building society and told them of Harry's death, adding that she would now shift the payments to her own bank account and would like the house to be in her name only. They replied that payments on the mortgage and remortgage were six months behind and they were considering taking legal action.

Iris went numb. Remortgage? She knew nothing about that. She sat at the kitchen table, horror creeping through her. She remembered Harry coming home with a bottle of champagne, bursting into this very room, joyous and red-faced. He'd had a win on the horses, he'd told her. Bit of a flutter. She knew he often had a bet. It was his recreation, he'd said. She had her friends, her nights out to the theatre. He liked to punt. 'It's fun,' he'd told her. 'And I'm good at it. Got a bit of a nose for a good horse.' Iris had thought nothing of it. She considered gambling a waste of money, but, if it gave him pleasure, what harm was there?

A lot, she was beginning to think.

Scott and Sophy had returned to school. Iris was due back at work, but phoned in to say she needed a few more days.

'Take as long as you like, dear,' said Miss Moffat. 'These things take time.'

Iris started with Harry's desk. Pulling out each drawer, examining every letter. Every note, every slip of paper. She found betting slips. A letter from his turf accountant. Turf accountant? Harry had a turf accountant?

Apparently he had, and owed him a great deal of money. She found Harry's record of bets and horses, a detailed record of their running on dry or heavy ground. Who'd ridden them. Who'd trained them. The bottom drawer was stuffed with old racing papers.

Now, she went on the rampage. She emptied Harry's sock drawer on to the floor; his tie drawer too. She went through his suits, every pocket, his sports jackets, his trousers. She looked inside every shoe. She searched on top of the wardrobe, under the bed, rummaged through his toiletries and went through his tool box. She found parking tickets for several race tracks. Restaurant receipts for lavish meals she'd never known he'd eaten. They were always for one. She assumed gambling was his only vice, he didn't seem to have had a mistress.

She stopped her frantic hunt and made a cup of tea. Where else? she thought, and went over their days together. Up at seven, he'd shave and dress while she made breakfast. He'd read the paper as he ate, bacon and eggs most mornings, though recently he'd started eating muesli, said he was watching his heart. His jacket was always draped over the kitchen chair. Two cups of coffee, then he'd put it on, plus a coat if it was cold. Pick up his briefcase. Kiss her cheek and go.

His briefcase had been in the car, Iris hadn't bothered to collect it from the garage it had been towed to. She didn't think there would be anything damning in it. He came home after six every evening. Took off his jacket, kissed her cheek. Washed. Ate. Watched television. Bathed. And went to bed. Weekends he did the garden . . . 'The shed!' she shouted. And ran from the kitchen, out of the back door.

The shed was pristine. Tools hung from hooks on a shelf the length of each wall. There were boxes of nails and screws, balls of string, weedkiller and rose fertiliser, and a green, mouse-nibbled box file. Iris lifted it down and opened it. And there, at last, were Harry's bank book, his statements and letters from the building society and the many other people to whom he owed money.

The bank book told her everything. Three years ago, when Harry had lost his job, he'd deposited fifteen thousand pounds, his pension fund and redundancy money. Over the following year he'd withdrawn it in instalments that were always of five hundred pounds plus, sometimes twice a week. Nothing had been put back in. About fourteen months after the first large sum had been deposited, he'd put in another fifteen thousand pounds, his life insurance. He'd gone through that in months. Nine months ago another ten thousand pounds had been put in, the remortgage, Iris presumed. Now he was overdrawn.

It was more than she could take in. The turmoil she felt ran through her whole body, weakened her legs. She went back to the kitchen, stood at the table, and feeling the box she was holding to be filthy – the mouse-nibblings, dust, its contents – spread out a newspaper to put it on. Doing so, she noticed an article about achieving perfect skin in six days by eating citrus fruits, and leaned over the table reading it, putting off the moment of sorting through the evidence. She made a cup of tea. Noticed when carrying it from the kettle to the table that she was shaking. She sat down and began pulling papers out of the box file. Bills, demands, bank statements, foul letters from the building society, were sorted into piles. Putting things into orderly heaps mildly soothed her. It was as if she was taking control of the calamity.

She worked through her layers of shock. Shock at the financial state they were in – about to lose the house, thousands of pounds of debt inherited from Harry. Shock at the amount of money he'd squandered, and what they could have done with it. Shock at discovering her husband's secret life. What had he been thinking of? How could he? He'd come and gone, kissed her cheek, eaten supper with her, chatted about the children, the garden, holidays they might take, lain beside her in bed, made love to her . . . and all the while he'd been living a secret life. To all those people who'd come to the funeral, he'd been a different Harry. The life and soul of the party.

'Well, he would have been with all that money to throw about. No wonder he had friends,' said Iris.

The sound of her own voice in the silent house, the fury and indignation in it, stilled her. She hid her face in her hands. 'What am I going to do?'

On the back of an envelope, she calculated how much she now owed. She reckoned this would be a more logical way to deal with it as she could not face adding up how much Harry had gambled away. He must have been obsessed, she thought. Crazed.

That final fatal moment, she realised then, was not the result of him absently putting his foot down and moving out into the stream of oncoming traffic. Dread had made him do it. Dread and worry had flooded his mind, and so he'd rushed ahead. No matter what she now thought of him, and the foul situation he'd left her in, contemplating Harry and the anguished nightmare he'd been living through, her heart went out to him. 'You poor sod,' she said.

She packed all the letters, final demands and bank statements back into the box file, then hid it under her bed. And, not wanting to think, she started furiously to clean. The physical business of vacuuming, wiping, dusting, the violent elbow movement, was cathartic. Sweatily cathartic. It helped her ignore the fact she was going to have to sell the house.

It took six weeks. Iris gave spare keys to the estate agent so that buyers could view the house when she was at work. She found the thought of strangers moving through her home, considering critically what was precious to her, too painful. This sharp reminder of why she was selling the house she loved hurt. But in time she signed the papers, and was given six weeks to find somewhere else to live. She told nobody about this. She had a secret, like Harry had had a secret, and it would have to come out soon. She still didn't quite know how to tell her children that they had lost their home and had no money to buy another.

It felt unreal. Was this happening? She was moving, slowly, heavily, through a tunnel. Voices, even those that were very familiar to her, seemed distant, hollow. She got up, bathed, made breakfast, went to work, came home, she made supper, she spoke to her children, she read the newspaper, she went back to bed again. Days folded into days. But if anyone had asked her what she had done, said or read, she wouldn't have been able to tell them. Nights, when Scott and Sophy were in bed or doing their homework, and she was alone in the kitchen – she always sat at the kitchen table, the sofa in the living room was comfortable, and she felt too disturbed and miserable for any sort of comfort. No, the hard chair and the draught that keened mercilessly under the door suited her mood – she would huddle over a cup of coffee. She was unnaturally tense, aware of every tick and click in the house. The slightest rustle – her arm brushing against the newspaper, her foot rubbing the calf of her other leg – alarmed her. She'd sit for hours, staring. Barely thinking. Then she'd go to bed, aching from exhaustion and convinced she'd never sleep. But she always did – deep, black, dreamless sleep that never refreshed her, never relieved the fatigue. She'd wake gritty-eyed, still aching, more tired than when she'd lain down, eight hours before.

A week after the sale of the house was agreed, Iris drove to work. Fresh start, she was thinking. Somewhere new. Far away. Australia. The furthest tip of Australia where nobody knew her name. Or Alaska, she thought. Cold, icy cold. I want to run away, fast as I can. Far as I can. She stood in the car park, key in the lock of her Mini, frozen in a moment of helplessness. Numb with grief and bewilderment.

'Are you all right?' asked Miss Moffat, who had seen her and come across to help.

'I want to go somewhere cold,' said Iris. 'Bitterly cold. Where the air is clean and icy, and there is nothing to remind me of all this.'

'They do say that after a death . . . a shock . . . you should take time before you do anything drastic. You have to allow yourself to heal.'

'My husband lost his job three years ago and didn't tell me. He spent all our money. Our savings. Our insurance policies. He wasn't paying the mortgage. I have nothing. Very soon I will have no place to live.'

Miss Moffat said, 'Ah. That's different.' She thought for a moment. 'You were interested in taking a rural school?'

Iris said yes, she was. Had been on a course.

'Only,' said Miss Moffat, 'my old school at Green Cairns is looking for a new head. Small place, about twenty or so pupils. They're having difficulty finding someone.'

It didn't occur to Iris to ask why. She just thought, Fresh start. 'There's a house?' she asked.

'Of course,' said Miss Moffat.

'How many bedrooms?' Iris needed to know.

'Four.'

'That's perfect. I'll take it.'

That was more or less that. There were formalities. An application. An interview. But with Miss Moffat's glowing reference it was all plain sailing.

Three weeks before they had to quit the house, Iris told Sophy and Scott they were moving. All their young lives, she had discussed options, put her case, listened to what they had to say. Now she gave them a simple statement, a parental decree, the hard facts.

'We're going.'

Sophy had a tantrum. 'I'm not going anywhere! I'm staying here with my friends. How could you do this to me?'

'I have to,' Iris said quietly. 'I don't want to talk about it. You'll just have to believe me, we must do this.'

Scott said nothing but drank it all in, watching Iris. Then he got up, and on his way through the kitchen door, said, 'Bummer.'

Through it all, Ruby had come and gone. Knocking at the front door, opening it, peering into the hall. 'Hello, it's me.' She'd made

26

meals, cleared up. Leading Iris to the living room, sitting her down. 'You've got too much to think about to be dusting. Let me.'

She'd watch Iris's face closely, studying her eyes. 'I swear,' she told her friends at the church coffee morning, 'that one has never cried. Not shed a tear for my son. I've wept buckets.'

Her friends would tut, and shake their heads. 'You've got to cry. Can't hold it all in.'

Ruby was scandalised, though she never let Iris know. She thought Harry deserved some tears, after the work he'd put in supporting his family. She knew nothing of her son's last years, the gambling, the squandered thousands. She only knew of her daughter-in-law's dry eyes.

Of course Iris hadn't wept for Harry. She worried that if she started she'd never stop. Only when the house was sold and she had the offer of a job in Green Cairns did she relax. Let go. Till then she'd been holding herself together, sometimes physically holding her sides as she moved around. At night, her sleep was black and deep, dreamless, but she'd wake knowing from her aching jaw that she'd been grinding her teeth.

On the day she'd received the letter saying the new job was hers she'd gone to Miss Moffat to hand in her notice and to thank her for all she'd done. It was lunchtime. Miss Moffat was sitting at her desk, in that comfortable room, drinking tea, eating sandwiches. 'Iris, come in.'

'I won't stay,' she said. 'Just wanted to tell you I got the job and I'll have to resign from the school.'

'Iris, that's wonderful! This is the turning point. Everything will work out, I know it will.'

The coals shifted in the grate. There was the soft sound of flames. The room smelled of lilies.

'Here, share my lunch,' said Miss Moffat. 'I always make too much. You'll be doing me a favour. I'll only eat it myself and feel bloated all afternoon.' She held out a plastic box, packed with food.

Iris thanked her, and sat by the fire to eat. They didn't say much. Miss Moffat talked about the weather, and how her garden was coming nicely into bloom. 'Lovely time of year,' she said. 'Full of surprises. Things shoving out of the ground.'

Iris nodded. Chewed. Looked out of the window. The warmth, the comfort of this room, the relief of knowing she had a home for herself and her children – halfway through a tomato sandwich, she started to cry.

Arriving

A small red Mini Traveller wound and heaved round the long bends in the road. It could be heard for miles: the crunching of gears, the whine of the engine. Swirls of dust rose and hung in the hot air behind it.

From the leafy depths of the sycamore tree, on a branch that stretched out beyond his garden, Colin watched it, his grandmother's binoculars wedged against his eyes. He held his breath, counting. Two hundred was his record so far, numbers speeding by as he galloped past one hundred and thirty, face reddening, lungs bursting. Hundred and ninety-two, hundred and ninety-three . . . four, five, sixseveneightnineten . . . He'd open his mouth and heave air into his throat.

The car disappeared round the long steep upward sweep that led into the village. Colin scrambled from the tree and hurried through the garden. Squeezing between the beech hedge and the side of the house. Lips pressed together. Breath held, again. Eyes shut against the new shoots that stung his face as he rushed past them to his secret place amid the thick tangle of redcurrant bushes that sprawled through the railings, dipped on to the pavement. He crouched, ready to watch the car as it skimmed through the village. He polished the lenses of the binoculars on his jumper as he waited, little mouth pursed, concentrating. He hated his jumper. It was a murky green. Granny green, he called it. The green that only grannies wore. A sludgy colour that made you unhappy. People never noticed you in a jumper this colour. Which had its compensations. But he preferred Christmas green. A bright green full of promises, good things coming.

He heard the car heave up the hill that led into the village and prepared himself. He opened his red memo jotter, stuck his chewed pencil behind his ear, held the binoculars poised. He'd get this car's number. He'd been collecting them for a week now. His new hobby. So far he'd got thirty-two. It wasn't a busy place, Green Cairns. But today, barely twenty minutes ago, there had been a furniture van, closely followed by a heavy, old-fashioned Rover.

The car stopped at the house opposite Colin's. He could hardly believe it. It was her, he knew it, and he'd been the one to see her arrive. He'd be able to tell everyone that she was here, and what she looked like.

Binoculars pressed hard to his face, he watched as she climbed from her car and looked round. She stared up the road, turned and looked back the way she had come. Put her hands on her hips. 'Where the hell are they?'

She swore. She said 'hell'; that was a rude word. Colin couldn't believe it. But he'd definitely heard it. Now he *really* had something to tell. She was wearing jeans, he noted. He wanted jeans, like the cowboys wore in films, but his granny wouldn't buy him a pair. Instead he wore grey flannel shorts, week in, week out, winter and summer.

The woman had short hair. Fair, like his. 'Mousy' his granny called it. But, even from here, he could see this woman was no mouse. Unlike him. He was shy, tubby, clumsy. He couldn't run fast. He was always last to be picked for games teams. 'Fatso' the other children in school called him. This woman wasn't fat. She was curvy. She had a crisp blue shirt tucked into her jeans. Now, that was a mystery to him. How did people manage it? His own shirt always worked its way out of his waistband and hung, half-in, half-out, and the out bit always got grubby. His gran was forever taking hold of him, spitting into her hanky, wiping his face, calling him a mucky pup, shoving the wayward shirt back down his shorts. She'd examine his chewed fingernails and tut, shaking her head. 'Filth.'

He reached down and scratched the eczema on his leg. He thought he smelled. He *knew* he smelled of the stuff his gran put on his sore patches night and morning. He wasn't very nice. But he'd got used to that. Didn't think about it. That was how it was. Some people were nice, like Lucy Hargreaves, and some people weren't. And if you weren't, you had to be careful. You had to keep your eyes averted. Or the big boys, mostly James Biggar, would shout, 'Who are you looking at?' They'd punch and kick. Lock you in the lavatory. Call you Blubber. Fatty. Names. 'Names can't hurt you,' Granny said. But they could. Besides it wasn't the names, it was the way they were used. Taunting, cruel. And you couldn't cry. Crying only made it worse. More names. More kicking.

Colin had his own little corner in the playground where he sat at breaktimes, reading, drawing in his red memo jotter, playing with his yo-yo, watching the big ones play. Though if James caught him doing that, he'd kick and slap then, too. 'Who're you looking at, Fatso?' Slap. Slap. 'Nobody,' Colin would say. 'Not you anyway.' More slaps. More punches.

'Where did you get them bruises?' his gran would ask.

'Fell,' Colin would say.

And his gran would give him a gentle mock smack on the head. Say softly, 'Clumsy boy. Mucky pup.'

He lifted the binoculars to his eyes to get a closer look at the new arrival. In fact, it would have been easier for Colin to spy if he hadn't been using them. They were old, hard to focus, heavy – holding them up made his arms ache. If he breathed hard, and he always did, they steamed up. Besides, he wore glasses, and, at that, glasses with one lens patched to cure his lazy eye.

But he managed to focus on the face across the road, and saw the curve of her cheek, the red on her lips. Her eyes were blue. Her hair wasn't mousy at all. It was pale, the colour of corn stubble, no grey in it. She was young. Well, youngish. Young compared to his gran, and Mrs Mitchell the last teacher, who'd had a crumpled face like a dried-up dishcloth left on the sink, and whiskers. He didn't know teachers could be young. He thought they were all old like Mrs Mitchell. Who loomed at him, told him him he was fat and lazy and hit him on the knuckles with her ruler. Called him 'Boy' sometimes, 'You, boy' other times, and 'Silly boy' most of the time. It gave him a quiet thrill to bring this woman so close. He smirked. She didn't know she was being spied on. He felt secretly mighty.

31

Iris shook her head. Repeated, 'Where the hell are they?' Looked up and down the road. She opened the gate of the house. It squeaked. In the unnerving silence of this deserted place it sounded horribly loud. God, it was quiet. It made her want to shout. Rude words would be best, she thought. She wouldn't have been surprised to see tumbleweed, drifting past the houses.

She walked up the path to the front door and rattled the handle. It was locked. She kicked it. She wanted in. Was desperate for a cup of coffee and a pee. Though not necessarily in that order. She sat on the steps to wait for the furniture van, and for Ruby and Sophy and Scott. They'd no doubt thundered straight on and out the other end of the village. It was that sort of a place. You would thunder through it. Thundering was the best thing to do when you looked at it. There was nothing here. A garage with a shop, a Coca-Cola sign sighing in the breeze. It had a row of pumps in the weedy forecourt, piles of tyres, and a tractor that looked like it had been dismantled years and years ago, then abandoned. A bashed Walls ice-cream sign stood beside the pumps; it looked as if it had been knocked into often by cars arriving, but nobody had ever thought to move it. The shop was painted red, peeling red, had a flat corrugated-iron roof, and a verdant growth of weeds sprouting from its gutter.

The rest of the village was really just two rows of houses. Big, small, old, new – or newish – in no particular order. Iris got the impression that if someone could find a space, they built a house. A garden, bounded by a hedge, in front of every house. A church at one end, a village hall at the other. And that was it. Apart from the road running through it. She could see it winding through the glen, disappearing behind dips and bends, reappearing again, stretching far, far into the distance.

There was, she noted, a strange-looking small boy crouched in the bushes across the road spying on her through a pair of binoculars. How odd. His hair stuck up on end, and he was wearing a horrible sweater in a muddy sort of green. On a day like this, the child must be boiled alive.

She thought of waving. But then, thought, No, he'll be lost in some private game. And acknowledging his presence would spoil it. He looked to be about six or seven. He'd be one of hers, no doubt. Come term-time, when school started, she'd have a word.

She listened to the silky movement of the trees. Noted how overgrown her new garden was, and then let the silence thrum through her. It was peculiar. No voices. Summertime – and there was a word she loved, summertime, it was laden with promise, hot days, indolence, the exhilarating expectancy of sweet things – and this place was eerily quiet. The only noises were a lawn mower somewhere, the breeze in the elder trees, chaffinches bickering in the hedge. But these were sounds that only made the human silence louder. That she could hear them so clearly made Iris realise how still this place was.

Locked Out

She leaned over the flowerbed and picked a marigold. Twirled it between her thumb and forefinger, thinking. Reviewing the past few months. The things that had happened. Things she'd discovered. How she'd got here.

Until that day in February, when Harry died, she'd lived. Yes, that was it, she thought, nodding, a life. A normal, ordinary life. Same as most other people she knew. A husband, Harry, fifteen years older than she, quietly witty, shrewd, generous, mild-mannered most of the time. Oh, there had been sudden eruptions of temper, but then, who hadn't had moments of wild frustration, fury? Now, knowing what she knew about him, she wondered why there hadn't been more such outbursts. She wondered about Harry. Nearly eighteen years married, she'd thought she'd known him. But no, she hadn't known him at all.

At first, in bed, she'd lean over the pillow and sing in his ear, 'I'm just wild about Harry.'

Then: 'Do you love me, Harry?'

He'd stroke her cheek. 'You've got a lovely cheek, there. Soft. I love your cheek.'

She'd asked it often, and over the years his responses had changed. Become more distant. Then hardened. 'Do you love me, Harry?'

He'd taken a flower from the vase on the kitchen table. Put it in her hair. Smiled.

'Do you love me, Harry?'

'I think we're past that sort of question now.'

'Do you love me, Harry?'

'For heaven's sake, stop asking me that.'

35

So he never said he loved her. All those years, and he never said it. Not once. For a long time Iris had thought he just didn't want to say it. That he'd thought it silly. Now she thought he hadn't loved her. Perhaps couldn't love anybody. Didn't know how.

But in their married time together, she hadn't given his reluctance to commit verbally much thought. That was just Harry. The way he was. She'd had a full life, though lately she'd realised she'd in fact had two lives. One full, one not so full. One with Harry, one without Harry. The full life was the one without him.

She had a job she loved, teaching. Her own classroom, that she filled with posters, information, plants, drawings, a hamster. She moved about the room exuding enthusiasm. She infected her pupils with it. She was that sort of person. She was loved, she knew it, but only allowed herself to revel in it when she was depressed. She'd lift black moods by revisiting lovely moments she'd had: the smiles, the little hands slipping into hers, the presents – chocolates, home-baked cakes, trinkets from Christmas trees – and feel cheered.

She had friends. Too many to list. One best chum, Morag, a few close pals, and many, many acquaintances. Evenings, when the phone rang, it was always for her. There were nights out, trips to the theatre, the cinema, restaurants, or just to sit in Morag's living room, drinking wine and chatting. Iris read, too. Was a regular at the library. Harry stayed home nights, sitting by the fire, feet up on the coffee table, a glass of whisky on the arm of the chair, watching television, sports usually, waiting for her to come home. He'd smile, nod, say, 'Hello.' But lately there had been scenes. Where the hell had she been? What time of night was this to come home?

'Half-past eleven,' she'd said. 'A reasonable enough time.'

'Out with your fancy friends, leaving me here to cope.'

'Cope? With what? The children are old enough to put them-selves to bed. And my friends aren't fancy.'

'Yes, they are.'

On and on into the night they'd argue. It would start with her friends then move to her job, her clothes, the books she read, the films she'd seen that he hadn't. Thinking about them now, she thought their fights limitless. They could turn a piece of burnt toast into a major conflict, hurling insults at one another. Once, at her insistence, they'd taken the altercation outside into the garden so they wouldn't wake the children.

'Why don't you just lighten up?' she'd shouted. 'Let things roll over you. Go with the flow.'

'What! Go with the flow?' he'd yelled back. 'No way. You'd be stomping all over me, bossy bitch, manipulative cow. This is me. This is how I am. And this is my home, too. I live here, Iris.'

'Who said you didn't?'

'You. The way you run things to suit yourself. You think you're going to turn me into a pipe and slippers man. Mr Cosy. Stay home and do the dishes. Speak when I'm spoken to, Mr Yes-dear, No-dear. Sit me by the television in my old cardy. Make me your ideal hubby. I'll be damned if you'll do that to me.'

She'd stared at him. Was that really what he thought she was doing to him? 'You prat,' she'd shouted.

And then their neighbour had shoved up his window, stuck his head out into the night and told them to be quiet. People were trying to sleep.

They'd slunk indoors, scolded and shamed. This was how it had once been with sex, she'd thought. Not shamed, or scolded, but sneaking off together to find places to do it before they were married. And later, after the children were born, making love in the dark, trying not to make a noise. Silent, secret love. Now they had silent, secret fights. Glaring at one another over the breakfast table when the children's backs were turned. They communicated about the necessities – the phone bill needed paying, the news-agent had sent the wrong morning paper, Sophy's school shoes had a hole in the sole. They could discuss such matters sounding matter-of-fact, but there would be, obvious only to them, they mistakenly thought, an intense undertow of wrath. In the last few months of their marriage, they'd been speaking, but not talking, to one another.

The child across the road, Iris noted, was still observing her. She smiled in his direction. Colin ducked down. Lay, face pressed to the earth. Barely breathing. Slowly he rose to peek at her again.

Iris saw his head rising, the hair sticking on end, the round glasses, and looked away, remembering the secrets and fantasies of her own youth. They'd seemed so important at the time, she'd taken them so seriously. Enjoying them hadn't been an issue. That was the trouble with childhood, she thought, you didn't realise it was meant to be fun till it was over and you looked back on it.

She couldn't say Harry hadn't been interested in his kids. He'd teased, joked, chatted with them. But she'd done all the ticking off, nagging, disciplining, feeding, cuddling, trips to the zoo, the cinema, pantos at Christmas, the letters to the school, parents' nights. Well, her hours – the same as her children's – suited all that. Harry had taken care of the financing. He'd paid the mortgage, the big bills – repairs to the roof, a new kitchen – kept up all the insurance policies. Or so Iris had thought. How could he deceive me? she wondered now. What gets into people? How could she live with someone, share a table, food, sleep in the same bed, sit evenings at home together, clothes jumbled in the same drawer, and know so little about him?

On her way here, Iris had stopped in Forham, a small county town about fifteen miles from Green Cairns. It was a tiny place, but compared to Green Cairns it seemed vast. It had, after all, two main streets. Buildings huddled against buildings. The streets were cobbled. The shops reflected the lives they catered for. A sports shop sold guns and fishing gear, top-of-the-range wellington boots and Barbour coats. There was a fishmonger's, with water flooding down the inside of the window and an array of haddock, plaice and fresh, gleamy-eyed trout on display. A butcher's with carcasses hanging and a sawdust-covered floor, in the window, plump pork chops and speckled brown eggs with feathers still sticking to them. A baker's complete with tearoom where fat-thighed country ladies took tea, ate brightly iced cakes and cackled at slightly smutty jokes. And there was a grocer's shop, Fergus Harris Grocer and Licensed Vintner. Iris went in. There were shelves of what Iris thought of as posh jams – Oxford marmalade, wild strawberry, quince jelly. And posh soups, lobster bisque, duck and orange consommé. Behind the counter on marble slabs were continental cheeses – Brie, Emmenthal, Camembert, Gorgonzola. There was a huge red machine for grinding coffee. In the back, a vast selection of wines – Beaune, Margeaux, Chablis. Iris thought it a wonderland. The thick rich smells, the exotic labels.

'Goodness,' she said to the man behind the counter. 'I never thought I'd find a place like this so far from the city.'

And Fergus, slightly miffed, had said. 'Why not? It isn't just city folks have palates. We supply all the estates round here. All the big houses. The McBride Estate. Glamis. Cortachy. Oh yes, people who know their cheese and wine shop at Fergus Harris. The rest of them go to the supermarket.'

Iris nodded. The state of her finances, she was a supermarket person. In her dreams, she was a Fergus Harris Grocer and Licensed Vintner person.

She passed the supermarket on her way out of town, and knew from the size of the car park that this was where most of the glen folk came on Saturday mornings to stock up. And this was where she, too, would come to buy her supplies of beans, cheese, breakfast cereals, washing powder and occasional bottle of cheap plonk and everything else she needed to get by. In time, she also knew, this huge sprawling place would see the baker's, the butcher's and the lovely old-fashioned grocer's off. Unable to compete, they would slip away.

Now, she looked across at the garage. It was tumbledown, not so much neglected as over-used. Peeling posters for soap powders, margarine and chocolate bars and local events – a barn dance that had been held six months ago, a jumble sale in the church hall last week, a bring-and-buy sale next Saturday – in the window. In the front was a flyer for a newspaper shouting a headline for something that had happened last year, Iris noted. The roof was of corrugated iron, painted rusty red. Harry would have called it rinkydink. He liked that word. Used it to describe anything small, old, countrified. Anything, in fact, that he didn't take seriously.

Iris knew the garage would be a dammit shop. Dammit, I've forgotten butter, I'll have to go to the dammit shop. Dammit, I've run out of cheese, I'll have to go get a sweaty lump, cellophane-wrapped, from the dammit shop. All the things she regularly forgot to buy from the supermarket, or used a lot, then ran out of, she'd buy from the dammit shop.

She had long had a notion to head a country school. A small place. Somewhere idyllic. A house with a view over a glen or a river. She'd once asked Harry what he thought about her taking over a country school, and he'd said, 'Hmm.' She asked what he meant, hmm. He said, 'Just, hmm.'

She knew that in the language they'd developed over the years – the language of ums and ahs and looks and sighs, the language of those who do not talk to one another – it meant he had no intention of moving to a small community. And also, no intention of discussing why. No need, she'd thought. He'd have had to leave his job. The places in her idyll were too far to commute from daily. That would reduce them to one income. Plus the children wouldn't take kindly to being suddenly taken from their school routines and moved to what would be, in their eyes, the middle of nowhere. No friends, no night life, no nothing. The country dream would remain on the wish list for the moment, for years and years, she had thought.

Well, here she was. She stood up, dusted down her jeans, looked round. She had an inkling this country school dream was not going to be the idyll she'd conjured up in her imaginings. The house was old, neglected. She walked up the path and peered through the front window. A large room, an ornate fireplace, the walls painted a pale beige. Iris pressed her nose against the pane, staring into the room, noted with sinking heart the lack of radiators. 'No central heating,' she said aloud. 'I don't think much of that.' Being cold had not been part of her daydream. She looked round at the hills, peaking in the distance. There would be snow. She imagined blizzards, and in that room, three chilled souls wearing layers and layers of jumpers, sitting before a meagre flickering fire, hands stretched out to glean some warmth to ease numbed fingers. There would be complaints. There would be bickering.

She went round to the back of the house and peeked into the kitchen. Another large room. But even more unused than the living room. She remembered being told that the last Missie hadn't lived here. She'd bought a bungalow further up the glen, then sold it when she moved away after she'd lost the job. This house had been empty for at least five years.

Still, it was a good kitchen, Iris could see that. The sort of kitchen she'd fantasised about. Except that in her dreams it had been painted white, with herbs hung in bunches near the window, gleaming copper pots lined the shelves. Children, lots of children, ran in and out of the back door. Supper time they'd all sit round a huge table, eating hot nutritious soups and stews. In her imaginings, the soups and stews just appeared. She did not deal with details – like who cooked them. Or, indeed, where all the children came from. They were hers, of course, but the actual business of giving birth six or seven times had not been gone into.

So taken had she been with this country farmhouse kitchen filled with ruddy-cheeked happy children, she'd enthused about it to Harry. 'Just imagine it. An old farmhouse with a huge kitchen, a range we could cook on, a stockpot always on the go, home-made jams and jellies, fruit in the garden. I could make my own pickles and chutneys. We could have lots of children.'

Harry had said, 'Yumph.' Which was what he said when one of Iris's suggestions filled him with such horror he dare not answer in words lest he said something so dire it would lead to divorce. Like the time Iris thought he might like to accompany her to a reading of existentialist poetry in The Assembly Rooms. 'Yumph.'

She sat on the old wooden bench by the back door. At times like this, when she was alone, when she wasn't busying herself, fending off memories, they came to her in a series of fragmented, snapshot moments.

Sitting in Miss Moffat's room with the policemen. How they seemed to fill it with their uniforms, the rustle of cloth unbearably loud. She wondered how they could function while wearing such cumbersome outfits.

'How do you function with all that on?' she'd asked. Still cringed remembering it. It had been nerves. She'd known from the look on Miss Moffat's face when she'd beckoned her out into the corridor that something awful had happened.

The first day after Harry's death had been terrible. She remembered waking up, hearing the world beyond her window preparing for the day. A car starting up, the children from three doors down going off to school, a dog barking. How dare everything beyond this house continue as normal, when this dreadful thing had happened to her. Scott thought so too. He'd stood at the window watching people pass and said, 'Isn't it funny? The rest of the world is carrying on same as ever, and we've sort of stopped.'

It had been a little while before her first rage engulfed her. But engulf her it did. It stormed through her. She wanted to scream and shout. Often she'd had to leave her classroom and stand outside in the corridor, fists clenched, nails biting into her palms, breathing, telling herself to calm down. Her pupils were children, they couldn't possibly understand what she was going through.

The rage she understood. The nausea alarmed her. Sitting now on the garden bench, she could count the places she'd thrown up in. Her own home, often. School. The library when she'd at last returned the books she'd had out when Harry died. They'd been two months overdue. The small Italian restaurant Morag had taken her to. 'My treat,' she'd insisted. 'You could do with a night out.' Iris had stood looking down at the lasagna she'd just parted company with, thinking that all in all it would have been less painful if she'd just taken the plate straight to the lavatory and emptied it down the loo. Still, there had been no sudden rages or nausea for a few weeks now. Maybe she was getting better.

Iris could clearly recall sitting in the solicitor's office signing away her house. And later, when the keys were handed over, and she finally got the money, sitting alone in her bedroom in Ruby's house, where they'd stayed for a few weeks before they came here, writing cheques. The profit on the house, once the mortgage was paid off, had cleared Harry's debts. She still had to pay the remaining remortgage. It would be years before she was free.

At first, after Harry died, Ruby had come over every day. She fussed, brought food and watched Iris closely, checking that her son was being properly mourned. She chatted with Scott and Sophy.

She took over. Iris would sit, listening to her children laughing with Ruby, feeling locked out of her own kitchen. Almost an unwanted presence in her own home. When she entered a room and caught Scott, Sophy and Ruby together, the distress that she took with her everywhere she went, the worry – Harry's debts – that hung round her, a shroud, reminded them of their own loss and their own mourning.

When at last Iris had told Ruby that she was moving out of town, she was going to a country school almost three hours' drive away, Ruby had been shocked, hurt.

'You can't do that. You can't uproot the kids just when their dad has died. They need the familiar.'

'And I need to get away from the familiar,' Iris had said. She could not bring herself to tell Ruby the truth. 'Harry's everywhere in that house. Too many memories.'

'Well, you could move in with me if you don't want to be in the house you shared with Harry. There's plenty room. I'm fed up rattling about on my own.' For a few moments, Ruby imagined it. Her house would be filled with noise, movement, people. She would cook meals. They would all sit in her dining room eating, laughing. Her evening table would be lonely no more.

Live with Ruby? Iris didn't think so. She imagined it, walking on Ruby's pink carpets. Washing up in Ruby's yellow and blue kitchen. Sitting in Ruby's lounge with the huge untamed ivy climbing the navy and gold striped wallpaper. Drinking from Ruby's cups. Ruby everywhere: talking, making comments about Scott's hair and Sophy's long telephone calls and the sound of her French horn as she worked on her scales; telling Scott to wipe his feet, clean up his homework books, turn down the din from his hi-fi. A swift cruel blast of reality. Iris didn't know what to say, feared that anything she did say would be so harsh Ruby would forever break off all relations with her and Scott and Sophy. At a moment like this Harry would have said, 'Yumph.'

But Iris had shaken her head. 'Thanks. But I need to go somewhere new. Besides, I've always wanted my own country school. The chance came along.'

Ruby had sighed. 'So be it. If that's what you want. But you know my door's always open if you change your mind.'

Harry was her son. And, yes, she was grieving. At night, alone in the dark, Ruby would feel tears running down on to her pillow. Her Harry, her lovely, lovely boy was gone. But sometimes, only sometimes, during the day when she was with her friends, she felt a sneaking triumph that she was ahead in the grief stakes. Many of the women she knew had lost a husband, but she had lost a husband and a son. When it came to gaining sympathy, Ruby won hands down. Of course, she felt guilty at the comfort this accomplishment brought her, but there it was. She would talk to her friends about her loss, and revel in their kindness and pity. 'So young,' she'd say. 'So much to look forward to. Cut down in his prime.'

Her friends would nod and agree. 'Terrible. Terrible.'

Ruby had outlived her only child. A widow and a mourning mother, now. In gatherings and meetings (and Ruby attended many – church committees, an Italian cookery class, a drama group, a literary appreciation society, keep-fit every Tuesday morning) she was unrivalled in matters of mortality and lament. She was the queen of sorrowers.

Iris got up, walked the length of the back garden. It was weedy, overgrown. But it would have to wait, all her time would be taken up with painting the house. It was a pity Ruby would not be around to help. She had certainly helped in the weeks after Harry's death. Iris had to admit she was grateful.

Ruby seemed to keen forward into tragedy, face fixed in a smile that was never tender, certainly not jolly. Just there, Iris thought, permanently there. Ruby welcomed catastrophe. It gave her something to do. Still, there was comfort in her bustle. In moments when Iris had not wanted to clean or cook, had wanted only to sit perfectly still by the fire in the living room that was slightly too hot, and stare, Ruby had been there for her, giving her time to do just that.

I'll sit and stare no more, thought Iris. I will paint this old house. I will make this school a place of joy and learning. There will be singing and dancing. Laughter. I will make a life here. Friends.

She walked back down the garden and to the front of the house. There had been other options. She could have rented a house, kept on her old job. But no, this was better, a new beginning. So here she was, marvelling at the silence. Locked out. Waiting for her family. Being spied on by a small boy in a strange jumper.

She went out into the middle of the road. Stared up and down it, wondering where everybody was. She breathed in the air, held it in her lungs. The smell of the place. Fresh. The air was silky-soft. She walked slowly back to the gate, felt the place. Sheets flapped on several clothes lines. A door banged. Gardens were either neglected or regimentally trim, clipped hedges, weedless borders. Swallows dipped overhead. But there were no voices. Nobody called out. No distant laughter. No songs pouring from radios propped on kitchen windows. She sensed unhappiness. A certain acceptance of not quite misery, but pessimism, vexation. She thought, What have I done, coming here?

About ten minutes later, the van arrived, thundering back from up the glen, Ruby, Scott, and Sophy in Ruby's car behind it. The dog, a border collie, Lulu, sat in the back. Ruby stepped out on to the pavement, singing, waving the keys. 'Ha. Ha. Locked out. And you've not been here five minutes.'

'It's been a lot longer than that.' Iris sighed.

'Well, we got lost,' said Ruby, her voice high, musical. She was excited. Moving house thrilled her, though it was not she who was coming to live here. Which was the best thing about this. She could have a good poke round the new place, make tea for everyone, dish out the sandwiches and cake she'd made, help unpack, then she could leave the whole upheaval behind and return to the peace of her own home. She rather enjoyed turmoil. Well, other people's turmoil. 'We whooshed right through this place. Well, you would, wouldn't you? It's so small, it's hardly worth the signpost.'

'If you saw the signpost, why didn't you stop?' said Iris.

'We thought it was the outskirts, the beginnings of the place. We didn't know this was it. It's so small. What on earth are you going to do here? It's . . .'

'The sticks,' said Sophy.

45

'It's where we are going to live,' said Iris. 'This is it. It's all there was.'

Not quite true. When Miss Moffat had told her about the position, Iris applied for it, and got it. It was only after hearing that she'd successfully gained the headship at Green Cairns that it had occurred to her there might be better jobs, in more desirable parts of the country.

The school came with a history. The last teacher had been forced to leave. The parents had presented the local authority with a petition complaining about her treatment of their children, demanding she be removed from her post. This worried Iris. What sort of a community was this? Would they do the same to her? She looked round. Not a movement, except for the little spy in the bushes across the road. She admired his patience. All that time, sitting perfectly still, observing her. The child had tenacity. Still, she had the feeling other people, too, knew she was here.

Iris turned the key and pushed the front door. It was stiff, wedged. She pressed her shoulder against it, bashed it with her hip and stumbled in as it burst open. The house smelled dank, empty, unloved. The air was thick, still. Nobody had moved through this house, breathed in it, for years. The walls in the hallway were covered in faded pink paper splashed with yellow roses. Iris hated it, but not as much as Sophy and Scott did. They said nothing. Their horrified silence expressed a disgust that was beyond words.

They stamped upstairs, elbowing one another out of the way, eager to be the first to inspect the bedrooms and claim the best one. Iris heard doors slamming and raised voices. The removal men barged into the house manoeuvring the sofa through the door. Iris pointed to the living room, and noticed another removal man open the cat's basket. The cat slunk close to the floor, top speed across the living room, and up the chimney. 'The cat,' Iris shouted to nobody really. 'Oh never mind,. I'll get it later.'

Ruby bustled into the kitchen, bags stuffed with sandwiches, cakes and packets of biscuits banging against her thighs. 'I'll put the kettle on. Assuming we have electricity.' She was in her element.

'For we certainly don't have central heating.' She turned to Iris, 'You'll freeze come winter. You need central heating.'

Iris shrugged. 'Well, we'll have to manage. People did not that long ago.'

They looked at one another. More unspoken rebukes as the bickering upstairs started to crescendo. 'If you had come to live with me, none of this would have happened. You wouldn't be in this musty-smelling unheated house in this God-forsaken place,' Ruby didn't say out loud. The words rattled round her brain along with all the other things she didn't say. What happened to my son? Why did he die? What was going on with the pair of you? Did you drive him to it? Did you make him unhappy? You have no right to take my grandchildren to this place, so far from me. You always were wilful and stubborn, Iris Grigor. For she never did acknowledge Iris as a true Chisholm.

'I know,' Iris said to the unspoken rebukes. 'But fresh start and all that.'

'On your own head be it,' said Ruby. 'I just hope you know what you are doing.'

Iris shrugged again. Turned and climbed the stairs. Into the din. Know what she was doing? No. She'd never done that.

Squoinks

Sophy's word, new to Iris. But, hearing it, she smiled. The morning after their arrival at Green Cairns, Sophy went across to the dammit shop for milk. Twenty minutes later she returned, moving through the scattered half-empty boxes and piles of books, shouting, 'Squoinks!'

'Squoinks?' said Iris. 'Good word. I like it. What does it mean?'

'It's what we have here. Squoinks. The people here are all squoinks. And you have brought me to live among them.'

'Squoinks?' Iris said it slowly. 'Right. But what exactly is a squoink?' She had a feeling she didn't really have to ask. The word itself said it all.

'I mean, they're slow. They don't speak. Retards. Inbreeds. Their eyes are so narrow-set it's like they have one big eye in the middle of their foreheads. They're vacant. They stare. Never blink. It's creepy. Squoinks.'

Iris buttered a piece of toast, considering this. She was impressed by her daughter's stream of rhetoric. Had she been given such an outpouring in a school essay she would have given it a red tick. Written 'Imaginative use of language' in the margin beside it. But, there was a certain prejudice there, too. A jumping to conclusions. An instant, cruel judgment of people Sophy had hardly spoken to – not an attitude she wanted to encourage in someone she was supposed to be bringing up.

'Don't you think you're being a little judgmental?' she asked.

'I'm only being judgmental back. They judged us first. When I was in the shop I thought I'd order a paper, them being the newspaper shop, the grocer, the garage *and* the post office. And the woman behind the counter said, "No need. We've already got you down for the *Scotsman*." So I asked how they knew we took it. And they said they were watching you sitting on the step yesterday and figured you for a *Scotsman* person.'

'They were right,' said Iris.

'Oh, I see. They're right about you being a *Scotsman* person. But I'm wrong about them being squoinks.'

'It does seem a bit harsh.'

'Harsh? I wouldn't say that. It's accurate. There was this little boy when I came out of the shop, where incidentally I had to go out and round the back to get the milk because they keep it outside in the shade 'cos it's cooler than inside – squoinkism – and he had on the most horrible jumper I've ever seen. It was lumpy and piggy green.'

'Piggy green? What sort of shade is that? Pigs aren't green.'

'It's the colour of pig's shit.'

'Is that green?' asked Iris.

'I don't know. I've never seen pig's shit. But if it's green, that jumper is the colour green it would be. Anyway, he was staring at me through a pair of binoculars even though I was only yards away. So I waved. And he lowered his binoculars and still stared at me. So I said, "Hello." And he turned and ran away. Squoink.' She took the piece of toast Iris had just buttered for herself, and ate it.

Iris stood looking at her. At thirteen she was so young, and so self-assured. Where had it come from? Iris knew she wasn't like that at thirteen. Harry hadn't been, either. So where did Sophy get it? Perhaps there had been a mix-up at the hospital, and one day her real daughter, the gentle, submissive, non-judgmental one, would turn up. Though she'd miss Sophy. You never knew what she'd say or do next. 'That's my toast,' she said. 'I think grabbing someone's toast without a please or thank you is an extremely squoinkish thing to do.'

Sophy nodded, chewing and agreeing. 'When in Rome,' she said. 'How long are we going to stay here?'

'I don't know. As long as it takes to get back on our feet. A couple of years.'

'Two years! In the mud with the squoinks? I don't think so. I'll run away.'

'Well, let me know when,' said Iris, 'so I can cut down on the shopping. And take the dog while you're at it.'

'It's not funny,' said her daughter. 'There's no shops. No cinema. There's nothing here. Nothing.'

'Well, there are squoinks,' said Iris. 'Maybe if you're not too judgmental you'll find a few non-squoinks to make friends with.'

Sophy said a dubious, 'Hmm.' And went upstairs to sit amidst her unpacked books and clothes and play her French horn. She was inept, but determined.

Iris thought it must be a comfort to make such a noise when bothered by the proximity of squoinks. And mud. She spent the day unpacking, carrying bundles – books, clothes, towels, sheets – to relevant rooms. And trying not to think about Harry or squoinks. But the word had lodged itself in her brain like a bad song heard last thing at night that was still there in the morning, humming tiresomely, endlessly, round and round her thoughts in the morning. Every now and then, when her mind was blank, she'd say it: 'Squoinks.' It wasn't that their presence in the village bothered her. She'd make her own judgment about that. But she knew Sophy. Once her mind was made up, it was made up. Getting her to reassess situations, people, was hard work. If she thought she was surrounded by strange folk with one eye in the middle of their forehead, she was surrounded by strange folk with one eye in the middle of their forehead. She'd nag, whine, moan to move somewhere else. She'd withdraw into herself. And refuse to settle in. Iris saw trouble ahead.

She still had to pay off the balance of the remortgage. They were facing frugality. Up till now she and Harry had been more than comfortable. Sophy and Scott had wanted for nothing. What they wanted, they eventually got. She didn't know how they'd take to this. Potatoes and bread in the land of squoinks, she thought. Then told herself to shut up. Removing plates from their waddings of newspaper, placing them on the shelves in the kitchen cupboard, saying, 'Shut up. Shut up. Shut up.' Over and over.

51

A moment came back to her. She was sitting on the bed, holding Harry's betting slips. She was numb. What to think? 'Harry?' she'd said, her voice small in the room. She'd seen herself reflected in the mirror of the dresser, face drained of colour, shocked. 'Harry?' She touched the bed they'd shared. Things they'd done in it. Kissed. Loved. His lips on hers. Hands on her. His tongue. His lying tongue. He hadn't said a word, and she told him everything. Everything. How much she'd spent at the supermarket. How she'd pranged the car. What people at work had said. When she had her period. Every little thought, she revealed to him. Silly fears. Doubts. She'd had no secrets.

Most of her friends kept things from their husbands. Morag had regularly bought new clothes, hidden them in the wardrobe for a couple of weeks before wearing them.

'Is that new?' her husband Bill would say.

'This old thing,' Morag would reply. 'I've had this for ages. Don't you remember it?'

And Bill would look blank. 'No.'

Sometimes Morag would leave it at that. Sometimes she would pursue it. 'There you go. You never notice anything.' Which was unfair. Because she *was* wearing something new, and he just *had* noticed it. They'd divorced after three years. And no wonder, Iris thought. Jean, a colleague at school, had put her husband on a diet without telling him. He'd lost a stone and told her it was the natural rhythm of his system and proved people didn't need to weight-watch. The body adjusted itself automatically.

Sue was having an affair. Rosemary went to her women's group and, since her husband thought feminism an insult to men and a waste of time, told him she was going to play badminton. Which was a double lie. Lying to her husband. Lying to herself and her group about her beliefs.

When she thought about it Iris found that everyone she knew had secrets except her. And, more than that, she was the one to whom her friends told their secrets. 'Harry and I keep nothing from each other,' she'd boasted. 'We can talk about anything. It just wouldn't feel right keeping something to myself.' More fool me, she thought. What as idiot. And how her friends would laugh when they found out. As they surely would. They would sympathise to her face. But, oh, behind her back, they'd bitch. She winced at the things they wouldn't say to her.

But the thoughts that tumbled through her mind were mostly of Harry. All the questions he was no longer around to answer. She thought about him, those last years with him, and what he must have been going through. The evenings he came home – where had he been? – took off his coat and sat at the kitchen table.

'Good day at work,' she'd ask.

'Usual things,' he'd say. Mildly.

And that would be that. She'd tell him about her day. Now she thought about it, they hadn't exchanged information at all. In their conversations, she'd done the talking. Wiping out his silence with words. Trivia. A child in her class had cut another's hair. Michael Wilkie, an uneducable boy, had written, quite out of the blue, a wonderful little poem. There was hope. She'd talked and talked. And he'd said, 'Um,' and, 'Ah.' And, 'That's nice.'

Now she'd never know if he'd been in turmoil. Or if he'd been laughing at her. She remembered how he'd picked up the post every morning, thumbed through it. 'Stuff from the building society. I'll see to that.' And she'd found it a comfort he was so confident. She'd thought such matters beyond her. Had doubts about her own ability to understand important financial matters. Thank God for Harry, she'd thought.

The more it went round and round in her head, the harder it was to find some sort of reason. And it was dawning on her, slowly, that the way Harry had treated her, saying she saw to the day-to-day things, the little things that kept the wheels turning, while he saw to the bigger picture, the long term, he must have thought her a fool. Even if that was not how he defined it. If he was boss, there had to be an underling. Her.

So here in her new house she frantically wiped the shelves of the kitchen cupboards, lined them with red and white checked oilcloth before stacking her cups and saucers and plates. On her knees, a bucket of water sudsy and steaming at her side, she scrubbed.

Elbows going. A rhythm. Scrub. Scrub. Harry, what were you thinking of? Scrub. Harry, you made a fool of me. Scrub. Harry, look what's happened to me. She sat back on her heels. Her face was scarlet with effort. Sweat glued her hair to her head, ran in thick streams down her back, and between her breasts. Squoinks, she thought. Hah, if there was any squoink here it was her.

'I am squoink of the year. Squoink of the decade. Squoink of the century. Squoink of the universe.' She shouted it out but it didn't help. She still felt a fool.

Shortly before five, realising how little food there was in the house, she went across to the dammit shop. Mrs McGuire, Jenny, who worked behind the counter, told Iris who she was.

'You'll be the Missie, then.'

'Sorry?' said Iris who was looking sadly at the shelves. The choice was limited. 'A tin of corned beef,' she said. 'And potatoes. And some cheese.'

'The Missie,' said Jenny. 'At the school.'

'The what?' said Iris.

'The Missie,' said Jenny, who was getting tired of repeating this. 'At the school. That's what you're called.'

'Is it?' said Iris. 'I don't know about that. I'm married. Well, I was. My husband's dead.'

'Well now, that's not so good. But still, married or no, you're the Missie. Don't make no difference. If you're head at the school, you're the Missie. All the women who've ever been there have been the Missie. Now it's your turn.'

'The Missie,' said Iris vaguely. She would mash the corned beef into the potatoes, and top the whole mush with grated cheese. Stick it under the grill. That would be filling. With Scott and Sophy it was quantity that mattered. Stuff them with food and they were bearable. 'The Missie,' she said again. 'I think I'm a bit young to be a Missie. It sounds sort of old.'

'Well, you're not that young. How old are you? Forty?'

'Thirty-nine,' said Iris. A year till she hit forty. Not long, but she was hanging on to those twelve months. They made a difference, they kept her in the thirties.

'Yes, we were talking about that today. You are a bit younger than most. Our usual Missies are in their fifties. This is the last stop before retirement. We thought maybe a bit younger's what we need. The last one was a demon. Hit them kids, had them scared out of their wits. Bit of discipline never hurts with the little ones, but she took it too far. That was why the mums and dads got up the petition and sent it to the education board. So she's out and now we've got you. Here's a tin of peaches. Just to say hello, like. A welcome.'

'Thank you,' said Iris. 'That's so kind.'

This was dismissed with a flap of Jenny's hand. She'd handed over the gift. That was that. Over with. Effusive thank yous were only embarrassing. The deal was, take it, don't dwell on it.

'Oh, that Miss Mitchell. A terror! Scared the pants off of me. And I'm sixty-two. Of course, teachers are all like that. Bossy. And once a teacher always a teacher. I was still scared of mine long after I'd left the school. The one you're Missie of now. Miss Blackwood, she was called. Came in for her paper and her milk every morning till she died eight years ago, and still set my heart pounding. Couldn't add up or nothing when she was looking at me.'

'Goodness,' said Iris. 'But times have changed.' She was backing towards the door. 'I have no intention of frightening children. It's not my way.'

'Glad to hear it,' said Jenny McGuire. 'Now after Miss Blackwood, my Missie, there was Miss Cromwell. She was worse. Then there was Miss Jewell. She was no jewel, I can tell you . . . then . . .'

'I've just remembered,' said Iris, 'I've left the kettle on. Better dash.' She ran, thinking, Going to the dammit shop can be Sophy's job. She's stroppy enough to make a quick get-away.

In the street, standing staring at her, was the boy who lived opposite them. It was a summer evening, and hot. He wore a thick jumper, underneath that a shirt. Iris suspected there were more layers under the shirt. His nose was running. There was a raw eczema rash round his neck and running up his legs. The soul, thought Iris. The child didn't smile but continued to stare, mouth slightly agape. He wore glasses, round, with one eye patched.

'Hello,' said Iris, holding out her hand, 'I'm Mrs Chisholm. Your new Missie.'

The child did not answer but looked at the outstretched hand.

'Do you go to the school?'

He shook his head.

'No? You go to another school?'

He shook his head.

'You don't go to school?'

He nodded.

Iris didn't believe this nod. 'Which school do you go to?'

He pointed to the school across the road. Iris's school.

'So you'll be in class when term starts?'

He shook his head. Then nodded.

'Right,' said Iris. 'One of those. What's your name?'

The child stared.

'You have a name?' said Iris.

He shook his head. Wiped his nose on his sleeve.

'Handy things, sleeves,' said Iris.

A woman appeared in the doorway of the house opposite Iris's. 'Colin, your tea's getting cold. Will you stop bothering that poor woman?'

She was small. Anxious. Had busy hands that kept moving as she spoke. Her hair curled eagerly in all directions, and looked as if it was brushed fiercely morning and night, then left to its own devices. It was treated merely as an irritation that sprang out of her head, though her face was kindly and humorous beneath its anxiety. She was wearing brown slippers that seemed to fold over the arches of her feet, a shapeless brown skirt, and pink shirt and a cardigan identical in colour to the boy's sweater. Pig green, thought Iris.

'He's called Colin. He doesn't speak,' said the woman.

The child looked at her. Then at Iris. Knowing they were about to talk about him as if he wasn't there. It was what grown-ups did.

'He's dumb?' asked Iris.

'Oh, no. He can speak. He just doesn't. Well, he does to me. But not a lot. And he speaks to Lucy down the road. And that's it.'

Iris looked at him. 'You don't speak?'

56

Colin nodded.

'Excellent ploy,' she said to him. 'The stupid things I've said in my life, I wish I'd thought of that. I'd have saved myself a lot of grief. That's very clever of you to decide not to speak.'

She thought she saw a slight movement of the boy's lips. Upward. He might have smiled, but she wasn't sure. Still, she smiled. Better one of them did. It cut the ice.

The woman took the boy's hand. 'I'm Ella Robertson. This is Colin, my grandson. His dad died, went under a tractor few years back. And his mum went off with a travelling salesman when he was two.' She rubbed the top of his head. 'He's a soul.'

Colin looked up at her, head tilted back. He didn't think he was a soul. The words 'I am not a soul' formed loud in his mind. But he didn't speak them out. He never quite liked to say the things in his head. You never knew how people would react. They might laugh. The words he wanted to say might not be the right ones. So he kept them to himself. Iris crossed to her gate. Looked back at the house opposite. The child was at the window, staring. Wiping his nose on his sleeve.

Squoink, thought Iris.

Colin stood alone. He seemed tiny, forlorn. Lost in a world of huge, shouting people, and locked into some sort of silent protest about his lot in life.

Oh, my God, thought Iris. How could I think such a thing? He's not a squoink. He's a little boy.

She opened her gate, walked up the path. Sophy was at the window, making faces. She crossed her eyes, let her tongue dangle out of the side of her mouth, and screwed her finger into her forehead. 'Squoink,' she was saying.

No, just a child, thought Iris. And so, my girl, are you.

Adjusting

Iris, on entering the school, was flooded with emotion. First impressions were depressing. The place was claustrophobic, exuding an inhibiting brownness, a staleness. It was loveless and forbidding. Iris hated it. She was five again, moving through the fear she'd felt in her first years at school. Even today the smell inside a school bag, of leather, paper, pencils, sent a shrill shiver through her stomach. She remembered her old schoolmistress looming over her, hot gusts of nicotined breath fanning from her mouth as she taunted, 'Iris is lop-sided.' Iris was left-handed. Her writing sloped backwards. Her teacher had a vision of producing forty five year olds who could produce pages of perfect copperplate working with over-used, blunt-nibbed pens. The dip and scrut, Iris called it. Tongue sticking out of the side of her mouth, face inches from the page she was to fill with rows and rows of perfect es and fs, she was all inky fingers, sweat and tears. Only now, over thirty years later, did she realise that immaculate writing with such tired and worthless implements was impossible. In fact, that she'd produced something that was even legible was a miracle.

She moved along the desks, set in regimented lines, noting their age and the graffiti carved into them. Years of carving, scribbling, blackened with age. So many bored children. New desks, she decided. A pity, in a way. Each desk told a story. They were inscribed with doodles. Exclamation marks. Question marks. Swirls, circles, loops, hearts. Names. Stickmen. Many claimed 'Elvis is King'. Others favoured John, Paul, George or Ringo. One had a deeply carved, time-worn vow of endless longing for Errol Flynn. These are really old desks, thought Iris. There were lines from songs. Names of footballers. Declarations of love. Outbursts of loathing. I hate mince. I hate school dinners. I hate sums. I hate school. One desk, interestingly, had inscribed on it, in meticulous lettering, I love cheese. Cheese was repeated down the lid, beautifully written, sixteen times, Iris counted. Now there's boredom, she thought.

Her own desk stood in front of the class. There was nothing in any of the drawers. The register lay on top. Iris looked through it. A lot of absences. Though she noted that little Colin from across the road had not missed a day. But a school register says a lot about the children. Their state of mind. Little people who had not learned the language of unhappiness always expressed their woes physically. There would be sore heads, sickness, bitten fingernails, all sorts of strange rashes, upset tummies. And, Iris was sure, damp sheets in the morning. She'd seen them blowing on washing lines every day. Green Cairns was a village of bad dreams and bed wetters. A little place that hoarded secrets. Fretting parents and cheerless children.

It had potential this room, though. A good coat of paint was all it needed. Large windows looked on to the playground and the small wood across the road. There was a partition down the centre. Iris went through a doorway set in it. The other side was empty. Dusty. A blind was pulled down over the window blocking the light. Iris opened it. Sunshine flooded in. 'Well,' she said, knocking on the partition, 'this has got to go. We will have space. Space is the thing to have.' She spread her arms, twirled. Halfway through her second sweep round she saw through the newly unshaded window a small gathering of women watching her. She was being discussed. So she waved. Her watchers looked away, and moved off, heads down. Iris got the impression they were giggling. Ah, right, she thought. I'm a teacher. The Missie. Not a human being at all. I'm expected to behave myself. I've been decreed to be a cut above the gigglers. Damn!

Back in the classroom, she looked through the cupboards. Tattered books, crayons, chalks, papers, posters, bricks, plasticine turned the lumpen colour only plasticine can attain when all its colours are compressed by small, sweaty hands into a thick, unlovely, unworkable sludge. And there was a wooden-handled brass bell. She knew she would have to step outside and ring this in the mornings, at the end of break and at lunchtime, and felt suddenly shy at the prospect. Iris sighed. She'd found her first visit to her new school as depressing and bleak as the pupils, the desk-scribblers, obviously found it.

She returned home and wrote a stiff letter to the County Education Department requesting new desks for her pupils and a fresh coat of paint for the premises. '*The school,*' she wrote, '*is presently tricked out in many shades of dirty brown. I cannot imagine the extent of the depression such a miserable place evokes in the young who have to spend many hours of their childhood in it.*'

Mid-July, the beginning of term, was two weeks away. Iris painted her own kitchen, living room and hallway. White. Everything white. It was the cheapest paint she could find. But the finished effect pleased her. The old house looked brighter. Why, she thought, it's almost like a home. It wasn't really the smell of emulsion that gave it a sudden familiarity, it was the noise. Everything was always on. The television. The radio in the kitchen. The hi-fis. They had three. One was Sophy's. One was Scott's. One was hers. Except that her one was everybody's, and kept in the living room. It played all day, alongside the television, though nobody was ever there to watch or listen.

The Grateful Dead, The Beatles' White Album, Joni Mitchell, Radio One, all boomed through the house constantly. Standing in the hall where all the songs and riffs converged into one cacophony, the jangle of guitars met voices, Iris was often overwhelmed by the din. Still, there was some comfort in it. It was the only way she knew her children were there. They had stopped communicating otherwise.

Scott had withdrawn into music. He was hooked on sound. It started before he got out of bed and finished just before sleep took him late at night or early next morning. It came down to specifics. He'd play one track over and over. And when the addiction bit deep he'd play one part of one track over and over. Sometimes, he'd leave the table in the middle of a meal, go to his room, play the desired riffs, and return to finish his food. He ate, head down, in a solid rapid movement of fork to plate to mouth. Huge mounds of food – anything, he never complained about what he was given, or voiced a preference for one thing rather than another – disappeared into him. Iris thought the way he jiggled, knee moving, fingers tapping, to something that was still playing in his head, he was burning it off as he chewed.

At times they stood facing one another. She'd be thinking of something to say, a conversation opener. He'd be looking vacant. For a while she'd wondered vaguely if there was something wrong with him. A stab of worry flashed through her. A vision, Iris and Scott at the doctor's, her saying, 'He's suddenly gone vacant.' The doctor snapping his fingers in front of Scott's face, saying, 'Interesting. Suddenly, you say?' And Scott staring mindlessly ahead, unaware of anybody around him. But no, Iris decided, it was just the Grateful Dead weaving sounds, hissing chants on and on in his brain, long after the record had stopped. He'd grow out of it, wouldn't he?

She opened her mouth with the intention of saying something to communicate with him. Something like, 'Hello. Are you in there, Scott? How're you doing? Are you happy?' But what came out was, 'Are you thinking of getting your hair cut?' Damn! She was nagging. She hadn't meant to do that. Though a hair cut for Scott had been what she was thinking about.

'Mother,' he said, enunciating each syllable. Irritated. 'I'm never going to get it cut. It isn't nearly long enough.' It was past his shoulders.

'Right,' she said. Then, 'I don't really mind long hair. As long as it's clean.' Hadn't she read that recently in the *Scotsman*? She wished she hadn't said it.

He shrugged.

'I wanted to tell you,' Iris continued, 'that we won't have very much money now. We'll have to be careful. I can't buy you anything.'

'I don't want anything,' he said.

'Well,' she said, 'that's good. I can't afford things anymore.'

'I don't want things.' Scott was adamant. 'All property is theft.'

Iris said. 'Ah.' It was all she could think of. She resisted the temptation to list his possessions – clothes, records, books, hi-fi, bike – and ask if owning them made him a thief. Perhaps he should give them away. He seemed to have gone up the stairs completely non-political, then come down them twenty minutes later a raging Marxist. The same thing had happened with food a couple of years ago. He'd disappeared into his room with a ham sandwich, and emerged, minutes later, a vegetarian. Iris sometimes wondered what had happened in such a small space of time to bring about this change in him. And had the decision come before or after he'd eaten the sandwich? And if before, what had become of the sandwich? She didn't like to ask. He'd told her that society's preoccupation with trivia would bring about the fall of mankind, so asking about the fate of a ham sandwich might belittle him as he wrestled with politics and philosophy, the thinking teenager's biggies.

She wrestled with the thinking mother's little things. Sandwiches, dirty socks, the whereabouts of cups, and how to make something edible for supper out of the absurd contents of her fridge. He was chasing thoughts, in search of the big one, the thought of thoughts, that would put all his other thoughts into perspective and set the world to rights. Meanwhile she struggled with mindless details, tiny day-to-day-getting-by sort of things, and desperately tried not to think. Thinking only led to one thing: Harry and his state of mind. Had spending all that money made him feel joyous, important, filled with rapturous, extravagant abandon? Or had it driven him deeper and deeper into despair? He bewildered her. In the midst of the rage and confusion she felt about him, she missed him. She missed his voice, the way he whistled in the mornings when he shaved – a tuneless drone that had irritated her when he was alive though now she ached to hear it. She wanted to talk to him again. Ask him what he thought of the new house. Lie beside him in bed, listening to him breathe. Damn him for dying!

'Marx was the man,' Scott told her now.

'I expect he was,' she agreed. 'But who washed his socks while he came up with all this stuff?' Oh, God, she thought, I sound like a mother.

'Socks,' he said, 'were not a major concern during the Russian Revolution.'

She thought to end this conversation now, before it dissolved into a heated discourse about men thinking while women laundered with the Russian Revolution floating in between. But said instead that Marx was German. And that he'd died in London some thirty years before the Russian Revolution started.

Scott said, 'Really?' He seemed interested. 'I didn't know you knew about Marx.'

Iris had clearly risen a notch in his estimation, and basked momentarily in this. 'Yeah,' she said. 'He was born in Trier, educated in Bonn and Berlin. Eventually moved to Paris where he wrote *The Communist Manifesto*. "The workers have nothing to lose but their chains . . ." ' She watched her son's face. She was losing him. She'd gone on too long.

He shifted his feet, hands in pockets, anxious to escape to his room. She knew she was irritating him. It was her voice. Not what she was saying. Just that it was there, penetrating his muse, his thoughts, daydreams, the music that played at all times in his brain. Scott lived in his head. Well, she thought, he spends so much time in there, it must be a happy place. Or maybe it was gloomy, and he was happy being gloomy.

Still, Sophy had settled in. She'd made friends with the girl next door. They'd come across one another, each standing in her own garden, and been amazed. It was love or hate. For a second the relationship could have gone either way. They looked identical. They both had poker-straight blonde hair, ashen faces with panda-black eyes. They both wore bell-bottom jeans that reached the ground, frayed round the bottom. (Scott's legs were similarly covered. Iris realised it had been a while since she had seen her children's feet, and hoped they were keeping well.) From behind it was hard to tell one from the other. Sophy and Jean had stared at one another. Then they seemed to decide they'd each found a soulmate, and from that moment appeared to be joined at the hip. They were rarely apart. Every day they walked the length of the village in perfect rhythm. Moving together. Talking. This took five minutes. It was a small place. Then they'd turn and walk back again. Talking. They'd go to the dammit shop for sweets, and sit on the wall outside eating them. Talking. Heads close. Their constant stream of chat interrupted only by squeals of glee and giggles.

Iris remarked to Scott that she was amazed that two people who gave the impression they had absolutely nothing in their heads could find so much to say. And Scott, surfacing momentarily from his daze, said that that was what it was like when you were young. He was barely seventeen. Iris did not comment on this.

She wondered what her children felt about their father's death. Sophy, if she was grieving, was hiding it well. And Scott seemed to be more upset about the demise of Otis Redding, a couple of months before Harry died than he did about his father.

'God,' he would say, 'I'm gutted Otis is gone.'

'I feel the same about your father,' Iris would reply, snippily.

And Scott would say, 'Yeah. Him too. But "Dock of the Bay" was the quintessential soul song.'

'Harry Chisholm was the quintessential father of Scott Chisholm.'

'Was he?' said Scott. 'I suppose.' He left it at that. But three days later he said, out of the blue, 'I don't know if Dad was the quintessential dad. I've nobody to measure him against. He was the only dad I've ever had. I mean, you couldn't say he was the quintessential husband when you've not had any other husbands to compare him to? You may marry another bloke someday and decide Dad was a crap husband. You see, to be quintessential . . .'

Iris cut him short. 'I loved your father.'

They left it at that. Nothing else was said. But thoughts, doubts, swirled through Iris's mind. What did her son mean, quintessential husband? Harry was Harry. That was it. Nothing more. Well, there had been more. But she didn't want to think about that.

Morag, her friend, said that Scott and Sophy were in denial and that when they acknowledged their grief all hell would be let loose. Iris should watch out for it.

And Iris said, 'Thank you for that.' And that she would keep her eye out for all hell breaking loose. No doubt she would recognise it when it happened.

She escaped to the garden or walked the fields behind the house, the dog racing ahead, the cat picking its complaining way behind, tail in the air, curious to know where she was going. Iris fooled herself this was her thinking time. Her planning time. But she did neither. She stared. Looked at the landscape. She trailed her hand along the soft ears of corn. Kicked stones. And knew she was letting her mind drift, float off on its own through the events of the past months. She wore Harry's shirt, open over a T-shirt, held it round her. Wished he was here. Harry the gambler, liar, hoarder of secrets. Didn't matter. She'd rather have that Harry than no Harry at all. 'We could have worked it out,' she said. To no one at all.

She'd see birds sitting on wires overhead and wonder what they were. Wild flowers, and realise she knew nothing of them. And she knew, too, that people in the other houses that backed on to the fields were watching her. People were curious about her. She could read it in looks. Sidelong glances. It hadn't occurred to her that this was more than a job. More than just a teacher, she was the Missie. It was a position in society. A way of life.

'I need to be positive,' she said to Morag on the phone. 'There are things expected of me.'

'What?' asked her friend.

'Well, I need to be assertive. Accessible, yet distant. Wise, yet friendly and comfortable. Cheery, but not silly with it. Aloof, restrained, yet down to earth.'

'Easy,' said Morag. 'Tell you what, think tall. That's all you need to be.'

'But I'm not tall.'

'Neither are you wise, assertive, accessibly distant, aloof, restrained or particularly cheery. So think tall. Act tall. And nobody will know it's only you.'

'I think they'll notice I'm not tall.'

'Pretend you're a tall person who knows what she's doing.'

'You think?'

'Yeah.'

'I am the Missie,' said Iris. 'I will be obeyed.'

'Now you've got it. It is a bird? Is it a plane?'

'It's the Missie,' said Iris. 'The planet is saved. OK, tall it is. Then nobody will know it's only me.'

Running through the woods opposite the house was a small stream. It tumbled down from the mountains beyond Green Cairns, rattled over rocks, curved round the bend and hurried away. The path beside it was well-worn, dusty in summer, squelched mud from October to May. Iris walked it most days, Eric the cat behind as always, Lulu the dog hurtling enthusiastically ahead. The dog, Iris decided, was the only member of her family who had truly settled in. She was in heaven.

Yesterday on this path she'd met a man. She didn't know who he was but he knew who she was. He nodded. Said hello in the way of saying hello that was local way of saying hello. It was an acknowledgment that she was in the world, in the same spot in the world as he was, that came out on a single breath: 'Aye.' And there was a sideways nod of the head that went with it. It was a greeting she knew she'd never master. If she tried, the greeted ones would think she was making fools of them. So instead she said, 'Hello.'

And he said, 'Aye,' on his breath again. Nodded sideways.

An old man with a weather beaten face, sun-reddened beneath his cap. There was a scorched triangle at his throat where his shirt was open at the neck and the day's heat had left its mark. He had a small dog on a long lead. His shoes were shiny. He looked at hers, which weren't, and he nodded at this. As if the state of her footwear told him everything. The footwear and the dog. Lulu was what Iris described as a mobile heap of hair. The breeder had said she was a spaniel, but some crazed gene from another breed had got into her system. She was long-haired, a mix of black and brown, with long ears and a hyper-active tail. She was ebullient, enthusiastic, and prone to staring absently into the distance which made her seem vacuous at times. Iris thought her dog had the makings of a children's television presenter.

'You're the Missie then,' said the man on the path.

Iris nodded. 'Yes. I'm looking forward to getting started.'

'I expect you are.' He eyed her up and down, scuffed shoes to tousled hair. His disapproval washed over her. It seemed to loosen her limbs, prickle in her stomach. She wanted to apologise to him. For what? She'd done nothing.

'Young, though, aren't you?' he said.

'Am I? I think I'm a little past young these days.' Iris, thundering towards forty, felt quite pleased at this observation, however. Young wasn't an adjective she ever used to describe herself these days. Forty, she'd think, staring in the mirror, noticing every microscopic change in her face. Creases round the eyes. A certain tightening of her lips. Forty. She had a grey hair or two. Forty. Her hands showed the strains of four decades of use. Forty. Gazing at her reflection, she thought she looked sad.

'Yes, you are,' he said. 'Young. We're not so sure of young round here.'

Iris snapped then. What the hell did he mean? Who did he think he was, speaking to her like that? 'Well, I expect I'll get over being young,' she said, and stamped off. The man, whoever he was, stood staring after her.

'You obviously did!' she called over her shoulder, heading for home. It only took a few steps before the flash of temper disappeared. She decided she shouldn't have said what she had. She should have found out who this man was before she upped him on the matter of her youth. Too late, she thought now. There will be repercussions, I know that.

Back in her garden she stood and sniffed the air. The smell of cooking. Lard, she thought. Chips sizzling in lard. Such an old familiar smell. It reminded her of her childhood home. Five o'clock, teatime, and she'd come into the living room. The table would be set, the fire glowing in the hearth, the news on the wireless and the whole house filled with the comfortable smell of hot lard.

'Have you been good?' her mother would ask.

'Oh, yes,' she'd say. For she had been. Unlike her own children, Iris had spent her days working hard at being good. Back then, good had been the thing to be. It seemed shiny and harmless now. And a little bit pathetic.

The air was still with that same silence she'd felt on her first afternoon, sitting in the garden waiting for Ruby and her children and the removal van to turn up. She usually found silence sweet, a lovely thing. But the silence of this place was curdled. It made her uneasy. She sighed, turned and went into the house to cook supper, chicken (for Scott's vegetarianism had lasted a month, then vanished as swiftly and suddenly as it appeared) and rice. No, she would never offer them the comfort of lard.

The School Marm

They came dragging through the morning, heads down. Glum, but shiny. They'd been scrubbed and pressed for the new Missie. But then, she'd scrubbed and pressed herself for her new pupils. Iris was as nervous as they were.

She was wearing a black skirt, that stopped just below her knees, a dark blue shirt, open at the neck, and sensible shoes. Her school-marm shoes, Sophy called them.

'My mum, the marm,' she'd said. 'You look very bossy.'

'I am bossy,' said Iris. 'It's my job. Are you ready for school? Got your lunch money?'

'Yes, Ma.'

'Good.'

Sophy was transformed, tamed. Her hair was swept off her face, tied back with a navy ribbon. She wore a white blouse and blue and red striped school tie, black skirt, polished shoes and white ankle socks. It had taken years off her. She looked thirteen again.

Scott still looked seventeen going on forty-five. Glum. Thin. Restlessly watchful. His school uniform seemed only to heighten his rebel stance. His hair reached past his shoulders. His face was winter-pale for, though the days had been hot, he'd stayed indoors this summer. Sunlight never touched his skin. Two spots glowed, red and sore, on his chin. He wore a white shirt, open at the collar, a tie the same as Sophy's loosely knotted below it. But something about him – his height – had overwhelmed him. He was, said Ruby, 'Too tall for himself.' The way his hands dug deep into his pockets, and his head moved slightly to the right, and his feet stuck out awkwardly at the end of his legs, made him look

71

constantly dishevelled, defiant. Ill at ease with his surroundings, the people he mixed with, but mostly with himself.

He ate a bowl stuffed to overflowing with Cornflakes. Finished it. Refilled it. Ate. Chewing, constantly moving his head, so Iris wondered what was playing in there this morning.

'Are you all right?' she asked.

He nodded.

'Got everything? Your lunch money?'

Still chewing vigorously, he patted his pocket. It jingled. No need to say more. Or anything, come to that.

At half-past eight both Scott and Sophy stood at the gate waiting for the school bus to come down the glen. It rumbled up the road just after seven, a long winding journey picking up children along the way. By the time it passed once again through Green Cairns, it was alive, filled with noise, movement, calls, jibes. Empty on its way up, vibrant coming down, it would take all the teenage children to the High School in Forham, the county town, fifteen miles away. A greying place of old buildings, cobbled streets, an assortment of old-fashioned shops and a gleaming new breeze-block school with spreading playing fields on the outskirts.

Iris, standing at her window, saw Sophy climb aboard with her new best friend Jean. Talking. They moved up the inside of the bus, talking. Sat next to one another, still talking. So much to say, they hadn't seen each other since ten o'clock last night. Scott got on slowly. Stared around, then moved up to the back where there was an empty seat. The bus moved off, Scott at a window. Alone. He put his forehead on the glass, and stared down at the road.

A few yards away the first mums of the morning were gathering at the school gates, children already in the playground. It was full of small people in constant motion, milling, shouting. A couple were standing pressed against and clutching the railings. Wanting out, Iris thought. She went through to the kitchen. More coffee. Then face the day.

She walked through the garden and into the school grounds. Unlocked the building and went, smiling, to introduce herself. Assorted mothers of the morning, she thought. Thin faces, comfortable faces, suspicious faces, smiley faces, sleepy baggy faces, made-up faces, all watching her approach.

It was a short walk to the front gate, barely thirty yards. But thirty yards was a long way to smile. Halfway there the smile staled, shifted into a grimace. She was moving towards the mothers, looking, she thought, slightly demented. Hair swept off her face by the forward thrust of her pace. And she hated that. The bit of her she least liked people to see was her forehead. Large and glistening slightly, she wanted to keep it a secret.

They all said hello. There was no 'aye,' on an inward breath, with a sideways nod. Iris wondered if that was purely a man thing, and was quietly glad she hadn't tried to master it. She might have given out the wrong signals. A tall woman in jeans and an old tweed jacket said she was Mrs Hargreaves, Lucy's mum, and she'd been the one who'd raised the petition to get rid of the last Missie.

Their eyes met. A long, cool, calculating look.

'Excellent,' said Iris. For she didn't really know what else to say. She decided here was the local mover and shaker, she'd better make a friend of her, and smiled harder. She noticed a cheery woman standing at the edge of the crowd. Years of laughter had given her face an upward tilt. She wore jeans and a huge checked shirt. A cuddlesome soul. The mum of mums, thought Iris. The quintessential mum. I've found her, I must tell Scott. As plainly I'm not the quintessential mum, he'll be pleased to know there is one.

'I'm Stella,' said the quintessential mum. 'There's my boys over there. The twins.'

Iris turned. Saw two identical children both in grey trousers and blue shirts. Both with brown leather schoolbags over their shoulders. Both with curly black hair. Both waving in unison. There was something about them that made her smile.

'I'm in the black books. I wouldn't let them cycle to school this morning. They got bikes for their birthday last week.'

Iris nodded, said she was Iris. Iris Chisholm. And it was worrying letting children loose on the roads. Even these quiet ones.

'It's the quiet roads do the damage. Folk see an empty stretch and put their foot down. Cars come out of the blue. And we know all about you. You've got two of your own and your man died a while back. You've painted the schoolhouse white, and your cat goes on walks with you. You've been discussed.'

'So I see. Not very interesting discussions, though.'

'Oh, no, you make good gossip,' said Stella. 'A new face always does. There's so much to speculate about.'

The school taxi drew up. Half a dozen children tumbled out, chattering, bickering, squealing. They saw Iris. Fell silent. And walked sedately through the gate.

Iris said she'd noticed how quiet the village was. But it was calming, and quite addictive once you got used to it. And it was time she rang the bell.

A Strange Thing Happened

They prayed, a morning ritual, Iris leading the chorus of mumbles. She looked up from her pressed palms. Some heads were solemnly bowed, most were turned towards the window. Staring out, dreaming.

She read the register, calling names. James Biggar. Here. Robert Soames. Here. Fiona Wilkinson. Here. Lucy Hargreaves. Here. Colin Robertson. Silence. Iris looked up. Colin was looking at his desk.

'Colin Robertson,' she said again.

He leaned over, whispered in Lucy's ear.

'Here,' she said. Not without effort, she stammered badly. Stood with mouth open, head nodding slightly as she struggled to force the word ringing in her brain to her lips.

'Good,' said Iris. One stammerer, one mute, she thought. What else have we got? She looked round. Small faces looked back at her. Several had fingers wedged in their mouths. They all looked anxious. Their stillness disturbed Iris. They hardly moved. She had been teaching for almost fifteen years, and knew the body language of infants. They wriggled, nudged, lolled, they fiddled with pencils, scratched, leaned. She had never, ever seen twenty children sit with hands folded on the desk in front of them, motionless. Freaky, man, Scott would say. She thought that got it in a nutshell.

'I'm Mrs Chisholm, your new teacher. C-H-I-S-H-O-L-M. I'll spell it for you,' she said and turned to the board. She stood with her back to the class, chalk poised, and a strange thing happened. There was a rustling. A creaking. It was the uniformity of the noise that alarmed Iris. The soft sound of small bodies moving in unison.

She turned. The whole class was sitting with hands on head, looking at her. Tamed. Obedient.

Iris sat on her chair. Put her own hands, fingers neatly laced, on her head. They all sat, frozen. Minutes passed. Silence. There was a gradual crumbling of resolve. Giggling. And Iris, hands still on head, said, 'What are we all doing?'

'This is what we do,' said Laura Gilvray, 'when teacher turns her back or goes out of the room, we put our hands on our heads so we'll be good.'

Iris said, 'Ah.' She remembered herself at school, years ago. She'd had to do this, too. She smiled. Wasn't it funny how you forgot such things? So immediate, so important at the time. Then it all just slipped away. 'I don't think we'll put our hands on our heads anymore. It's tiring.'

Colin was sitting with hands set idly on his skull as he looked out of the window, master of the schoolboy art of acquiescing to demands while doing what he wanted in his head. Iris knew of such things. Had she not wiled away many a schoolday herself, years ago, staring out of the window? She remembered how contented she'd been during those dreaming interludes. It always seemed a pity to her to rouse children from their idling. People needed to muse, fantasise. And she had no doubt that the reverie was a lot more interesting than anything she had to say about multiplication and division. But there it was, her pupils were here to learn and musing had to be kept to a minumun.

Colin fascinated Iris. He walked with his head tilted slightly to one side, looking at nobody, hands in pockets, laces untied. He was a soul, she thought, wandering his tiny world. From home, across the road to school, then back again. Was that all? The boundaries of the space he inhabited were horribly narrow. She hoped the plains of his imagination were boundless.

During the course of her first morning Iris spoke several times to him. He always answered through Lucy. 'What are four fours, Colin? Do you know?'

He leaned over, whispered into Lucy's ear, loud enough for Iris to hear: 'Sixteen.'

And Lucy told Iris the answer. Stammering, so it took a while. 'S-s-s-s-six—,' long gap while she gulped breath and swam through her obstacle vowels '—teen, Miss.'

And Iris waited. 'Excellent. Well done, Colin. And Lucy.'

The girl beamed. Two missing front teeth. Colin looked out of the window. And floated off to the happy place where he lived.

Iris joined him for a few seconds. A small gaze towards what was for Colin a far better place – the world beyond the window. And she had to agree with him there. Wasn't it the damnedest thing? School started and the days turned hot and golden. Sunshine pouring down and here they all were sitting scrunged at old desks, working out sums with chewed pencils. Except, that is, for Lucy. Lucy of the perfect pencils, her precious pencil case neatly placed at the top of her desk.

The child lifted out a glossy red pencil, freshly sharpened. She looked at it. 'No, Mr Red Pencil. I'm not using you now. It's Mr Blue Pencil's turn. You go back to bed.'

Iris stood behind her, and smiled. Now there was a thing. Lucy conversed perfectly with her pencils. Only people made her stammer.

She wandered on, looking over shoulders. James Biggar, a large boy in his last year at primary, was leaning over his work, arm shielding it from her view. Iris reached over, removed the arm. The page was thumbmarked, filthy. There was a hole where he'd written in a wrong answer, rubbed it out, replaced it with another wrong answer, rubbed again, wrong again, rubbed it out again.

'Long division is a trial, James, is it not?'

'I hate it.'

'Take a new page and start again.'

'You get the belt for that.'

'For what?'

'Making a mess of your jotter.'

'Well, you won't be getting the belt from me. I'm not in the habit of hitting people smaller than I am.'

This business of hitting children alarmed Iris. She found it humiliating to lash out at small outstretched hands with a leather belt, and had always refused to do it. It was inherently nasty, and also she feared she would miss one day and whack herself on the leg. She never therefore disciplined her pupils with pain, but resorted to subtler methods. Mostly she tried to keep the children she taught so busy they had no time to get up to mischief.

'That's 'cos I'll soon be bigger than you,' said James.

'Exactly.' She fixed him with an authoritative eye. A rebel. But she liked rebels. 'But growing taller than someone is hardly a great achievement. We are the height we are. So soon I will be someone smaller than you who can do long division.'

'So what do you do, if you don't give the belt?'

Iris knew this question was coming. 'I glare,' she said. 'And a glare from me, James Biggar, is a painful thing.'

And she glared at him. He looked down at his page, got on with his struggle. But when she continued her tour of the class he raised a single defiant finger to her departing back. Iris felt the shiver that ran through the class. There was sniggering. 'I saw that, James. I have eyes in the back of my head. I glare with them too.'

Just before eleven o'clock, lunch arrived. It came, clanking, in large metal containers, delivered by taxi. Cooked in Forham at eight in the morning and sent out on a long circuitous route, down tiny, twisting roads, taking in all the country schools for miles and miles around. Green Cairns was tenth on the list.

Iris watched it being carried in with sinking heart. The smell of it, deeply, fattily unappetising, lined the insides of her nostrils. She hadn't thought about school lunch when she'd applied for the job of head teacher. She realised now that if she had, she would have taken her other life option – she'd have gone to Australia.

The meal was served by Effie Jeffries, who told Iris there was no need to introduce herself. She was Iris Chisholm, lost her man a wee bit back, and she'd painted the schoolhouse white, and her cat went on walks with her.

Iris said, 'That's me.'

Effie was a thin woman whose face seemed fixed into lines of disapproval. It was a surprise, then, when the look of censure melted into smiles every time the woman looked at a child and pressed a steaming plate of glutinous stew, watery mash and pebble-hard, greying peas into a small outstretched hand. That change in expression, the swiftness and contrast of it, almost made the unpalatable palatable.

Iris looked down at her own helping. So, it had come to this. Years at teachers' training college. The books she'd read. Exams passed. People she'd taught. Constant achievement. And it all led to this static stew, rigid on the plate and with a worrying rim of shiny fat round the edge.

It had been served up by Effie using the school ladle, an item of cutlery that was intriguing enough to take Iris's mind off the ordeal ahead – the eating of the stew. The ladle was uncompromisingly utilitarian, a dulled steel colour. Its size, though, was a wonder. This was the biggest ladle Iris had ever seen. A king ladle. The ladle of ladles. Cartoon huge. Iris marvelled at its size and watched the way Effie could, with a flick of her wrist, manage to deposit child-size portions on to plates with it. The skills we master, she thought, mesmerised. She could do things with a ladle like that. A ladle to drown in. She could talk to the class about size. The bigness and littleness of things. Now, she thought she would say to them, this is huge to us, but to a giant it might be but a teaspoon. That was the thing to do this afternoon. Get the class talking. And children's perception of size was fascinating. A puddle could be the sea. A distant mountain, a pimple. Children, she mused, small people with no real grasp of infinity. Yet often they thought themselves invincible. Adults, now, wrestled with infinity, could just about imagine it yet always came to know how fallible they were. She looked up from her thoughts. The children were gathered at the table, stew in front of them, steaming vilely. They were all looking at her expectantly.

'What?' she asked.

'You have to pray,' said Effie.

'Pray? Who, me?' said Iris.

'Yes. Grace before a meal. I don't know about you, but that's how we do things around here.'

'Of course, of course,' said Iris. All her teaching life, she'd worked at avoiding school meals. A sandwich and a think were her usual lunchtime fare. 'I was dreaming.' She pressed her hands together, bowed her head. 'For what we are about to receive, may the Lord make us truly thankful. Oh, and please, God, do something to the stew quickly. It looks like it needs a bit of divine intervention. Thank you.' She looked up. Her pupils were still sitting in praying position. She put her own palms together again. 'Sorry, God. Amen.'

Well, thought Effie, she's certainly got a new take on praying. I've never heard the like in my life.

Iris lifted her fork, jabbed it into the meaty mound on her plate. And, as heartily as she could manage, stuffed a smallish lump into her mouth. The children watched.

'Oh, my,' said Iris. 'Oh, yum, it's worked. He has intervened with the stew. It's delicious.'

The news of divinely intervened stew spread around the table. The children started to eat.

'It's lovely,' said Eileen Barton.

'Lovely,' agreed Laura Gilvray.

They all silently ate. Only James Biggar looked dubious. Well, he would, thought Iris. She gave him a swift glare lest he say something. A grade-three glare, she thought, not the full-on grade-one hostile glower. She'd save that for when she really needed it.

Effie watched. Fourteen years serving school dinners and she'd never seen stew disappear so quickly. Well, she thought, that new Missie's not as daft as she looks.

The afternoon passed slowly. August heat thickened the air. Iris opened the windows, though it made little difference. Nothing moved. The heat was relentless, inside and out. Black harvest flies swarmed at the window. Tractors grumbled past on the road outside, rumbling and clanking. Everything that was happening on the land, the harvest, seemed close. These lives she was now part of were governed by the seasons.

Children sprawled over their desks, heads resting on their arms. It seemed as if there was not enough oxygen in the room to supply them all, and what little there was was being squeezed out by the gases escaping from little bodies full of stew, mash and gritty peas followed by rice pudding, which hadn't been quite as dreadful as Iris had imagined it would be.

'I'll read you a story about a giant,' she said. 'Laura, please sit still. Then I want you to write a story about if you were very, very big, or very, very small. What would it be like? What problems would you have? Laura, stop wriggling.'

'Can't.'

'Why can't you sit still?'

'I've got a splinter.'

'Well, come here and I'll have a look at it.'

'No.'

'No?'

'No,' said Laura again.

'Why not?' said Iris.

' 'Cos no,' said Laura.

Iris looked at her. And had a sinking feeling about the location of the splinter. 'Would you like to go into the dinner hall, and tell me where the splinter is?'

Laura nodded.

'Get out your reading books,' Iris told the class, wondering vaguely at the lack of sniggering. And she took Laura through to the dining room. 'OK. The splinter.'

The child indicated it by clutching her dress and swivelling round, trying to see it. 'It's in my bum.'

'I had a strange feeling about that,' said Iris.

'Same every lunchtime,' said Effie, standing with her back to the sink to watch the small medical procedure. 'It's them benches. Chipped and old. Plain dangerous if you ask me. Splinters in bums all the time.'

There was a large sliver of wood piercing Laura's knickers and wedged into her left cheek. Iris removed it. 'That's a nasty one.' She dabbed the wound with TCP.

The child seriously inspected the offending sliver of wood. 'This is big.'

'Must have been sore,' agreed Iris, heading back to her other pupils. Outside in the corridor between dining room and classroom was a small queue of similarly afflicted pupils. Iris had to tend to half a dozen pierced bums with tweezers and TCP, thinking, First stew, then this. The life of a Missie.

At three the infants left. They had a shorter day than the older pupils. The heat in the classroom became intolerable. Colin was turning a worrying shade of red. Beads of sweat glistened on his upper lip and forehead. His hair clung damply to his skull.

Iris thought he was about to faint. 'Colin,' she said, reaching for him, 'you can take your jumper off. It's terribly hot in here.'

Still seated, he flinched. Almost reeled away from her, clutching his jersey to him. A sound, 'Sheeek,' squeezed from his lips. This was the first thing he'd ever said to her. And such was his discomfort at being told to remove the hot, thick and rather dire garment, Iris didn't pursue it. He must feel secure in there. Little boy under the layers. Layers and layers he hid beneath. The jersey, the shirt, the vest, and then there he was, peering out at the world, safe in the secret harbours in his head. Luring him out was going to take time and care. It would be hard work.

By half-past three her first day was over. The children spilled out into the sun. Free at last. They'd go home, and their mothers would ask, 'How was school? What's the new Missie like?'

Iris knew children. They'd say, 'OK.' And, 'She's fine.' And disappear out to play. Into gardens and fields, in the world that was theirs. Outdoors. Only Jane Woodman said to her mother and father that the new Missie was a wonder. That she spoke to God, and he fixed the stew for her. 'She prayed to him to make it tasty. And He did. He intervened with school dinners.'

'Oh, did she?' said her father. 'Well, there's a thing.'

It was a pity, really. Iris had only sought to make the children eat. She knew that full children are easier to teach than empty ones. But Jane's father was Minister of the parish of Green Cairns, and he was surprised to hear of someone summoning the Divine Being to intervene with the stew.

The Folks who Live at
the Foot of the Hill

At four-thirty the school bus dropped Scott and Sophy off at the gate. Scott slung his bag down the hall and headed for the fridge. 'Anything for eating?'

'Cheese,' said Iris. 'How was your day?'

'Yeah,' said Scott.

'Yeah? Is that an answer?'

'Yeah. How was yours?'

'Yeah,' said Iris.

'Great. Yeah,' said Scott.

Iris supposed one of them knew what they were talking about. It wasn't her. He cut a thick wedge of Cheddar, wrapped a slice of bread round it and disappeared upstairs. Music. Interwoven jangling guitars and soulful voices moved through the house, filled every room. Iris shouted, 'Turn that down.' Nothing happened. He couldn't hear her. Ten minutes later he reappeared, transformed from school-boy into the mass of hair and denim Iris knew and loved.

'Going out,' he said.

'Out?' said Iris. 'That's a first. Careful, there's daylight and fresh air out there.'

He grinned. 'Yeah.'

'Where are you going?'

'Jake's.'

'Who is Jake?' asked Iris.

'Met him in Forham at lunchtime,' said Scott.

Iris assumed the meeting had happened at school. It hadn't. Scott had met Jake in Woolworth's, looking at LPs.

83

Iris was heartened Scott had made a friend. Someone interesting enough to lure him across the threshhold must be interesting indeed. She thought no more of it, she had a letter to write.

To the Director of Education, County Buildings
Dear Sir,
Following my request for new desks and a lick of paint for Green Cairns School, I feel I must now ask for new benches for the dining hall. I cannot overstate the urgency of this. The existing benches are ancient. Their seats have been sat upon too often, by too many writhing hungry children. Time has taken its toll. Now my pupils are suffering the pain of rough wood on their posteriors. Or splinters in the bum, to put it plainly. I spent a deal of time this afternoon removing said slivers of wood from several juvenile bottoms, and feel this to be a waste of valuable educational time. Indeed, I would point out that my teacher training did not extend to such activities.
Let us not ponder what might happen should a sharp piece of wood enter any child's body a little further round their tender anatomies. Lovely as my pupils are, there are bits of them I have no wish to see, far less operate on. New benches, please.
Yours sincerely,
Iris Chisholm

Excellent, she thought. Witty and to the point. The new benches would arrive within the week. She put the letter in an envelope, addressed it, stuck on a stamp and went across to the letter box outside the dammit shop to post it.

Colin was standing by the old and fading news-stand, solemnly sucking an ice lolly.

'Hello, Colin.' Iris tried to sound cheery. 'That looks good.'

He looked at his lolly, then at her. Said nothing.

'Can I have a lick?' said Iris, already slightly regretting this. What if he gave it to her?

But no. He licked steadfastly on. Looking worried.

'Thought not,' she said. 'If I want a lolly, I should get my own.' She posted her letter.

Colin's grandmother appeared from the dark interior of the dammit shop, carrying a loaf of bread. 'Lovely day,' she said.

Iris agreed, indeed it was, and wasn't it a pity the children were all cooped up in school when the sun was shining?

'Best place for them. Keeps them out of mischief. The holidays are too long, if you ask me.'

Colin, anticipating a lengthy conversation (his grandmother rarely had any other kind), took the loaf and went home.

'Was he good, then?' asked Mrs Robertson.

'Of course. He's a lovely boy. I'm a little worried that he doesn't speak, though.'

'He speaks at home. Though not a lot. He's a quiet lad, like his dad. He's a thinker.'

'Nothing wrong with being quiet. Or a thinker, come to that. But I'd love to know what he's thinking about. It might do him good to communicate his thoughts.'

'I don't see the problem,' said Ella. 'What's he needing to speak for? When he does speak, he never says anything worth listening to. People like us, we're not great talkers. We work on the land. Always have – my dad, his dad, and his dad before that. That's what Colin will do. I left school Friday after my fourteenth birthday. Monday I was planting potatoes. It never did me no harm.'

'I have a sneaking suspicion Colin might be very bright,' said Iris.

'He is that. His dad before him, too. Top marks in everything. Didn't hold him back. Didn't stop him working on the farm up the road. It won't stop Colin either. Where does being bright get you? Off into the world. Living goodness knows where, among folk you don't know. It leads to disappointment and heartache. We've always been here. There's people we know, friendly faces. We're happy here. And happiness is the main thing.'

Iris nodded. She looked Ella Robertson full in the face. When, a couple of weeks ago, she'd first met her, Iris had thought her to be in her sixties. But now she could see the woman was only in her late-forties. Her cheeks were weathered, hardened by wind and rain. Tiny, tiny flecks of earth were embedded in the creases and folds of that face. But the eyes were blue and their expression unyielding. Years without moisturiser, thought Iris. And held her teacher's tongue about where being bright might get you.

'I worked on the land twenty-five years till my back gave out. And then all the lifting did for me, I had to have a hysterectomy. Still, they were good years. I've never seen no need to travel. There's everything I want here. Haven't left the village since nineteen sixty-two. If Colin needs faraway places there's his books. He's reading *Treasure Island* at the moment. There's adventure enough in that.'

'*Treasure Island*?' said Iris, impressed. 'Is he enjoying it?'

'Can't get him to put it down. And the book with tiny print, and him reading it with one eye.'

'See,' said Iris, 'I knew he was bright.'

'He's bright right enough. Just don't you go telling him that. Giving him ideas above his station.'

Iris didn't know what to say. She considered it part of her job to give little people ideas above their station. In fact, she thought it her duty to point out to anyone who would listen that there was no station. Anybody can do anything, she always thought. You never know till you try, she said regularly to her own children. This was a yeah moment. She suddenly understood the language of Scott. The non-committal, enigmatic teenage 'yeah' was the thing to say here. She could dish out the word and be on her way, and Ella wouldn't have a clue what she meant.

In the overgrown, neglected hedge behind them, that heaved branches out into the air, birds squabbled. Hot dust rose in the garage forecourt when the occasional car swirled in and stopped. Ella Robertson wrung her hands slowly, anxiously. Her eyes never let Iris's go. A long steady gaze. Don't you go meddling with my boy, she was silently saying. Though the shifting of palms over wrists said she was sure Iris would. And it worried her.

She doesn't want Colin to leave this place, thought Iris. She thinks if he goes away, he'll never come back. Leave her behind, forget about her. She'd face pity and disgrace in the community – her wee lad's gone, never gives her a second thought – and loneliness.

Iris looked about her. The day was turning exquisite. Afternoon melting into evening. The heat was less savage, though the pavement beneath her feet was still hot. The world around her was on the cusp of autumn, scented and succulently over-ripe. So she didn't say anything about Colin and his silence. She didn't even say yeah. She said instead that it was a lovely day, and she thought she'd go for a walk. And smiled.

Ella smiled back. A reluctant twitch of her lips. And said, that was the thing to do on a day like this. After all, it would probably rain tomorrow. She seemed relieved to be talking about the weather. Iris knew that here was a woman who did not welcome the discomfort, pain even, of discussing more meaningful, personal things.

She went home, collected the dog. Climbed over the fence at the end of the garden, and walked round the edge of the field beyond. It was thick with barley, browning ripe, that rattled as she dragged her fingers over it. Larks rose, trilling noisy alarmist songs, straight into the air. The dog rushed ahead, nose to the ground. The cat trailed a few yards behind, tail in the air, yowling its displeasure at feeling obliged to follow her.

'Well, why come if you feel like that about it?' she asked it.

It sat, tail curled round its bum, staring at her. Now, thought Iris, there's a glare. If I could glare like that, not a child would stir in my class. Homework would always be done. People would step aside for me. The world would be mine.

She walked on, making her noisy way, cat yowling, dog yipping, to the end of the field, over the fence and on round the next. Beyond that was bogland. And beyond that Couttie's Hill, tempting, lush. Iris could see it from her kitchen window and wanted to climb it. One side was steep, tree-lined, the other a long gentle slope. Every evening the sun set behind this hill, and set the trees in black outline against its dying red light. Iris had been told badgers lived there, and foxes, and longed to go watch them. But getting there meant crossing the bogland, a huge area that was always left uncultivated. It undulated deeply, was dense with whins and gorse, raddled with boulders. Iris had always stopped her walks at this point previously. The ground was soggy, water squeezed over the sides of her shoes. There were cow pats, dried heaps of dung randomly scattered. This whole place, she thought, is squelchy and hazardous. Take your eyes off the way ahead and you could put your foot into a sinking swamp, or worse.

But Lulu had caught a whiff of rabbit, had wriggled beneath the fence and was now gloriously coursing after it. The rabbit panicked. In a brown blur it flew across the ground with the dog in joyous pursuit, yipping as she went. They topped the first undulation and disappeared, though Lulu's boisterous exhilaration could still be heard. It pierced the hot afternoon, echoing, brazenly gleeful. Iris found it embarrassing. The rabbit reappeared, scudding up the slope then over the top and away. The dog, still howling its joy, steamed after it.

Iris called. Her voice seemed small against the open spaces. Shrill. Lulu hurtled into the distance. Not a backward glance. Iris puckered her lips to whistle, and a slow, breathy, barely audible high-pitched 'Wheeep' came out. 'Bugger,' she said. Licked her lips and tried again. But fury made further whistling impossible. All that came out was a futile spit. 'Sodding dog,' she said. Then slid through the fence and set off across the wasteland, cursing. The cat sat neatly watching her go with a superior feline air. Iris was a fool, he wasn't.

The cow pats were easily avoided. Well, the consequences of landing an angry foot in one of them was dire. Crispy on top, rancid underneath. Iris didn't think so. But mini-bogs were deceptive, tiny areas of grassland that seemed safe and dry but were, in fact, saturated. Several times she stepped into one. Felt the rush of chilled water over her feet, and the thick sucking sound of wet mud. Heard the squelch as she heaved back on to dry land. And she cursed even more. 'Taxidermy's too good for you,' she shouted. Not that the dog heard. It was a good half-mile away. Heading for the hills.

At the top of a grassy ridge she stopped, looked around, and saw to her relief Lulu coming back to her, tail wagging, tongue hanging out, no sign of penitence at all. Iris gave her a glare and turned away. She sensed she was being watched.

Tucked down at the foot of Couttie's Hill was a cottage. She hadn't known it was there. Standing outside was a woman with long fair hair and bare feet. Her hand was raised, shading her eyes. A Volkswagen van, painted in multi-coloured whorls and flowers, was parked at the door. Wind chimes tinkled. The garden in front of the cottage was filled with jostling sunflowers. There were two men sitting on the doorstep. One got up and disappeared inside. Iris had hardly caught a glimpse of him, but could have sworn it was Scott. The other, in jeans and T-shirt, also barefoot, waved. His hair, she noted, was longer than Scott's. A child came out. She was more than barefoot. She was wearing a pair of pink knickers, nothing else, and was eating a slice of bread. Iris recognised Gracie, one of her new pupils. Primary one, and, Iris thought, clever and argumentative. She liked the girl. From inside the house came the sound of Captain Beefheart. Sounds like Scott, thought Iris, looks like Scott. It *is* Scott. What is he doing there? And who are these people? And what is Scott doing hanging out with them?

She took Lulu by the collar and headed home. In time, no doubt, she'd find out.

Sophy was in the living room when she got in. 'Where have you been?' she asked. 'I've been home for ages. I'm starving.'

'Oh, my,' said Iris, 'call the tabloids. Teacher starves daughter. You could have peeled some potatoes if you're that hungry.'

'Nah,' said Sophy. Peel potatoes? She wasn't that hungry.

Iris looked at her own mud-caked feet. Bath? Feed hungry child? She had vile memories of howling infants needing to be fed. She decided to cook first, then a long bath with a glass of wine. The best way to end the day. 'Do you know who lives in the cottage at the foot of Couttie's Hill?' she asked.

'The Lynnes.' said Sophy. 'He used to teach at some university, but dropped out. Or something like that.'

'What did he teach?'

'Psychology or something. Dunno.'

'What you dunno is a lot,' said Iris. 'Do you have homework?'

'No. Well, yes. But it doesn't matter. It's chemistry and I don't want to be a chemist.'

'It matters. No wonder there's a lot you don't know.'

'I'll do it after dinner,' said Sophy.

Iris sighed and went into the kitchen to peel potatoes.

❈   ❈   ❈

The next day was cooler, but the children were restless. Iris had noticed that day two back at school was always worse than day one. It was as if they had realised that this business of coming here, sitting still, listening, learning, was going to go on for weeks and weeks. And it was not that pleasant a prospect. Sausages for lunch, after a prayer asking for enlightenment in the matter of long division. 'It's proving tricky for some of us,' Iris explained, palms pressed in front of her. For pudding there was a funny spongy thing in pink custard. Four splintered bottoms. And in the afternoon the library van arrived.

George, the librarian, brought in a large box of books. Dropped them noisily on the floor. 'I hardly think these suitable,' said Iris, turning over a copy of *Fanny Hill*.

'They're not for them.' He dismissed Iris's pupils with a wide sweep of his arm. 'They're for the mums and dads.'

'They come here to choose a book?'

'Nah. Doesn't work like that. They tell their kid if they want one and you dish them out.'

'How do I know what people want?'

'Just give them a book. Thrillers for the dads, romance for the mums. That usually does it.'

Iris said, 'But . . .'

Her small protest was ignored. 'You'll get the hang of it. I'll pick up the books again at the end of term.' And he was gone.

All Iris could do was repeat, 'But . . .' She moved the box into a corner and said that if anybody's mum or dad wanted a library book, there they were. She presumed that she was not required to date stamp any borrowings, or take charge of any library cards. She felt a flash of resentment that she was expected to do such a chore – hand out books, keep a note of what had gone where. Here she was – Missie, nursemaid *and* librarian.

There were other things she was expected to be, but refused. She knew herself too well. She didn't have the temperament to bake cakes to help feed the starving in India. She'd buy cakes other women baked, but sifting, mixing, the movement of eggs and butter, sugar and flour, did not interest her. Nor did showing off flower arrangements, or knitting, or any kind of needlework. So she wouldn't join the Women's Rural Institute. And she wouldn't join the local historical society, and she wouldn't sit on the church committee. 'No,' she'd said to all of them. She had just lost her husband, had two kids who had just lost their father. She had the school. She did not think she could, right now, give any sort of group the attention it might need. 'Besides,' she added, 'I'm not a joiner.'

'But,' said Angela Marshall from the Rural Institute, whose son was one of Iris's pupils, 'the Missie always joins the Rural Institute. It's a tradition. It's expected.'

Kathy Jackson from the historical society understood and said, 'Well, when you've come to yourself – perhaps then. The Missie is always part of our group. It's tradition.'

Alan Woodman, the minister, smiled, patted her arm. 'Of course,' he said. 'But it has long been local tradition that the Missie plays an active part in the community. The committee was always part of her duties.' He had been going tactfully to bring up the matter of the prayer for the stew, but thought now was not the moment. One thing at a time. And besides, had she shown interest in his committee, he'd have overlooked the matter. Prayer was wonderfully calming. It was an act of trust, solace, a communication with the Divine. It was not to be abused by asking God to make stew more tasty than it already was. That Iris had done this, and that she had done it in front of children, bothered him. But no, he would not mention this now. Not here in her living room when he was inviting her into the community. He would wait. So, when Iris refused the invitation, he said, 'You must take your time. You are grieving your husband.'

Grieving my husband, thought Iris. And my home, and my job. My whole life has gone. I have lost everything. She didn't under-stand what was happening to her. Thinking about Harry was painful. It was like a wound that she could not bear to touch, it hurt too much. Mourning was such a physical thing. She'd always thought it was a silent sorrowing, a suffering that passed, eased with time. But it was more than that. It was an actual ache in her heart. She wanted to howl loudly in public places. Nights, when Sophy and Scott were in bed, she would, still clothed, roll herself in the duvet and cry. Cry till her nose ran, and she was shuddering with sobs, sick with the effort of it. She wanted to scratch herself, cut herself, bang her head on the floor – anything, anything, to make this awful longing for Harry, and the pain of losing him, go away. Yes, she was grieving.

But there was something else, and this had crept up on her only recently. It astounded and bewildered her. She was filled with lust. She wanted someone to make love to her. More than holding, kissing. She wanted heat, sweat. Tongues. Sex. It snuck up on her, this longing, at all times of the night and day. In bed, in the dark, she let it roll over her. She pulled her duvet round her, moaned, sighed. But in the daylight hours, at work, when she was gripped with the need, she would close her eyes, breathe deeply and banish it. Sometimes, when the class was busy, and she was marking a set of maths books or a spelling test she'd set, she'd find herself looking out of the window and near as dammit twitching with this hunger. A man, hands on her, lips, teeth on her nipple. Then the rush and abandon, the mindless movement pursuing pleasure. She wanted that. She'd swallow, and look round at the class. 'James, get on with your work. Susan, stop dreaming.' A crisp, schoolmarmish voice when who was she to scold anyone for dreaming? She'd feel shocked at herself, slightly ashamed she was thinking erotic thoughts when she should be working. Stop that immediately, she'd tell herself, her voice even more schoolmarmish. When chiding herself she showed no mercy.

What bothered her was that the man in her daydreams wasn't Harry. He was nobody. A faceless man, but handsomely faceless. In her dreams he was beside her in bed, holding her, kissing her, loving her. Their sex was hot, passionate, abandoned. Sweaty. She did things with this man she'd never done with Harry. She shocked herself with her own torrid imaginings. She was meant to be mourning. Lust? She would have none of it. She would throw herself into her work, expend her passions by making this school the best in the land. There would be projects, plays, trips, a nature table, a dressing-up corner, a reading corner. She would make the stutterer loquacious, the mute speak. And when she was not fixing everything, she'd walk. Walk till her legs ached, and every longing, all her sexual itchings, were gone, cleaned away, sweated out of her.

Charles Harper,
and the Perfect Shade of Yellow

She was walking when Charles Harper called. It was raining. Wearing wellington boots and on old raincoat, Iris tramped through the woods watching the river, swollen from early-autumn trickle to a rushing brown torrent, that swirled and gushed over rocks and spread over its banks. The path she trod was thick with mud, the dog filthy. Rain soaked her hair, and seeped in small rivulets down the back of her neck. She didn't care. Walking, with deliberate movements, one foot in front of the other, helped expunge the images of the faceless man and the things she wanted him to do to her.

'I think about sex all the time,' she'd told Morag on the phone.

'Well, you're not getting any. It makes you like that.'

'My husband just died, I shouldn't be having wet dreams. Especially when I'm not sleeping.'

'Maybe you're missing that side of your marriage,' said Morag.

'Hmm,' said Iris. She didn't know about that. That side of her marriage had been more than lacklustre over the past couple of years. It had been non-existent. Occasionally Harry had turned to her in bed, put his hand on her – his opening ploy – and she had turned away. Or else had pretended to be asleep. But mostly it had been Harry who hadn't been interested. He'd started coming to bed hours after her, sitting in his chair, drinking, telling her he'd be up in a minute as she lingered in the doorway, saying, 'Well, goodnight then. I have to go to bed, I'm knackered.' He'd wave goodnight.

'You are realising you're going to be celibate from now on, and subconsciously you aren't at all happy with the notion,' said Morag.

Iris said, 'Hmm,' again. Celibacy? She was used to that. Harry would sit alone downstairs in the living room, she'd sleep alone upstairs in the bedroom. Alone, she realised, they were both always alone. Well, when you've got a dire secret, it's best to be alone. The less communication the better, it reduces the chances of it slipping out. 'Yeah, well. See you next weekend,' she said.

Yeah? She was always saying that. It was a habit she'd picked up from Scott. The non-communicative, non-committal yeah. She was slipping into herself. She'd walk, the sounds of the world about her, her breathing, the soft swish of her coat, moving along the path by the river, up the steps across the road, round the back of the school, over the fence and across the fields. Walking till her mind was emptied of confusion, loss and sex. Then she'd turn and go home to a deserted house. Scott would be at Jake's and Sophy next door with Jean, talking about boys and school and perfecting their rendition of 'Hey, Jude' which they sang in harmony, sitting on Jean's bed swaying together, eyes blank, as they chorused . . . *na na na nana na na* . . . over and over. And when they'd done, they'd start once more at the beginning, never tiring of the song. Though those around them shut their eyes, covered their ears and mumbled, 'Oh, God, not again.'

Today, however, Charles Harper was sitting on the front step waiting for her. He was a smallish man, wearing blue overalls. Dark hair, but it was his eyes that caught Iris's attention. They were bright, impish. There was a mischief about this man. The way his body seemed to be in constant motion, he couldn't stand still. The way he looked at her. His smile.

'Come to move the partition,' he said, jerking his thumb towards the school. 'Tony sent me.'

'Who?'

'Tony, Head of Education at County buildings.'

'Anthony Smith?' Iris said. And this man called him Tony. He must be well connected with friends in high places, she thought. 'It's quarter to five,' she said. 'The school's closed.'

'Well, you'd not be wanting me to be taking down a partition when it's open and all the children are there, would you?'

There seemed logic to this, so Iris led him across the lawn to the back door and opened the school for him.

He walked round the classroom, inhaling deeply. 'Smells like a school. Same smell as when I was a kid.' He shook his head in disgust. 'I hated it. Most miserable time of my life, school. Place of misery.'

'Well, mine won't be. Not when I'm finished with it.'

He nodded, turned to examine the partition, running his hands along the wooden panels, whistling softly. 'No bother,' he said.

'If you're so friendly with Tony,' said Iris, 'can you put in a word for me about having this place painted? All this deathly brown is depressing.'

'I'll get that done for you at the weekend,' he said. 'No bother.'

Nothing seemed to be any bother to this man.

'Won't it need the go-ahead from some committee, then forms and chitties? That's how things seem to work.'

'There's that. But the best thing is to paint it first, then let the committee decide it should be painted and let the forms and chitties take their own course through the system. That way you get the benefit of the paint job while the decision is being made. Works for me. I'll put in a bill for it when I'm billing them for taking down the partition. Then they'll pay me. Then they'll decide your school should be painted. That's the way of it. You shouldn't be bothering yourself with officialdom. You'll spend your life drumming your fingers, getting all hot under the collar, and end up having a heart attack.'

So far Iris had noticed one thing about this community. People either spoke or they didn't. Those who didn't confined their communications to a look that was either hostile or friendly – nothing in between – and a few brief remarks on what she was doing. As in, 'Going for a walk, then.' Which would be obvious as she would be outside with the dog, walking. She'd reply, 'Yes, nice day for it.' Or, 'Yes, dreadful day for it,' according to the weather. And that would be that. Those who spoke – spoke. Endlessly, it seemed, moving through opinions, speculations and observations with verbal ease and an alacrity that kept the person they were speaking to silent.

This Charles Harper was one who spoke. Iris was surprised. She'd spent eighteen years with a man who rarely opened his mouth, and had almost come to the conclusion that all men were like that. She'd been wrong.

'What colour will you be wanting?' he asked.

'Something soothing, comforting, cheery and warm. And light.'

'Yellow, then.'

'Yellow? I'm not awfully keen on yellow.'

'Children love it. 'Course they grow out of it but not till they're up a bit. All children like yellow.'

'You have children?'

'Five and they all love yellow, or did when they were wee. And now their children do, too.'

'You have grandchildren?' He didn't look old enough.

'Three. I started young, had my first at seventeen. Father gave me a hammering for that. Then mine did the same. I didn't hammer them, though. Now they're all grown, fled the nest, leaving me and yellow behind.'

'And your wife, too, no doubt.' Iris felt an important person had been left out of this scenario.

'She's gone, too.'

'Oh, I'm sorry. I didn't mean to be nosy.'

'No bother. She lives down the road, still comes by when she needs her bills and things sorting out. And sometimes I babysit her new wee one, Paul.'

Iris said, 'Ah.' And thought briefly about other people's lives, other people's messes. Could there be existences out there more complex and absurd than her own? This man's seemed to be.

'Yellow, then,' he said.

'Fine. But not fried egg yellow. Or buttercup. More pale green yellow, going into grey.'

'Right, yellow. No bother. I'll come by Saturday morning and get it done for you.'

She left him to it.

On Saturday, at half-past eight in the morning, he turned up. Iris, woken by the sound of his car engine, stood watching from her bedroom window as he unloaded the trailer he towed behind his car. Still wearing her nightdress, she folded her arms, leaned against the window frame, drifted into an observer's gaze, thinking, wondering, forgetting she was staring.

There was a calm about Charles Harper. His movements weren't slow, just untroubled. Iris always felt she moved through the world with difficulty, at odds with it. This man seemed to be part of it, at one with it. Not slow, she thought, but unhurried. Easy. She, on the other hand, rushed through her life like a demented hen, clucking, tutting, nagging. Picking things up, fussing. 'Homework, Sophy.' 'Will you turn down that noise, Scott?' 'Colin, tie your shoelaces.' 'There are two fs in daffodil, Laura.' 'We have been talking about Captain Cook all week, doesn't *anybody* in this class know the name of his ship?'

'The *Mayflower*, Miss.'

Aaaah! 'No, it was *not* the *Mayflower*. That was the Pilgrim Fathers.'

Compared to this gentle being walking through the school play-ground, carrying paint, brushes, a huge dust sheet, she was deranged. A prickle of jealousy ran through her. Why couldn't she be like that? Walking peacefully in old suede boots and dungarees, smiling serenely as she went.

On his way back to his car for a second load, he stood and looked closely at the wall enclosing the playground. Why is he doing that? Iris wanted to know. It's a wall, there's nothing to it. A wall, that's all. He walked on a few paces, stopped and watched a blackbird that was sitting on the railings, watching him. He seemed to tighten his lips. Was he whistling? Iris couldn't quite hear. But the bird seemed to be answering. Nature boy, she thought. He finished his communication with the bird, walked on to his car, paused by his trailer, noticing Colin in the bushes across the road, spying on him. He walked, slowly, over, peered into the under-growth, Colin's secret place, and started to chat. Colin rose from the depths of greenery and stood, hands in the pockets of his grey shorts, listening. Iris was guiltily relieved that the boy didn't seem to talk to Charles any more than he did to her. He was staring at

Charles's mouth. Yes, Iris thought, Colin did that, he watched words form, the movement of lips, as if fascinated more by the business of talking than by what was said. The child was trapped in his silence. This worried Iris, since his grandmother said he spoke at home. It seemed as if Colin had just given up on talking to anybody other than Ella, his gran, and Lucy. He certainly had nothing to contribute to the conversation with Charles.

From where she was watching, it looked to Iris like this didn't bother Charles at all. He was happy to have a chat, one-sided though it was. He took Colin's binoculars. Turned them over in his hands, admiring them, then put them to his eyes and swept the horizon, gazing at the bluing peaks miles away. He turned and looked down the road, then, still with the binoculars, scrutinised Colin, waved to him. Iris saw the child smile, lift his hand slightly to wave back, but, overcome with shyness, change his mind. Turning again, Charles examined the school, and the schoolhouse, and finally Iris, standing at the window watching. He laughed.

Embarrassed, caught gawping, she backed into the room. She dressed and went downstairs. In the hall, on her way to the kitchen, she looked across at the school. Charles was sitting on the step, rolling a cigarette. She bustled to the sink, filled the kettle. 'That man who has come to paint my school is just sitting on the step rolling a cigarette. No attempt to get on with his work at all. Just sitting there.'

In fifteen minutes her attitude to Charles Harper had moved from muted admiration, to envy, and now he irritated her.

'He's probably waiting for the keys,' said Scott.

'Well, why doesn't he come and get them?'

'He's probably waiting for you to go and give him them. He'll have seen you watching him from the bedroom window in your usual teacherish proprietorial way.'

'I am neither teacherish nor proprietorial,' she said, taking the keys from their hook by the back door. 'Good word, though, proprietorial.'

'Teacherish, Mother,' he said to her back.

Jingling the keys, walking swiftly across the garden to the school with small steps – the demented hen again – she thought, My God, he's right. That *was* teacherish.

She handed over the keys with a crisp, 'Good morning.'

Charles nodded. 'You were watching me.'

'I happened to be looking out of the window when you arrived.'

He unlocked the door of the school and went in. Iris followed. He stood looking round the classroom, hands in pockets, examining the walls. 'Couple of days. First coat today, second tomorrow. You'll be wanting to see the colour.'

It was yellow. Vibrant, lurid yellow.

'It's hideous,' said Iris, too horrified to consider tact.

'Children like bright colours,' he said. 'They'd choose this.'

'It's hideous,' she said again.

'Do you know?' He looked her in the eye. 'I thought you'd say that.'

'I have to live with it. It'd make me nauseous. All day – nauseous.'

'I like a woman who speaks her mind.'

She thought he was smirking. He knew she'd hate this paint. He'd done this deliberately. 'I like men who have taste. Who appreciate subtlety.'

'You like subtle, do you?'

'On walls, I do.'

He poured a stream of nauseous yellow paint into a large metal bucket, opened a tin of white, stirred it in, then added a small amount of black. 'Subtle,' he said.

The paint was transformed into a yellowish, greenish-grey.

'If you wanted sage, you should have said sage.'

'I did. I said yellow going into grey. I just didn't say the word sage.' Teacherish, she thought, proprietorial.

'Right enough,' he agreed. 'It is an easier colour to look at. Well, I'll get on.'

She said she'd leave him to it.

As she walked back towards her house, he said, 'It'll be no bother moving all the desks and taking your pictures off the wall.'

'Excellent.' She nodded and walked away.

At lunchtime Iris returned to the school to see how work was progressing. Coming in the back door, she heard Charles talking. 'I've always had a notion for a Jaguar,' he was saying. 'Looked at one the other week. Three years old. Thirty-two thousand on the clock. But the accelerator was worn down, well-trod on. I didn't believe that at all. Nah. Nice red, though I prefer green myself. What about you?'

Silence.

Iris went into the classroom. The children's desks were stacked in the centre, along with her own and the cupboard, covered with a dustsheet. The woodwork was undercoated white. One wall was painted sage. Charles was working, his back to her, talking to Colin who was painstakingly covering a small area level with his good eye. There was paint on his jumper. Occasionally he would turn, gaze steadily at Charles whose arm moved fluidly covering the wall in front of him with an even coating of paint, bending to dip his brush into his bucket of paint, spreading the silky liquid, bending, dipping, brushing, talking incessantly.

'Some say cars are like women. You know, you keep them in good working order, maintain them, a coat of polish, bit of oil when they need it. Lock them up at night. And you shouldn't get obsessed with them. Don't let them take over your life. But I don't think so . . .'

'I should think not,' said Iris.

Charles and Colin turned. 'Eavesdropping?' said Charles.

'I came to see how you were getting on. And to ask if you wanted some lunch.'

He shook his head. 'Brought something with me.' He looked at Colin, put his hand on his head. 'Got a helper.'

Iris nodded. 'Hello, Colin.'

The boy looked at his foot, then moved his head so that he could squint at her, a momentary glance from behind the thick lashes on his single seeing eye. His glasses were dotted with tiny specks of yellow paint. He returned his gaze to his foot.

'Time for some food, then. You want some lunch, Colin?' said Charles.

The boy put his brush carefully on the dustsheet. Walked slowly from the room. But once outside, he took off. Iris and Charles watched him hurtle across the playground, over the road and into the safety of his own garden, up the steps, through the front door and out of sight.

'No road sense at all, the children round here,' said Iris.

'Doesn't say much, does he?' said Charles.

'No. He says nothing at all. A self-elected mute, it's a worry.'

'Is that what they call it? In my day it was quiet. He'd have been a quiet lad.'

'There is a difference between quiet and not saying anything. I think it must be lonely in his head.'

Charles shook his head. 'Nah. It's lonely out here with us. It's fine in his head. That's why he lives there.'

Colin had just arrived in the classroom, apparently, and sat on the floor watching Charles. The child seemed to feel no need to announce his presence by asking, as children usually did, 'What are you doin', mister?' He did not ask endless questions but sat following Charles's every movement. Till he had said, 'Well, if you're going to sit there, you might as well give me a hand.' He'd given Colin a small brush, some paint poured into a plastic tub, and pointed at the wall. Colin started work. For an hour he'd carefully covered the area Charles had pointed to before Charles realised what he was doing, and pointed to another bit. Which Colin worked on for another hour. Then Charles gently took him by the shoulders, moved him on again.

To ease the stiff silence that happens when two people come together and one is too inhibited and distrustful to utter a word, Charles had spoken, continuously. He'd talked about cars, farming, the modern methods of growing and cropping potatoes, his army experiences and women – one of his favourite subjects. The child had said nothing, but everything Charles said to him soaked into his mind, swirled round and stayed. Colin decided he would save all this new information up – things about cars and the army and women – keep it in his head till night time when he was in his bed, alone in the dark. He'd take it all out then, and think about it.

Are Missies Real People?
And What Happened to
Randolph Scott's Potato?

The next day he slipped back across the road. Came silently into the schoolroom, picked up his brush and started to paint again. Occasionally he'd look across at Charles, but he said nothing. There were things Colin wanted to ask, questions crowded into his mind. How do you know about paint? How much black and white to add to yellow to make this colour? Did you have a gun when you were in the army? What's the fastest you've ever driven your car? He thought and thought about his questions till they all seemed silly to him. Charles would laugh at him if he asked them. So he kept his own counsel, said nothing, stood painting his allotted square foot of wall and watched the brush moving up and down, the new soft coating spreading before him. He liked the bright yellow that Charles changed to this greeny one better. He thought to say that. But probably Charles didn't want to know.

At half-past three in the afternoon the Missie came with a tray, on it two mugs of coffee, a plate of biscuits and a glass of orange juice for him.

Charles was talking about life. 'D'you ever think about life, Colin?'

Iris paused outside the door to listen.

Silence. Colin stopped painting to look piercingly at Charles. A slow dawning spread across his face. As a matter of fact, he did think about life. Like what was he going to do when he grew up? Work on the farm up the road, his gran thought. But he didn't want to do that. And he thought about other people's lives, Lucy's, for example, which seemed clean and cosy with a mother who baked biscuits. But Lucy's mum was bossy, spoke all the time. Colin thought she was an in-charge sort of person. She knew everything. Not like his gran who was always losing things and often forgot what she was saying, 'What was I talking about again?' she'd ask. But sometimes, when Lucy's mum was speaking to him, he got a funny feeling in his tummy. Sometimes he thought she was saying one thing and thinking about another, and the other thing was something that made her sad. He thought about his gran's life and how some nights he'd hear her cry, and know she was missing her son John, his dad. His gran cried buckets. It was interesting to hear Charles say he thought about life, too. Colin had thought it was only him.

'I was driving along the other day and having a think to myself, the way you do when you know the road. And I was thinking about my life.'

Colin stared, mouth slightly open.

'And I was thinking about a man's life. How it's the same for me as it is for other men, even rich blokes who run big companies. It comes in three stages, I thought. One,' Charles raised his thumb, 'you're the young upstart. That was me in the army. Thought I knew it all. Two,' his index finger joined the thumb, 'you're guilty provider. Me with a wife and kids trying to earn the money to feed and clothe them all. Worked all hours doing that. Then, three,' his middle finger joined the other two, 'you're a grumpy old git.'

Colin stood, astounded by this. Paint dripped from his brush on to the dustsheet.

'Well, I've done the first two, but I'm buggered if I'm going to be a grumpy old git.'

Just beyond the door Iris felt something stir in her stomach. Was that how Harry had felt? Years of guilty providing coming to an end, he'd felt the first flush of old gitdom and, unable to bear it, gone on a spree? She coughed and came into the classroom, laying her tray on one of the desks.

Colin looked at the biscuits. There were six of them, two each. That was fair. He took his orange juice carefully. At home he never got a glass, except at Christmas, or if people came to tea, but people hardly ever came to tea. He usually drank from a pink plastic beaker. The Missie had orange juice just like his gran had. He didn't think that Missies had ordinary things. He clasped the glass, the Missie's glass. Special. She'd touched it. He gazed into it, two melting ice cubes floating. That was special, too. His gran didn't have a fridge. Filmstars had ice cubes in their drinks, he'd seen them on the telly. Heard that fabulous clink, and wished he could have drinks like that. The drinks on telly seemed so much tastier than the drinks he had at home. So, too, did the food. It always puzzled him why people in films never finished their dinners. On Sunday afternoon Westerns the cowboy, often Randolph Scott, would be sitting in the salon at a table with a checked cloth and a woman who was often called something like Mayanne would bring him a steaming plate of steak and potatoes. He'd often say she made the finest steak and potatoes this side of the Colorado River, and she'd say, 'Ah, go on. I do believe you're flirtin' with me.' You'd know then that soon they'd be kissing, which was really boring. But Randolph Scott would plunge his fork into a potato and lift it, whole and round and perfect, to his lips, when there would be a gunshot outside. Someone would shout, 'It's the James boys.' And Randolph Scott would put down the fork, take his six-shooter from its holster and head for the swinging doors. And he'd never, ever get to eat that potato. Or the steak.

This bothered Colin. 'But what about his potato?' he'd say to his gran.

She'd say, 'He'll come back and eat it up when he's seen to the baddies.'

Colin watched, waited for him to do that. But he never did. Instead he'd jump on his horse and start trailing the James boys. Colin always wished he was there; he'd sneak into the saloon and eat that potato. He looked at the Missie, now talking to Charles about her garden.

'It's a bit neglected,' she was saying. 'But there's a lovely old clematis growing over the shed. And it's been a good year for the roses.'

That was the sort of thing his gran said. It was as if the Missie was a real person, which she couldn't be on account of her being a Missie. Colin watched her. The bit of her that he liked best – the bit between her chin and the top of her T-shirt – was burnt red by the sun. She should put some calamine lotion on that to cool it down. He wondered why she and Charles weren't eating the biscuits. Chocolate on both sides, and, Colin could tell, a creamy bit in the middle. He wanted one. He stared and stared at it, willing it to come to him. Longing to bite into one, lick off the chocolate. But you couldn't just reach out and take. You had to wait till you were told. There were rules about biscuits.

Iris turned and saw Colin standing alone, carefully holding his juice with both hands, gazing with forlorn longing at her plate and the six little chocolate offerings on it. 'Help yourself, Colin.'

A shy hand snaked out. The plate was down to five biscuits. Colin bit, and sipped. The trick was to get just enough liquid in your mouth to make the biscuit soft, mushy, and get all the tastes at the same time: chocolate, coffee cream filling and orange juice. His fingers were covered with paint. The Missie was saying how hot it had been today. Just like his gran. Maybe she *was* just like his gran. Maybe all woman were just like his gran. Did the Missie fart? He grinned. Then, worried that he might be caught grinning and asked to explain what he was smiling about, tried to stop. Which made him grin more. He took another biscuit. This one he deconstructed. Eating the top layer, then scraping off the creamy middle with his teeth, before putting the bottom bit in his mouth whole. He had chocolate on his fingers, too, now. He wiped them on the seat of his pants. Four biscuits left.

The Missie said she'd never known it so hot this time of the year. She'd been planning to do some ironing but in the end decided it would be a crime to stay inside and miss the sun, so she'd taken a book and sat on a rug on the lawn reading. 'If you can call it a lawn,' she laughed.

Colin knew his gran would never do that. She always ironed on a Tuesday after washing on a Monday. He liked coming home on ironing day. The smell of clean clothes, the homey piles of newly pressed towels and sheets, the soft creak of the ironing board. On ironing days Gran would cook something easy for tea. Beans on toast with a cup of tea. Now he thought about it, American cops never finished their food either. They'd be sitting in the car, eating a burger, when a voice would come on their car radio: 'Armed robbery in progress at twenty-seven and sixteenth.' And the cops would throw their burgers out the window and drive off, top speed, sirens wailing. That was littering, Colin thought, and took another biscuit. Three left. He'd been greedy and eaten more than his share. 'Yer eyes are bigger than your belly,' his gran would say.

It was Saturday. Saturday was sausages. Gran bought them from the butcher's van which came round the glen in the morning. Sometimes she bought steak, for a treat, which she fried with onions. This morning the Missie had gone to the van, Colin had spied on her. She'd bought sausages, too, and steak. He wondered if she fried it like Gran, and if the onions made her belch like they did Gran. And if she did, did she bang her chest with the side of her clenched fist and say, 'Oh, sorry, pardon. Onions'? He took another biscuit, pondering this. Sucking the chocolate till it rimmed his lips.

The Missie had her hand on her chest as she spoke. Her fingers were spread, a wedding ring shone. Her husband was dead, Colin knew that. His dad was dead, too. When he'd died Gran had cried and cried. He wondered if the Missie had cried and looked at her eyes to see where the tears would have been, if there had been any. He doubted Missies cried. They were always bossing people about, scolding them for staring out of the window or doodling on the desk while they were saying something important about Captain Cook. He couldn't imagine the Missie crying.

She was talking about digging the bottom of the garden in the spring and growing vegetables. 'Potatoes, peas. I love fresh peas,' she was saying. Fancy a teacher liking peas. It was strange how grown-up people could talk for ages and ages about boring things. They never said anything interesting. Except Charles, he said things about the army and cars and stuff like that. Colin wondered if Charles would like to see his collection of model cars. But thought not. His gran said they cluttered up the place. He took another

107

biscuit. Swigged his juice. Looked at the plate. There was only one biscuit left. He'd eaten five. A whole five biscuits. He flushed with panic. It rumbled through him, sent prickles of fear through his tummy. When the Missie saw what he'd done, she'd give him a smack. And when his gran found out the Missie had given him a smack, she'd give him a smack, too. Maybe if he ate the last one, hid the plate, the Missie would think she hadn't brought out any biscuits after all. She'd meant to, but forgot. Gran was always doing that. 'Did I bring my cup of tea through here? I'd forget my head if it wasn't screwed on.'

Colin gulped the last of his orange juice. Crammed the remaining chocolate biscuit into his mouth. Stuffed the plate up his paint-streaked jumper and ran from the school, across the road and into his garden. He ducked behind the wall, and hid the plate in his secret place behind the redcurrant bush, where he kept his other secret things in a tin box with a picture of labrador puppies on the front. In the box was a metal puzzle from a Christmas cracker, a television pencil sharpener with Fred Flintstone on the screen – when he moved it back and forward Fred waved his arms. There was a bullet from his father's gun that he'd found and stolen before his gran had given the gun away, plus several dud cartridge shells. A cigarette stolen from his gran's packet. A jay's feather. A bird skull. A ram's horn. And there was a compass. He was keeping it so he'd know the way when he ran off to America, to Hollywood, to uncover the mysteries of uneaten burgers and Randolph Scott's potato.

Iris and Charles watched him scuttle across the road, bent forward, arms folded in front of him, keeping the plate in place.

'Top speed beetling,' said Iris. 'What's got into him?'

'Your biscuits,' said Charles, looking round. 'All of them.'

'And the plate,' said Iris. 'He's stolen my plate. I liked that plate.'

'He's eaten all the biscuits. Then buggered off with the evidence. Christ.' Charles remembered sins of decades ago. 'I used to do things like that.'

'Did you? I'll have to watch out for you. I never did.'

'Never?'

'No. Never. I was what you'd have called a goody-goody. I did my homework. Helped my mother in the house. Always did my piano practice – an hour every afternoon after school. I was the perfect child. Never in trouble.'

'Well, then, I'll have to watch out for you. You've got all your sins to come. Do you want me to go get your plate?'

'Leave it. That child is suffering enough already without us reminding him of what he's done. That one is a guilty conscience on legs.'

Six o'clock the following evening, Charles loaded his trailer and went to tell Iris he was finished. 'Had to do it all myself. My little helper is still in self-imposed disgrace.' He walked back to the school with her.

She wanted to view the new paintwork. 'Lovely,' she said, rubbing her hands. 'What a beautiful job.'

'Lightens the place up fine.' Nodding and smiling, he congratulated himself on a job well done. 'Space and light, just what you need. Well, some of what you need.'

'It's wonderful,' she said. Then, not knowing till the words were out that she was going to invite him, asked if he'd like to have supper. 'We'll be eating at about seven o'clock.'

He said that would be grand.

He sat at the table, across from Sophy who glared at him.

Scott, however, found him fascinating. 'What is it you do?'

Charles shrugged. 'Anything. Everything. Harvest coming up soon, I'll be driving a combine for Ted Williamson up the road. Then I'm putting in a wood-burning stove for the Hargreaves. Him that works at the university. Then it'll be October and I'll be getting the garden at the Manse settled down for the winter. After that,' he shrugged again, 'something will come up.'

'You just take it as it comes?'

Charles nodded.

Scott said, 'Cool.' And asked him if he had dropped out.

'Out of what?'

'Life.'

Charles chewed his sausage, thinking about this. 'I came home from the army and I couldn't get a job. Not round here, anyway. So

I started doing things, this and that. Painted someone's kitchen, cleaned gutters, fixed cars. And that was it. This is me now. I do things.'

And Scott said, 'Wow. You just tuned in to who you were.'

Charles said he had no idea what Scott was talking about. Sophy told him that her father had been a warehouse manager, and that her mother had a degree. 'An MA,' she said.

Charles said you could never go far wrong with a bit of education.

But Scott disagreed you had to drop out of school, out of everything, to tune in to what you really were.

'What *are* you talking about?' said Iris. 'No way are you going to drop out of school.'

'I think he's been talking to the Lynnes. I put in a wood-burning stove for them last winter. They live on lentils and muesli. Sacks of them in the kitchen. They're part of a cooperative.'

'Yeah,' said Scott, 'Jake dropped out of university lecturing to come here. To listen to himself, and find out what was really in his head. Get rid of the stuff other people had put there.'

Iris said, 'Oh.' It was all she could think of, really.

'I was thinking of dropping out of school. There's nothing there for me. History, maths, English, what is it all? Just stuff other people want me to learn. I want to learn about things, life. I could work on the land. Grow things. I could tend sheep, be a shepherd. Something real.'

Iris said nothing.

Charles said that being a shepherd didn't pay much.

Sophy refused pudding – apple pie – on account of watching her weight, then she was off to study Keats. 'I'm going to university. I'm having a career. I'm not going to be a peasant.' She was talking to Scott, looking at Charles.

Iris said that studying was an excellent thing to do, while glaring at the girl. Scott ate a huge slice of pie and said he was off to see Jake.

'How old is this Jake person?' asked Iris.

Scott shrugged. 'Same age as you. Pretty old, except he doesn't act it.'

'You mean, I act my age.'

'Yeah. Old.'

'I am not old. I am thirty-nine.'

'Old,' said Scott, and headed for the door.

Charles affably took a second slice of pie and started eating it. He said nothing.

'Thirty-nine isn't old,' said Iris.

'Jake's cool,' said Scott. 'He doesn't act or talk like he's old. Like you.' He disappeared down the hall and out the front door.

Iris called, 'Just a minute. You come back here!'

But Scott was gone.

Charles ate quietly.

Iris apologised to him. 'Sorry about that.'

'What?' he asked.

'My children.'

'They're just kids. They seem pretty normal to me. Do you want a hand with them dishes?'

She shook her head. She was going to sit outside, it was too nice an evening to contemplate washing up. They sat on the ancient, weather-bleached bench by the back door.

'It's a dying thing, this bench,' said Iris. 'We'll get splinters in our bums, like the children.'

'They get splinters in their bums?'

'From the benches in the dining room.'

'A quick going over with the sander would fix that.'

'I am a teacher. I do extra duties as nurse and a librarian, I'm not adding any DIY to that list. I've asked for new benches.'

'Fair enough.'

The sun paled in the sky. A thrush perched far above them on a rowan at the end of the garden opened its throat, let everyone know this was his place in the world.

'No wonder they're called song thrushes,' said Charles.

'Yes.' Iris nodded. Sunday night. Here she was, sitting in this overgrown garden, far from anywhere familiar to her, far from anybody she knew. Sunday, when the weather was like this, soft, balmy, she and Morag used to go to sit in Morag's garden and talk.

111

Conversations about past times when they were different people. They'd lament lost weekends, laugh about the swift, fierce passions of their youth. How they'd fretted about the importance of the palest shade of lipstick they could find and the little flicks they drew at the corner of their eyes. And the music they'd played, the dances they'd done together in Morag's bedroom. The floor shook as they wiggled and jived, serious-faced. This was important, perfecting the dance. Weekends back then had been golden. Friday a day of heady optimism. Who would they meet tonight? Whose kisses would come to them? Their sex lives vibrant, and lusty, and, in the end, innocent. They neither of them went *all the way* but were getting close. They'd compared notes. Sunday evenings back then had been filled with bittersweet gloom. They'd gloated over the revelries, follies and glories of the Saturday night, wallowed in melancholy over Monday morning, looming.

The air tonight smelled of warm earth and new-mown grass; someone nearby was trimming their lawn. The cat walked by.

'He is getting fat,' said Iris.

'He?' said Charles. 'Are you sure it's a he?'

'He's called Eric,' said Iris. 'After Clapton. He's Scott's.'

'Well, it certainly sounds like a he.'

From across the road came sounds of children playing. They were swinging across the river on a Tarzan rope tied to a tree. The tarzie, they called it. Squeals. Sophy's squeals, Iris heard. She hadn't studied for long. So much for going to university, not being a peasant. Iris asked if Charles would like a glass of liqueur. She thought she had brought some Drambuie left over from Christmas with her when she moved.

'Liqueur?' He didn't much like the stuff. 'That would be nice.'

She fetched them both a glass. Sat down, sipped. Slipped back into her memories. She'd been eighteen when she'd met Harry. He'd been a friend of her father's. How flattered she'd been at the attentions of an older man. He'd taken her to the theatre, to dinner. Her life divided into two – before Harry, after Harry. Before Harry dates had been what she and Morag called P and Gs. Pictures and a grope to follow. Not that she minded the grope, there had been something thrilling about kissing and fumbling in doorways. After Harry dates were flowers or chocolates (he never turned up empty-handed), dinner and a kiss in his car. Harry had a car. This was a coup, a man with wheels. He seduced her on a weekend away in, of all places, Liverpool. She never could think of Liverpool afterwards without thinking of sex. She hadn't known what to pack.

'Should I take a nightdress?' she'd asked Morag.

'Of course. You want to have something on that you can take off. It's sexier.'

And after that, she had been Harry's. She moved into Harry's life, mixed with Harry's friends (not that he had many) and drifted away from Morag. She meantime had taken up with a boy called Richard and had moved into his life, his circle. They met afterwards, Iris and Morag, on Tuesday nights, spoke about books, their university studies, music they liked and sex. They didn't compare notes, though. They thought themselves too sophisticated for that. Comparing notes came later when they thought, To hell with sophistication, fun's the thing. Morag married Richard, divorced Richard, and started having the sort of sex life her friends gossiped about.

'If you had a million pounds,' Sophy had once asked, 'what would you have? A big car or a house with a swimming pool?'

'If I had a million pounds, I could have both,' said Iris. But what I really want is Morag's sex life, she'd thought. By then Harry had lost interest.

And by then she and Morag had once again started to meet on Sunday nights. Though now they did not perfect their jive in Morag's bedroom. They sat in a pub and chatted about everything, but mostly about Morag's complicated love life. And they did not gloat about the glories of Saturday night; for Iris they were no longer hectic. Sometimes she entertained, sometimes she did the ironing. Neither of them dreaded Monday morning. They both looked forward to escaping back to the sanity of work. And here she was now in Green Cairns, missing those chatty evenings with Morag. And that was Harry's fault.

'My husband gambled away all our money,' she said. 'Every single penny. I have nothing.'

Charles let this roll round his mind. He didn't think she had nothing. She had a comfortable home, she had her children, a good job. Didn't seem like nothing to him. 'That was an awful thing to do,' he said. 'But he must have had a grand time doing it.'

Iris supposed he had. She sighed, watched a spider crawl up the wall beside her. From the tarzie by the river, a yowl and a splash. Someone had fallen in. The scream was familiar, Sophy. Iris didn't move. Neither Charles's comment about how Harry must have enjoyed his gambling spree nor the cry of woe from her daughter would shift her. She was comfortable here, with the Drambuie, the fading sun, the thrush singing, the smells of earth and grass, the gentle rattle of ripe wheat in the field beyond. Charles sitting next to her, sipping his drink saying nothing. This was pleasant.

The front door slammed shut. Someone stamped up the stairs into the bathroom, a rush of water, the bath being run. Sophy was fine. Angry, humiliated, but fine. Iris sighed again. No need to move. She drifted back to her thoughts.

Scott licked salt from the back of his hand, downed his third tequila and sucked a slice of lemon. 'Excellent.'

Jake Lynne sat sprawled in the armchair, one leg draped over the arm. He pointed at the bottle, inviting Scott to have another. Which Scott did, then handed the bottle to him.

The stove burbled softly. The door was open, scents of honeysuckle and burning wood filled the room. Music wove into the air. The Incredible String Band. In the kitchen, Emily Lynne baked bread. Scott thought this cottage the coolest place in the world.

The hi-fi was Bang and Olufsen. It was treated with reverence. The furniture had all come with the cottage and sagged, sighed whenever anyone sat on it. The chairs were all brown chenille, and covered with the Lynnes' selection of Indian throws. An Aubrey Beardsley print hung on the wall behind the sofa. The other walls were taken up with several thousand immaculately alphabetised LPs and books. Scott would eye these walls with envy. So far he had seventeen records in his collection, and that included his dad's collection of Perry Como, Rosemary Clooney and Mario Lanza which he never played, but in the pile beside his bed they added bulk. The record stopped.

'Em!' shouted Jake.

Emily appeared, wiping her hands on the back of her jeans. She lifted the record from the turntable, holding it tenderly, hands spread so her thumb was at the hole in the centre, and her fingers gripped the rim. She wiped it with the record cleaner, placed it in its sleeve and put it back on the shelf in its allotted place, after Janis Ian and before Iron Butterfly. Briefly, she patrolled the shelves looking for something that suited her mood. She paused at the Bs, considered the Beatles, settled for Buffalo Springfield which she thought just about hit the mark. She took a swig from the bottle and returned to her bread.

This cottage was never silent. The first thing Jake did every morning was put on some music, before he even went to the bathroom or made a cup of coffee. He believed that somewhere, either in his vast collection and yet undiscovered, or out there yet to be bought, was a song, a track – the track of tracks – that would be the ultimate piece of music. Once found, and played, that would be it. He would be cured of his constant need for sound, and could move on with his life. Meantime, the quest continued.

Emily, while recognising this, and feeling, too, the addiction to rhythm, wasn't sure about the move they had made to this place, to lead this life. They had wanted to find themselves, live simple lives, grow their own food. But secretly she found it boring. And messy. Things weren't working out. Out in the garden their crops came to nothing. Slugs decimated their cabbages, some plague of flies had ravaged their carrots, blackbirds helped themselves to their strawberries. Their onions were small and slightly soft. Nothing had grown as promised on the seed packet. Only the potatoes were edible. Emily wondered how long they could survive on them before going insane. Potatoes and rock and roll were, somehow, not enough. She had an excellent crop of mint, which went well with potatoes, and had boasted about this in the dammit shop. There had been a silence. A scornful scathing silence. Mint, she had been told, grows anywhere, is invasive and should be torn from the ground and burned. They lived, then, on muesli, lentils which they got from the health food cooperative which they visited once a month, and potatoes.

Gracie and Jake seemed happy enough. Jake seemed to think he'd stumbled on the perfect life. But then, perhaps he had. He went off twice a month to score, sometimes to Aberdeen, sometimes to London, and usually with GIs from the army base forty miles away. American men with cropped hair came by often and smoked with him. They'd sit, stoned, and listening to music, searching, too, Emily supposed, for the perfect track that would be better than any other track and would cure them of this lethargy and longing they all seemed to feel. Sometimes they brought food from the base, Twinkies and Hershey Bars. But mostly they brought giant bottles of tequila and vodka and Jack Daniel's, all one hundred per cent proof. And, in truth, they came not to see her but Jake, who was the local pusher.

They had come here from London where Jake had been a lecturer. Emily had been one of his students. She had fallen for him the minute she clapped eyes on him, though her friends couldn't understand why. Jake was thin, his hair a mass of unkempt curls; a thick black moustache flourished on his upper lip and drooped towards his chin. She was exquisite, frail, blonde. One day, in a tutorial, he had declared himself to her. 'I find you extraordinarily lovely,' he'd said.

And that had been that. Within a week she'd dropped out of her course and moved into his busy flat. What a time that had been. 1962. The floor littered with people, talking, drinking, sleeping off too much drink, and Charlie Parker on the hi-fi. In the days before Dylan and the Grateful Dead, jazz had been Jake's passion. Brown rice, smoky saxophone riffs and her in his bed. At nineteen she was pregnant. Jake's lady, they called her, and moved aside when she swept by. She always sat on the best floor cushion. Jake's young acolytes lusted after her, adored her. They said her face was achingly beautiful and wistful, with a child-like wisdom.

Then Jake wanted to drop out of everything. Life, work, society. They'd come here towing their dreams and three-year-old daughter behind them. Jake would work the soil, grow their food. She would bake bread and they'd have children who'd run through the mornings, free and wild. It would be wonderful. And others would follow, Jake had been sure of this. Soon they would have their own commune. They'd live freely with one another, an open, honest existence. In the cottage he had removed all the doors so that people could move from room to room easily. 'It'll flow,' he'd said.

But Jake hated the garden. And Emily, though she never admitted it, hated baking bread. And nobody came to join the commune. And the cottage, with no internal doors to stop draughts, was cold. Gracie grew and now she was at school. Emily walked her there every morning, and could see the hostility on other mothers' faces as she approached. She should wear shoes, she told herself. Arriving barefoot, her cheesecloth skirt trailing on the ground, was, apparently, unacceptable. Gracie, blissfully unaware of this disapproval, bounced ahead. She glowed with vitality, a boisterous talkative child. She knew she was loved and oozed confidence.

Emily didn't. She shrank inside herself. She thought she wore her loneliness like a disease. People could tell just by looking at her that she was a solitary soul, and avoided her lest they too find themselves chatting to the cat and to the sunflowers and seeking companionship in voices on the radio. Jake disappeared for days at a time; Emily cooked, tried to do imaginative things with brown rice, nuts and potatoes, and when nobody was home, danced alone on the rush matting to the songs of Joni Mitchell. What will become of me? she thought. I am twenty-six years old, I talk to nobody, my lover sits stoned out of his brains reading *The Tibetan Book of the Dead*, waiting for the perfect track to come into his life. And I am pregnant again.

In the room beyond the kitchen she heard Scott down his sixth or seventh tequila, the slurp of lemon being sucked. She knew him well; the curve of his thoughts, his quest for the knowledge he imagined only Jake possessed. She, too, had once thought Jake a god, just as young Scott did now. She had come to the conclusion that she had brought all this mess and solitariness on herself. Only the shy and insecure and inadequate seek idols. Then again, she thought, only the insecure and inadequate and arrogant take pride in becoming one.

Iris mused and drifted, sifting through her memories. Aware, but only slightly, of Charles at her side. His quiet breathing. Sometimes he would break their silence to comment on the activities of the evening. A chaffinch on the fence. 'Chaffinch,' he would say. And she'd agree, 'Chaffinch. So it is.'

Across the street, Colin was alone. Sunday nights, his grandmother played cards with her friends the Browns. She'd lay out a glass of milk and some biscuits for Colin to eat before he went to bed. 'Seven o'clock, mind. You be in bed by then. School tomorrow. I'm just down the road if you need me.' Of course, she knew she shouldn't go out and leave such a young child alone. But in a tiny place like Green Cairns, where doors were never locked, what harm could come to him? And Colin was a quiet boy, he'd put himself to bed, and be sound asleep when she came home at ten. She stroked his hair, and said, 'You be good now.'

Colin was in double torment tonight. He'd eaten all the Missie's biscuits, and stolen her plate. His little round face reddened at the thought of it, and of the pain of punishment to come if his gran found out. Then there was the hall. Only a few yards of patterned carpet between the living-room door and his bedroom, but it was dangerous out there. A madman was waiting for him. He knew it, could hear his presence, his breathing, his menacing patience. He knew Colin had to come out of that room sometime, and he was waiting. Colin had read *Kidnapped*, drinking it in. The adventures, the life he wanted to lead. He wanted to be Alan Breck, striding the heather, cunning, stylish and brave. Then he'd read *Treasure Island*. But this book had stirred his imagination in a different way, it had filled him with terror. Blind Pew. The very words stopped him breathing. His throat choked with fear. Blind Pew. He was out there now, a grim smile on his ancient face. He'd grab Colin's hand and, laughing, disappear into the night. Colin would uncurl his palm, and there it would be – *the black spot*. He'd be doomed. He regularly refused to go to bed on account of Blind Pew in the hall.

'He's out there,' he said to his gran. 'He's going to get me. With the black spot.'

'Get to bed,' she said. 'You'll be getting a black spot all right, but it'll not be from Blind Pew.'

The threat of an enraged grandmother was worse than that of a demon blindman so Colin always sloped off into the darkened hall, ready to shout should anyone appear out of the shadows, cackling menacingly. Gran would see them off. Only she wasn't here tonight. He'd have to face the dark alone. Now it was almost ten, and his gran would be home soon. He had to get to bed before she arrived. For four hours, since she'd left at six, he'd sat bolt upright in the chair by the fire, his gran's chair, and, therefore, safe. He'd hardly moved. The lights were on, and Colin knew that burglars and bogey men and Blind Pew only struck in the dark. Finally, fearing the wrath of his grandmother at finding him still up more than the vile Blind Pew, he ran from the room. Down the hall, into his room, he threw himself, still fully clothed, into bed. He lay still, listening for the dread tap, tap, tapping. The blindman's cane feeling its way towards him. Clicks and movements in the house. The pipes, the wind under the front door. Soon he'd fall asleep with his clothes on. But still, it didn't matter. It would save time. In the morning, he wouldn't have to get dressed before he had to leave for school.

Charles put down his glass and stood up.

'Better be getting down the road.'

'OK, Charles,' said Iris.

'Thanks for the supper and the drink.' He would have added, 'And the chat,' but there hadn't been any. Instead he said, 'It's Chas. Not Charlie or Charles. Chas.'

Iris said, 'Thank you too, Chas.'

'No bother.' He walked down the path at the side of the house. Stopped. Thought a moment. Turned and came back. 'What are you thanking me for?'

'For sitting here. Keeping me company. Not saying anything.'

'Oh, that.' He hadn't said anything because she hadn't said anything. This had puzzled him. He liked to chat, and had presumed when he'd been invited outside and offered a drink that some chat was in the offing. He'd plenty to say. He wanted to mention that her guttering needed cleaning out before winter and the rains came. Her garden needed digging. If she didn't paint her back door, damp would warp it. Then there was the business of her daughter near as dammit calling him a peasant. He had a lot to say on the subject of being called a peasant. But he smiled and said, 'No bother.'

Iris sat for fifteen minutes, thinking, shifting through her memories. Then went inside to do the dishes. She left them to dry on the rack beside the sink, she needed a bath.

On the way to the bathroom, she tapped on Sophy's door. 'Are you all right?'

'Yeah,' called Sophy, 'fell in the river. Got soaked.'

'But you're fine?' said Iris.

''Course,' said Sophy.

Lying soaking, Iris heard Scott come home. He locked the front door, and slowly climbed the stairs. He shut his bedroom door, very quietly. Iris got out of the bath, dried herself and went to bed. She lay in the dark, pulled her blankets round her. Sophy was home and hadn't hurt herself. Scott was home and in bed.

Outside the world beyond this room an owl called, a long resonant cry. It was starting to rain. A late-night car howled down the long straight road that stretched beyond the village. In the street outside, footsteps, someone running to get out of the wet. None of it mattered, to Iris.

Her children were here, near her, safe and warm in their beds. She could sleep.

Being Real

Iris walked everywhere with a ghost beside her: Harry. She had not shaken him off, he was with her always. Everything she did, she felt he was watching. Faced with dilemmas she'd think, What would Harry do? He'd been her mentor, and mentors, she found, were hard to shake off.

But on the back of the Harry question came another. She'd ask herself, What would a real person do? She chastised herself for this, telling herself she *was* real. As real as they come. 'I am real,' she'd say, walking about the house, duster in hand. 'What do I mean, "What would a real person do?" They'd do what I do. Deal with things.' But still, it stayed with her, this lingering thought that out there in the world were the real people who knew the secrets of dealing with things, all sorts of things, better than she did.

In school this did not happen. Teaching had become a part of what she was. She did it well from a mixture of experience and instinct. She knew when she had the class listening to, hanging on to, her words, and when she'd lost them – from movements, rustlings, fidgetings. She knew when she had her back to her pupils, writing on the board, who was being the class comic.

'What is the adverb in this sentence: The cat ran quickly across the road? Stop that, James Biggar.'

She could deal with sudden outbursts of childish naughtinesses. When Jean Simpson painted a red streak down Laura's face. When Richard Graham glued Fiona's ruler to her desk. There were temper tantrums, bullyings, teasings, sore tummies, cuts and bruises, tears, fits of giggles. A child looking glumly at her feet complaining they'd suddenly got smaller. 'I think, perhaps, Lorna, you have put on the wrong shoes.' Nothing fazed her. In the classroom she reacted, dealt with everything that came up. This newly painted room was her domain, and here she was real. As real as they come.

Outside the school, in the dammit shop or in the street, she was the Missie. Capital letter. And treated with a reverence she found unnerving. Mothers would stop her as she was emerging from the shop with a bottle of milk looking forward to making herself a cup of tea, and apologise for their children, and their own feeble attempts at parenting.

They would explain that their child was inept at spelling because spelling didn't run in the family. Or they would tell her that Susan or William or whoever had suddenly stopped eating meat or vegetables, and would only eat fish fingers and beans, and could this be why they were so fidgety? Iris would reply that the child would grow out of it. Hers had. And would reassure whoever she was talking to that their child was fine, normal and doing well in class.

Eric the cat, who had recently extended his following Iris habit from shadowing her on her walks to walking behind her wherever she went, would sit at her feet, waiting for her to return home – so he could follow her. He followed her to school in the mornings, lay outside waiting for her to come out, and followed her home. His weight increase bothered Iris. 'Are you over-eating because you're unhappy?' she asked. 'Are you taking comfort in food because you have not settled in your new home?' The cat would sit, tail wrapped neatly round his legs, and say nothing. 'It takes time,' Iris told him, 'to become accustomed to a new place.' In fact, the cat was fine. 'Look at Scott and Sophy,' she said. 'They've settled in, made friends. They're fine.' In fact, they were not.

Today had been absurd. It had started when the school phone – an ancient Bakelite thing that stood on a table by the door – rang. Iris had been standing on a desk pinning up a poster, and had asked James to answer it.

'Who was that?' she asked.

He shrugged. 'Dunno. He didn't say.'

'Didn't you ask?'

'No.'

'So what did whoever it was say?'

'He asked if you were here. And I said you were and put the phone down.'

Iris said, 'Ah.'

There followed a ten-minute lesson on phone-answering which was interrupted by Fiona Wilkinson pointing to the window and screaming.

A wasp, thought Iris. It was, after all, wasp time of year. Dazed by the scents of oncoming winter and the sudden chill they came indoors and then buzzed frantically against the pane, trying to get out again. Their presence in the room, however, caused havoc. Children yelled, hid under their desks, some ran into the dining room. Iris had come to hate wasps. But this howl of despair had nothing to do with insects and their stinging powers.

'It's MENTAL DENTAL,' shouted Fiona. Moans horror, electrifying dread, spread through the class. The children whipped themselves into a frenzy of anguish, as children do. Making mock jittering sounds. Hands over mouths. Self-induced tremblings. Iris turned and saw the mobile dental surgery at the gate.

Mr Buchan travelled the glens in a van equipped in the back to carry out all the fillings, extractions and polishing little mouths needed. Unfortunately, he could not get this van into Iris's playground. The gates were too narrow. He had to set up shop inside the school.

On the roof of the dammit shop, Chas sat and watched. He was putting a patch over the leak that had sent water dripping on to the packets of washing powder (now being offered at half-price) that lay below. Then he would paint over the damp stain on the ceiling, using a very tasteful shade of sage, he'd told Jenny.

It was a perfect day for sitting on a roof. The view was excellent. He could see down the road, cars coming to the village, and then beyond, the road stretching for miles and miles. It was what this place was about, he thought, the road. It took people away, hundreds of them over the years, and none of them came back. They went to Australia, New Zealand, Canada and America. Places he'd visited, and was thinking of going back to one day.

Wasn't life strange? You started off thinking that nothing mattered except having a good time, then you married, had kids and started to sweat with worry trying to earn enough to keep them. And one day you looked at your wife and thought: Who the hell are you?

Of course, he'd married too young. By the time he came home from the army both he and his wife were different people. Strangers sharing a home, a bed, with little to say to one another. The divorce had been affable because they'd both been relieved to say out loud that the marriage was over. Now he passed her in the street and they said 'Hello', or 'Lovely day', as if they were acquaintances. As if there hadn't been a time when they'd clung to each other, declared undying love. Time had erased the intimacies they'd shared and now they were nothing to one another. There was never so much as a meaningful glance, a moment when their eyes met and they engaged in small tender memories, mutual nostalgia – the way they were. Their conversations now were brisk, to the point. If her husband was away she might ask him to unblock a drain or mend a fuse.

He'd say, 'Well, that's that done for you.'

She'd say, 'Thanks, Chas.'

And that was all. Last week he'd painted her living room. 'A lovely shade of sage,' he'd said. 'Got some left over from a job I did the other day.'

The Missie's subtle shade was turning up in all sorts of places. He'd had a lot left.

He watched a skein of geese flying over. Waved to Hugh Stone the farmer from down the way, and watched the dentist arrive at the school. He wondered what the Missie would make of that. Mental Dental, they called him. They said he could do twenty fillings and several extractions in half-an-hour. The man was brutal but swift. Chas didn't like him.

He did, however, like Iris. He liked her quick movements and the way she spoke. He liked her house, the books lying everywhere. She lived, he thought, messily. But it was an organised mess. He sighed and stretched, took a bag of mints from his pocket, opened it, peered in and selected one which he popped into his mouth. He slowly sucked it, watching a blackbird rummaging amongst fallen leaves in the garage forecourt, rabbits in the newly harvested field beyond the school frolicking, a buzzard hovering over the tops of the trees on Couttie's Hill. He thought about going across the road and cleaning out the gutters on the Missie's house, but wondered if she'd think he was interfering. Besides, it wasn't really her house, she probably didn't care about the state of repair it was in. So how did he let her know he was interested? Woo her, he thought. Funny word that – woo. He'd had affairs since his divorce. But with women he'd met in bars or at parties who'd let him know with a look, a smile, that they were willing. They were lonely, like he was lonely, and looking for romance, someone to talk to at night, a voice answering theirs in the dark, someone to hold, a presence across the dinner table. But nothing had lasted. He took another mint from the bag. Let it lie on his tongue. Maybe he was too old to be pursuing someone. Maybe he should be doing more with his life. At his age he should be a businessman with a big car and a big house. But he enjoyed the way he passed his days, coming and going as he pleased, chatting to people. Yesterday, putting new windows into a cottage far up the glen, he'd seen a herd of deer. Hundreds of them running, hooves over soft heather, then jumping a fence, as one, like a wave. Then on, and out of sight. He smiled, remembering that. Oh, it's a fine old life when you think about it. Really he should be getting on with repairing the roof, but it was a grand day. Fine weather for sitting and staring and musing.

'Where is the partition? I always treat my patients behind that partition,' said Mental Dental.

'I had it removed,' said Iris. 'I needed the space. And do you usually turn up without giving any warning of your arrival?'

'Third Tuesday in September, that's when I come. Everybody knows that. I don't have time to send out notices.'

He wheeled round and went into the dining room. 'In here will have to do.'

He took the children in alaphabetical order, booming out their names, summoning them to him. Some came back smiling, no cavities. For, others, the grim whine of portable drill, the smell of antiseptic, the cries of pain – and Mental Dental shouting, 'Rinse.' And, 'Next.' Iris knew the morning was lost.

Scott stood in the headmaster's office, hands behind his back.

'Chisholm,' the head said, waving his ruler, 'it's six inches over the collar. Get it cut.'

'Not keen on that, sir,' said Scott.

'That is obvious. You've been told four times since you came to this school, and four times you have failed to comply with our rules. Hair must be no longer than half an inch past the collar.'

'I don't see what difference the length of my hair makes to my academic ability.'

'Probably you don't. But I have no wish to see long-haired louts in this school's uniform. It gives a bad impression.'

'I'm not a lout, sir,' said Scott. 'I have just let my hair grow. And I don't want to have it cut. This is me. I am my hair.'

'Looks loutish to me. Get it cut. What would happen if everyone grew their hair?'

Scott shrugged. 'People would all have long hair,' he said. 'And barbers would go out of buisness, I suppose. But what's the problem? I don't see why people get so uptight about it. I mean, I don't mind you having short hair.'

'There's something snide about you, Chisholm. I'll see you back here in my office Monday morning and you'll have had a haircut.'

Scott shrugged again, and left. He did not bother to return to the geography class he'd been summoned from by the headmaster for his lecture on hair. Instead he went to the lavatories, leaned on the wall and lit a cigarette.

On the second floor of the same building a voice cut through Sophy's daydream. 'Sophy Chisholm, what did I just say?'

She looked up, alarmed. 'You asked what you'd just said, miss.'

'Excellent. And what did I say before that?'

Sophy said, 'Um. Can't remember, miss.'

'It was only seconds ago. You must have a very short memory.'

Sophy agreed, indeed she had. But she'd been dreaming of Jean's father, Kenneth. Not that she called him that to his face, only in her daydreams. They'd been, in Sophy's golden driftings, walking hand in hand along a moon-drenched beach, barefoot at the edge of the sea. Sophy carried her French horn, and had stopped to face the glisten of light on water and play an exquisite slow rendering of Mozart. Kenneth had been enraptured. He'd taken her in his arms, told her she was beautiful and wonderful and that he would take care of her for ever.

'You haven't been listening to a word I've said, girl. You will write out "I must not daydream in class when the teacher is discussing French grammar" five hundred times,' Miss Jackson, her teacher, told her.

'Please, miss,' said Sophy, 'I can't do that. I have to practise my French horn.'

'From what I hear about your skill on the French horn, no amount of practice will make you any good at it. A virtuoso you aren't, my girl. Five hundred lines tomorrow morning, first thing.'

Sniggers sounded round the room. Sophy's heart lurched. She looked down at her fingers, red-faced and humiliated. She hated French. She hated her French teacher. She hated school. She hated everybody, except for Jean, her best friend, and Kenneth, her best friend's father.

'Well,' said Mental Dental, 'that's me done for the moment. See you again in six months.'

'No, you won't,' said Iris. 'This is never going to happen again.'

He stared at her. 'And how are we going to care for these children's teeth?'

'I suggest your surgery would be the more hygienic option. You can send them appointment cards. And, by the way, don't you use anaesthetics?'

He shook his head. 'Well, for extractions, a little gas. But other than that it is a well-documented fact that children's nervous systems are not fully developed. They don't feel the same pain as adults.'

'That will explain the screams,' said Iris. Suddenly infuriated, she poked him in the ribs, hard.

He yelped.

'Oh, sorry,' said Iris. 'I thought the way you treated my pupils, perhaps you weren't acquainted with pain. I presumed it might be an underdocumented fact that dentists didn't feel it.'

'I get the impression you don't like me very much, Mrs Chisholm.'

'Oh, no, you're wrong about that, Mr Buchan. I don't like you at all. Now excuse me, I have a phone call to make.'

Iris liked the old, black Bakelite school phone with its large round dial. Her voice, however, was not welcome when people at the County Buildings heard it. This was the woman who phoned regularly to demand to know what had happened to her request for new desks, new dining-room benches, new books, new paint, new sports equipment, new everything. She heard the sigh when she gave her name.

'It's Mrs Chisholm,' someone said, with horror.

'I want to speak to Mr Smith,' she said. 'I have just had a visit from the school dentist. Unannounced, I might add. And that wasn't dentistry, that was barbarism. It is not happening in my school again. I demand that Mr Smith put a stop to this.'

'He's in a meeting.'

'Well, you get him to phone me when he comes out of his meeting. Or I'll be down to see him at half-past three.'

Lunch, that day, was gloomy.

'Whose turn is it to say grace today?' said Iris.

'James, miss.'

Praying for something to be done about school dinners had been just the first step. Dinner time prayers had become a problem line where children were encouraged to voice their predicaments. Iris restricted her own communications to pleas for the custard to be lump-free and the mash not too watery. She asked for the weather to be fine for the weekend, but kept her real worries to herself. The twins prayed for permission from their mother to cycle to school. Lucy prayed for a baby sister, since her mother was pregnant and she didn't want a brother. 'Boys are smelly and rough, except Colin,' she said. Snorts of wrath rang round the table.

Boys were a fascination and a mystery to Lucy. Their knees were scabbed, fingernails bitten and dirty, when they spoke they made noises of cars and planes and explosions, waving their arms, 'Caboosh!' She never knew what to make of them.

Iris knew because Lucy had confided this once before fish fingers, congealed beans and flaccid chips. She knew all sorts of things about her pupils through their pre-dinner prayers. Such as the fact that the Hay children's mother drank and regularly forgot to feed them. This because Lorna Hay had asked that there be more to eat today and not just school dinners. Lucy lived as perfect a life as her mother could make for her. Freshly ironed clothes every day, cocoa and a cuddle and a story at night before she slept. Iris knew Lucy's mother put herself through a private hell of guilt and parental ambition for her daughter. Lucy's life had to be blissful, a dream childhood, and she had to be a wonderful mother. Such aspirations, thought Iris, only lead to Valium. James had a father who beat him.

'Please, God, let my dad be in a good mood.'

So Iris knew who had unhappy homes. And who came from happy, caring, easy houses. Most of it she could have guessed anyway. But speaking some of their problems and woes out loud proved to be some kind of blessing for the children. Of course, Iris could find out nothing about Colin, who pressed his hands together and prayed silently, lips moving.

'Excellent prayer,' she would say. 'I'm sure the Powers That Be heard.'

Today, James put his hands together and said, 'Hello, God. Thank you for our dinners. And please let the dentist die.'

'Veto that prayer,' said Iris. 'Thank you for the food we are about to eat. And please keep Mr Buchan safe. Just, we don't want him here again. At least not in any sort of dental capacity. Amen.'

The mighty ladle was wielded. Stew.

'You forgot to ask him to make the stew nice,' said Fiona, a fierce urgency in her voice. 'Quick, get in touch again.'

'And please make the stew tasty. Amen again,' said Iris.

'Phew!' said Fiona. 'That was close.'

'A little dramatic,' said Iris. But then, she thought, children filled their little lives with drama. They revelled in it. Were good at it.

129

They made dramas out of all sorts of ordinary, mundane events. Adults, on the other hand, went to great lengths to avoid it.

Stella and John Vernon lay in bed. With the twins away at school, they were free to be naughty in the afternoon. Outside the weather was soft, balmy. A robin chipped a small song in the rowan tree that grew outside their window. A gentle September breeze sifted through the curtains.

'This is the life,' said Stella. 'We should do this every afternoon. It's terribly good for us. Good for the skin, the hair and the circulation.'

'If we had any visitors we wouldn't have time to do this.'

'See,' said Stella. 'There's an up side to everything. No business, plenty of sex. If you've got too much business and are working all the time, you have no time for sex. You get all grumpy and have a heart attack. I'm keeping you healthy.'

'Healthy but broke,' said John.

'Things will pick up.' Stella was sure of this. 'We have lovely holiday homes. We have games, gourmet food. Once word of mouth gets about we'll be overflowing with bookings. We'll be turning people away. Who could resist coming here?'

'Just about everyone in the country. We've got nobody coming for an autumn break. We hardly had anybody all summer. We're seriously broke.'

'Oh, no,' said Stella. 'Broke, yes. But not seriously.'

They had no idea how broke they were since they had stopped looking at their bank statements. A small pile of them lay in unopened envelopes in the desk in the living room. It was their way of dealing with problems. What they didn't know, they figured, couldn't bother them.

'We have so much,' said Stella. 'We live in this beautiful place. We have our own business. We have each other. We have the twins. John,' she said, 'we are blessed.' She turned to him, touched his cheek. 'We are the people with everything. And we have an hour before I have to go collect Stephen and Simon from school.'

So they kissed for this was a wonderful way to pass a gentle autumn afternoon. Better than repairing the broken window in

Lupin Cottage, better than doing accounts, and much, much better than worrying.

Chas, Iris noticed, had spent most of the day on the roof of the dammit shop. Some of the time he'd been busy doing whatever it was he was up there to do. But mostly he'd just sat, looking around him, breathing in the view and the day. Iris marvelled at the man – so calm, so self-contained, at peace with himself and his surroundings. Sitting on a roof, sucking mints, watching the world go by, busy being happy. Peace . . . what was that again? How did one attain it? She continually likened herself to a demented hen, always moving, fussing, bossing. Tie your laces. Pick up your shoes, Scott. Turn that music down. Have you done your homework? Nag. Nag. Nag.

Half-past two. Soon it would be time for the younger pupils to go home. She told them to draw their daddies at work, since yesterday they'd done their mummies at work. Gracie wanted to know how to spell anarchist because that was what her daddy did.

Iris wrote it on the board. 'Anarchist? Your daddy's an anarchist?'

Gracie nodded.

What did an anarchist do all day? Iris had to know. She looked over Gracie's shoulder. A naive, innocent, multi-coloured drawing. Here was Gracie's dad, the anarchist, long hair, beard, bare feet, sitting on a sofa, staring into the middle distance. Iris supposed the drawing was accurate. That would be what anarchists did, these days, dream.

Walking round the room, Iris started a small speech about anarchy. After all, the word had come up, her pupils should know what it meant.

'Anarchy,' she said, 'is . . .' She stopped. How to explain? She picked up a pink hat that had fallen from the dressing-up box in the dressing-up corner, twirled it in her fingers. Then became aware of someone standing in the doorway, watching, listening.

Anthony Smith, head of the county education department, fearing the threatened visit, had driven out to the school. What he saw was a bright sunny room with windows open, walls aglow with new paint and covered with posters and children's drawings. He saw a group of eager pupils, felt a sense of business and purpose. Energy.

Iris thought he saw little innocents getting a lecture on subversion from a woman idly playing with a pink hat, and felt defensive.

'Mrs Chisholm,' he said, 'I got your message and came to visit. I thought I'd let you do battle on your own ground.'

'Excellent,' said Iris. 'So where will we start? Desks? Dinner benches? Or dentistry?'

'I am well aware of your desk and dinner bench situation. Let's do the last D, dentistry.'

'Barbarism, more like,' she said. 'And unhygienic barbarism at that.'

'I didn't think barbarism ever was hygienic.'

She glared. He smiled.

'I'm not prepared to have a discussion on the niceties of barbarism. What I am saying is, it isn't going to happen in my school to my pupils.'

He said, 'Hmm.'

Which she hated. 'What do you mean, hmm? You're verging on the patronising with that remark, Mr Smith.'

'Since when was "hmm" patronising?'

'Since two seconds ago when you said it.'

'Mrs Chisholm, the county pays Mr Buchan to come to all the rural schools and care for the children's teeth.'

'Mr Smith, Mental Dental came to my school and rummaged about my children's mouths with his big hands in my dining room. Children could be heard screaming. The sound of the drill echoed round the classroom. A tooth was extracted through there,' she pointed extravagantly, 'only yards away, in the dining room. If that isn't barbarism, you tell me what it is.'

'A procedure that's part of maintaining dental health.' He paused. 'Mental Dental?'

The children sniggered. Reminding Iris that they were there, listening. She should have conducted this confrontation in the hall, outside the classroom.

'Mr Buchan's nickname. Quite fitting, I think.'

'I'll pretend I wasn't told that.'

She started manoeuvring him from the room. Heads turned, watching. And when Iris shut the door, the class erupted in to whispers.

'If she talks to her boss like that she'll get the sack,' Lucy told Colin.

He frowned. What did that mean – get the sack? Was it like getting the belt? When you held out your hand and the teacher whacked it with her leather strap. That hurt. This Missie never did it to you but the last one had. His hand had felt hot and sore for hours afterwards; he'd blown on it to cool it down, and kept it in his pocket at home so his gran wouldn't see the huge red weal. Maybe this man would hit the Missie's with a sack, only that wouldn't hurt much. Unless it was filled with stones or bricks. His face contorted with worry.

Lucy put her arm round him. 'It'll be all right.'

Iris took Mr Smith into the dining room, ran her hand along one of the benches. 'Look,' showing him her palm, and the two slivers of wood the small sweep had gathered. 'This is what happens every dinnertime. Only not to their hands. I have to remove splinters from their bottoms. And, quite frankly, it's not my idea of fun. I believe in hands-on teaching, but there are places these hands have no wish to go.'

'We'll get you new benches.'

'When?' she said.

'As soon as possible.'

'Sooner,' she said. 'As soon as possible is not soon enough.'

The whispers in the classroom gathered steam. The fevered murmurs grew into shouts, yells, a babble of hoots and squeals.

Iris opened the door, shouted, 'QUIET! Get on with some work and stop malarkeying about.' Shut the door. 'Damn! I said "malarkeying". I always swore I'd never say it. It's such a teachery word. I've only ever heard teachers say it.' She started pulling the splinters from her palm. 'These children are lovely. But I have a severe stammerer, a mute, two who look pretty underfed, one who is beaten at home. And that's just what I know about. For the most part they lack self-esteem. I think not having to have bits of wood pulled daily from their bums could be the start of building some self-confidence. But that's only me. What do I know? I just said malarkeying.'

Mr Smith moved towards the door. 'So, you want new benches, new desks, books . . .'

'. . . art materials, no dentist, and our sports equipment at the moment is seven hula hoops, three balls and a selection of bean bags,' Iris chipped in.

'Right.' They were walking across the playground towards his car. 'And how do you propose we manage that on our budget? There are other schools competing for money.'

'My needs are greater. No mercy,' said Iris.

'How do you imagine your pupils are going to get to the dentist?'

'Taxi. You pay.'

'You write to us weekly. You phone. You demand. You are making a name for yourself at the County Buildings, Mrs Chisholm,' he said. 'I have a tight budget. I have to treat all schools equally. Show no favours.' He smiled at her. 'It's tough at the top.'

'I know,' said Iris softly, patting his arm. 'I know, it's hard. But take comfort, Mr Smith, it's even tougher at the bottom.'

At the classroom window, heads jostled for a view.

'Oooh!' Big dramatic gasp from Lorna Hay. 'She touched him. They must be in love.'

'Maybe they'll get married and have babies,' said Lucy. An idea so sudden, so spontaneous, she forgot to stutter.

There was a fleeting silence as the children considered this. Then speculations and imaginings soared. They'd live in the schoolhouse. Sleep in a big bed. Together. They'd do it in the schoolhouse. She'd wear a pink nightdress. Or maybe nothing.

'They'd both be naked,' shouted James. 'BOLLOCKY BUFF.'

Iris turned to walk back into the school, saw a crowd at the window, little glassed-in faces, red with mirth, watching, speculating.

'Oh, pardon me, Mr Smith, I just farted.' Fiona paraded up and down, holding her left arm out, hand limp. 'Shall we take our clothes off and have sex now?'

Iris entered the school. In the fleeting time it took for her to walk the short corridor to the classroom, the children scattered, running from the window back to their desks. When Iris came in, they were silent. That intense guilty silence of little people who have been naughty, saying rude things, thinking even ruder ones.

Iris knew it well. Tiny, grubby minds have been working overtime, she told herself. She'd been the same, and, given the opportunity, still bellowed at dirty jokes. 'You've disgraced yourselves,' she said. 'What sort of noise was that to make when Mr Smith was here? Not nice. Not nice at all. Extra homework, I think. You will all write an essay for me, The Nicest Thing In The World.'

Outside at the gate mothers were gathering. Iris clapped her hands. 'Pack up your school bags, everyone. Time to go home.'

She walked out into the playground, felt the soft September sunshine. Not hot, just warming, and a chaffinch somewhere chirping a defiant little song. Children running like jubilant puppies, spilling out into freedom. Time to play. Voices carrying into the afternoon – Iris watched them go.

Stella was late. Her aging Land Rover rumbled and clanked into the village after all the children except the twins had gone. She clambered out, apologising. 'Sorry, sorry.'

The twins were already protesting at being kept waiting. If they could cycle to school, she wouldn't have to come for them.

And Stella said, 'I already told you, no.'

Iris wondered what Stella had been up to, she looked rumpled, flustered. Her hair was tousled. 'You all right?' Iris asked.

'Oh, I got caught up, is all,' said Stella, not meeting her eye. 'Forgot the time. Busy, busy.'

Chas climbed down from the roof of the dammit shop. Wiped his hands on the seat of his jeans, crossed the road, smiling. 'Been a grand day, hasn't it?' He'd seen everything from his vantage point, and knew that, for Iris, the day hadn't been grand at all.

'No,' she said. 'It has not been a good day for me. Though, I'll agree, it has been for you, sitting on a roof dreaming.'

'Well, I've been fixing the leak as well as dreaming. But what's a day if it hasn't got a little dream in it?'

135

Iris stared at him. She supposed he had a point, but this was not the day to make it. 'A very normal day for those of us who have a lot to do, Mr Harper,' she said, turned and walked back across the playground.

Still smiling, Chas watched her go. He loved the way she walked. Head up, small and busy yet naturally graceful. The chaffinch still sang, the world about him was ripe, warm and lazy. Iris moving purposefully back to her classroom . . . He would remember this moment for the rest of his life. He thought that today, watching her, the way she spoke to her pupils, made them laugh, the way she stood up to Mental Dental and made demands of Anthony Smith, was the day he fell in love with her.

That night in houses in the village and all the way up the glen stories were told. The Missie had told a man who'd come to the school that the dentist wasn't to come anymore. And she wanted new desks. And then she'd touched the man. Was she in love?

'No, don't be silly,' said Fiona's mum. 'It was a gesture. People touch all the time. The Missie's a touching sort of person.'

Not good enough for Fiona who needed drama, attention. 'But she kissed him!'

'Kissed him?' said Mrs Wilkinson. 'What do you mean? What sort of kiss?'

'Like this,' said Fiona. She folded an imaginary man to her, puckered her little lips and kissed him, long and passionate, head to one side. 'Like in the films.'

'Did she now?' Mrs Wilkinson didn't approve of this. That Fiona might be exaggerating didn't cross her mind. Fiona wouldn't do that. No child of hers would do that.

Rumours flew through the community. Phones rang, tongues wagged. What sort of a person would kiss like that in full view of anybody who might be passing, in full view indeed of her pupils? And what about the children's teeth? Nobody likes going to the dentist, but this was something else. Denying these poor little ones proper dental care. And having an affair, and her recently widowed. Goings-on in the schoolhouse. It was a scandal.

The Nicest Thing in the World

The front of Iris's house looked out on to the street. Green Cairns only had one. At night the brightest light, the gathering place, was the phone box. It was a bikes and Coca-Cola sort of place, and you had to be under eighteen to join in. Sophy qualified. Kids would sit along the wall behind the box, their banter spinning out into the dark. Every now and then one of them would break away from the group, cycle the length of the street, whirl round and come back again. And, until the dammit shop closed at nine o'clock, they'd wander back and forth buying Coke, and more Coke.

From her kitchen window Iris could see fields, and the hill she kept promising herself she'd climb one day. Occasionally a tractor would rumble by, and sometimes she'd see the Mad Woman striding purposefully. To where? Iris didn't know. The Mad Woman, Iris had been told, was married to a local farmer and had become demented after their crops failed three years running, their barn had burned down killing a prize bull inside, and the child she'd been longing for, after fourteen years of trying to get pregnant, had been stillborn.

'That would do it,' said Iris.

'Well,' Jenny McGuire at the dammit shop told her, screwing her finger against the side of her forehead, 'she's always been a bit thon way. She lives up on Blawcotts. Wind never stops there. Cold, and the sound of it sweeping round the house makes you want to shout at it to stop. Nothing grows in a gale like that.'

She wore pearls, the Mad Woman, and her face was always made-up. Though it seemed as if she never looked in the mirror while putting it on. Her lips were a thick slash of crimson. Iris got the impression she took her lipstick and rubbed it furiously in the general area of her mouth. The Mad Woman wore a tweed skirt and matching jumper, and a green anorak. On her feet, wellington boots. Draped over her left arm, a black leather handbag. Striding, she stared straight ahead. She moved at speed across the fields, appearing on the horizon walking directly to the hedge at the edge of the lane behind the school. She did not skirt the fields, but ploughed through the barley or wheat, eyes fixed on the distance.

Once, Iris had met her when she was on one of her walks: dog darting ahead; complaining cat, tail in the air, behind. The woman had appeared not to see her, and the two of them had nearly collided on the path. They did that nearly-bumping-into-someone dance, each moving aside for the other. Only in moving aside, they'd both moved to the same side, then repeated the nonsense when they both moved to the other side. It was a ducking, diving sort of meeting, with Iris laughing and apologising, 'Sorry, sorry.' The Mad Woman had said nothing, and as soon as the way ahead was clear had strode on, silently. No eye contact, no acknowledgment that Iris was even there. Weird, thought Iris. And remembering the crowded stations and bustling streets she'd manoeuvred through without colliding with anyone, laughed to think she'd almost banged into someone in this vast, empty space. Only the two of them, and the wind shifting through the crops. The woman had heard the laugh, turned to glare and mumble then strode on. Iris shivered.

Iris's favourite view was from the landing at the top of the stairs. She could never just pass this window. On every trip upstairs, or downstairs in the morning, she felt compelled to stop and stare. From here she could see everything. The village. Hills in the distance, mountains peaking behind. She could see the phone box and the gathering of kids its light attracted. Teenage moths, she thought. She could see the back gardens where washing hung and vegetables grew, sun loungers sat on lawns waiting for weather suitable for people to come lounge on them. Greenhouses and sheds. Some gardens were neglected, weed-covered and littered with old tyres, bits of bicycle and abandoned toys. Others were immaculate, mowed and trimmed. They were divided by long stone walls, shrubs and ivies spread over them creeping into new territory, gardens tumbled into gardens.

Beyond the village, scattered over the landscape were farms and cottages. At night, when the sky turned indigo, lights came on, pools of yellow gleaming in the dark. Mornings, now that autumn was here, mist lay along the earth, enveloped trees. Deer coming down from higher ground walked slowly, single file across the fields. Iris saw it all from above, looked down on the soft wrapping of still foggy air, holding her breath. It was beautiful, here.

'Beautiful to look at,' Sophy said. 'Not to be in.'

It was another of Iris's promises to herself that one day, soon, she would drive up into those distant hills and walk them to see what was there, move through the perfect air and discover if there was, somewhere deep inside her, peace.

One Saturday morning Morag arrived. Iris watched her keening up the path, moving, as she always moved, at speed, shoulders bent, head forward, as if that bit of her had to arrive first. She was wearing a gypsy peasant outfit: a low-cut blouse with ruffles round the sleeves, a long denim skirt and leather boots. Her hair, naturally curly, had been allowed since Iris last saw her to grow into a long, thick and messy tumble. Unwilling to make two trips from the car she carried two bulging overnight bags that banged against her leg in one hand, and two plastic carriers in the the other.

She dumped everything in the kitchen, kissed Iris, said, 'You're looking great. Country life suits you.' Looked round and added, 'Fantastic room. Such potential. It'll be wonderful once you do it up.'

'I've done it up,' said Iris. 'This is as wonderful as it's going to get. Coffee?'

Unabashed, Morag said, 'Absolutely.' Sat at the table, put her cigarettes and lighter in front of her. 'So, how long are you going to stay?'

The kettle boiled. Iris made coffee, gave herself the cracked mug and sat down. 'Shut up, Morag. How do I know how long I'll stay?'

'Only,' said her friend, 'it's so quiet here. There's nothing. What do people do?'

'They get up in the morning. Go to work. Come home. Eat. Watch television. Then go to bed. What do you do?'

'The same,' said Morag. 'Only with twiddly bits in between.'

'Yeah, well, there's twiddly bits going on here, I suspect. Probably not as complicated as yours, though.'

Morag smiled. 'Years of practice.'

They sipped hot coffee. A tractor rumbled past in the field beyond the garden.

'Very pastoral,' said Morag.

'Noisy,' said Iris.

'But you like it?' said Morag. 'You could be happy here?'

'I'm coping. That's the mood of the moment. I cope. I have Sophy and Scott, and I have the school. I cook food, I do the motherly stuff, I teach the kids. I cope. Sometimes I pick up the newspaper and read about a film I'd love to see, but know I'll never get near a cinema to do that. There's books I can't get to a shop to buy. Make-up the shops in the local town won't sell. Wines. Foods. Everything. So I do a little bit more coping, and don't think about any of it.'

Morag nodded. 'And how's the Harry situation?'

'I thought about him yesterday. And the day before. And the day before that. But a week ago I had a whole day when I didn't think about him, till I was in bed when I realised I hadn't thought about him. Which reminded me of him, so I thought about him. But I figure one day I'll have a Harry-free day, then another and another. Then I'll be cured of him. But still I wake up in the night and reach for him. Sometimes I'm in the kitchen at the time he used to come home from work and I'll turn and expect to see him, there, in the doorway. But I see a different door, and I remember where I am. Here. So I do a little more coping.'

'Coping?' said Morag.

'Coping,' said Iris. 'Head up, going forward. But coping, right now, is as good as it gets.'

In the afternoon they headed for the hills in Morag's car. She drove the way she walked, head forward, leaning towards the windscreen. Talking constantly, now and then she'd expound too much and let go of the steering wheel while she gesticulated.

'Sheep, there's nothing but sheep here.'

'What did you expect?'

'I don't know. But somehow the baa-ing of sheep makes it seem so desolate. Lonely. I bet people go insane here. Wind, rain and nobody to talk to.'

'You really know how to put a girl off.'

'Sorry,' said Morag. 'I'm a city person.'

'Noise and pollution and traffic jams,' said Iris.

'Mud and incest,' said Morag.

'Crowds and bus queues and rude people,' said Iris.

'Red necks,' said Morag.

'Squoinks, Sophy calls them,' said Iris.

Morag nodded. 'Good name.'

'They're just people,' said Iris. 'They live a different life at a different pace, but they're still people.'

Morag conceded, 'Suppose.'

They parked at the end of a rutted path and started to walk into the forest. The path was tree-dark, brown pine needles underfoot. They didn't speak, but fell instead into a mutual, companionable panting. Fifteen minutes later they came out from the trees and moved into light and space. The path ahead was thickly heathered. They turned to look back the way they'd come. Treetops, then a wide spread of farmland, patterns of fields, scattered cottages, farmhouses and outbuildings. The river slid and wound through it.

'OK, it's beautiful,' said Morag. 'But I don't think I could hack it here.'

'No Chinese takeaway for miles,' said Iris.

'Yeah,' said Morag. 'Face it, I'm tacky.'

They walked on. In the distance curlews wheeled, shrill cries. Once or twice a hare, startled by their approaching steps, sprang up and scudded into the distance. A small wind shifted round them. Morag complained, 'Christ, I'm not fit. I'm in a lather.'

'Your sweat must be worth a bit, though,' said Iris. 'It'll be a mix of pure alcohol and nicotine.'

'True,' agreed Morag.

They trudged, bent against the incline of the path, panting and cursing their aching limbs.

'I think I truly hate the outdoor life,' said Morag.

The track swept round the side of a hill. They followed it, though by now Morag was protesting, 'This isn't for me, just walking. No shops. No pubs.'

'Oh, shut up,' said Iris. 'Fresh air to unglue your lungs. Breathe. Lighten up.'

'There's absolutely nobody about. Not a soul,' said Morag. 'I feel vulnerable. There's nothing to protect me. No buildings to cower beside. I feel perpendicular in a huge landscape.'

'It must be hard for you,' said Iris. 'You being such a horizontal person.'

They rounded the long bend, and there, before them, was a small loch. Reeds sprouting round the edges, a little wooden boathouse, willows trailing down to the surface of the water. A heron stood icy still at the far side. A single swan moved towards the middle. They sat, squeezing their bums on to a single boulder, watching the view, sharing a Mars Bar.

'This is better,' said Morag. 'Sitting down's more my thing. And if it was in your living room, by the fire with a glass of something, it'd be perfect.'

'Stop whining and tell me about your love life,' said Iris. 'I need details, the more intimate the better.'

So they spoke about Morag's current lovers, her job, the reports she had to write, the people she worked with, her worries, doubts, fears, but mostly about her lovers.

'I think I'll never have a man again,' said Iris. 'I think I'll never make love again. I'll be an old maid. Missies usually are, you know. I get the feeling that's what's expected of me.'

'Don't be stupid,' said Morag. 'It takes time. You'll get over Harry and move on. Then you can show people round here how sexy a Missie can be. Now I'm going home.' She stood up and started back down the path. Over the hill, turned the wrong way, took the wrong track back. Iris followed.

An hour and a half later they arrived back at the road. But it was

142

not the same bit of road they'd started from. The car was not there. They stood looking up the road, then down the road. One pointing left, the other right. Which way? Neither of them knew.

'Look at us,' said Morag. 'We're like a couple of yokels.'

'This is your fault,' said Iris. 'You took the wrong path. I thought that at the time.'

'And didn't say! So it's *your* fault. You're the local here. You should know your way through the hills.'

'I've never been this far up the glen before. I have no idea where I am.'

'Well,' Morag panicked, 'how do we find the car? I need a pee. I need a drink. I need to sit in a comfortable chair. Food, I want that, too.'

'Well, which way?' said Iris.

'This way,' decided Morag. 'It's on the way home. It's downhill. As a choice of direction it has everything going for it.'

They set off. Ten minutes walking. No car. Glumly they were both beginning to think they were headed away from where they'd parked. But neither of them spoke their fears out loud. They stumped homeward. To their left tall pines shifting in the wind, to their right a vast spreading of fields. Sheep crowded by the fence to watch them pass. They were the only thing happening. The road was pitted, rough underfoot. The sunny afternoon was darkening into evening. It was starting to rain.

'Fucking countryside,' said Morag.

'I'm beginning to agree,' said Iris. 'It's getting dark, and we're in the middle of nowhere.'

The Land Rover, when it appeared, had its lights on. Morag heard it coming, stepped into the middle of the road, stood waving her arms above her head. No way was it going to go right past them. It was Stella Vernon, mother of the twins. The quintessential mum.

'I've been sent to get you,' she said. 'At first we thought you were just walking down the road a bit. Then we realised you were probably lost from the way you were stumbling along, waving your arms about. Sort of bickering. Your car's four miles back up the road.'

'You've been spying?' Morag accused.

'Oh, yes.' Stella knew no shame. 'Of course we have. It's always fun watching you townies stump about and lose your way. Actually your car's just yards up the road from where you came out of the trees. We had quite a laugh when you both pointed in different directions. I won a fiver. I bet you'd head downhill.'

'Well, good for you,' said Morag.

Stella turned the Land Rover, headed back up the road. Lurching, crashing gears. 'I hate this thing.' She steered into a long weedy drive, rhododendrons spilling on to the tarmac. 'You'll be coming in for a cup of tea.' Hard to know if this was an invitation or a command. And since they were in the car and already headed towards the Vernons' house, neither Morag nor Iris could refuse. 'Only it's raining. And we never let visitors go by without a little something.'

'Fine,' said Morag. 'You belong around here?'

'Oh, my, no. We're incomers. Like the Missie.'

'How long have you lived here?'

'Not long,' said Stella, manoeuvring the Land Rover over potholes, swinging round boulders. Inside the cabin the passengers swayed, gripped their seats. 'Ten years.'

'Ten years!' said Morag. 'That's ages.'

'Not to the people round here. You have to be here longer than that to be accepted. Fifty years, I'd say. In fact to be really accepted you'd have to live here over fifty years, then die here. That'd do it. But then, of course, you'd be dead and you wouldn't know you'd been accepted.'

'Not much of a deal,' said Iris.

'Yeah, well, folks here – set in their ways, y'know,' said Stella. She jammed on the brakes, they all lurched forward. Stella jumped out and bustled into the house, leaving Iris and Morag to lumber out, stiff from sudden exercise. Chilled. Through the evening gloom they saw a large courtyard, potted plants, bikes, washing hanging, damp and limp, on the line.

The Vernons' house was a row of cottages, knocked together into one long, low home. Steadings adjoining the cottages had been converted into the holiday homes the Vernons rented out. Each had a withering potted plant on the front step, and a pokerwork name on a piece of varnished wood nailed to the door. The Hollyhocks, Rose Cottage, Lupin Cottage, Daisy Corner, The Heathers. They all had a small patio with wrought-iron tables and chairs. But it was jolly, in a dilapidated sort of way. The lawn in the middle of the courtyard was worn thin and bare like a neglected football pitch. At one end was a basketball net. In front of the Land Rover was an old Ford, both of its back wheels replaced by a pile of bricks.

Iris looked at Morag. 'This looks like someone had a dream, then thought better of it and let it go.'

They went inside. Iris was hoping the twins would be there. She loved getting glimpses of her pupils' homes, and always imagined when talking to individual children what sort of place they went back to at the end of the day – their kitchens, living rooms, bedrooms. She prided herself on her skill in this. She hadn't visited many of her pupils at home, but her imaginings about those she had, had been right. She thought this home would be untidy, filled with aromas of baking and an enfolding, comforting cosiness, a soft wall of heat. She imagined an old besplattered Aga, children's pictures pinned to the wall. A kitchen that needed a coat of paint but was too stuffed with books, furniture, homey mess, for anyone ever to get round to redecorating.

She'd been right. The kitchen was large, warm, busy, cluttered. Dishes on the draining board, pots on the Aga, a grouping of odd chairs round the table which was littered with newspapers, books, a set of accounts, toy cars. Either side of the range was a bashed, deeply seated armchair. On one a cat lay curled and sleeping; on the other was a labrador, head between its paws, watching, tail thumping behind him. He yawned, fat, friendly, and too lazy to get off the chair to extend his welcome beyond the tail-thumping. This room had, as Iris had imagined, the soft enfolding wall of warmth. The windows were steamed.

'Take a seat,' said Stella, flapping her hand towards the already-occupied chairs.

Iris and Morag sat at the table. Stella put a chocolate cake down among the clutter in front of them, then a plate of scones, flapjacks, an apple cake, bread, butter, jam. Fitting each new treat in the gaps between the spreading litter. She stood, hands on hips, considering her offering. 'Cheese,' she said. Fetched a cheeseboard heavy with a selection of goodies – Camembert, Brie, Cheddar and a heap of crackers. She stood back again. Considered again. Clapped, pointed. 'Brownies. Made them this morning.' She piled some on to to a plate, placed it amidst the clutter. And stood back again. 'What am I thinking of? You must be hungry.'

She surged towards the Aga, shifting up a gear into full bustle. A clattering of pots and heated sizzle of fat drowned Iris's protest: 'Please, don't bother.'

'No bother,' said Stella, standing with her back to them, elbows working. Swift darting forays to the fridge for eggs, bacon, tomatoes, mushrooms. She tossed eggshells into the bin under the sink, made tea. Placed a plate before each of them, filled mugs with tea, and said she was off to tell everybody they were here. 'Eat up.'

Iris moaned that she had a beef *bourgignon* in the fridge at home.

'Excellent,' said Morag. 'We can have that when we get back.'

'I have a sinking feeling we're not going to get back. We've been captured and lured here, forced to stay with promises of cakes.'

'Sounds good to me.' Morag ate. 'Look at this food. D'you think she'd adopt us? Who is the everyone she's off to tell about us being here?'

Iris shrugged. 'Her husband and family, I suppose.'

'Fresh farm eggs, you can tell the difference,' said Morag.

'Fresh farm eggs straight from the supermarket,' said Stella, coming back into the room. 'Everyone's coming. Soon as I told them who was here,' looking at Iris, 'couldn't keep them away.' To Morag, 'Iris is quite the celebrity round here. She's the youngest Missie we've ever had.'

'Goodness,' said Morag. 'The rest of them must have been pretty old. Iris is looking at forty.'

'You're never forty?' said Stella. 'You don't look it.'

146

'I don't look it because I'm not it. I'm thirty-nine. I've got ages before I'm forty.'

'A whole six months,' said Morag.

'But what a six months they'll be,' said Iris. She was struggling to finish her two fried eggs, four slices of bacon, tomatoes and pile of mushrooms. But she toasted the six months ahead, the hoped-for naughtiness of them, with her mug of tea.

Morag's plate was clean. She'd started on her second brownie and was planning to have some chocolate cake next. She figured she'd walked enough today to justify a vast amount of food. Her appetites for everything – food, cigarettes, sex – seemed boundless.

'A drink,' said Stella. 'Before everybody arrives.'

'Who is everybody?' asked Iris.

'Everybody,' she said. 'I phoned everybody.' She pulled a bottle of whisky from the cupboard and filled three tumblers. Placed one before Morag, one before Iris, and sipped the third herself.

The hospitality here – bacon and eggs, a vast selection of cakes, whisky – overflowed. It was thrust at them. It was almost aggressive. Iris protested, perhaps a little mildly, that she didn't drink whisky.

But Stella said, 'Of course you do.' Tilted her glass towards Iris, then swigged. A demonstration of whisky-drinking.

Behind them the door opened. The twins slid into the room and stood, side by side, smiling shyly. It had taken Iris a while, but now she could tell them apart. Stephen had a stillness, a steady gaze, was marginally taller, more serious, ten minutes older than Simon, who had an impishness about him. His face was more mobile. He seemed to be in constant motion, not fidgety, just energetic. Whenever the twins got up to mischief, Simon was at the root of it. He had that eager childish curiosity that led him to poke his finger into holes – any hole anywhere, in walls, sheets or the ground – and into bowls of creamy puddings, and to pick icing from cakes. He wasn't naughty, he just faced the freshness of every day on a need-to-know basis. Need to know what this tastes like, need to know what the inside of the telly looks like, need to know if I can climb this tree, need to know if I can ride my bike without holding on. And Stephen followed.

'Look who's come to see you,' said Stella.

Two identical faces with identical grins acknowledged Iris. 'Hello, Miss.'

'Hello, Stephen and Simon,' said Iris. 'Where have you been? I've been here for ages. You haven't been avoiding me, have you?'

They shook their heads. Morag snorted. 'Of course they've been avoiding you. You're their teacher. They probably don't even think you're human.'

The twins grinned.

'They probably think you live in the school.' Morag was enjoying this.

'No,' said Simon. 'She lives in the schoolhouse. We see her. When we get dropped off early, we see her in her pink robe thing bringing in the milk.'

'Simon!' said Stella.

'Well, we do.'

'And absolutely gorgeous I look in it, too. Don't I, Simon?'

'Yes, Miss.' Reddening. But eying the food on the table.

'Oh,' said Iris. 'You didn't come to see me at all. You came to see if you could wangle some cakes.'

'Oh, no,' they said in unison, looking at the spread.

'Thought so,' said Iris. She would have invited them to help themselves. But it wasn't her food. They weren't her children.

'Go on,' said Stella. 'Fill a plate each and take it to your room. We've got people coming.'

Excellent treat. Cakes in the bedroom. They took a plate each from the cupboard, Stephen a small one, Simon's huge.

'Simon,' said Stella.

He shrugged, replaced the huge plate with a small one. It was, Iris knew, another need-to-know thing. Need to know if I can get away with a great big plate. She helped them with their selection, holding up the biggest brownies and flapjacks. 'Lovely brown brownies.' Iris in her element, talking to, playing with, children. She loved children. Their seriousness when selecting the choicest cake. Little faces furrowed with indecision.

'Big brown brownies,' said Stephen.

'Beautiful big brown brownies,' said Simon.

'The beautiful bouquet of big brown brownies baking,' said Iris. She thought to mention alliteration, decided against it. It was the weekend. But they'd do alliteration on Monday for sure.

She phoned home to tell her own two she'd be late. 'I've got caught up here. At the Vernons'. There's food in the fridge,' she told Scott.

Scott said, 'No bother.' He'd get something. And tell Sophy who was staying next door tonight anyway.

He took a couple of spoonfuls of Iris's beef *bourgignon*, and several glasses of the wine she had bought for Morag's visit. Told Sophy Mum would be out late, and went to see the Lynnes. Sophy went out to the phone box gathering, told them her ma was out for the night, they could all come to her house.

For Iris, the night became a blur of people, music and whisky. Handshakes. Faces: old faces, and young, beautiful faces, faces weathered by years of working on the land, red faces, faces with the white line across the middle of the forehead where the cap stopped, smiling faces, curious faces, suspicious faces, friendly faces. Iris knew none of them But they all knew who she was.

'So, you're the Missie.' Fiery breath.

Roy Orbison on the stereo. 'Only the Lonely'. Stella moving through the crowd, filling glasses, handing out sausage rolls, sandwiches, canapés. A row of women wedged on the sofa in the front room, talking loudly about people Iris didn't know. A man squeezed into a tweed jacket, fiercely pressed trousers and shirt collar so tight a small roll of skin on his neck folded over it, called, Iris thought, Tam, came to complain about the noise. And stayed. Iris decided he'd known when he came to ask for the noise to be turned down that he'd be invited to stay. Why else would he dress up? He was giving a one-man demonstration of the correct way to do the Dashing White Sergeant. Morag was in the hall kissing someone.

People stumbled from room to room, and when they came across Iris they'd tell her she was doing a grand job with the kids, even if she didn't know about dentistry. It was hot. The windows were wide open, Rob Orbison sang. Iris had had enough. She went

149

outside into the courtyard, sat on a bench by the kitchen window, and worried. She wanted to go home, and didn't really know how to get there because she wasn't sure where she was. Whisky did terrible things to her. She had a batch of essays to read and a maths test she had given the older children to correct.

By the door a couple were arguing about a goat, as Iris passed on her way to get outside to escape the noise and heave some fresh air into her lungs.

'It's a waste of space,' he was saying. 'I hate it. It has to go.'

'You're not going to kill it,' she said. 'I won't let you.'

'It's a bloody animal. You can't be sentimental about animals in this game,' he said.

'I know. But I won't let you kill that goat.'

The rush of air. The whisky. The food. The music. Iris's head reeled. 'Don't kill the goat,' she said. 'Poor old goat.'

The couple looked at her. And went inside.

Iris sat, heaving in soft silky air. Breathing herself sober. A man carrying a bottle and two glasses came and sat beside her. 'I know who you are.'

'Well, you have the advantage,' said Iris. 'I've never seen you in my life before.'

'Michael Kennedy.' He held out his hand.

Iris shook it. 'The two hundred and seventy-fifth hand I've shaken tonight.'

'Really?'

She shrugged. 'Feels like it.'

He was tall, with a mop of thick, curly hair. Houndstooth checked jacket, blue shirt, open at the neck. Chelsea boots. 'How do you like living up here?'

'Haven't decided yet. A bit quiet. But lovely kids. How long have you lived here?' She thought he looked like a poet. The hair.

'Born and bred. Left to study law in Edinburgh. Came back. I have a law practice in town. I like it. I like the smell of things here. And I love these parties. They just sort of break out, happen.'

'Do they?'

'All the time.'

'What do you like about them?' Iris said. And put her hand over the top of her glass as he made to fill it. 'Oh, no, I've had enough.'

'I like the crack,' he said, raising the bottle. 'Sure?'

'Absolutely sure. The crack? You like the conversation.'

'Ah, now, no. The crack isn't conversation. There's more to it than that. You can have a conversation about the weather, or your chrysanthemums. But that's not the crack. Unless the weather or your chrysanthemums are amazing beyond belief. There are no rules to conversation. It can be interesting or boring, depends on what you make of it. But there are rules to the crack – it can never be boring.'

'So what are the rules to the crack?' said Iris.

'First rule of the crack,' he raised a finger, 'you can't talk about the rules. That spoils it. The crack can be about anything. Shoelaces, ducklings, unidentified flying objects, meetings with pop stars . . . as long as the thing you're talking about is amazing or unusual. It has to be interesting. But it can never be about yourself. You can't whine or complain or talk about your illnesses, unless of course you have an amazing illness, never before seen in these parts. If you picked up your illness in some strange corner of the world, then it's the crack, all right. You can talk about yourself . . .'

'I thought you couldn't?' said Iris.

'I'm just defining the boundaries of talking about yourself. You can do that if you have something strange about you that sparks others off to tell you something strange about themselves or one of their relatives, or someone they met in China. You can say, for example, that you have webbed feet . . .'

'I don't,' said Iris.

'Neither do I, but that's by the by. Or you can reminisce. As in, "When I was a lad my grandfather grew the biggest turnip known to mankind. It was ten feet wide . . ." '

'Did he?' said Iris.

'No. He hated gardening, my grandfather. I'm just letting you know the sort of thing you can say about yourself.'

'Ah,' said Iris. 'I wish my wings hadn't withered. I'm so fascinated, I could fly round this courtyard.'

'Now you've got it. That's the crack. You can tease, banter, joke, lie, exaggerate. But no self-pity. When you talk about yourself, keep it light, keep it interesting.'

'Lie? Exaggerate?' said Iris. 'And you a lawyer. You could give up the law and take courses in the crack at the university. Invitation to the Crack: A Study in Embellishment, Hyperbole, Fabrication and Ballyhoo.'

'Now there's a thing I'd like to do. Actually I did take a course once. Music and Maps: Communication Through Symbols. Dots and squiggles, if you like. Emotions, locations, expressed without words.'

Iris looked at him, disbelieving. 'Did you?' Eyebrows raised.

'As a matter of fact, I did.'

'Funny subject for someone who seems passionate about words.'

'I'm passionate about communication. Maps and music included.'

'Perhaps you could orchestrate the crack. Crescendos and whispers. Dots and squiggles.'

'There's an idea. Music and the crack. Two of my favourite things. Orchestrated crack, that'd be the nicest thing in the world.' He smiled.

Iris smiled back.

Michael said, 'There you go. You smiled. You should do that more often. That's the first time you've smiled all night. I've been watching.'

Iris smiled again. She looked up. The sky was clearing, a huge moon sliding out from behind the clouds. Wind rattled through the autumn trees. Far away a curlew called. She wondered what Sophy and Scott were up to. The noise of the party swelled inside the house, women singing along to 'You've Lost that Lovin' Feelin'? Shouts, laughter, shrieks, the clashing of glasses, swirling music.

The party heaved up a gear, everyone singing. Though it sounded like they were all singing a different song.

'What gets into people?' said Iris.

'Drink and loneliness. People in a landscape. Tiny figures in an open space, hugging all their thoughts and frustrations inside. So they get together, and the heat and the drink – it all comes pouring out. Tonight they'll say your name, and hug you, and tell you that you are fabulous. Tomorrow you'll see them alone in the middle of a field with all that vastness around them and they'll give you a quick glance and say, "Aye",' Michael told her.

'Shy?' asked Iris.

'Shy, and no need to say more. Shall we return to the fray?' He stood up and held out his hand.

Iris ignored it, moved past him. Take the hand of someone older than twelve? Someone male? She didn't think so. She wasn't ready for intimacy like that.

Six miles away, in the schoolhouse, Sophy surveyed the debris. Bottles, cans, stains on the carpets, cigarette ends. The pictures on the walls were askew. Things had got out of hand. Word had spread through the village and beyond that there was a party on, and older kids had turned up bringing beer and vodka bought from the pub in Forham. The street outside had been lined, both sides, with cars. There had been dancing and wildness on the lawn. Roars of young voices spinning into the night. Neighbours had watched and some had tutted. The new Missie may have got the school painted, but she couldn't control her own children. Jenny at the dammit shop had said, 'Young ones today. It was never like that in my day. Damn.'

Sophy put her head in her hands, said, 'What is my mother going to say?'

Jean, her best friend, said she didn't know. Didn't like to think about that. She had seen Iris in full flood once, berating her children. The woman had a tongue, there was no doubt about that.

In the tiny cottage at the end of the rutted track, Scott lay back. He stroked Emily's hair, and kissed the top of her head. He sucked a spliff. Joni Mitchell sang on the hi-fi in the next room. He was content. Guiltily content. And triumphant. First time. And with an older woman – what a coup.

Several hours before he'd arrived to visit Jake. To hang out, chat, smoke a little, drink, shoot the breeze. But Jake wasn't there. He'd left a week ago, to 'sort out some business,' he'd said. And hadn't come back. That he hadn't returned didn't bother Emily unduly. She knew he'd be back eventually. He always came back. The moment he walked through the door and opened his arms, calling. 'It's me, babe,' she'd run to him.

His absence upset her, though. She ached from the lack of him. The lack of anybody, really. She'd stand listening. Were those footsteps? Jake's? She'd run to the door and look out. Nothing. Several times a day, she'd walk up the path to the village, hoping to meet Jake's van coming towards her. She never did. She was lonely. Seven days, and the only person she'd spoken to was Gracie. And not a lot of conversation there. Gracie spent most of her free time with Lucy, since she had a television. The Lynnes also had a television; what they didn't have was television reception since the cottage was in a hollow and couldn't get a signal.

Gracie's chat, then, was about Lucy and Lucy's toys and Lucy's mother. And programmes Gracie watched on Lucy's television. As Lucy never came to Gracie's house, Emily had never met her. She'd seen Lucy's mother at the school gates, but had never spoken to her. Every day now, after school, Gracie would go to Lucy's house, picked up by Lucy's mother. At ten-to-five Lucy's mother would put Gracie in the back of her car and drive her home. She never came in. In fact, she'd drop Gracie off at the end of the rutted track and leave her to walk the rest of the way alone.

Not that Gracie minded. That couple of hundred yards often took her half an hour. More. She'd stare up at trees, watch their branches waving far above her. Listen to the soft calls of wood pigeons. She'd pick flowers – dandelions, buttercups, wild garlic in the spring. Once she saw a frog. She'd run after the rabbits that scudded away as she approached, stand staring into the under-growth they'd disappeared into, hands by her sides. 'Oh, don't go, bunnies. I won't hurt you.' The nicest thing in the world, the Missie wanted to know. It was walking alone down the path, going home.

Emily felt that Gracie was slipping away from her. Now that she had gone to school, other people, new people, had entered her world. The tiny cottage with its rush matting, wind chimes and sea of sunflowers by the door, was not enough. Lucy had opened

Gracie's eyes to the world of owning, and now Gracie wanted. She wanted a Barbie doll, like Lucy's. A nurse's outfit, like Lucy's. A skipping rope, like Lucy's. A hobby horse. She wanted to eat the food Lucy ate – fish fingers and creamy puddings.

It made Emily sigh. And that she couldn't afford to give Gracie any of it – not even the fish fingers – filled her with guilt. Conversations of late had been strained. Yesterday Emily had snapped, 'I can't bloody afford bloody fish fingers, so stop asking for them. And anyway they're full of preservatives and junk. I want us to eat pure organic food.' And she'd stamped outside and punched a sunflower. Watched, wracked with guilt, as it swayed, reeled, sent a yellow shudder through the whole cluster. A rain of tumbling golden petals scattered through the air. She apologised to the victim flower.

'Sorry.'

Emily wore long skirts that trailed on the ground, their hems heavy with mud. She wore peasant shirts or T-shirts. Winter she put on one of Jake's jumpers that had fraying sleeves. On her feet, she wore sandals in the summer or went barefoot. Wellies in the winter. Her appearance said poverty, drugs, free love. In Green Cairns she was a dangerous presence. Few people spoke to her. When she walked along the street, people averted their eyes. Small groups of gossiping women would silence as she passed, then, as she moved on, a small ripple of heated whispers would follow her. She huddled into herself, fending them off. Sometimes, rather than face the silence that greeted her, she would put off going to the village shop, though Jenny was friendly enough, thinking it was easier doing without milk, toothpaste, soap, whatever she needed.

When Scott turned up, asked for Jake, found out he wasn't there, he turned to go. Emily said, 'No, stay. Have a cup of coffee. I need someone to talk to.'

So Scott had accepted a mug of Nescafé and stayed to talk. He spilled out his worries about school. He was going to be expelled for refusing to get his hair cut.

Emily was shocked. 'They can't do that. It's your hair. Nobody can tell you how to wear it. It's an abuse of your freedom. What does your mother say?'

155

'She doesn't know. I haven't told her.'

Emily nodded. 'You think she'd be on their side?' She reached out, stroked his hair. 'It's lovely.'

Scott nodded. He told her that her hair was lovely too. And they smiled at one another in mutual appreciation of long and unkempt hairstyles. Then they kissed. And kissed some more. Emily thought, It's just a kiss, it's nothing. Just someone to hold. Scott thought, Cool. The kissing sitting down led to kissing lying down. Emily thought this uncomfortable and suggested they move to the bedroom. After that everything Scott had ever dreamed of happened. Naked with a woman in bed, skin against his skin, the pleasure of it was perfect. Now he lay, Emily sprawled over him, head against his shoulder, arm draped across his chest, thinking how wonderful this Saturday night had turned out to be. The air was charged and thick with love and longing. Outside trees moved, a late bird sang. If he wasn't half listening for Jake coming through the front door, this would be exquisite. The nicest thing in the world.

Iris got home at four in the morning. The house was silent, Sophy next door and Scott, she presumed, asleep in his room. He wasn't. He was in Emily Lynne's bed. Easing her loneliness.

Iris sniffed. Alcohol. Cigarette smoke. 'There's been goings-on here,' she said.

'There would be. You've got teenage kids and went out for the night,' said Morag.

Iris opened the living room, looked round. The scent of naughty doings deepened, though the room was immaculate. Too immaculate, she thought. The smell of cleaning fluids was added to the earlier naughty scent. Sophy had stayed up long after her guests left and cleaned up. Well past midnight, she had vacuumed and wiped. All the bottles and cans were in plastic bags in Jean's dustbin, so Iris wouldn't find them. The glasses and cups had been washed and put away. Pictures on the walls straightened. The bathroom had been scrubbed. But there had been goings on, Iris could feel it. She just knew it. But was too tired to do anything about it. She went to bed.

Next morning Morag left, vowing to come back soon. Keening forward, the way she did, down the garden path, moving swiftly. Noticing a child hidden in the bushes across the road, observing her through binoculars, she looked at Iris.

'Don't ask,' said Iris. 'He's our little spy.' She went indoors. 'What did you get up to last night?'

'Nothing,' said Sophy. 'Why?'

'The house reeks of alcohol and smoke. That's why.'

'Does it?' said Sophy. 'I don't smell anything.'

'Well, you are to stay in for a week,' Iris said.

'Why?'

'You are being kept in for doing whatever it was you did last night. And you are also kept in for telling me you didn't do it. Lying to me.'

'That's not fair.'

'Fair?' said Iris. 'When did I give you the impression life was fair? Don't waste your time looking for fair. It doesn't exist. Except for now, when you are being kept in for getting up to something behind my back.'

'What am I going to do?' said Sophy.

'Do your homework. Study. What are you doing at school anyway?'

'Jane bloody Austen. *Pride and* bloody *Prejudice*.'

'Excellent book. Just the thing for a kept-in girl to read.'

Late afternoon, the doorbell rang. When Iris opened the door, she met a rather dowdy young couple: he in worn cavalry twill trousers with checked shirt open at the neck, she in jeans that looked from the fit of them, gathered at the waist, rolled up at the ankle, to be his. She decided all this with a swift flick of the eye, took it in. Really, though, her attention was taken up by the large white goat that stood between them.

The man smiled. 'We've brought the goat.'

'So I see,' said Iris. 'Will it take tea?'

'He quite likes a cup,' said the woman. 'Though I don't think it's very good for him.'

'Probably not,' said Iris. 'So, what can I do for you?'

'We've brought the goat,' the man said again. 'Remember, last night you said you'd take it?'

'No, I do not remember offering to take a goat last night. Remind me.'

'We were at the party. You said, "Don't kill the goat."'

'I remember that. But I don't remember offering to take it. What would I do with a goat?'

'Keep it. He's a fine goat.'

'I have no doubt. He is a handsome fellow. But I have no need of a goat.'

'Only,' the woman said, 'when you said, "Don't kill the goat," we sort of took it to mean you'd take him. So he wouldn't get killed.'

'I meant nothing of the sort,' said Iris. 'I simply meant that it seemed to me the goat would he happier if kept alive rather than put to death. I know that's how I would feel.'

She said, 'Please.' And handed Iris the end of the length of rope that was tied round the animal's neck. 'We're leaving tomorrow.'

They were going to Canada, their dream of self-sufficiency over. Their crop of vegetables had been eaten by snails and flies, their hens hadn't laid, the goat which they'd bought unseen, hoping for milk, had turned out to be male. They could no longer pay the rent and had sold everything they owned to pay their air fares. The Lynnes had taken the hens, Michael Kennedy the dog, and now here was Iris taking the goat.

'Thank you.'

They both turned and walked back up the path.

Iris called, 'Wait!'

But they had climbed into their car and gone.

Iris still didn't know who they were. 'I don't want a goat,' she said, feebly.

She led the animal through the kitchen to the outhouse at the back. Sophy and Scott came to look over the new arrival.

Scott said, 'A goat.'

Iris said, yes, indeed, it was a goat.

Sophy asked what it was for.

Iris said, 'Good question.'

Scott said, 'What will we do with it?'

'I thought we'd have it curried with chips tomorrow for supper.'

Scott said, 'Cool.'

Sophy said, 'You can't do that. I'm not eating it.'

Iris said, 'Neither am I. I just don't know what you do with a goat.'

'Well, why have you got it?'

'The people who left it presumed I wanted it.'

'Why?' said Sophy.

'I can only presume it is a truth universally acknowledged that a middle-aged widow in possession of a good outhouse must be in want of a goat to put in it.'

'What?' said Sophy.

'Go read your Jane Austen,' said Iris.

She went inside, made herself a cup of tea, and took her batch of essays to read at the kitchen table. 'The Nicest Thing in the World . . . well, it isn't a goat.'

Lorna said the nicest thing in the world was waking up on your birthday. Fiona said it was waking up on Christmas morning. James said it was cheese. Iris thought, Now I know who doodled on the desk. Quality doodling, though. Didn't know he had it in him. Lucy said it was tasting snow. Then Iris came to Colin's essay.

My mum ran away. Then my dad died under a tractor. And my gran cried. I found a ram's horn and that was nice. I'm scared in the dark and my gran still cries. She must cry buckets. And here he'd drawn lines and lines of perfect buckets. Rows and rows of them. 'Good buckets, Colin,' wrote Iris on the side of the page, in red ink. *I like in the morning when I lie in bed and hear Gran making tea. I like the sound of trees outside my window. The sound of morning is nice, and the smell of green in trees. Sometimes my gran makes me tea with sugar in, and cake with jam in. And we sit by the fire. That is nice. The nicest thing in the world is when she rubs my head and she calls me a mucky pup.*

Iris read this through twice. She wrote, 'This is lovely, Colin.' Put two gold stars at the top of the page. Then she put her hand to her mouth, and cried.

She Did Not Know What Was
Happening in her Heart

Iris had a routine. She walked every morning, through all weathers, the small distance from her back door to the back door of the school. The path was cracked and old, long grasses trailed against her ankles. She'd open the door of the school, go into the classroom, put the corrected tests and homework on her desk, and go to the window to watch the children. They'd be in the playground, standing in groups or kicking a ball about. Sometimes the girls skipped using an old washing line, singing songs she'd sung years ago, different time, different place.

> On a mountain stands a lady
> who she is I cannot tell
> all she wants is gold and silver
> all she wants is a nice young man.

Colin would usually be alone. He'd be running a toy car along the ground, or dropping stones into a puddle, watching ripples. He did not seek to fill the puddle with stones, it was an idle little game. Something children did.

Watching them, Iris noticed how they all seemed to play separately. For football they did not form two teams, but kicked the ball about, each boy trying to get it and keep it. Skipping or running, chasing or throwing a ball, they were not little people bonding, seeking fun together. They were a group of isolated individuals all doing the same thing, but none of them had learned the simple trick of joining in. Iris supposed that was how it was for these little ones.

They lived in lonely places most of them, and had no other children near them, only adults who had long since lost the art of puttering about.

So here she was teaching a group of young people who had not mastered the simple art of playing, and did not know the secret rules of being children. You did not tell tales, you were fair to your mates, you gave others a shot of your football or a chance to skip. Iris decided she would teach them to dance. Wild hot fast country dances. Whirls and shouts. Living here, she knew why these dances, barn dances, square dances, country dances, were the way they were. When people came a distance to meet, get together, there was no time for polite warm-ups. They got on with it swiftly. Heat, passion, link arms and twirl. Break the ice and dance.

So she'd watch her pupils for a few minutes every morning, but always at nine o'clock she'd take the brass bell from the cupboard, go to the front door, and clang it wildly. And her pupils would come running.

In October the school broke up for the potato holidays. Children whose parents owned or worked on the land were expected to help gather the crops. Multi-coloured lines of people bent double moved slowly over fields behind tractors ploughing up the ground, picking potatoes. The lane behind the school was lined with the caravans of people, tinkers, who came to pick, then, once the picking was done, moved on again. Smoke churned from their little chimneys, and some came to Iris's door selling pegs.

Colin and his grandmother picked potatoes, they needed the money. James picked because he had to, as did the Hay children. Sophy, on hearing that huge amounts of money could be earned in a week of picking, went. And came home after a morning spent face to the ground on a bitter day, cold, stiff and dirty. Wind had driven swirls of dirt into her face, her mouth, nose, hair. Her nails were grimed and filthy. Her back ached. She refused to eat potatoes for a fortnight, saying that if that was what it took to get them out of the ground, then it wasn't worth it. And why couldn't everyone just eat spaghetti or rice?

When school resumed, two weeks into October, the world had turned cold and wet. Children arrived bundled against the weather in anoraks and woolly hats. Iris turned the heating on. As she spoke about capitals of the world and long division and prepositions, rain hammered against the window panes. The pupils watched the rivulets stream down the glass, huddled against the wind, glad to be indoors. Still, without the lure of sunshine outside, learning was easier.

A week into the winter term, the letter arrived. It was a circular sent to all the schools in the country. Thick, glossy paper, expensive printing. It was from the Lunan Lemonade Company – Loony Lemonade, the children called their fizzy, gaudily coloured drinks. It said that it was promoting good health and safety in young people, and was running a campaign called In The Swim. It offered a prize of two thousand pounds-worth of sports equipment to the school that produced the highest percentage of new swimmers by next spring. Plus, it glowed, we are giving each child who enters a free can of Cream Soda. Just send in copies of the elementary swimming certificate along with numbers of pupils in your school. Iris, who normally tossed circulars into the bin, read and re-read this. Two thousand pounds. She ran the sum round her mind. Savoured the words. Two thousand pounds-worth of sports equipment. She dreamed of trampolines, footballs, hoops, benches, goalposts, mats, badminton racquets, shuttlecocks, ping-pong bats. She felt her eyes widen with want. The things she could do. Movement, children learning, at last, to play with one another. Team spirit, she thought.

'How many of you can swim?' she asked the class.

No hands went up. The children looked round, checking hopefully that they were not the only one with their hands by their sides.

'How many of you have been to the swimming baths?'

The twins had, Lucy had, Fiona had. That was all.

Iris nodded. 'Well, I think it's time we all went to town and learned to swim.'

She wrote off to the Lunan Lemonade Company for an entry form, and to each child's parents for permission to take them to the swimming baths in Forham. 'The highest percentage', the circular had said. She certainly could not get the highest number of pupils with an elementary swimming certificate. But with only twenty pupils she had a good chance with percentages. Why, if she worked at it, she could teach them all to swim. One hundred percent – she'd surely be the only one with that.

'I could win,' she said to Sophy.

'Pigs could fly,' said Sophy. 'The world could turn orange overnight. Face it, Ma, we don't win things. We're just not the type.'

'I don't like your attitude,' said Iris. 'To win something, all you have to do is take the first step. You never know if you're a winner if you don't try. Trying's the main thing.'

'Mother,' said Sophy, 'I'm not being rude or anything, but these kids . . . the ones you teach, they're hardly athletes. I mean, they're all lop-sided and shy with funny hair and always wearing hand-me-downs.'

'Not all of them,' said Iris. 'They're good kids. All they lack is confidence.'

'They're a hand-me-down bunch.' Sophy was sure of that. 'Inhibited.'

This was a new word to her, she was using it a lot. It had been pointed out to the girls in her class, S1, by the girls in S4, the fourth year and therefore very sophisticated, that their geography teacher Mrs Kramer was inhibited. Frigid, said Elizabeth Cummings of sophisticated S4. The S1 girls had picked up on this new word, and now a great many people were inhibited. Though nobody was as inhibited as Mrs Kramer, who Sophy had nicknamed Virgin Kramer. The name had caused a deal of hilarity, and had swiftly spread through the sniggering corridors. Someone had daubed it large on the wall, so it could be viewed by all entering the building. 'Virgin Kramer's out of luck. Nobody's going to give her a f . . .'

Now the hunt was on to find out who the culprit was. Who had written this verse, and defaced the wall, and brought shame and disgrace to the school? The headmaster, at Monday morning service, said the guilty party would be found, and when found would be dealt with severely. So, too, would anyone who knew who had done the deed and not come forward. The honour of the school was at stake.

Scott had shuffled and yawned and shoved his long hair from his face. He was due to report to the headmaster after registration. But he would not go. He would register his presence then slip away, to wander the streets of Forham till it was time to go home. He would not cut his hair. He would not be punished for not cutting his hair. His own honour was at stake. But he knew the name of the dauber of the silly verse. It was the colour of the dripping message he recognised. It was pale, greying, greenish-yellow. A subtle shade of sage. The graffiti artist was Sophy.

She didn't know what had got into her. Emboldened by the squeals of glee and mirth when she'd come up with the rhyme, she had put a small amount of paint from her mother's classroom into a coffee jar, and early one morning had printed it large for everyone to behold and laugh at. She now thought it fortunate that she'd run out before she could finish the final word. She could hotly deny she'd been going to write fuck. Though what she might say the word had been going to be, she did not know.

But then Sophy felt she did not know anything any more. Not wanting to be associated with the secret grafitti artist, all her friends had abandoned her. All she'd wanted was popularity, to be one of the girls. Even Jean had turned her back on her. Though she was friendly enough back home in Green Cairns. Now she walked the corridors alone, spent breaktimes and lunchtimes alone, her trusty French horn at her feet. Not that she needed to bring it to school. She had been refused entry to the school orchestra. Her playing, the music teacher told her, had a long way to go before she was up to standard. In fact, he confided, he thought she had very little musical ability. He said he'd only mentioned this to save her disappointment later. 'Your desire to make music is commendable,' he'd said. 'But I don't think you'll ever make a horn player.'

Sophy nodded, bit her lip. And, once home, had lain on her bed and wept till she was sick.

Scott heard, and went to her. 'Stuff them,' he'd said. 'Crap little orchestra anyway. You're too good for it.' He'd patted her shoulder and given her a piece of his chewing gum.

But not wanting her mother to know of her musical disgrace, Sophy still carried the instrument back and forth to school, and on orchestra practice days came home late. She'd wander Forham, music case in hand, in and out of shops. She stole sweets from Woolworth's. Regularly she got thrown out of her classes for causing disruption. She was getting a reputation as a rebel, and she didn't like it. Sometimes a strange rage took hold of her. She'd walk about her room furiously mouthing things she wanted to say, but could not.

Nights she lay in bed and thought about her best friend's father. She imagined him holding her. Kissing her. Whenever she saw him she felt a heat that flushed her face red. If he spoke to her she could hardly answer him. He was, in her estimation, an old man. Almost forty, Jean said. But Sophy thought him wonderful. Every time she saw him, or heard his voice across the garden wall, she'd catch her breath. She did not know what was happening to her. She did not know what was happening in her heart.

Now, standing in the kitchen, Iris looked at Sophy. There was something fragile about the girl. Yes, she was bold, lippy, but never really impudent. 'Lively in class,' her reports from her last school had said, 'a pleasure to teach'. Iris knew nothing of Sophy's current problems. Any mother would be proud, she thought. Then considered the accusation that her pupils were all hand-me-down kids, inhibited, and denied it. 'My pupils are lovely,' she said. 'Every single one of them.'

Over the weeks Iris had been putting a lot of what she called emotional elbow grease into getting to know her children. She took them on nature trails – 'In twos, boys and girls' – a chattering ragged line walking along behind her. They gathered leaves and flowers, and laid them on the nature table to look up and draw. They stood staring into the chestnut tree, stooped to pick up conkers with which they filled their pockets. This was Iris's favourite tree, she visited it often as if it was a person whose company she sought. She taught her children poems by Spike Milligan and Edward Lear, and got Lucy the stammerer to read them aloud. The stammer was slowly healing. Iris made her children run around pretending to be chickens or ducks, playing the fool in unison. She made them sing at the top of their voices. 'All Things Bright And Beautiful' could be heard from one end of Green Cairns to the other. And when they were listless, or when their morning energy was bursting within them, she would open the school door wide so that they could run three times round the playground, to get air into their lungs and burn off overly high spirits.

Oh, yes, she thought. I am getting there with these children. And soon I shall teach them to dance. And then I shall teach them to swim.

The Reverend Woodman stopped his car and sat, watching. The children of Green Cairns School were running round the playground, waving their arms and singing. 'All things Bright and Beautiful.' It was a windy day, tree tops heaved and October leaves were thick on the ground. The children were high on the swish of air and sparkling autumn sun. It had been raining for days, and all the pupils had been stuck indoors. Now they were wriggling, restless and gigglish. Iris had opened the door and set them free to run and wave and give vent to their wild spirits. Then they would settle down and learn a little history, which, the way Iris told it, was not a list of dates but tales of valour and disgrace and treachery and swaggering bravery and the agony of being misunderstood. She'd told them to sing anything they wanted as they ran, to shout and yell and tire themselves out. 'There's learning to be done,' she told them.

She thought it was Fiona who started the hymn, or maybe it was Lucy, but they'd all joined in. Unusual, for normally when asked to pick a song to sing the class chose something by the Beatles.

Reverend Woodman watched for a while then drove away. He was bewildered. Why would the Missie do such a thing? What sort of woman would make a mockery of a such fine old song? If rumours were to be believed, and he rarely did believe them, she was having an affair. There were wild parties at her house. She never came to church on Sundays. He would have a word. He drove on, and found the hymn running through his head. He hummed it. Then started to sing at the top of his voice: '*The purple-headed mountains, the river running by . . .*'

Jenny in the dammit shop pulled tins of tomato soup from a cardboard box, and stacked them on the shelf behind her. ' *"The cold wind in the winter, the pleasant summer sun, the ripe fruits in the garden . . ."* Damn and blast me, George,' she said to her husband who had come in from doing an oil change on a Ford Cortina. 'I've got that song in my head now. And it's not a hymn I'm particularly fond of. In fact, I'd go so far as to say I hate that hymn. *"He gave us eyes to see them . . ."* There I go again! Stop it, me.'

Michael Kennedy phoned that evening and asked Iris out for a meal.

'I don't do dates,' said Iris. 'I'm sorry. I'm not ready for that sort of thing.'

'I'm glad to hear it,' he said. 'I don't do dates either. Haven't since I was seventeen. A fine age to stop dating.'

'You think?' said Iris. 'You must have started young if you stopped at seventeen. I think that was when I started.'

'No matter that. You've stopped now. As well, I'm not asking you on a date. I'm asking you if you'd like to join me for a chat. That's not a date.'

'A chat sounds nice,' said Iris. 'Not a date, though.'

'Certainly not. But with our chat, I thought we'd have a little drink. And with the drink a bite to eat would go down a treat. But not a date, just eating and drinking and chatting. How's the goat, by the way?'

'The goat is fine. He's called . . .' she paused. Thought. So far the goat didn't have a name. He was called The Goat, mostly because she feared getting attached to him. She was tempted to say he was called Michael. But no, a drink, a bite to eat and a chat were tempting, best not insult the man. 'He's called Willoughby. He's a handsome fellow.'

'Good. Well, I'll pick you up half-past seven tomorrow night.'

'I haven't agreed to come yet,' said Iris.

'Yet,' he said. 'Note the yet. It implies you haven't refused. I take a non-refusal as a yes. See you tomorrow.' He rang off.

They went to a pub in Forham. Walked along narrow cobbled streets between old grey buildings with small-paned windows. Rain threatening. Iris pulled her coat round her and struggled to keep up with Michael. He strode, taking two huge paces to Iris's six. It was always to be this way. Every time she went out with him she was always slightly behind, and he'd be half turned to her, talking, gesticulating, not really looking where he was going. That would be the nature of the relationship.

The Deer and Thistle was tiny but crowded. People squeezed in, jostling at the bar, taking drinks, held high, back to tables. There was a thick babble of voices, laughter. Smoke hung in a blue pall in the space between the top of heads and the ceiling. The walls were panelled in old, old wood. Wooden bar, wooden floor, wooden chairs and tables. The place smelled of beer and cigarettes and curry. This was not what Iris had imagined. The evening she'd had in mind was plusher: chilled wine, crisp table linen, the discreet chink of expensive china. And from around a high-ceilinged, candle-lit room the murmur of polite but charming conversation. This place was noisy.

When Michael's face appeared amidst the throng, people called his name.

He grinned, waved. In tweeds tonight, thick jacket, checked shirt, brogues. Smoking. He sat Iris at a table by the fire. Raised his cigarette hand to the bar. 'Two,' he mouthed. For what was the point of actually speaking? In this din who would hear him?

'Two whats?' asked Iris.

'Two of everything. Two beers, two whiskies, two curries.'

'I don't know about that,' said Iris. 'I'm a wine person. I never touch whisky. And I don't know if I'm in the mood for a curry.'

'Course you are. When is one not in the mood for a curry?'

'Most of the time,' said Iris. 'I'm more often not in the mood for a curry than I am in the mood for a curry.'

'This is a curry place. They only serve curry. Ian, the barman, was in India for thirty years. Curry's all he cooks.'

'Curry it will be, then,' said Iris. She contemplated complaining about the beer, which she rarely drank, but decided against it. It would wash the curry down.

The drinks arrived. Iris sipped. Michael swigged, said, 'Aaah.' Wiped his mouth with the back of his hand. 'Grand. So tell me your day?'

'Usual sort of day. Fiona took hysterics when she saw a spider. James punched Simon. Lucy cut off a chunk of her hair with the scissors, which she shouldn't have had. And little Colin wrote a lovely poem about grass. "I like grass because it's green, and my feet makes marks where I've been." And someone spilt a pot of glue on the floor. Nobody's telling me who. Which is fine.'

'Why is this fine?'

'They are acting communally. A united front. They didn't used to do this. Someone would have told. I like this spirit of being a class.'

'But they are united against you.'

'Only in the matter of spilt glue. Which is as it should be. People shouldn't tell tales.'

'Ah, neither they should.'

Their food arrived. A heap of rice, pale yellow with turmeric, a generous dollop of brown saucy stuff on top. Iris looked at it suspiciously.

'It's the taste that counts,' said Michael. 'Surely a woman of your perception and wit isn't swayed by appearances?'

'Depends on what I'm looking at,' said Iris. But she took a mouthful nonetheless. 'Good,' she said, surprised.

'Good? Good doesn't get it. This is bloody marvellous.'

'If you say so.'

'I say so.'

She asked if he was married.

'Was. Divorced five years ago. No kids.'

'Messy?'

'Civilised. If divorce is ever civilised. We even shook hands at the end. It started with something more intimate, though.'

'I'll bet. My marriage started with a handshake and ended with a shock.'

'No passion?'

'Oh, yes, in between the handshake and the shock we had two children and a shudder now and then.'

'A woman such as yourself, I think you'd want more than the occasional shudder.'

'I'm very strait-laced,' she told him.

'Never. The lunchtime prayers? Kids flapping round the playground singing hymns? I don't think so.' Forking up his food, eying her.

'You've been talking about me,' she said.

'Only nicely. Everyone's talking about you.'

'The prayers are to get the children to open up. The flapping hymn thing was to get them to let off steam so they'd settle down to some history.' She looked round the room. What was she doing here in this sweaty room? With this man? This wordy person, wild-haired and full of himself, she thought. A noisy, smoky pub filled with conversations, and nobody knows I'm a stranger here. A stranger even to myself now.

'Penny for them,' he said.

'My thoughts? Oh, no, I think they're worth more than that. But they're private.'

'Well, some thoughts are.' So he changed the subject. 'I hope you're feeding that goat more than grass. Don't want it to explode.'

'Explode? A goat? Don't be daft.'

'No, really, they eat grass and fill up with gas and one day – whoosh! Bang. End of goat. When I was a lad . . .'

He started on a story about a man on the MacBride Estate at the top of the glen who'd had a goat that exploded. And the mess! And Iris smiled. A little, it wasn't a very nice story. She wondered if it was true, you never could tell with Michael's stories. She wondered what would happen at the end of the evening. They'd leave this place, go out into the rain, walk back through the glistening streets, through the wet. Him a few paces ahead of her, turning to speak; her struggling to keep up. He'd drive her home. Wipers squeaking against the windscreen, the hiss of tyres on water-logged roads and the sweep of headlights through the dark, rushing light falling on hedges and trees. The radio on. And would she invite him in? If she did, what would he expect? Coffee, and perhaps a kiss? He'd get no more than that. After all, she had two children. And besides, it was too soon after Harry's death. She was not ready, was not able to cope with anything more than a kiss. But she'd invite him in, yes, definitely that.

In the end he accepted the coffee. He sat at the kitchen table, patted the dog. Spoke about his young life. The house he lived in now, he'd always lived in. He'd gone, before he was sent to boarding school, to the school where Iris now taught. 'Circles and loops, my life,' he said. 'Round and round.' When he left, he did not offer Iris a kiss. He touched her arm and said, 'Goodnight.' Iris did not know if she was relieved or disappointed. She wouldn't have minded a kiss, but nothing more. What she'd really wanted, though, was the chance to say no.

It rained for days. Endless damp, endless grey. Rivers running down the windowpanes. And the small stream that all summer had idled through the wooded den opposite the school turned into a frothing brown torrent. It gushed, tumbled and overspread its banks so that Iris could no longer walk there. Purple faded from the hills and the fields turned murky. Mud underfoot everywhere she walked. At night she lay in bed, listening. Foxes barked and in trees somewhere not too distant, owls called. It seemed to Iris they wept into the dark. That was the mood she was in.

Mornings, she would stand at the top of the stairs staring out. Rain swept down from the hills, in moving, drenching sheets. The last of Iris's roses, clinging on to life past the first frosts, drooped under the force of falling water, a scattering of pink and yellow petals on the sodden ground. There were rows of dripping water-proofs in the hall beside the school door. And underneath, catching a deal of the drips, no doubt, a line of wellingtons.

And it rained. The radiators banged. The room got stuffy. It smelled of hot little damp people. The primary ones chanted their two times table. Primary twos and threes wrestled with subtraction. The metal canisters containing school lunches were covered with tiny droplets. The windows steamed.

On Sunday Iris was woken by the chime of spade on earth. The rain had stopped and birds were singing, a glorious warble outside her window in time, almost, to a steady chip, chip, chip. Someone digging in her garden. Or so it sounded. Iris got up, wrapped herself in her pink chenille dressing gown, padded across to the window and pulled the curtains. The morning was crystal clear, a thin jagged frost shining. At the far end of the garden a man in blue overalls was working rhythmically, heaving his spade high, thrusting it into the ground and shoving it deep with his foot. He lifted the earth, then turned it over, and moved on. Lifting, digging, turning. A thin, hand-rolled cigarette hung from his mouth. Charles Harper. What was he doing here?

She dressed, ran downstairs and out into the garden. In the chill air she crossed the grass, the crunch of frost underfoot. Her face was morning pale. 'What are you doing?'

'Digging,' said Chas.

'So I see.'

'Well, no need to ask, then.'

'OK, I'll put it more precisely. Why are you digging my garden?'

'It needs digging. First time I saw it, I thought, That needs digging. And it's been nagging me ever since. Hate to see a garden going to waste.'

'I didn't ask you to come into my garden and start meddling with it.'

'Neither you did. But I was thinking you wouldn't mind since you had no intention of doing it yourself. Had you?'

She looked at the ground, kicked a lump of weeded earth. 'No. But that's by the by.'

'Good ground like this. You can grow all sorts,' said Chas. 'Potatoes, cabbage, spinach.'

'That's as may be,' said Iris.

'Carrots,' said Chas. 'Peas.'

'Still, you had no right just to come here and start ploughing up my ground.'

'I'll give you that. I should have asked. But when I got here there was nobody up and I didn't want to wake you. I got bored hanging about waiting for someone to open the curtains. So I got started.' He smiled. 'Good to dig it now. Let the frosts get in, clean out the weeds.'

'I can't pay you,' said Iris.

'I never asked you for money. What I was thinking is, I'll do the digging, weeding and planting. And you can take whatever you want as a way of me paying for using the ground. 'Course, I'll be taking what I want, too.'

'I don't know if I want someone doing my garden.'

''Course you do. You're just annoyed I got started without asking. You like to be in charge. You're a teacher. Bossy.'

He was right. Iris glared. How dare he be right? 'I expect you'd like a cup of tea.' Changing the subject so she didn't have to comment on his rightness.

'I'd prefer coffee. I'm not really a tea person.'

'Fine,' said Iris. Hoping she sounded crisp, and heated, and slightly annoyed. She turned and walked back to the house.

Chas leaned against his spade watching her go. He liked her from the back. He thought she had a fine bum.

Iris wheeled round. 'What are you looking at?'

'I was just thinking that a cup of coffee, right now, is exactly what I need.'

That evening Iris stood at her back door. The air was crystal sharp, glittering, above her a vast scattering of stars. She watched them and thought of Harry. If he was up there, some sort of spirit, and looking for her, she thought he wouldn't know where to find her.

She longed for city things. Movement in streets, clatter and bustle and calls of strangers. But it was lovely here. Geese flew by, honking through the dark. Going up the glen, she thought. The first time Iris had heard geese, she'd been a child on holiday. Suddenly everything around her had been filled with that noise. Wild clanking and hooting. At six years old, she'd thought it was the end of the world. But now, standing breathing in the chill, listening to the call of wild geese travelling east, the sound made her breathless and full of wonder. Thinking about Harry and if he was wondering where she was, and Michael, and Chas, and all her pupils, and how small, quiet and lovely this place was, and how much she missed the clamour of busy streets, lit at night, and the rustle of passing cars and cabs, she did not know what was happening in her heart.

Swimming

Three weeks after the letter came, Iris took the children swimming. She had been refused the use of the education department mini-bus, but been given use of the Forham swimming pool for one hour every Wednesday afternoon. The swimming instructor had also been put at her disposal. Well, she thought, a proper swimming instructor. More than I'd hoped for.

She took six children in her own car. Not that the car was meant to take any more than four people, but with a squeeze they managed. Stella Vernon loaded the rest into her Land Rover.

'Is this legal?' she worried.

'What could possibly be illegal about taking a bunch of kids to swim?' said Iris. Worried also but not admitting it.

The twisting miles to Forham were filled with stifled giggles for though it was on the curriculum that the children should go each year on a school trip, this was the first time they had actually gone anywhere. They huddled together and made jokes, with gurgling sound effects, about swimming and drowning.

The pool was in the same street as the pub Iris had gone to with Michael. She parked, and as the children tumbled out, waved to Stella in her Land Rover and caught a glimpse of Scott disappearing into the Deer and Thistle. She froze. Scott? Children milled round her. Some rushed up the steps of the municipal swimming baths, and some moved out into the road. She shrilly summoned them back. 'Not on the road. Come back here.'

The moment was gone. Could that have been her son? She had the impression he'd seen her and dodged away. No. She was being silly. Scott would be at school. All young men had long hair these days, or so it seemed anyway. It had just been someone who looked, from a distance, like Scott. She shook her head and conducted her babbling charges into the swimming pool, through the solid metal entrance gate and up the stairs to the changing rooms, shouting, 'In twos, children. In twos.' What was the point? The children milled and chattered and shouted with excitement.

The water silenced them. A long pool, deep shimmering blue. In assorted swimming costumes, they gathered round it. The girls wore swimming caps that clung to their skulls with straps that bit into their chins. Fiona's was blue and bedecked with pink rubbery flowers. Other girls eyed it with envy. Iris could see a swimming cap war developing. There would be rivalry.

Chas Harper was the swimming instructor.

'You?' said Iris. 'You are the swimming instructor?'

He told her, yes, he was. Had been for the past four years, two afternoons and four evenings a week. Taught hundreds to swim and drowned nobody. 'It's the way of things. We do what we do. We make a living. Get by.'

He turned to the children. 'Right, let's get used to the water. And Colin, I think you should take your glasses off.'

Colin was wearing maroon woollen swimming trunks. Once wet they'd become heavy and sag horribly. His gran had knitted them yesterday evening by the fire, needles clicking in the glow. They were at least two sizes too big for him, he'd pulled them up well past his waist. His legs and body were winter-white, though summer was only weeks gone. He slowly, carefully, removed his round spectacles, handed them to Iris and looked round, mouth open. Seeing in stereo for the first time in three years. He looked at Iris, mouth still open, and for a fleeting moment she thought he was about to say something. But no. Colin turned, and carefully descended the steps into the water.

It was the first time Iris had seen him really smile. He jumped through the water, arms aloft. Then stopped, yanked up his swimming trunks, and started jumping again. Chas stood beside her, watching. 'You can tell right off who is going to be at home in the water.' Then, 'You're not coming in yourself?'

Iris shook her head. 'I thought it best to let you have free rein.'

'Maybe you're right there. You being you, you'd be muscling in. Telling me what to do.' Iris snorted and went to sit beside Stella on a bench beside the pool.

Chas dived in and swam up to join the children. He demonstrated the breast stroke. This was what they would learn. Standing at the shallow end, they practised the arm movements.

Iris watched. 'There's always one,' she said, her eyes on James. 'One?' said Stella.

'One who chances his luck. Note I said his. It's usually a boy. There will be one who thinks he is invincible and strikes out for the deep end.'

'So, are you ready to jump in and haul him out?'

'I am ready to make enough noise that Chas jumps in and hauls him out.'

'Who is your money on – James?'

'At the moment. It won't be the either of the twins. Not with their mum watching.'

'It could be Fiona. She's a bit cocky.'

'Nah. She's breezing into womanhood. Too vain to risk being rudely yanked on to the side of the pool, red of face. She is discovering that swimming caps do nothing except fill up with water. That's enough for her. She's busy playing up to Chas.'

The girl was making perfect breast stroke movements on the surface of the water, eyes on Chas. Look at me, I can do this.

In fact, it was Colin who broke away. The one nobody ever watched. He'd mastered the arm movements. Then arm movements with one leg on the bottom of the pool. Then arm movements with two legs lifted from the bottom. At first, he'd sunk. Had paddled furiously, spitting water. Then found he could near as dammit swim. Fiercely working his arms and legs, holding his head achingly high, he managed to get from the middle of the shallow end to the edge. He hung on for a few minutes, gathering his breath, then struck out again. Flailing and splashing, he reached the middle. Chas was busy taking pupils individually, holding heads above water, instructing them to work arms and legs in unison. Other pupils had partners. But there being an odd number, Gracie Lynne off school with a cold, there was one pupil left over. It was Colin. It was always Colin.

'Colin's enjoying himself,' said Iris. 'I think he's going to be quite the swimmer.' Then she watched Chas get the thing. She had no idea what it was called but all swimming baths she'd ever been in had 'the thing'. It was a long pole with half a rubber tyre attached by ropes to one end. Apprentice swimmers lay in the tyre and swam, held afloat by the instructor walking along the side of the pool, holding the other end of the pole.

'I don't really like using this,' said Chas. 'But it gives them confidence, and helps them coordinate arms and legs.'

Colin had just plunged, spat and spewed across his first breadth. Gasping. Sending glistening showers round him. He could swim. There was nothing to this. He thought to try out his new skill in deeper waters. Flailing, he set out for the far end, where the diving boards were. He wasn't seeking glory. He simply wanted to see if he could.

Iris was shouting at James, telling him to stop ducking Fiona underwater. Chas was holding Lorna. Colin, gasping, arms working furiously headed out into the middle of the pool. He was swimming, and this was his only thought. He was experimenting with his new skill. Kicking his legs. Straining to keep his head above the surface. Swallowing, gulping. He looked back. It seemed a long way to return to the safety of the shallow end. His woolly trunks became heavy with water. Too big for him already, they suddenly felt enormous. He sensed them slip towards his ankles. And panicked. He stopped the flailing and floundering that was keeping him afloat, reached to pull them up, and sank.

Water filled his ears. Eyes wide, bent double yanking at his swimming trunks, he saw the tiled bottom of the pool looming up. He shoved against it, and still holding his trunks, started rising to the surface. He burst back into the world. Sudden sounds, the hollow sodden echo of children playing. He heaved air into his lungs, still holding on to his trunks, started to sink once more. And Iris saw him. She jumped to her feet, pointing at him, shouting, 'My God, Colin!' She flapped her arms at Chas who swam easily down, scooped him up and deposited him at the side of the pool. Colin suffered all this and never let go of his trunks. He stood spitting and coughing, bent his head to the left, then the right, hoping the water would run out of his ears. He looked up at Chas and Iris, thinking he was in for a serious scolding.

Chas said, 'Don't do that, Colin.' Then went back to the class.

Iris wrapped him in the huge bath towel she'd brought in case some child turned up without. She gently rubbed him dry. 'Colin, you never cease to amaze me. But don't do that again.' She rubbed his hair. 'Did you get a fright? Do you want to get dressed?'

He was quite enjoying being towelled. The Missie's towel, he thought. Softer than his gran's and bigger, and red. He liked red. But no, he didn't want to get dressed. Not ever, really. He wanted to get back into the water. And swim. Here was something he could do.

'He's keen,' Iris said.

'He's got worrying shorts on,' said Stella. 'He can't do anything for keeping them up.'

Colin was, they agreed, a soul.

There was a small group of mums waiting at the school gates when they arrived back at the village. The children poured from the two cars, shiny-faced and still damp. Fiona told. Her news burst from her as she descended from the back of the Land Rover, it was out before she hit the pavement. 'Colin nearly drowned.'

There was a hush. Everyone looked at Colin, who reddened deeply and stared at his feet. Shoelaces untied. Ever since he'd known he was going to the swimming baths, the shoelace business had worried him. He could not tie them. This worry had lain long in his mind. That, and taking his clothes off at the baths. Then putting them back on again. He'd solved the first problem by wearing his swimming trunks under his trousers to the baths. But getting his clothes on again had proved a problem. While other boys played in the changing room, flicked one another with towels, Colin sweated and struggled behind the curtain of his cubicle. He scrubbed himself roughly with his towel, then pulled his vest and shirt over his damp body. He hadn't removed his saturated swimming trunks, but instead put his trousers on over them. He fretted. What if he took too long to get dressed, and everybody forgot about him? What if they went away without him and he was left here, alone, all night? In the dark. He didn't bother with his socks, put his shoes on the wrong feet, wet feet. Left the laces to trail along the ground, stuffed his towel into his school bag and trudged down to the foyer.

Normally Iris would have spotted the laces and lack of socks and tidied him up, but today her attention was taken up by the little ones who needed help to dry their hair and dress.

Now, with Fiona's announcement about the near drowning, everyone turned to look at Colin. There he stood, sockless and dripping. Damp from his soaking swimming trunks had spread through his trousers, and a small river of water ran down his leg into his shoe. Eyes followed that river to his feet wedged into the wrong shoes. On the way these eyes noted that he'd forgotten to zip his fly, maroon swimming trunks plainly on view. Colin looked at his feet, searched the quizzical faces for the one that belonged to his gran. It wasn't there. He took off, across the road, through his gate and into the house. Safety.

Fiona's mother watched him go. 'The boy's brainless.'

Iris fixed her with the glare. 'I've been a long time teaching, and I've met a few brainless kids. Colin's not one of them. Brainless he ain't.' She stared across at the front door Colin had run through, slammed behind him, and her heart went out to him.

At four Scott came home. He dropped his bag in the hall and headed for the fridge. Stood staring glumly into it, selected some cheese and set about making a sandwich, hacking at the loaf with a bread knife.

'Good day?' said Iris.

He cut a wedge of cheese, slapped it between two hunks of bread, took a bite, said, 'Uh-huh.'

'The funniest thing happened today,' she said. 'I was driving the kids to the swimming baths, and I saw you going into the Deer and Thistle.'

Scott swallowed. 'Me?'

180

'It was very like you.'

'Was it?'

'Yes.'

He stopped chewing and looked at her. Guiltily.

'You're looking guilty,' said Iris.

'I always look guilty when I've been accused of something. People do. It's what happens. Someone asks you if you did something, and you start looking guilty.'

'I suppose,' said Iris, 'you must have a double.' Then, changing the subject, 'Remember those yellow swimming trunks you insisted I bought for you then never wore?'

'Yeah,' said Scott. 'I hated them.'

'Then why did you want me to buy them?'

'I liked them in the shop, then when I got them home, they were yellow.'

'They were yellow in the shop, too.'

'Yeah, but they were a good yellow in the shop. Once I got them home I could see the colour for what it was.'

'What?' said Iris.

'Yellow,' said Scott.

'Do you still have them?' asked Iris.

'Yeah. Upstairs in my drawer. They won't fit me now.'

'Get them for me. I have a home for them.'

Scott gladly went upstairs to find the discarded swimming trunks. Anything to avoid being quizzed on the subject of being seen going into the pub. Though he thought he'd handled it well. He'd expounded on the matter of behaving guiltily. He hadn't denied going for a drink when he should have been at school.

'I hear you almost drowned my boy,' said Ella Robertson.

Iris looked sceptical. 'Hardly.'

'I heard he had sunk to the bottom for the third time when Chas Harper saw him and brought him to the surface in the nick of time.'

'No,' said Iris. 'He was just starting to go down for the second time when Chas got hold of him. He'd struck out on his own, heading for the deep end, when he got into difficulties.'

'Difficulties? Is that what you call it? We could have lost him.'

'I doubt that, Mrs Robertson,' said Iris. 'I very much doubt that.'

'Well, he's not going swimming again.'

Iris sighed, and fingered the plastic bag she was carrying. It contained Scott's discarded yellow trunks. Gold more than yellow, Iris thought. A sunny colour. Colin would love it.

'He sank right in the middle of the pool, down to the bottom.'

'Yes, he sank in the middle of the pool. But why not ask yourself how he got there? He swam, Mrs Robertson. He swam. One small lesson, and he took off. None of the others could do it. Actually,' enthusing now, 'it's wonderful. Even if he did get into difficulties.'

'I don't think so,' shrilled Ella Robertson. 'It's hardly likely Colin could do anything the others can't. He's daft. Lovely, mind, but daft. He can't tie his own laces. He reads all the time. Unhealthy that is. No, you've got it wrong.'

'I have done nothing of the sort. The boy swam. And he would have swum further than he did, and certainly would not have sunk, if he'd been wearing swimming trunks that fitted him.'

Ella Robertson frowned.

'His trunks came down and he grabbed them and wouldn't let go. That's why he sank. For goodness' sake, I think Colin is a very remarkable boy. I brought him these.' She handed over the bag.

Ella took it, turned it over in her hands. 'I don't take charity.'

'Well, I do,' said Iris. 'If there were some kindly people out there with funds to dispense to stressed-out school teachers with teenage children, then I'd be banging at their door.' She turned and stumped down the path before turning back to Ella. 'But that's not charity. That's a pair of swimming trunks that haven't been worn, that my son has long grown out of, and would just lie unused, and might give Colin pleasure.'

She went out the gate. Across the street, she saw Scott heading off to visit the Lynnes, or rather Jake. She thought it grand he had a friend.

The night was chill and lovely. In the gathering dark a slip of a moon moved up the sky.

'I don't want to go in,' said Sophy.

'Me neither,' said Jean. She took a drag of her cigarette and handed it to Sophy. Though she shunned Sophy at school, here in Green Cairns they were still best mates.

Sophy took it, inhaled, and felt a rush of nausea and giddiness. They were in the field at the back of their homes, pressed against the hedge at the end of Jean's garden where they could not be seen. Their cigarettes were stolen from Jean's mother's packet.

'Do you miss your dad?' said Jean.

'Sometimes. I used to in our old house. But not so much here. I think about him and how I'll never see him again. Then I try to remember what he was like. I shut my eyes and try to see his face. But it won't come.'

Jean said, 'Yeah,' sympathising, but not understanding.

'He was just always there. He came and went to work and that, and sometimes we'd have a laugh. But I didn't really know him. He was distant.'

Jean said, 'Yeah,' again. She wished her dad was distant. He nagged her about her clothes, her hair. He checked her homework, always wanted to know where she was going when she went out. He cuddled her, rubbed his unshaven cheek against hers. She was his little princess.

The air smelled cold, a breeze curled round them. They shivered. Thousands of stars above, and beneath them the earth was damp. Faraway hills stood dark, shouldering the sky. From the copse across the fields an owl called. They saw him move, a silent flight, out of the trees. Far away up the glen, a curlew called.

'Your dad's cool, though,' said Sophy. 'I like him.'

'Do you?' said Jean. She wrestled with the notion of her father being cool. The man was nearly forty. How could someone so old be cool? 'He's old,' she said. 'I'm not going to get old. I want to die before I'm thirty.'

'Me, too,' said Sophy.

Jean took the cigarette. 'I want to marry someone like John Lennon.'

Now it was Sophy's turn to say, 'Yeah.' She reached over, took Jean's hand in hers, felt the softness of her palm. 'I'm glad you're my friend.'

'Best friend,' said Jean.

'Yeah,' said Sophy.

Michael Kennedy phoned Iris. How did she fancy another curry? A night out would do her good, calm her nerves after nearly drowning one of her pupils. Iris sighed, said that nobody had nearly drowned and the rumours in this place would drive her insane. And, yes, another curry would be fun.

She went back to her pile of corrections. 'Bloody hell, this place! Rumours have wings.'

Scott lay enfolded in Emily's arms. He could hear her heart beat, and was thrilled at the sound. So close, so close he didn't want this night to end. But soon he would have to get up and go home. He hated that, leaving Emily lying sleeping, her hair spread on the pillow, mouth slightly open. He'd stand at the door watching her. He thought her beautiful. He loved her, was sure of that. 'I love you,' he said.

'No, you don't,' she said. 'You're just infatuated, you'll get over it.'

'No, I won't. I love you and I want to take care of you.'

'How could you do that? You're a boy. You don't earn any money.'

'We don't need money. We could get a place like this. We could grow things. We'd be happy.'

'I already have a place like this,' said Emily. 'And you do need money. Everybody needs money.'

'We would have each other,' said Scott. 'We'd get by. I could do things. I could get odd jobs. It wouldn't be much, but we'd get by.'

She sighed, didn't answer. It would be the same old conversation. His hopes, dreams, plans. Her denial. 'We could do it,' he'd say. 'We'd be happy, that's all that matters.'

'No, we wouldn't be happy,' she'd say. And she lay and stroked his hair, listening to the hiss of the wind in the trees outside and scolding herself because she hadn't locked up the hens. A fox would get them. 'Shouldn't have taken them,' she said.

'What?' said Scott.

'Nothing. Just the hens. I shouldn't have taken them. I felt sorry for them. I thought we'd get some eggs but they don't lay.'

Scott felt heavy. He was warm, happy. He'd just made love to Emily and was pleased with himself. After his first few energetic efforts, he felt he was getting better at this. Better and better. He was getting to know her body, her needs. He was drifting into the dreaming. Couldn't fight it, didn't want to fight it.

Emily looked at him. 'You're sleeping,' she said. She looked at the window, the glimmer of moonlight at the edges of the curtains. She didn't want this. An affair with a boy. But the comfort of it, the feel of a body next to hers, a voice – somebody to talk to. She thought about the life she'd left behind, so gladly. Bedrooms she'd known. A mattress on the floor in her student flat, a silk scarf draped over the naked light bulb to soften the glare, grey blankets, clothes in heaps, her radio, postcards and notes propped on the dresser, books, posters and record sleeves on the wall. And a memory beyond that memory: her childhood bedroom, a patterned quilt, a teddy bear to cuddle in the dark, shelves of books. It had been so perfect, she'd turned her back on it.

'Your parents are bourgeois,' said Jake. 'Their lives are full of possessions. Status symbols. Come the revolution they won't know what to do.'

She had readily agreed. Come the revolution, everything would change. She didn't know much about the revolution, other than it was coming. Nobody was organising it. 'We are anarchists,' said Jake. 'We don't organise anything.' It would just come. It was in the air, you could feel it. Hear it in a thousand songs. It would sweep through the land, this mood – freedom, love. Everything, everyone, would change. She'd tried to tell her parents, Miriam and Eric, about it. But they had told her not to be silly. In ten years' time, they said, Jake would have cut his hair, be wearing a suit and tie and working the nine to five like everybody else. Meantime, he appalled them. They'd told her if she dropped out of university and went to live with him, they didn't want any more to do with her. She'd have made her own bed, she could lie on it.

The allure of this making and lying on her own bed was irresistible. She left university, moved in with Jake. Now her mother and father didn't know where she was. They didn't even know about Gracie. A tear slipped from the corner of her eye, ran down on to the pillow. She wanted to go home.

In the depths of the night Colin got out of bed into the shivering cold. He put on the light, tiptoed across the room to the chest, opened the top drawer and pulled out his new swimming trunks. Gold. The colour of honey, buttercups, the crowns princes wore in fairy tales. It was a colour that could enfold you, you could fall into it, be swimming in gold. Just like he wanted to swim in the music they played on the radio on Saturday mornings. The Beach Boys, the man had said. He'd turned it up loud so it would fill every corner of the room and would swirl round him. He'd spread his arms to feel it.

'Are you deaf?' his gran had said, storming into the room from the kitchen. 'What'll the neighbours think, music like that coming out of our house?'

Colin had said nothing. He'd gone outside to his place in the sycamore tree, to sit on his branch watching cars on the road coming and going. But the music was still in his head, layers and layers of voices, quickening his heart. It thrilled him.

Tonight, his gran had fretted. Knitted and fretted. 'I was rude to her. I shouldn't have said that about you drowning. Well, you didn't drown, did you? But swimming, you?' She shook her head. 'No. That can't be right. Still she brought a gift, and I should have just said thank you. She's got her bad points – these men of hers, and her children are wild. That boy sneaking off to the Lynne woman. And there's them prayers. But you're besotted with her so she can't be that bad.'

Colin had looked up from the giant butterfly he was drawing, and nodded. He loved the Missie, he knew that. Last week she'd leaned down to tie his laces. 'Now, Colin, it's time you mastered the art of laces. How are you going to grow up to marry me if you can't? I'm not marrying a man who can't tie a simple knot in his shoelace.'

He'd looked down at her busy fingers. Long nails, painted palest pink. He wondered now about marrying her. He thought he'd quite like to. But by the time he grew up, she'd be old. It was a worry. Still, he had the swimming trunks. He slipped off his pyjama trousers and put them on, then pulled on the pyjama bottoms over them and went back to bed. He lay in the dark, feeling the trunks against his body. He loved the way his pyjama bottoms slid against the shiny material. They were wonderful, truly lovely. He thought he'd never take them off.

The Things We Do for Love

Two o'clock in the morning. Stella Vernon sat at her kitchen table with her accounts book and adding machine, bills, receipts and bank statements scattered around her. It was raining, bitter lashings against the windowpane. She wore her husband's thick red dressing gown, her feet wriggling with worry inside a pair of sheepskin slippers. Two hours ago she'd woken from a thin nagging sleep, sweaty and bedevilled by apprehension. They were broke.

She normally dealt with her vexation over money matters by putting unpaid bills and demands into orderly piles, tamping them on the table and stapling them together. Maybe she couldn't pay them, but at least she could arrange them neatly. This way, she felt she was doing something about them. Addressing them rather than ignoring them. But tonight she'd lain awake, counting. Sums made from lettings this year and last, minus sums used to run their business over the same period. Only she couldn't do that piece of maths, since the amount they'd made was infinitely smaller than the amount they'd spent.

Ten years ago, when John had left the army where he'd been a captain, they'd looked about for a small business they could run together. They'd considered a cleaning company, a chicken farm and this one – Cairn Cottages. Three cottages and six wooden chalets they'd lease out to tourists on self-catering holidays. They didn't think they'd make a fortune, but they'd make a living amidst fabulous scenery. They had a vision. It did not come to them, complete, this dream. It arrived in their separate minds in a series of fragmented visions which they'd holler out the moment they arrived.

'Honeysuckle round the doors,' Stella yelled one morning on waking.

'Pony rides,' John enthused as he packed their crockery.

'A children's farm, with chickens and stuff,' she said.

'We can rent out bicycles,' he said.

'Gourmet meals,' she cried out. 'I can cook gourmet meals and keep them in the freezer. Folks can buy them, save them cooking and cheaper than a night out.' They whooped with glee.

This was going to be fabulous. They'd be happy making other people happy. In their dreams they went to a sunny place filled with the laughter of frolicking children, apple blossom, air scented with honeysuckle. They sang as they drove north.

Over the next year they had painted the cottages and the chalets. Furnished them from Habitat. Installed a new washing machine and drier and television in each one. They planted honeysuckle, bought a couple of Shetland ponies. Stella cooked and filled the freezer with gourmet meals packed into plastic cartons, labelled in her tidy script 'Duck in orange sauce', 'Sole Veronique'. They built a play area complete with swings, a basketball net and trampoline.

The twins, too young to go to school, played on the grass in front of their new home. The sun was warm on Stella and John's faces as they worked. They were filled with the frisson of the new. They opened. Visitors arrived, stayed, and didn't come back. Nobody bought a gourmet meal. They brought their own burgers and beans, kid's food. The ponies bit. Children howled and had to be taken to the doctor for treatment. Parents threatened to sue. The Vernons let them go home without paying.

The farmer, Jack Binnie, who lived at the end of the rutted track that led to the cottages, also owned it. Tourists' cars enraged him almost as much as tourists. 'This land is working land,' he said. 'These people are ignorant idlers.' He parked his tractor across the entrance so that nobody could get in, or, once in, leave. When people couldn't reach the Vernons' cottages, they drove to the chalets up the road which were cheaper, had views of the river and belonged to Jack Binnie. He still thought them ignorant city idlers, but was partial to their money. Besides, he was local. The Vernons were incomers who still had to earn his respect. Nobody who hadn't lived in these parts for four generations at least got that.

Stella learned, on passing the travel agency in town, that it was cheaper for a family to go to Spain or France for a fortnight than it was to stay in one of her cottages for a week. No wonder they don't come, she thought. And glumly admitted to herself which she'd prefer. Spain was sunny. The weather at Cairn Cottages was unreliable, but every holidaymaker was guaranteed at least three or four days of rain.

A month ago, a cheery middle-aged couple had turned up and stayed for a week. They joked, and laughed, shouted friendly good mornings. Each day they set off to tramp the hills, breathe the air. They even bought a gourmet meal – duck in orange sauce – which they said was the tastiest thing they'd eaten in a long time. 'It made the holiday,' they said. Stella glowed. One morning they were gone, and at first she thought they'd driven into town to get some supplies. But there was something silent and final about their absence. She carefully opened the door to their cottage. It was empty. Stunningly empty. The jolly couple had taken two mattresses, the television and the fridge. They'd emptied the wardrobe of clothes hangers, taken the sheets from the beds. Everything movable had been removed. When Stella checked the freezer in the corner of the communal games room – a place where people could play ping-pong – she found it empty. Every single gourmet meal gone. She listened to the chilled hum, stared into the frosty void, and cried. The honeysuckle thrived, though. It scented the air, just as Stella had hoped it would. There was still hope.

So, Stella sat, the solid clicking of her fingernails on adding machine keys punctuating the dark. She whispered her additions, subtractions and multiplications as she worked. Put bills into must-pay and can-wait piles, and stapled them together. There, that was something, at least. Her still face shone slightly under the pool of angle-poise light. John, at the door, where he'd been standing unnoticed for the past few minutes, watched her. He thought her beautiful. He loved her calm. It seemed to radiate from her, a stillness, serenity. He'd hardly ever seen her angry. In moments of family crisis, she brought peace. She could scoop up a wailing child, hold him, rock him silent. She could stroke a fevered brow and kiss sores and cuts better. 'Oooh,' she'd say, in a soft croon,

'that's a nasty one. Kiss it better, kiss the pain away, kiss it gone.'
And the child would turn into her, clutch her, snuffling back tears.
'Kiss it gone,' Stella would say. 'There, there, all better.' John would
marvel at this. Faced with wounded knees, cut fingers, he'd say,
'That's nothing to cry about. It's only a scratch.' Even when,
sometimes, it plainly wasn't. Once, when Simon had badly sprained
his ankle and fallen to the ground, writhing in agony, John had
said, 'Now, now. You're not going to cry, are you? Boys don't cry.'

Not that he could blame his sons for seeking those healing lips, that
soft bosom. There was such comfort there, such comfort. He nightly
sought those lips, those breasts, could lose himself in Stella then
sleep. 'What are you doing?' he said now. 'It's the middle of the night.'

She turned. Smiled. See, he thought, she hadn't known he was
watching her, yet when he spoke, she didn't even start, she smiled.

'Going through our accounts,' she said. 'Trying to find ways of
staying alive.'

'Alive? It isn't that bad?'

She nodded. 'It is. We're broke.'

'How broke?'

'Seriously broke. We have nothing.'

Silence. They looked at one another, considering their plight.

'Something will turn up,' said John. 'Always does.'

'Your belief in things turning up is touching,' said Stella.

'Things always turn up,' he said. 'You'll see.' He crossed the
room, stood beside her, hand on her shoulder. 'You're cold.'

'I know,' She sighed, rubbed her tired eyes. 'We shouldn't have
bought the twins those bikes, we couldn't afford them.'

'Well, when you're a kid you've got to have a bike, even if your
mother won't let you ride it to school.'

'I worry.'

'You shouldn't molly-coddle them. Let them go. They'll be fine.
Think of the petrol you'll save not taking them in the Land Rover.'

Wearied, she said, 'All right.'

He leaned over, switched off the light. 'Come to bed.'

Too tired to protest, she let him lead her by the hand up the stairs
to the bedroom. She lay in the dark, John's hand on her. She

turned to him, kissed him. They would make love, it was what they always did. They celebrated with sex and sorrowed with it. Different moods, different sex. Slow, almost mournful, tonight. John's lips on her neck, he breathed her in. Whatever it was that was troubling him, Stella could kiss it better.

Afterwards she lay looking into the dark, listening to the rain. If it was up to her, she'd cut their losses, sell up and go south to a city where she and John could find jobs, start again. But he would never agree to that. 'Give up?' he'd say. 'The Vernons never give up. We are winners.' He'd clench his teeth, his eyes would shine. He would look fiery and noble, if a little foolish. He might even slam his fist on the table. Defeat was not even a consideration. Tomorrow she'd make an appointment with the bank manager, ask to extend their overdraft. She'd tell him they'd had over two hundred enquiries about renting next year. If he asked to see them, she'd forge them. She would go and see Binnie and try to reason with him. Maybe she could offer to cook him gourmet meals as part of the fee he demanded for the use of his track. Maybe she could offer her services as a cleaner in the farmhouse. She knew his wife, Elspeth, hated chores. She sighed. My God, she thought, the things we do for love.

It was something Iris had said that made Scott choose this night.

'Isn't it funny,' she'd remarked, 'that you always sleep like a log when the weather's foul? When the night is warm and clear, you're restless. I don't know.'

'Must be primal,' Morag had said. 'On a warm night your ancient senses are telling you that you should be out hunting or gathering crops or berries or something. But when it's cold and rainy you're husbanding your strength against the elements.'

'Hibernating,' said Iris.

Tonight was a night for hibernating. Bitterly cold, sheeting rain. Iris would be sleeping like a log, and so, he hoped, would Hugh Stone. It was a night for bravery. At two o'clock he got out of bed, dressed and slipped downstairs. He took Iris's old hessian shopping bag from its place on the hook at the back of the kitchen door, the torch from the kitchen drawer, and lifted Iris's car keys from the table in the hall where she always dumped them when she came in. Scott sneaked out of the house and into the car. It was, to his huge relief, pointing the right way. He had never driven a car before, but figured, hell, his mother and father could do it, Mr Blacksmith, head of the school, could do it, Jake could do it, dammit, his grandmother could do it. If all these folks could drive a car, there must be nothing to it. He could do it.

He turned the key in the ignition, pressed the accelerator and lurched forward. Stalled. He tried again, this time remembering to release the handbrake. The car moved in a series of jerks before stalling again. He started to sweat, rubbed his palms on his jeans, wiped his brow with the back of his hand, started again. This time he slammed the accelerator hard to the floor and shot forward. In first gear, he roared up the road and out of the village, into blackness. Feverishly, he flicked switches. The heater howled, the radio came on, and, at last, the lights and the windscreen wipers. Hunched over the wheel, staring fixedly ahead, he crawled and lurched down the road. Long silver needles of rain streamed through the beam of the headlights, the tyres hissed through the layer of water deep on the road. Scott could hardly see where he was going. But he would do this. He would show Emily how much he loved her.

He saw the henhouses every morning on the way to school. Eight of them, tall wooden structures on wheels. Every week Hugh Stone of Coppie's Farm would trundle them to a different field, open them up, and let the hens out. Every night his wife, Maisie, would herd them into their mobile home and shut them up, safe from foxes. What Scott had noticed were the cockerels. He thought them splendid. Befeathered, strutting, gleaming kings, he liked their style. He did not know these creatures were championship stock, or that their polished trophies lined the shelves, pride of place in the Stones' farmhouse kitchen. To him, they were just cockerels. That was all. The Stones' hens laid large speckled brown eggs that they sold to the butcher in Forham where they were displayed in the window: tempting, double-yolked, small feathers and straw still clinging to their shells. Emily's hens didn't lay. They needed, as Scott put it, a man.

He parked at the roadside next to the field. Squeezed through the fence and set off towards the henhouses, torch flickering a thin shaft through the teaming night. The rain sheared into him, soaking him. He could barely see but didn't care. He was on a mission. Water seeped through his shoes, flattened his hair, ran down the back of his neck. His T-shirt and jeans clung to his body. This is how much I love you, Emily, he thought.

He selected the nearest henhouse, opened the door and stepped in. It was, he thought, a comforting place. Rain drumming on the roof, the soft clucking of contented hens who eyed him beadily but did not move. Perches stretched the length of the interior, lined with hens; below them the dropping boards that were removed and scrubbed daily by Maisie.

Scott saw a cockerel, a White Leghorn, a fabulous bird. Snowy white with a deep red comb. White for my lady, thought Scott, and lunged at it. It hadn't occurred to him, as he'd planned this, that the bird would resist. In his imaginings, he'd grab it and scarper. The bird did not see it that way. As Scott reached for it, it squawked and screeched, and flapped and flew upwards. This sudden protest set the other hens off. They flew from their perches and flapped round him, objecting loudly. It was more than clucking, it was a cacophony of shrill shrieks, cries, wing beatings. Nothing, Scott thought, could make a noise like disturbed hens. This was awful. 'Shut up! he yelled at them, fending them off, waving his arms.

He finally got hold of his quarry and tried to stuff it into Iris's hessian bag. The bird had other ideas. It spread its wings and refused to be stuffed anywhere. It squealed, shrieked, cackled, writhed. It dug its feet into Scott's arm. There was blood. He gave up on the bag, clutched the violent creature to him, and ran out. He plunged forward into the dark and rain, hugging the bird. He ran. Tripping, stumbling, squelching through mud. The bird, volubly objecting to this sudden cruel removal from its cosy home, squawked, scratched, writhed in his arms, pecked his face. But still Scott clung on.

He squeezed back through the fence and crossed the road to the car, the bird pressed hot against him, clucking its discontent. He threw it on to the back seat, climbed in himself, and sat there, ashen and shaking. At last he turned on the ignition, flicked on the lights and wipers, and started his beginner's jerk down the road. The bird stirred, and perched imperiously on the back of the passenger seat beside him. It was only now that Scott realised he did not know how to reverse the car. The road was narrow, too narrow for a U-turn. He would have to drive on till he found somewhere he could sweep round and head for home.

Twelve miles down the road, he came to crossroads. Slowly, wrenching the wheel, he eased the car in an awkward circle, and, crashing the gears, headed back the way he'd come. This sudden and alarming change of rhythm panicked the already startled bird. It leapt from the back of the passenger seat and ran amok in the rear of the car, attacking the back of Scott's head. Then it switched its frenzy to the front, throwing itself against the windscreen. He swiped at it, making it worse. The car careered across the road, skidding on the watery surface. At last the bird settled on the floor at his feet, in between the clutch and the footbrake. Changing gear was impossible. They completed their journey, slowly, noisily, in second gear. By the time the car crept sluggishly into Green Cairns, it was filled with a worrying burning smell.

As he opened the car door, the courtesy light came on and he could see the damage. There were feathers everywhere, lifting, clouding, settling, but the truly horrifying thing was the liberal scattering of bird shit. How was he going to explain that? Splatterings on the outside were fairly common, but on the inside of the windscreen? Cursing, he picked up the bird by the feet and headed for the Lynnes' cottage. It was five in the morning. He'd thought the whole exploit would take half-an-hour. Now the sky was turning grey, pinking round the edges of the clouds. The first birds were stirring. He no longer needed his torch. The cockerel, however, had numbed into silent shock. Toted upside down for the last part of its journey, it was too traumatised to utter a sound.

Emily was not pleased to see him. 'It's fucking five in the fucking morning!'

'I brought you this.' Scott held up the cockerel.

She was wearing Jake's Frank Zappa T-shirt, looking small and thin, shivering at the door, sweat-shiny from sleep. 'I do not need another hen. I do not need a hen at this bloody hour. For God's sake! A hen! At dawn!'

'It's a cockerel,' said Scott, triumphantly. He couldn't understand this, he'd thought she'd be pleased. 'It's why you don't get eggs. Your hens need a man. And here he is.' He'd been practising this last sentence all the way home, in second gear, cockerel squawking at his feet, car smelling of deranged bird, droppings and burning oil, rain whipping against the windscreen. 'White for my lady,' he said.

'I am nobody's lady,' said Emily. 'Least of all yours. Go away.'

'I thought you'd be pleased.' Tears pricked Scott's eyes. 'I went through hell to get this for you.'

'I didn't ask you to.'

'I know. But it's for you. So you can have eggs. You and Gracie.' And the tears he was fighting so hard to keep back slid down his face. He sniffed. He was soaked, scratched, pecked, covered in mud and bird shit. He was shaking with exhaustion and nerves. He was miserable.

'Take it away,' said Emily. 'I don't want it. I don't want a cockerel. I don't want hens. I don't want to be here.'

'I love you,' he said.

'Get over it,' she said, and shut the door.

He stood, cockerel dangling by his side. He didn't know what to do. So he carefully placed the bird by the tree at the bottom of the garden where the other hens were clustered by the hedge, trying to keep dry, for it was still darkly raining.

He went home, a slow and mournful trudge down the path. Birds were singing now. The sky scarlet, dawn and foul weather in the offing. He dumped Iris's car keys on the table in the hall, and in his room peeled off his saturated clothes. Oh, the relief of bed, warmth and softness. He slept, plagued by dreams of being chased. An hour later, Iris woke him. A voice ringing through the black depths. He rose, pulled on his school clothes and went downstairs where he sat at the breakfast table. Pale, gaunt, looking wild-eyed, haunted. 'My

God,' said Iris, 'look at you. Where did you get those scratches on your face?'

'Dunno,' he mumbled. 'Must've done it in my sleep. I had a nightmare.' In truth, he was still sleeping. The only thing that made Iris think he was awake was his eyes, which were open. But they were red still, swollen from tears.

'You look awful,' she said. 'I think you should stay home today. I don't think you're well.' She placed a concerned hand on his brow. Felt the heat. 'You've got a temperature. You're burning up.'

He nodded. He was burning up. He went back to bed. Heard Sophy leave. Heard the school bus stop at the gate.

Iris looked round his bedroom door. 'I have to go, will you be all right?'

'Yeah.'

'I'll look in at breaktime. You sleep. I brought you some orange juice and aspirins. Take care.' She thought, This is it. He is having nightmares, he is disturbed. The truth has hit him. He has finally realised his father is dead, and he's been brought to this new place. Morag had said he and Sophy would erupt one day. She looked at him, and thought, What have I done to you?

He thought, Just go. Leave me.

He heard her shut the kitchen door and walk across the garden to the school. Then he rose, took the vacuum from the cupboard in the hall and the long lead that would stretch to the car. He had feathers to clear away, bird shit to wipe. He was bone-sore, head aching. He was sweating, fevered, shivering with oncoming flu. His heart was broken. Numbly, he gathered last night's soaking, mud-encrusted clothes and took them downstairs to put in the washing machine. He plugged in the extension cable for the vacuum and carried it down the front path to the car. The roaring hum of the machine matched the hum of flu in his head. He'd made a fool of himself, stealing the cockerel, taking it to Emily in the middle of the night. Maybe right now the police were hunting for him. Maybe Emily would never talk to him again. He felt tears spring anew to his eyes, and gulped. With a damp cloth he scrubbed at the droppings on the car floor.

The things we do for love.

Knowing, Loving and
Seeing with Eyes Shut

Iris marvelled at Michael Kennedy. The liveliness of him. It wasn't just his eyes that twinkled, he twinkled all over. They went to the same bar, heard the same greeting as he entered. It seemed to Iris that everyone shouted, 'Michael!' He made his way to the same table by the fire, raising two fingers at the barman: 'Two of everything.' Two beers, two whiskies, two curries. Iris doubted her digestive system's ability to cope.

He seemed to feast on rooms, the people in them, their noise, banter, their doings. He loved the intricate rambling fiddle music a band was playing in the public bar. Heartiness radiated from him, touching everything, everyone, including Iris. He'd bathe her in a fond look that made her feel cherished, wanted. 'I like your face,' he said. 'I especially like that bit.' He leaned over, touched her chin. 'Just there, at the very point. It's as if God was going to give you a dimple, then changed his mind.'

'You think?' said Iris, touching where he had touched. From this moment, and for the rest of her life, Iris would like her chin.

'Oh, I think.'

She smiled.

'And I like that, too. Your smile. The dimples don't end at the corners of your mouth, they spread in little ripples across your cheek. Nice smile. Well-flexed smile muscles. Good sign, I think.'

Their drinks arrived. Michael rubbed his hands, lifted his beer and downed half of it in one. 'Ah.' He put his glass down, wiped his lips with the back of his hand. 'I needed that.' Then he swigged at his whisky. 'Perfect.'

Iris sipped. 'So,' she said, 'when you and your wife split up, was it nasty?'

'It was inevitable. She was older than me. Twelve years. I was but a boy. But a boy who wanted to stay here, had no desire to wander. She wanted other things – parties, restaurants, the hum and bustle of the city. She couldn't stay round here. And there was another thing: I settled down. When we wed, she was older than me. But when we split up, I was older than her. She got younger.'

'I don't understand?' said Iris.

'She wanted all the things of youth. She got the Sunday papers and read about books and films and places to eat and things to do, clothes to buy, clubs to dance in. And she wanted them. So she upped and went to get them. I couldn't go with her.'

'Where is she now?'

He shrugged, smiled. 'Who knows? She went to Glasgow, then London, then Rome. I think she might be in New York now. She went to a city, then she needed a bigger city, and a bigger city after that. To get lost in, to find herself in, to believe she's part of whatever the bigger city offers. What was your husband like?'

The food arrived. Michael gazed at it, beheld it. 'This is the stuff. I've been looking forward to this all day.' He dug in.

Iris dipped a polite piece of naan bread in her sauce. Nibbled. Sipped. 'I always thought he was reliable. A bit boring, staid. Funny sometimes. But when he died I found out all sorts about him, and now I think I didn't know him at all.'

'Oh? Is that because he lost all your money?'

'Yes,' said Iris. How did he know that? The man seemed to know everything.

Michael caught the look. 'Ah,' he said, 'it's the way of things. Your old head, Miss Moffat, told Anthony Smith all about you. He told me. It hasn't gone any further.' But it had. Most people in the district knew of Iris's plight. A secretary had seen Miss Moffat's letter and word had spread. Talk in bars, in shops, on street corners. Tongues had wagged.

'I was angry at him. But then someone said how happy he must have been in those last years, living his secret life, letting his alter ego rip. So now I think, Well, good luck to him. He's gone, I'm still here. I can cope. I am coping.'

Michael downed the other half of his pint, raised his hand at the bar, pointed at the table, called for another. 'Good for you,' he said to her.

Iris looked about her. It was a good pub, unpretentious and frothing full. Conversations bubbling, a blue filmy cloud of smoke drifting towards the ceiling. Every now and then a shout of laughter would sound above the buzz of chat. Drinks were being downed, people were smiling. She thought it good to be out, seeing a little bit of life. And there was Michael across the table, and what would become of this going out together? Friendship? Bed? She didn't know, and wasn't really prepared to think about it. For the moment, this was good.

'Good, isn't it?' said Michael. 'Getting out, letting some unhealthy air into your lungs. A little drink, some food and chat. Better than staying in fretting about bills and filling surly young minds with grammar and arithmetic.'

Iris smiled and said indeed it was.

It was after eleven when they left, and Iris worried about the journey home. She wasn't drunk, but was certainly drunker than she'd been when she went into the pub, and knew she wasn't sober enough to drive. Michael, on the other hand, was drunk, plain and simple. She asked if he was sure he wanted to drive.

'Of course I want to drive. I've been driving that road home for years and years. I know every inch, every turn, every pothole. I can do it blindfold.'

'I'd rather you didn't,' she said. 'At least, not when I'm with you.'

He sat in the car, looking round beatifically. Pointed to the tobacconist's shop on the corner. 'Bought my first cigarettes there. Had my first grope round the back after a dance in the town hall – Mary MacGregor, lovely girl. She's a nurse now, married, three kids. Down there, by the drinking fountain, smoked my first dope. Stoned and happy. And the fruit shop, scene of my one and only crime, apart from the dope. I stole three oranges. Loveliest oranges I've ever eaten. Stolen fruit. And over there, Woolworth's. My pal

Francis stole a Mars Bar, and felt so guilty about it, he asked me to put it back next day. Lovely Catholic boy, he went and confessed to the priest who said I was a bad influence and he shouldn't be friends with me. Broke me up. God, memories. How could I ever leave this place?'

'The joy of the familiar,' said Iris.

'You said it.'

They drove out of town, Michael pointing out his life's landmarks. A large house with a huge monkey puzzle tree in the garden. 'Big party there. Great time. I went upstairs to the bedroom with Rosie Chapman. Oh, my.'

A bus stop on the edge of town. 'That's where Rosie told me she'd found someone else and didn't want to see me any more. I stumbled away from her because I didn't want her to see I was crying. Missed the last bus home. Poor boy, me.'

They drove out of town, past the last street lights, plunged into dark. Michael driving with his lights dipped. Miles they went, Iris wondering if she should point out that he'd see the way ahead better with the headlights on.

'Then there's other things,' said Michael. Driving slowly, sliding the wheel through his fingers as they rounded corners. 'There's the place by the river where I caught my first trout. Lovely day, but cloudy. Balmy. Me on the bank and the water moving slowly before me. Then a tug, and the rod jerked in my hand, and I pulled it out, high in the air, gleaming, a fat brown trout. My first brownie. The pride of it. Cooked it there and then, on a little fire and ate it, and after that me and Rosie . . .'

'Maybe we should leave you and Rosie to it. She deserves a bit of privacy,' said Iris, thinking how good it was to be with such a safe driver. The careful speed, the gentle cornering. Yet, she thought, he'd see the road better if he put on his headlights, and debated with herself about mentioning this. She didn't want to appear a nag, but it was a little disconcerting.

'I've walked all the hills.' He waved his hand towards the distance ahead of them. 'Got to the peaks, and walked. On my own. It's lovely up there. Silent, cool. And it's quite level after the climb, you can just walk as if you were in the High Street. Scorching day, took all my clothes off, put them in my rucksack, and walked. Kept me boots on, though. Saw not a soul. Only a herd of deer running across my path. A thousand hooves moving together, and hardly a sound. All moving, the oneness of it. I'll never leave. There's the scene of the week's big crime,' pointing towards Hugh Stone's field. 'Someone stole a prize cockerel, Snowy the Leghorn.'

'Why would someone do that?'

'It's worth a bit. There's rivalry between breeders, don't ya know?'

'I'm worried,' Iris said at last, 'that you are driving with your lights dipped. Shouldn't you have your headlights on?'

'Technically. But I know the road. Also, I didn't notice. I've got my eyes shut. Wanted to see if I could do it without looking.'

'You what? For heaven's sake, how long have you had them shut? I didn't see.'

'Ever since we left town, soon as we got past the street lights.'

'What if someone steps out in front of you? Or something? A deer?'

'I'm thinking that nothing would. And if they did they'd see me coming and get out of the way. It's what you do if you see a big lump of metal bearing down on you.'

'Please, please,' said Iris, 'open your eyes! Don't do this.'

'I'll open my eyes when we get to the village. I don't need them open. I know this place. Every bump in the road, every sound from outside the car, every smell, everything. I know it. I don't need to look, it's all burned into my mind. I love it.'

'Oh, my God!' said Iris. 'Don't do this. We could crash. I could get hurt. I have children, a job. For fuck's sake, will you look where you're going?'

'I know where I'm going. I don't need to look. Sometimes it's just lovely to feel your way forward and let your senses take you where you are going.'

'You're drunk,' said Iris. 'Let me out of the car.' She was trying not to sound hysterical. Which was hard. Because she was.

'No, I won't. Shut your eyes. Enjoy the thrill of moving forward in the black. The hum of the engine and the night.'

She sat staring ahead, ready to shout out if she thought he was about to hit a tree or veer over into a ditch, gripping the door handle. Ready also to leap out to safety when the accident happened.

They stopped in the village, on the other side of the road and two or three yards short of Iris's house.

'See,' said Michael, 'I did it. I knew I could. Wasn't that grand?'

'No,' said Iris. 'It decidedly wasn't. It was terrifying.'

'Nonsense.' He leaned over. Took her by the shoulders. 'You're shaking. Don't shake. It was fine. You were perfectly safe.'

She turned to open the car door and get out. But he pulled her close, big comforting arm round her. He rubbed her back slowly. 'It was fine. I won't do it again.'

'Not with me in the car, you won't.'

'But didn't we have a good time? I did. You did, too. Apart from the drive home. And part of the way you didn't even notice I was driving with my eyes shut.'

'That's not the point, noticing. It's the doing of it. Endangering other people.'

'You're right. In future I'll only do it when I'm alone in the car.' He looked down at her. Smiled. Then he kissed her.

At first, she thought to resist. Then, she wasn't feeling particularly well – the curry, the drink, the precarious ride home. But lips on her lips, new lips, strange lips. So soft. Something deep within her stirred, a longing. Human touch that was not a routine goodbye or hello peck on the cheek from a departing or arriving child. For a few fleeting moments there was bliss, and here was Iris, not mother, not teacher, but woman, sexual being. There was a gentleness about him. She let him kiss her. More, she kissed him back. When they moved apart, he still held her. Looked at her. 'There,' he said, touching her chin, 'my favourite bit of your face.' He kissed it. 'And I won't do it again.'

'Kiss me?'

'Oh, I'm planning on doing that again. No, the other, the driving thing.'

'Fine,' she said. And got out of the car.

He said he'd pick her up next week, same time. She nodded. Waved goodbye and crossed to her gate, the click of high heels on frosty pavement resounding along the empty street. Inside her house, the curtain moved. She noticed this and was aware of other curtains in other houses moving.

Ruby was sitting in the living room. She was on the chair by the fire where Iris usually sat, leaning back, hands firmly gripping the arms. For a few seconds, just after she came through the door, before she got control of her face, Iris's shock showed. 'Ruby! What are you doing here?'

'You haven't invited me so I thought I'd just come. I wondered how you all were,' said Ruby.

Iris got control of herself, her shock. 'Well, it's lovely to see you.' She walked into the room, arms spread, embraced Ruby and felt her disapproval. The old woman stiffened. Iris knew she'd been spotted kissing a man, and now that her face had been at cheek-pecking distance from Ruby's, her boozy breath had been noted.

'Who was that?' said Ruby.

'Who was what?' Iris knew perfectly well who she meant. Acting innocent gave her a few moments' grace to plan her defence, plus having to ask twice made Ruby feel as if she was prying.

'That man you were with out there in the car?'

'Oh, Michael,' in a throwaway voice. 'He's a friend.'

'A close friend by the looks of it,' said Ruby. 'And you've been out gallivanting while your boy here is at death's door.'

Scott was lying on the sofa, head on a pillow, cocooned in blankets. On the floor was a cup, filmed and frothed with the remains of hot chocolate, on the plate beside it the crusts of hot buttered toast. Ruby had been ministering to him, and Iris felt a flush of guilt.

'He's hardly at death's door if he's been downing hot chocolate and toast. He's got a touch of the flu. By the looks of it, he's getting better.'

'No thanks to you and your gadding about. What time of night is this to come home?'

'It's before midnight, and I can come home whenever I like.'

'Leaving two children to fend for themselves,' said Ruby. 'And you've been drinking. I can smell it from here. You reek like a pub.'

Scott smirked. This was wonderful. His mother getting ticked off for coming home late and smelling of booze. He smirked harder.

'Go to bed, Scott. And take your cup with you. Put it in the kitchen.'

'You get to bed, son. I'll wash your cup,' said Ruby.

'Scott can wash his own cup. In this house, my house, if you're fit enough to stay up till twelve o'clock watching television, you're fit enough to wash a cup.'

Scott threw back his blankets, rose slowly from the sofa, picked up his cup and plate and headed for the door. He nudged Iris as he passed her. 'Naughty, naughty. You'll be kept in for a week.'

'Get to bed,' said Iris.

As soon as he had closed the door, Ruby rounded on her. 'I can't believe what I saw just now! You cavorting with a man in a car in front of your neighbours. And my son, your husband, not cold in his grave.'

Iris drew breath. She was tired. She wanted to go to bed. 'I was not cavorting, I merely gave Michael a goodnight kiss. A polite, social peck on the cheek, a thank you for a lovely evening.' Bullshit, she thought. 'And I can go out when I please. My son is old enough to be left in charge of the house. And I am aware of how long my husband, your son, has been dead.'

'It's not decent,' said Ruby. 'Going out with a man, and you recently widowed.'

'There is nothing indecent about it,' said Iris. 'And my marriage was . . .' She stopped. Her marriage had been in ruins, only she hadn't known it. Her marriage had been lifeless, and she'd become used to it. How could she say this to Ruby? How could she tell her that her son had squandered thousands, had lived a secret life? She sighed. 'My marriage wasn't always happy.'

'No marriage is.' Ruby was indignant. 'We all have our ups and downs.'

Seeing her about to elaborate on the ups and downs of matrimony, Iris said, 'You'll have to excuse me, I'm very tired. I must go to bed. Please put out the lights and switch off the television before you come up. The bed in the spare room has fresh sheets.' She left Ruby standing alone in the middle of the room, looking resentful, hurt and surprised at being abandoned. For a fleeting moment Iris felt sorry for her.

She climbed the stairs. Opened the door of Sophy's room and looked in. The girl was lying spread out, her bedclothes kicked off. Iris crossed the room and pulled them over her, tucked her in, stroked her hair. Kissed her sleep-damp forehead. She washed, cleaned her teeth, then in her own room undressed, pulled on her nightdress and climbed into bed. She lay listening to Ruby downstairs, switching off the lights then clumping slowly up the stairs. The evening was still with her, its highlights – the absurd drive home, the kiss, Michael's admiration of her chin, Ruby's fury at her cavorting with a man and coming home smelling of drink. It was all so absurd, bizarre, Iris started to laugh. It boomed suddenly out of her, breaking through the dark, ringing through the house. Ruby, poised outside the bathroom, clutching her towel (she'd brought her own, not trusting Iris's to be quite up to her standard) and toothbrush, scowled. The woman's lost her senses, she thought. It's a disgrace. She thought she would get up early tomorrow morning and leave without saying goodbye to anyone.

In the end she didn't leave. She rose shortly after six, when the house was quiet, and tiptoed down to the kitchen, pausing, holding her breath at every creak. She was filling the kettle for a cup of tea, because it didn't do to set off anywhere first thing in the morning without a cup of tea inside you, when she saw Chas in the garden.

Before the frosts, he'd put in onions and spring cabbage. Now he was here to plant garlic. Ruby had noticed Iris's garden and thought it messy. Messes bothered her, so she was delighted Iris had taken the trouble to employ someone to come clean it up. And someone who would start so early. Impressive.

Chas visited Iris's garden long before she was up as he had to do it before he went to work. After he finished, it was too dark.

However, he'd been observed coming down the front path at seven, and it had been assumed he'd been in the house, or more specifically in Iris's bedroom, Iris's bed, all night. This didn't particularly bother him, he thought people who spread scandal a waste of time. Then again, it hadn't occurred to him what these rumours were doing to Iris's reputation. His mind was full of the vegetables he planned to plant in the spring, and the roof he was repairing for the Stones who'd recently lost a cockerel and who had asked Chas to fit double padlocks on all of their movable henhouses. These were the things he thought about, along with the early arrival of the geese this year, and the rowan trees which had been stripped of all their berries before the end of September and what that might mean in terms of the winter ahead. A sign, he thought, of a freeze to come. He thought about the book he was reading about the life of early settlers in Montana, and how he'd like to go there one day.

Ruby plugged in the kettle then set off up the garden, mind set on telling this gardener chap about the importance of pruning roses, weeding flowerbeds and clipping hedges. The necessity of these chores and the shame their neglect might bring on Iris crowded into Ruby's mind as she strode up the lawn. By the time she reached Chas, she did not bother with niceties. 'I hope you're planning to do more than fiddle with my daughter-in-law's vegetable patch when there's a deal to be done round here. These hedges are a disgrace, the flowerbeds need seeing to and I don't know when the grass was last cut.'

Chas looked at her. 'I can see all that.' He continued to plant the garlic, ignoring her.

Ruby stood waiting for a further response, some affirmation that the jobs she'd mentioned might get done. When that didn't come, she asked, 'Don't you speak?'

'Oh, yes,' said Chas, 'I speak. In fact I'm known as quite a speaker. I like a chat. And when I chat, some of the words I use are "hello" and "good morning" and even "nice day".'

Ruby considered this. She felt a little embarrassed, she had been rude. 'I stand corrected,' she said. 'Hello. I'm Ruby, Iris's mother-in-law, and are you going to prune the roses?'

'Hello, I'm Chas. I don't know what my relationship with Iris is or how to define it. And I am not going to prune the roses. Rose pruning is not part of our deal.'

'Deal?' said Ruby.

'We have a deal, and roses weren't mentioned in it.' Chas split a garlic bulb into cloves, laid them out across the area he had prepared and started planting.

Ruby stood watching, then said, 'I see.'

Chas straightened up. 'I plant the veg, look after them, and she gets to use whatever she wants in exchange for the use of the land. That's the deal. She'll save a bit on the grocery bills come next summer which will be fine considering . . .'

'Considering what?' said Ruby.

'Considering she's a bit pushed for money with her man passing away,' said Chas.

'I'm sure Iris is perfectly comfortable, teacher's pay, no rent on the house . . .'

'Look,' said Chas, 'I know all about it. She told me. But it's all right, I don't gossip. I know about her husband and his gambling.'

'Gambling? I don't know what you mean,' said Ruby.

Chas knew then that he'd blabbed. He returned to the garlic and said no more.

Ruby went in to make her cup of tea. By now it was almost seven o'clock, she could hear Iris moving about upstairs. Ruby thought it too late to steal away. She sat, keeping her own counsel, staying out of the way while the morning moved into full bustle.

Once Sophy was away, Iris collected her books and handbag and told Ruby to make herself at home, she'd pop over at lunchtime to see how Scott was.

Ruby could not, however, wait till lunchtime. 'Did Harry gamble?'

Iris nodded. 'Yes.'

'Well, lots of men like a flutter.'

'Harry liked more than a flutter,' said Iris. 'He gambled away everything. We lost the house, everything.'

'I don't believe you,' said Ruby.

'No, I don't suppose you do. But he did. I had to sell the house to pay off his debts. So I came here because there was a house with the job.'

'You could have stayed with me.'

'I needed to come somewhere new. Fresh start. That sort of thing. Look, I have to go.' She stopped at the door and stared at Ruby who was sitting at the table looking pale and bewildered.

'I don't understand,' she said. 'Harry wasn't like that. He wouldn't do such a thing.'

'That's what I thought,' said Iris. 'I'm sorry, I really must get across to the school. We'll talk about this at lunchtime, or tonight when I've got more time.'

Ruby watched Iris walk through the garden, stop and chat to Chas. She heard their voices chime through the chill air.

'Morning, Chas.'

'Morning, Iris.'

'What's this you're planting?'

'Garlic.'

'Oh, yum. I love garlic. Don't suppose you're free next Friday? We're having dancing classes and I need a man to make up the numbers.'

'That'd be fine. I like a dance.'

'So do I,' said Iris. 'It's friendly, don't you think?'

Chas nodded.

Ruby watched. Iris seemed so different now. Not the quiet girl Harry had married. There was a confidence about her, a no-nonsense cheeriness. The morning breeze lifted her hair. She stood with all this scenery about her, hills and trees, and the way her skirt flapped round her legs, and she carried her books in the crook of her arm, smiling at that gardener fellow, you'd think she hadn't a care in the world.

Chas finished planting the garlic. He picked up his trowel and bag of compost and walked down the path to his car. Waved goodbye to Ruby. Colin was coming out of his gate, face newly scrubbed, hair dampened flat to his skull. He looked at Chas and a little smile creased his face.

'Morning, Colin,' said Chas. 'See you at the swimming next week.'

Colin did not speak, but he nodded, and the little smile deepened into something impish and cheeky. Chas felt something within him stir. People thought Colin a soul. Not Chas. He thought Colin a little silent fighter, a keeper of his own counsel, a stubborn boy who was, in the face of loneliness and loss, surviving. Chas liked him.

Colin, still smiling, crossed the road and entered the school gates. The Missie was standing at the door ringing her bell. 'Come on, Colin. Lazy bones, you live nearest the school and you're always last to arrive.' She patted his head as he passed. Colin, still smiling his little smile, went into the classroom. He was feeling fine today. He was wearing his yellow swimming trunks.

Emily walked sourly back down the track to her cottage after dropping Gracie off at the school gates. It was damp. Long grasses soaked her canvas shoes. Her skirt hem felt heavy. Trees moved in the breeze and the sound of leaf against leaf and the slow creaking of branches heightened her isolation. Pigeons burbled throaty conversations from the depths of the boughs overhead. Lonely, lonely, lonely, she thought. She crossed the garden to the cottage, past the browning, dead sunflowers and the neglected vegetable patch. Hens clucked and scurried away from her. She stopped to watch them, vaguely ashamed of not locking them up at night. A fox could get them, or they could get chilled. She was sure it couldn't be good for any animal to spend nights outside in the deep of November. Tonight she'd see them safely tucked up in the coop they'd been in when they were brought to her. She went to pick up a hen that was sitting in the flowerbed beside the hedge. It watched her approach, moving its head slightly, beady eyes alert. She picked it up and crooned, 'Poor old hen.' Then she spied it on the ground among the thyme she'd planted, small and brown and perfect. Oh, joy, an egg.

It Has Been a Day

When Iris returned home at lunchtime, Ruby was gone. Scott was at the kitchen table, eating a sandwich.

'Has Ruby gone home?' Iris asked.

Mouth packed full, he nodded.

'I said I'd see her at lunchtime,' Iris said. 'I'd hoped she'd stay for a chat.'

Scott swallowed. 'You had a chat last night.' He smirked.

Iris made a face. 'She thinks I'm being a gadabout. Frolicking in the backs of cars when I should be sitting, face to the wall, mourning her son.'

Scott snorted. 'Were you frolicking?' This was hard. Iris was, after all, his mother.

'No, I was not. I have a perfect right to an evening out. I like going out with Michael. He's good company.' She was sounding indignant. As if Scott too was about to accuse her of indecently flirtatious behaviour.

But he wasn't. In fact, to Iris's surprise, he agreed with her. 'Yeah, Michael's great. But I wouldn't want him for my dad.'

'I have no intention of marrying him. Good heavens, we've only been out twice.'

She had been flustered by Scott's words, the suggestion that she might marry Michael, a man she hardly knew, had merely dined with two or three times. How irritating. You have a curry with a man, and a swift kiss, and there you are on the verge of walking up the aisle together. She was giving vent to her exasperation when the full implication of what Scott had just said dawned on her. 'What do you mean, Michael's great? You know him? How do you know Michael?'

Scott thought, Oh, Christ. I should keep my mouth shut. He knew Michael from the Deer and Thistle where they were both lunchtime regulars. Before Jake had left, he and Scott would meet in the pub at lunchtime for a pint. Or two. And they'd run into Michael who knew he was called Scott, but had no idea he was Iris's son. To him Scott was simply Jake's young and callow hippy pal, whose name had slipped past him when they were introduced. Scott had sat at the table where Iris had sat, had quaffed beer with Michael and Jake. They had spoken about many things, but mothers was not one of them.

Now, he swigged deeply from his mug of tea and wildly tried to think of some acceptable place they might have met. He couldn't say Michael had given a talk at school because Iris would surely mention it next time they went out together. So he shrugged. 'Don't actually know him. I've just seen him about.'

Iris said, 'Hmm,' and left. She didn't believe him. Something odd was going on, she thought. But the suspicion melted into the heat of a dreadful afternoon. Maybe because she was worried about Ruby's disappearance, or because she was occasionally revisiting that kiss, or because she was looking through a theatre programme planning a Christmas outing, for a few minutes she was engrossed in something that took her mind off the class. And a few minutes was all it took.

They had been making lentil pictures. Lucy had got carried away, and had used up all the lentils she had been told to share with Fiona. Fiona had been infuriated by this as the sudden dearth of lentils meant she could not add a final flourish to her picture of an autumnal tree, leaves turning to shades of brown. Fury boiled suddenly, redly, and Fiona, never a child to stifle her emotions, emptied a jar of water over Lucy's head. Lucy screamed, and retaliated instantly by setting about Fiona, fists flailing. Fiona defended herself by pulling Lucy's hair.

'Girls, girls!' shouted Iris, jumping from her chair.

Meantime James seized the moment. Billy Ramsay, a year younger than James, bore the cruel nickname Pig because, facially at least, he resembled one. It was a monicker Iris discouraged, though she could see why it had arisen. Billy had not been fortunate when his nose had been formed, there was definitely something porcine about the boy. And how, when Iris was not about, he suffered. James, though, had recently revealed his own weakness. He hated water. At this week's swimming lesson, he had refused even to enter the swimming pool and had sat on the edge, wearing a vest as well as his swimming trunks. Chas had advised against coaxing and cajoling the boy. 'Let him come to it himself on his own terms,' he told Iris. 'We could put him off for life.'

But children can be brutal, pitiless. Billy, seeking vengeance for his own heartless nickname, had been taunting James all day whenever Iris was out of earshot. 'Chicken,' he'd said. 'Scaredy.' And worst of all, 'You're a girl. Yellow.'

Now that the class was in uproar shouting, 'Fight, fight,' James turned and grabbed Billy's pencil case. In one easy movement he emptied it, snatched up all Billy's prized pencils which had been sent to him by his Aunt Peggy in Philadelphia and were decorated with the American flag, with BILLY RAMSAY inscribed in gold letters up the side, and snapped them all in two. He put the fragments back into the pencil case and swiftly, violently, dumped it back on Billy's desk.

Billy responded to this by shouting, 'Ya bastard!' The child had a powerful voice – Iris had the notion it would have its uses in the end-of-term play she was planning next summer – and strength enough to start hitting James over the head with his school satchel.

'Boys, boys!' shouted Iris. 'Stop that immediately.' She rushed up the class towards them.

Maybe it was the excitement. Or the heat in the room. But Lorna Hay, who was at the best of times a thin, pale, sickly-looking girl, threw up. Mid-rush, Iris heard that unmistakable sound of regurgitated food hitting the floor. Her heart sank.

'I don't feel very well,' said Lorna.

Indeed the girl had turned a worryingly green shade of pale.

Iris laid a hand on her brow and felt the fever. 'We'd better take you into the dining room.' She summoned Lucy to come too. 'Let's get you dried off. James, Billy, I'll be talking to you later.'

215

Effie appeared from the kitchen with shovel and bucket and mop. 'It's been a day.'

It had indeed. Iris was glad when it was over. She had scolded James and Billy roundly, thought about insisting James buy Billy new pencils. But these particular ones were not easily replaced, and the boy had been taunted. She decided they would both stay in class at breaktime and lunchtime for a week and do extra work. Lucy and Fiona would join them. She hoped there would be some bonding. She phoned Lorna's mother, but got no reply, so the child was wrapped in a blanket and excused lessons for the rest of the afternoon.

Scott went to see Emily, praying he was forgiven for arriving in the middle of the night with a cockerel. She was looking, for the first time in over a week, happy. She'd just eaten a fried egg sandwich. Yolk had run down her chin and she had moaned pleasure, scooping the runaway streams of yellow back into her mouth with her fingers. Christ, she was sick of baked potatoes and lentils.

Mellowed by food, and needing to celebrate her good fortune further, she allowed Scott into her bed. When their passions were spent, they did not talk but lay together listening to the sounds of the November afternoon outside. Leaves moving, hens busying themselves just beyond the window, and from somewhere the smell of autumn burnings. This, thought Scott, was all he would ever want.

'It was wonderful,' said Emily. 'I don't remember enjoying it so much.'

'Really?' Scott glowed pride. He was getting better at this. 'Want to do it again?'

Emily looked away so he wouldn't see her smile. She'd been talking about the egg.

Iris, for the first time in her life, poured a drink as soon as she got home. From the depths of her strict Presbyterian childhood there remained the notion that it was somehow immoral to take alcohol before five in the afternoon. Except, of course, at Christmas, then she could drink whenever she wanted. But today, as Effie had so eloquently put it, had been a day. And, come to think of it, so had yesterday. So, she considered a drink necessary. Vodka in large measure, tonic in small. She lit the living-room fire, watched flames lick round the coal and disappear up the chimney. Wriggled her feet free from their shoes, put them up on the sofa, lay back and sighed. Soon she would phone Ruby, and sort things out. But now, a moment to herself.

The doorbell rang.

'Scott,' she called. 'Answer the door, will you?'

In the house nothing stirred. Scott was not here. Cursing, Iris put down her drink and went to open the door herself.

It was the Reverend Woodman. 'Mrs Chisholm, I hope I'm not disturbing you. I thought I might have a word.'

'Of course, come in.' She stepped aside to let him past.

In the living room, he smelled the drink. He was a drinking man himself, mostly whisky. But he was partial to the odd gin if it was offered.

'I just poured a drink,' said Iris. She'd considered, though only for a tiny moment, apologising for being caught taking alcohol before five in the afternoon. But then she thought this was her sin, her hangup. And why should she excuse herself, anyway? She was an adult, she could do what she wanted. So she invited him to join her.

He refused. 'A bit early in the day for me.'

Iris thought to say it was for her, too, but it had been a day. But didn't.

He sat in the armchair where only last night Ruby had sat looking censorious. 'I wanted to talk to you about a number of things,' he said. 'There has been some concern expressed about your teaching methods.'

Iris said, 'Oh? Perhaps those who are concerned should speak to me personally.'

'Perhaps. But we have our ways of doing things round here. And usually they elect me to pave the way, as it were, to do the talking.'

Iris said, 'Right.'

'There is the matter of the prayers at lunchtime. I believe you let the children all have a turn at saying their own little prayer?'

'Yes. Though it's hardly a prayer, more a communication. To get them to open up. They were a closed and silent lot when I came. It's a way of getting them to talk openly about anything that's bothering them. I don't imagine God would object.'

'No. It just seems at times a little . . . jocular.'

'It *is* jocular. Why shouldn't prayers be jocular? I always thought God had a sense of humour.' She was about to elaborate on this but demurred. Something told her this was not the time for frivolity. 'And I think children should be introduced to religion gently. A prayer is a plea for forgiveness, or an offering of thanks, or a reaching out for help. But they all have their problems and speaking them out loud gives a little ease. It also makes them eat their lunch, and I always find a full child is easier to teach than an empty one.'

'I think the swimming lessons are a wonderful idea,' he said, praising her before tackling his last concern. 'And Jane, my daughter, loves coming to school.'

'She's very bright,' said Iris.

'She's learning poems by Spike Milligan. I'm more of a Wordsworth and Keats person myself.'

'Indeed,' said Iris. 'Keats isn't your normal nine-year-old fare. They need to learn some poems by heart. They love Milligan. Though I'll be touching on Wordsworth later on, when Jane's about to go to the High School. We won't be doing any literary analysis, just a bit of language appreciation,' she said, lowering her voice, sounding firm. She swigged her drink. 'Would you like a cup of tea?'

He shook his head. 'We never see you in church on Sundays.'

'That's because I'm never there.'

'Don't you think you should set an example to your pupils?'

'I set an example every day. But on Sundays I leave the example-setting to you professionals and have a lie-in.'

'I was wondering, Mrs Chisholm, about your faith. Do you have faith?'

'Yes, Mr Woodman, I do. I have faith in many things. Religion's one of them.'

'Fair enough,' he said. Then braced himself for the trickiest matter he'd been saving till the others were dealt with. 'I'm sure you won't like my mentioning your private life . . .'

'How right you are. No, I won't like you mentioning my private life. But no doubt that won't stop you.'

'You could say it has nothing to do with the people in the village.'

'I could indeed. In fact, I will. My private life has nothing to do with the people in the village.'

'But, Mrs Chisholm, this is a small community and things are noticed. And you are, after all, in charge of our children.'

Iris swigged deeply. 'What on earth do you mean?'

'Your affairs, Mrs Chisholm.'

'Affairs? S, plural? I'm having more than one? Well, lucky me.'

'There is Anthony Smith.'

'Anthony Smith!' Iris exploded. 'I've met him twice. And though I'm clearly meant to be a woman of loose morals, they're not *that* loose. I met him once at my interview for this job, and there were other people in the room. I'm sure they'll confirm that Anthony and I did not get up to anything naughty then. Second time was in the classroom with all the kids present. I like my sex in bed, lights out, nobody watching. And I prefer it with someone I know, not a vague professional colleague.'

'What about Charles Harper?'

'My God!' said Iris. 'He does the garden. Comes early in the morning. Often he's gone before I even see him. He's been spotted, hasn't he, leaving my house at dawn? And so the conclusion has been reached that he's been here all night.' She tutted. 'People with narrow lives and narrow minds. I don't know.'

'There's Michael Kennedy.'

'That's it,' said Iris. 'Enough. What I do in my own time and with whom is my business. No more.'

'We are concerned for our children, that's all.'

'You think I'm going to start having orgies in front of my class somewhere between multiplication tables and elementary geography? Rumours,' said Iris. 'Rumours. I have been out with Michael twice and nothing improper has happened, but if it did, and it might, I think I'm allowed. Who exactly has been spreading lies? And who has been listening to them, wide-eyed, tongue hanging out? This is pure gossip, foul and nasty. And, oh, isn't it lovely to believe vile things about other people? Things you wouldn't do yourself. It reaffirms your goodness. For good you surely are – except that you listen to and believe tittletattle about other people.'

'*I* do not believe in or listen to gossip. It is my job to come here and talk to you about the concerns that have been expressed to me about you, and to remind you of your position in this community.'

'Well, thank you for that. Now, I think you've had your say. I'll take heed. And if, or when, I start engaging in any untoward activities, I'll let you know by hanging a large pair of bloomers with "consummation has occurred" written on them from my bedroom window. And then you can come tick me off about my lecherous behaviour.'

Reverend Woodman put his hand to his mouth. He thought he might laugh but didn't want to show it. 'They would have to be extremely large bloomers to get all that written on them.'

'I shall ensure,' said Iris, 'that the fellow I choose has the where-withal to buy them before I allow any naughtiness to take place.'

He said that would be fine, and he'd look forward to seeing her message when she hung it out of her window, and now he should be going. Iris showed him to the door.

The Manse was not far from Iris's house. He walked. He did it at a measured pace, along the street, through his gate, up the drive, in at the front door – and only when it was shut behind him did he burst out laughing. He thought Iris fun, he liked her and wished he had accepted a drink or a cup of tea. It would have been more friendly. He had the impression they'd parted amicably, that he'd been diplomatic. It didn't cross his mind that revealing the gossip going round about her had made her furious.

Iris stamped about her house, full of impotent rage. There was nothing to be done, nobody to vent it on. She went into the kitchen, circled it a couple of times, then walked up the hall into the living room. She sat down. Got up again, and fumed. Poured another drink. 'Affairs? Me? Are they mad?'

'What affairs?' said Scott. He'd just come in, heard the word 'affairs', and needed to know more.

'Mine,' said Iris. 'Apparently, according to local gossip, I'm having three. Well, that was at last count. I passed a man in the street yesterday and said good morning to him. Maybe now *he's* been included in the list, whoever he is.'

'Who are you having affairs with?' Scott needed to know this, too.

'I am not having an affair with anybody,' said Iris, and stumped to the kitchen. Scott thought, I am. He wished he could tell. Share this thrill, this boundless joy he felt whenever he thought of Emily. But he couldn't. His only friend was Jake, and he could hardly tell him he thought his wife fabulous in bed. Besides Jake was not here to tell. Scott couldn't bear to speculate what was going to happen when he returned.

And he was not about to confess to his mother he was carrying on with the mother of one of her pupils. So, he had a secret. Actually, now he thought about it, he had more than one. Not only was he the cockerel thief, but last week he'd been told not to return to school unless he had his hair cut. He'd thought, Fine, I'll quit school. Drop out. He was sure that in time, with love and gentleness, he could persuade Emily to run away with him.

Iris, in the kitchen, started to peel potatoes. 'Affairs, plural, with an S. Me. Hah! Cheek of people. How dare they?' She put down the potato, looked out of the window. Affairs? If only. 'God, it's been a day.'

Everybody Knows

Iris always believed that everyone was special, in some way, even if only a little. Some people shone openly, vibrantly, and some people flowered shyly in secret. In any school class there were always stars, and Iris worried about them. It did not do, she thought, to shine too young. To peak at ten seemed, to her, pretty near tragic. So many children had she encountered who at six or eight or eleven seemed to have the world at their feet, kings and queens of their classes, then at fifteen or sixteen seemed confused, defeated by life in an older school world, wrestling with algebra or French. They'd slipped from glory. Pretty girls with bows in their hair who turned into gum-chewing backrow lurkers, too caught up with teenage traumas to look inside books, or brash playground boys who frittered away their schooldays giving their whole selves over to sex, cigarettes and God knows what else, she thought, instead of keeping their natural lust for unhealthy follies to the weekends. Oh, my, she thought, say a prayer for the silly ones.

And there were the shy ones, who said little and hid from the limelight. Then they'd find themselves, who they were, what they wanted to be, and quietly shine. And she'd scold herself for not noticing them sooner, thinking they'd been shining secretly for long before it had become apparent to her. There were also, and these children worried her most, the undistinguished, the middle-of-the-road kids who turned up to school day in, day out, and never showed any real aptitude for anything. They came and they went, they did their sums and did enough to get them by, nothing less and certainly nothing more. She feared for them. If they did not push themselves, did not try for greater things than ordinariness, they might never know failure, but then, they'd certainly never know the joys of triumph.

There was Rosalind Jackson, for instance, who sat beside Lorna Hay and day in, day out, hardly said a word, rarely bothered to put her hand up when Iris asked the class a question. Yet she did her set work adequately. She seemed to sit in a small daze, not totally lost in her own world but not quite with the rest of the class either. Regularly, Iris would stop speaking, mid-sentence, turn to Rosalind and ask, 'What did I just say, Rosalind?'

And, word-perfect, Rosalind would tell her.

I also teach those who only sit and stare, Iris thought.

And there was Billy Ramsay, an outwardly unremarkable child. He also sits and stares, Iris thought. He did his work in school and his homework. He joined in class activities. His accomplishments were right on line for his age. He was behind in nothing, neither was he ahead. Not that Iris expected any more than that. She just thought everyone was special in some way, and looked to find that special thing in every child she taught. She didn't care what it was, she was not seeking genius, just something to let the little ones who crossed her path know they mattered.

So the day that Billy Ramsay sang was a good day. Friday afternoon, a chill fog outside, curling and shifting slowly, and inside the class was running on empty. Spirits were flagging, children were lolling over their desks, arms spread.

'What a sleepy lot,' Iris said, crisply. 'What's got into you all?'

'It's Friday, Miss,' said Simon Vernon. 'We're knackered.'

'Oooh, knackered,' said Iris. 'Good word, but don't use it if the School Inspector is here.'

Usually, on Friday afternoons she read her class a story. But today, she thought not. They'd just fall asleep. 'We'll sing,' she said instead.

There were complaints. 'Awww, miss!'

'We'll sing.' She was adamant. 'What will we sing?' Crossing to the piano.

The class was resigned. She was going to do this. And they were going to sing.

'Campdown Races,' shouted Fiona.

'Yes,' agreed James.

They liked this song, they liked the words. 'Oh my Sal, she is a spunky gal'. Lyrics that made them giggle.

Iris knew this, but, well, they would giggle, wouldn't they? Fiona and James were on the cusp of growing up. Giggling was part of that. 'Fine,' she said. 'Good choice. Get out your song books.'

She was not a piano player of note, but she could bang out a chord or two. She struck up. Then Billy did that embarrassing thing, he came in too soon, starting several bars before everyone else. 'Oooh, de Camptown ladies sing this song . . .'

A voice that was pure and crystalline and lovely filled the room. It soared. It was golden. A silly stomp of a song was transformed into something flawless, nearly sacred.

Iris stopped playing. 'Who was that?'

She turned, surveyed the class. No need for anybody to own up. Billy was bright red.

'Billy?' said Iris. 'Was that you?'

He nodded.

Iris gazed at him. Don't gush, she told herself. Don't embarrass the boy. Don't put him off. 'You naughty boy. You never told me you could sing.'

He looked down at the desk. 'Sing all the time,' he told it. 'Sing at home.'

'But, Billy, you have a voice. It's wonderful. What do you sing at home?'

'Songs.'

'Of course,' said Iris. 'Silly me. What sort of songs?'

And unbidden Billy sang 'Hard Times'. The sound of woe filled the room. ''Tis the song, the sigh of the weary, oooh . . .'

Every head in the room turned. And when he'd done, the children and Iris clapped. It was a rendition so pure that when it was over she looked out of the window to see if the mist had lifted. But it was still there, hanging on to the branches of the trees across the road, shifting, swirling, soaking.

'It was wonderful,' Iris told Sophy that evening. 'I didn't know he could sing.'

'Why should you? Bet you never asked. Bet you hardly noticed he was there. Bet you've got your favourites that get to do all the teacher's pet things like clean the board.'

'Not true. I have a rota for that. Everyone gets a turn.' Iris defended her egalitarian attitude to blackboard-wiping.

'Well, you should have noticed he could sing. All sorts of people sit unnoticed in classrooms. Winston Churchill . . .' she searched her mind for other maligned pupils '. . . and other people. John Lennon. Albert Einstein. P.J. Proby.'

'I think you're making things up to make your point,' Iris accused.

'Am not,' said Sophy. Then rushed on before Iris asked her to prove her claims. She knew nothing about P.J. Proby's education. 'Anyway, the Ramsays are quite well-known, they go out singing all over the place. Folk songs. They play instruments, the guitar and such like. Everybody knows that.'

'Do they?' Iris had an image of the Ramsay family sitting of an evening round the fire, singing mournful songs about the crops failing and sailors lost at sea. She supposed it wasn't really like that, but knew now why Billy hadn't mentioned his singing. No need for approval from the teacher when he had plenty at home.

'And you're planning to use the poor Ramsays in some way in your school, getting them along to give a concert, or to teach folk songs. Or something.'

Iris didn't reply for it was true. She was.

'You teachers,' said Sophy. 'You all think you're God. Bullying people into doing things. Manipulating people. Bossing people about. And then, with other people, not even noticing they're there.' And with that, she got up and left the room. And, Iris heard, the house.

'What's up with her?' she asked Scott.

He shrugged. 'Dunno. Maybe she wanted more than fish fingers for her tea.'

'Well, that's all I could get from the dammit shop,' said Iris. 'I was sure I had lamb chops. I just couldn't believe it when I opened the fridge and they weren't there. In fact, I was positive I had them. How could something like that disappear?'

Scott shrugged again. Then looked away so Iris wouldn't see his guilt. For, indeed, she did have lamb chops. Scott had taken them to Emily, feeling the poor woman needed more than eggs and potatoes. She needed meat to keep her strength up for the baby she was expecting that Scott vaguely thought might be his.

In the cottage at the end of the muddy winter path Emily and Gracie had just finished the lamb chops along with a cabbage stolen from the garden next to Iris's and rosemary that Emily had grown. And very good it had all been, too.

Sophy stood in her favourite place at the edge of the field by the hedge where her garden met next-door's. A sycamore grew there, old and comforting. She would lean against it. When she'd arrived in Green Cairns, she'd look up into its branches and see nothing but dark boughs and green. Now what leaves the wind had not taken were fading, dried, curling yellow and brown at the edges, and looking up Sophy could see the sky, a gleaming moon shafting through the mist.

'I want to go home,' she said. She said this several times a day. When her mind idled these words slipped into it. She wanted to go home. And home wasn't the schoolhouse in Green Cairns, it was that house miles and miles away where she'd lived with her mum and dad. She had been happy there. Or at least, the way she now remembered it, she had been happy there.

Now her days were filled with dread. It was only a matter of time before she was unveiled as the writer of the dirty message on the school wall. By now, in her imaginings, the punishment was dire. She'd moved from public humiliation, being beaten, expelled, to being reported to the police for defacing a government building. She pictured herself in the dock awaiting sentence. Borstal, a remand home for unmanageable girls. She imagined her mother visiting on Sundays, tutting and scolding, telling her this was what happened to vandals.

Eric, the cat, came to see what she was up to. Pressed against her legs, purring. Sophy picked him up, and wept into his silky coat. She'd miss him when she was put away. He was all she had to talk to these days for Jean, her very best pal, had a new love. He lived three miles away, up the glen, and evenings she'd cycle to his house where they'd play his Rolling Stones records, and kiss till his mother knocked on the door with a mug of tea and a plate of biscuits, a sign that it was getting late. School tomorrow.

So Sophy hugged the cat, and dreamed. She dreamed her father came to her, here beneath the tree, and said, 'It will be all right. Don't you worry.' And sometimes she dreamed that Kenneth, Jean's dad, found her here, and took her to him, and said, 'We'll go away together. You'll never have to go back to that school ever again.' This was her favourite dream. She sighed, wiped her damp eyes on her sleeve and went indoors. She'd play her horn. She didn't care if she wasn't musical. It helped, in the midst of worry and despair, to make a very loud noise.

By the end of November, Iris and Stella were friends. On Wednesdays, swimming days, Stella would come to school before it was time to leave for the baths, and join Iris for a cup of tea and a chat in the dining room.

Seeing this as favouritism, other mothers started to drop by for tea also, though they did not come without an offering, a chocolate cake or a tray of flapjacks. 'For the little ones,' they'd say. They'd be invited in, and soon found themselves coerced into helping in class, sorting out lentil pictures, joining in the dressing-up, reading a story, taking a turn in the dancing class.

Music hurtled, on these dancing days, from the open windows of the school, skirled through the frosted winter air, and outside people passing would quicken their steps in time. Stella danced. There was freedom in movement. She'd take a young partner and join the jig, whirling. Iris's voice would soar above the din, shouting instructions as she danced. 'Twirl in the middle, and twirl the person on your right. Now into the middle again.'

228

Chas chastised her. 'You're such a boss! You'll put them all off dancing for life. Dancing's meant to be fun.' And he took her in his arms, waltzed her the length of the room. Twirled her, and waltzed her back again. And let her go.

The swiftness, suddenness, of this took Iris by shock. He left her breathless and flustered.

'Don't do that,' she said. 'You took me by surprise.'

'Don't you like to dance?' he asked.

'I do. I love to dance.'

'Well, then.'

'What do you mean, well then?'

'I mean, well then.'

They stared at one another.

'Well then, dance. If you like it so much.'

Iris walked away, trying to smile. Trying not to let the people around her see how unhinged this swift cavorting up the classroom, past desks swept aside for the afternoon, had made her. Later, alone, she would think about this. Not the dance, but how it had made her feel. Rattled, disconcerted. She realised why this was: Chas had made her join in. Of course she joined in dancing with the children. But when she did that, she was in charge, she called the instructions. She led the way, it was her party.

Then, for a few fleeting seconds, she had danced the dance, what it was really about. Looking someone in the eye, moving with them, twirling with them, smiling with them. Contact. She hadn't allowed herself that with anyone since Harry died. Oh, there had been Michael's kiss, she'd given herself to that. But all the time his lips were on hers, she'd known she could just open the car door and run away. So she hadn't given herself wholly. And, very, very briefly, she had to Charles in a joyous, cheeky waltz. She had joined in, and kept nothing back.

She usually kept something back, something of herself. Something private. She laughed, she smiled, she taught children, but there was always a little bit of her that kept back, looked on. All the swift comments, all the telling people what to do, went on despite her grieving. That long mourning persisted, a constant hum in the recesses of her life, in the background. So, she never, ever, except for that dance with Charles, really totally joined in.

It was what teachers did. They performed in the name of maths, English, history, geography, basic writing and reading skills. And they performed in any way that worked for them, strictly, jocularly, in a friendly manner or a distant one. Whatever it took. Which was why so many pupils were surprised to find a human being with private passions, hobbies, a family, lurking beneath the front. There had been a moment when he was whirling her round and round and she'd been breathless, pink-cheeked, laughing, feet off the ground, when the teacher, the private mourner, had been forgotten and she'd been Iris again. And that had upset her. Turning, moving, frenetic music battering out, she hadn't been in control. Iris thought about this, thought about the look on Chas's face, determined, concerned, smiling but not mocking, and she thought, He knew. The wily bastard knew exactly what he was doing.

Stella had laughed. 'Ooh, Iris, you've been swept off your feet!'

'Not at all,' she'd said. 'Just showing how it's done. Just letting Chas know I can keep up with him.'

And Stella had laughed some more. She laughed a lot on dancing afternoons. At herself, her mistakes, mostly. The laughter, she worried, was sometimes near to hysterics. There was so much to worry about when she wasn't moving in time to music, taking hold of little hands and skipping past lines of clapping people. She fretted her way through every waking moment, and at night, in the dark, that fretting turned into crazed anxiety. She worried about worrying so much. Her health would fail, she'd get an ulcer. Be whisked into hospital, and what would happen then? Now she worried about those dancing moments when her worry lifted and she laughed sometimes till tears ran down her cheeks. Those tears of mirth, she knew, could easily turn into outright weeping, then convulsive sobs, and she'd collapse in a whimpering heap in front of everyone in the classroom. When times are hard, she thought, it does not do to laugh too much.

She had been to see the bank manager to plead for an extension of their overdraft. She'd told him there were many enquiries about bookings for next year, and in fact many people had simply booked when leaving this year. She'd lied. Aware of Stella's exaggeration, the bank manager asked if the bookings had been firmed up with deposits.

'Not as yet,' she said crisply. 'We don't ask for that until February. Things are a little tight at the moment, and if we don't move forward with our plans and make necessary repairs they could start going downhill. It's important to keep up the standards our guests have come to expect.'

He'd stared at her mildly. He was used to bullshit. He knew the Vernons had a good business idea, knew they worked hard and knew why things weren't working out. He would have a word with Binnie when he next saw him. He extended their overdraft for a year and added a thousand pounds to their limit. He doubted it was enough to see them through the winter.

Stella, meantime, had gone to speak with Binnie. She had asked if he would please not leave his tractor halfway down the track to the cottages, thus stopping her guests from entering or leaving. She told him they couldn't afford to pay for the use of the track, but perhaps she could do something else by way of payment. 'I could clean for you,' she offered.

He stared.

'Or perhaps John could do some sort of farmwork. He's very good at repairs. All sorts of things.'

Binnie had stared harder. He had no intention of letting Stella clean. He didn't like strangers in his house, poking at things, meddling. But repairs, farmwork for free, he'd think about that. So he'd said, 'Aye, well.' No more.

Stella had left in a state of apprehension. She'd expected a yes or a no. This slow 'aye, well' disturbed her. What exactly did it mean? She told her husband about it.

'He said "Aye, well"?' said John. 'That's encouraging. I like the sound of that. At least he didn't say "No".'

Stella had looked at him in disbelief. Sometimes she thought it hell to live with a perpetual optimist. If only he'd come into the hole she was in, join her in her darkness and despair and worry, she wouldn't feel quite so lonely. Binnie is going to exploit us, she thought. He knows how broke we are. He knows. Sometimes when she took the twins to school and met other mothers at the gate, caught their looks, Stella thought, Everybody knows.

So Wednesday afternoons she swam. Joined the children in the pool, spread herself into water, lay on her back floating, working at not thinking. And Thursdays she danced, hot and sweaty, and sometimes only music and movement filled her mind. Sometimes she would look at her watch and think, Oh, my, how wonderful. I have had fifteen whole minutes without worrying.

Iris wrote to Ruby. Six in the evening, the sounds of Sophy's French horn booming painfully through the house. Iris shut her eyes. If she'd known it would sound like this, she'd have veered Sophy gently in another direction. Sometimes the noise, the force of it, drove all reasonable thought out of Iris's mind, and the only words she could muster were, 'Shut up!' Though she never voiced them out loud. Who knows? she thought. Maybe one day it will start sounding sweet, musical even. Maybe the girl had hidden talent, maybe she'd grow up and join an orchestra, play solos. Then a slow, deep, long and laborious blast would halloo out, and Iris would think, Then again, maybe not.

Dear Ruby, she wrote. Upstairs the horn blasted and blew.

I'm sorry you left before we could have a chat. I realise how hard it must be for you to think that there was a side to Harry that you, or indeed I, did not know. But, I'm sorry to tell you, he was a gambler.

Before he died he lost all our money. I had to sell the house to pay off his debts. There was no life insurance or pension left. He'd lost it all. I appreciate this must be a shock to you . . .

. . . Not nearly the shock it was to me, though, Iris didn't write.

It is hard to learn new and disturbing things about someone we love. But there it is, Harry was a gambler. And not a very good one, considering the amount I now have to repay.

I came here to escape. Not my responsibilities, they follow me. But I do not want to be in the place where Harry moved about, living his other life. I do not want to think any more about why he did this. I do not want to think that he might have been unhappy with me, or his children. And I love those children. They are both doing well, here. They have settled in and made friends.

Yes, Iris thought. We are, all three of us, settling down. And she believed this, her children were getting on with life.

I came here, to think. To be the Missie. I wanted a fresh start. I'm sorry if you think I've been speaking badly about Harry. It's not true, I haven't. Please get in touch, so we can talk.

She stared at the letter now. Couldn't think of anything more to say. She'd end it there.

Hope you are well . . .

And here was a problem. She couldn't write 'Yours sincerely', it sounded too formal. 'Love?' No, Ruby wasn't a love person. And I don't love you, Ruby. Not at all.

Best wishes, Iris.

There. She put the letter in an envelope, sealed it, addressed it. Thought, Well, at least I've tried. And decided to reward herself with a cup of coffee and crackers and cheese.

Only there were no crackers. She was sure she'd bought some yesterday. Sophy and Scott must have eaten them. These children just eat and eat and eat, she thought. The food I'm going through. There was also no cheese. Knew it, thought Iris.

In the smoky cottage, Emily and Gracie finished their crackers and cheese and leaned back replete, patted their bulging stomachs and sighed.

Panto Night

By the end of the first week in December, Iris had been out with Michael four more times. Four curries and four kisses. And they'd all been splendid. The curries filled with exotic aromatic flavours, the kisses warm and moist.

'It's as far as I want to go,' she said to Morag on the phone. 'A kiss is all the physical contact I can take. It's far too soon after Harry to go further. I don't want to go all the way.'

'All the way? Listen to you,' said Morag. 'So old-fashioned! You sound like something out of nineteen fifty-two.'

'Nineteen fifty-two was a very good year,' said Iris. 'I enjoyed nineteen fifty-two. Though I don't think there was a lot of sex about then.'

'Course there was. People didn't talk about it. Didn't analyse it. Just did it.'

'It would appear I was missing out way back then as well,' said Iris.

'Yep,' said Morag. 'Everyone about you has been having a wild old time, and you have been content with kisses.'

Nothing wrong with kisses, Iris told herself when Morag rang off. Anything more is too complicated.

The school was caught up with Christmas. It always came too early for Iris who often considered campaigning for Christmas in February. Such a dreary month, it could do with something to brighten it. But now there were things to do. The children always made cards, and ornaments for the tree. They had to practise their carols for the service on the last day of term. There was a party to organise. And there was a trip to the panto, next week.

This trip, this panto business, had got a little out of hand. Iris had written to every parent asking for written permission to take their children to town by bus to see *Cinderella*. As a footnote she'd added that she'd appreciate help from some mothers to keep an eye on the pupils. All the mothers had offered to come along. Knowing that if she invited a few chosen mums to join the panto trip it would be seen as favouritism, Iris asked them all to come. Problem solved, she thought. Ordered a bigger bus, and changed the block booking at the theatre.

But then Stella asked if her husband John could come. The twins were going. She was going. John would be left alone. 'A night out would do us good,' she told Iris. 'Things have been a bit fraught lately.'

'Of course John can come. The more the merrier,' said Iris.

On hearing that Stella's husband was going, other mothers asked if their husbands could come, too. Then, with both parents going, younger children who were not of school age and could not be left at home alone had to come along. As did some older children who had gone on to the High School but were still not of an age to be abandoned for an evening. After that a few grans, grandads and aunts thought a night at the theatre might be fun, and asked if they might join the party. All this was conveyed to Iris in notes brought in to school, in phone calls to her at home, and in the street when she was shopping across the road at the dammit shop. In the end almost everyone in the glen was going on the school outing, three buses and a huge booking at the theatre.

The only mother who did not want to go was Emily. Scott said that Christmas pantos were boring, he didn't want to go either. On the tenth of December he and Emily would have the cottage, indeed, it seemed, the whole glen to themselves. He was counting the days. Not that Emily did not let him into her arms, and her bed, at the moment. In fact Scott was very much in favour right now. His acne had completely cleared up. He suspected his welcome in Emily's bed probably had a lot to do with the food he was supplying.

As well as the lamb chops, crackers and cheese, Scott had provided Emily and Gracie with an apple pie, several cartons of yoghurt, bacon, sausages, some fish, tomatoes, lettuce, tins of tuna and a deal more. Iris was puzzled by all this. She knew growing children ate a lot, but this was absurd. Her continually emptying fridge meant she had to stock up from the dammit shop, which she could ill afford, especially as prices there were considerably higher than in the supermarket in Forham. This was made worse by the number of people who waylaid her on her way to and from the shop asking if they, their mother or some other relative could join the party going to the theatre. She didn't, in theory, mind being waylaid. But in practice what should have been a brief conversation lasting a few minutes took a long time as it was explained to her who the relative was, where he or she lived, what they did for a living. And, along with all that, there was usually a rundown of the relative's personality, quirks, fads and previous history. Iris now knew that Fiona Wilkinson's aunt had been married twice, worked as a vet's assistant in Forham, had three children all too old to attend her school, grew a wide range of exotic rockery plants, made her own wine which was lethally strong, especially the parsnip, and had been arrested when she was twelve for shoplifting two pens from Woolworth's. More than I need to know, thought Iris. Her smile would glaze on her face, for as she listened, and tried politely to excuse herself, she imagined that in her kitchen her children were standing at the open fridge slowly munching their way through everything it contained.

When the evening eventually came, Scott was ready. Using four weeks' pocket money, and two weeks' lunch money, he had bought two bottles of wine, lying to the assistant in the supermarket in Forham who'd asked how old he was. 'Twenty-one,' he'd said. Adding that everybody asked him that, he had a young face. A nice touch, he thought.

He watched as the three buses slowly filled. Jokes and laughter filled the crystal, frosted evening. Iris moved through the throng with her list of panto-goers, shouting names, checking everyone was here. Scott felt proud of her, which surprised him. He usually thought of her just as Mum. But there she was, taking charge. Bossing. Which was something she did extremely well, he thought.

Not long ago, he'd seen her pale and gaunt with worry and grief. Now, she seemed like a different person.

That was what old people were like, he thought. You never really knew where they were in their heads. There was his mother moving through her life, talking, laughing, making new friends. Anyone would think she was light-hearted. Yet sometimes, when she thought she was alone, her face changed, darkened, as she wrestled with her ghosts. Then she'd catch him watching her, and her face would light up, she'd smile. 'How was school, today?'

And his face would change as he wrestled with his own ghosts. 'Fine,' he'd say. Hoping she would not notice the worry. The lie. How would he know what school had been like? He hadn't been there. He'd passed the day wandering about town, sitting in the park. He'd spent his lunch money on a pint in the pub, and some chewing gum to hide the smell of alcohol on his breath. This was what he'd come to, wandering aimlessly, worrying and hiding his secret life behind his face when his mother asked him what he'd been doing.

He wondered if Emily hid her own secret thoughts behind her face. She always seemed pleased to see him. If Gracie wasn't about she'd come to him, put her arms round his neck, kiss him. He suspected this had more to do with what he might have brought her than any pleasure his presence gave her. He thought he might be buying her favours, and cursed himself for that. Every time he left her, sleeping in her bed, he vowed he would not return. But he was always drawn back. The excitement, the wrongness of it, the heat, her body, those moments of being lost in passion when he forgot everything, the warmth of her bed, there was so much he couldn't resist. Then he'd come home again, stick his head round the living-room door, say 'Hi' to his mum, if she was still up. And his face would not show all the things he'd been doing.

That was the thing. When he was little, if he had any pain he howled, any joy he laughed and squealed. Now he tried never to cry. When he laughed, it was a short snort, rarely did he let go and guffaw or giggle. All the pain and joy he felt, he hid behind his face. Iris did that, too. Maybe sometimes, as she was standing teaching, she wanted to double up with pain at the loss of her husband, but she couldn't. She just carried on. Maybe all those faces clambering on to the buses hid secrets, sorrows. Maybe that was why all the grown-up faces he peered at looked taut. All the things people knew, all the things they did, were concealed.

But tonight he was not going to conceal his happiness. Tonight he and Emily would eat together, a candle-lit meal. He'd brought candles from Iris's kitchen cupboard. They'd talk softly. Listen to music. Then they'd move to the bedroom. Light incense sticks, and make love as the night glistened outside and the room filled with musky scents. Tonight nothing mattered. And there would be no secrets hidden behind his face. He'd let his love show.

It was a beautiful night. A night for doing beautiful things. He walked the track down to Emily's cottage, the ground beneath his feet frosty hard, his breath splaying into the air, bottles heavy in the plastic supermarket bag. He dreamed the coming evening in his head, what he and Emily would do, what they'd say, how it would be. He was electric with anticipation. Erotic anticipation.

It made him shy when he entered the cottage. 'Brought you stuff,' he said, handing over his bag of goodies.

She took it, peered inside. Glowed appreciation. 'Wine, great. Steaks, wow.' She went into the kitchen, emptied the bag on to the table. Then sat down.

Scott had been hoping for more than this. In his mental rehearsals of this evening, she had thrown her arms round him, kissed him, then started to cook as he opened the wine. Their talk would be as mellow and rich as the fermented grapes they'd be drinking. She'd lean on the cooker as the steaks fried. Glass in her hand, she'd look at him with longing. Instead she sat. Not long before Gracie had left to go to the panto, they'd eaten omelettes. Emily wasn't hungry.

Scott offered to open the wine. Emily nodded, but made no attempt to fetch the corkscrew or glasses. They sat, at opposite ends of the table, saying nothing.

That was how Jake found them when he entered the kitchen. 'Hi,' he said. Quietly, coolly. He'd thought to come into the house casually, as if he'd only been away for ten minutes, not months.

Emily glared at him. 'Where the hell have you been?'

'Around,' said Jake. 'Aren't you glad to see me?'

'No,' said Emily.

Scott didn't know what to say. He thought, Fuck you, Jake. Turning up now.

Jake spotted the goodies on the table and went to inspect them. 'Hey, wine. Steaks. Cheesecake. Cool.'

Scott had bought a slice of chocolate cheesecake as an afterthought. He knew Emily liked chocolate, while he preferred cheese. This seemed an excellent compromise which they could share before bed. Or maybe even in bed. Afterwards, in a mutual orgasmic glow, putting forkfuls into each other's mouths. This evening had been planned down to the smallest detail. Now it was all going wrong.

Jake put a hand on Scott's shoulder. 'Thanks for taking care of my lady.' He rolled his eyes towards the door and jerked his head slightly, indicating he wanted Scott to leave.

So Scott said, sheepishly, 'I'll be going, then.'

'OK,' said Emily.

And Jake said, 'See ya.'

And Scott stepped out of the kitchen, through the living room and out into the night. The track was cold, in the trees an owl called. Grasses rustled. Everything that had on the way to the cottage heightened his excited, yearning senses, now added to the ache in his trembling heart. He walked backwards, staring at the way he'd just come, thinking Jake or Emily might rush after him, call him back to share, at least, the wine he'd brought them.

But no.

Home, he climbed the stairs to his room, and lay on his bed. He was a fool. Jake and Emily would be drinking the wine, kissing, making up for their months apart. She'd be sitting on his knee, arms round his neck, fingers in his hair. She'd be saying his name. Jake would have one arm round her, and in the other hand a glass of wine. Or maybe he'd just drink from the bottle. Scott pulled his pillow over his head and cried like he had done when he was little. Only now he knew nobody would come to hold him, or kiss the sore bit better. He couldn't tell his mother what had happened.

He had nobody to tell. He would have to hide his grief behind his face.

His tortured imaginings about what was going on in the cottage at the end of the track were wrong. Emily and Jake were fighting. Their dispute was chaotic. They moved from room to room, shouting.

Emily was at full rant. 'You didn't get in touch! I didn't know where you were. You could've been dead!'

'I'm not dead,' said Jake. 'Look at me.' He waved his arms about, danced a tiny jig to prove there was still life within him. 'I've got a pulse.' Hands on his chest. 'My heart still beats.'

'Well, fuck your heart,' was all Emily could think to say.

'Aaaw, Emily. That's a shit thing to say.' Jake moved towards her.

Emily walked out of the kitchen, into the living room. 'Where the hell have you been?'

'Went to the anti-war demo. Got my ribs kicked in. Went to Cornwall. It's great there.'

'You went to Cornwall! What about me? I've been alone here. Nobody to talk to. It's all weather here, that's all there is. Fucking weather. You could have phoned.'

'We don't have a phone,' he said, reasonably, he thought.

'You could have written.'

'I don't want the postman coming here. I don't want people to know we're here. You know there's stuff I don't want people to find out about.'

'You could have phoned Scott, and he'd have come and told me where you were.'

Jake shrugged. He hadn't thought of that. 'I stayed in a squat in the Cromwell Road for a bit.'

He'd stayed in a squat. Caught a dose of clap. Been to a clinic. And was never going to tell Emily about it. For the most part, his months away were a haze. He vaguely remembered going to Cornwall. Looking down from some cliff into sea so clear he could see fish moving through perfect water, and sitting on an ancient

241

wall outside a pub, drinking beer. Living in a cottage up a winding street. A girl with long black hair, and eyes heavy with mascara. Her name, however, was gone. For the most part, it was a blur. In fact, he wasn't sure how he'd got there. He thought he must have driven, because he had driven home from there. He knew he'd done that because the van was at the door. And as there was nobody else here, he must have been the one behind the wheel.

Trying to piece things together was difficult. He'd gone to Aberdeen to get some dope. There was always stuff there on account of the oil. He'd been in Union Street and someone had said there was going to be a big anti-Vietnam demo in London. And he'd said, 'We should go.' So they had. He must have driven to London. When he was there, moving carefully, on account of his broken ribs, someone had said there was a great scene going on in Cornwall. So they'd gone. That was it, really. There was a multi-coloured hole where his summer ought to be. He wished now that he'd thought to phone Scott to tell him to tell Emily where he was. But recapping on his past months, he didn't think he'd been capable of thinking anything. 'I had a great time,' he said now. Stupidly.

'Well, I'm glad someone did,' said Emily. 'I've been living here on this broken bit of land, reading Sylvia Plath, watching rain.'

'Cool,' said Jake. 'That's so beautiful.'

Emily picked up a cushion, which was the only thing to hand, and threw it at him.

He went back to the kitchen. Opened the wine and started to drink. Then came back into the living room. 'Hey,' he said. 'This is how it is. Didn't we say we wouldn't chain each other down?'

Emily agreed. They had. Only she hadn't known at the time what it would be like to be alone with a small child in a cold cottage with very little to eat and no money. 'I couldn't go anywhere. I was living on lentils and potatoes I picked up from the fields. I hate it here. I hate it. Hate it, hate it, hate it!' She stormed from the room, into the bedroom.

Jake followed.

'Get out of my bedroom,' said Emily. 'Go away.' Then she let go, lost control, started screaming, 'Get out! Get out! Get out!'

Hands raised in a show of innocence, Jake backed out. 'I hear you, OK? Don't lose your cool.' He took Scott's wine, sat on the sofa, swigging. He hated arguments. Why didn't Emily just chill out? He wasn't going to hold her down. She could do whatever she wanted. She could have gone away, too. Except that she had no money, but apart from that she was free. That was the deal, they were both free. And then – the long journey north, the fight, wine – he passed out.

Hearing the silence, sensing it was more than Jake not speaking to her, Emily emerged from the bedroom. She saw him deep in a semi-coma, poked him. He barely stirred. She put a tentative hand in his pocket, felt some money and pulled it out. A pile of used and grubby notes, not what she'd wanted. She rolled him over, rummaged in his other pocket, and found some change. She pulled on the mutual fisherman's jersey and set off up the track. The village was a graveyard still. Not a sound.

Emily opened the door of the phone box, lifted the receiver, and dialled. When she heard the familiar voice at the other end say, 'Hello,' Emily said, 'Mum?'

A Baby

The panto, Iris thought, was a success. She had spent most of the evening watching her pupils. Their faces reflected events on stage. Except for James, who slumped in his seat and considered every-thing with detached scorn. He's too old for this, thought Iris. Too old for obvious, trivial and silly things. He would have to wait till he was old enough to want to be young again. There he was, with his face waiting for life to happen to it, nicotine stains on his fingers already. He had what Iris called television eyes, slightly bagged from hours of staring ahead expressionless at a small screen. She had never come across a pupil who could so completely remove himself from class proceedings. He could dance, and somehow manage to make the jig look like nothing to do with him. She could read stories to the class that excited the other children, made them ask questions. Made them, indeed, want more. All except James who would sit at his desk, chin cupped in palm, looking past her. Hearing, but not listening. He was never openly insolent. His disregard for adults was displayed in small gestures, a shrug, a sigh, a slight curl of the upper lip.

'Wipe the board, James.' And he'd do it. But only just. He'd always leave a bit for her to have to come over and finish for him. In the way he moved, the way he spoke, he showed his contempt not just for all grown-ups but for his own childhood. He couldn't wait to leave it behind, and waiting for his youngness to be over bored him. He was so bored, he'd turned boredom into an art form, Iris had to give him that. He was very good at being bored. She worked hard at hiding her disapproval. She knew that the young and surly thrived on it. Reproach the sulky, and they will only strive for new heights of sulkiness.

So she praised James for his sullen inadequate blackboard wiping, 'Excellent job, James. Only a small patch for me to clean up.' And for his morose dancing. 'Well done, James. A whole eightsome reel and not a smile has cracked your lips. Glad you're taking this so seriously.' And on trips to the swimming baths, 'Fantastic! Another swimming lesson and you're not a bit wet. I like to think you're mastering the theory of the crawl before attempting it.'

James responded to this with the usual upsweep of his eyes and tiny snarl. But Iris said nothing about that. She figured she was winning.

The rest of the class was lively enough. Though, of late, Colin had started to bother Iris. She had congratulated herself on having lured him out of his shell but now he seemed to have stuck halfway in, halfway out. He was communicating, only not verbally. He had mastered the art of speaking volumes by moving his eyebrows, his lips, his shoulders. He keened forward over his desk, obviously bursting with information.

'What's the capital of Spain?' Iris would ask.

And the room would be filled with raised arms, little voices saying, 'Miss! Miss! Me, miss!'

Iris would see Colin alive with the answer. 'Colin?'

But he would still whisper the answer to Lucy, who would say, 'M . . . Madrid.'

'Excellent, Colin,' Iris would say. And Lucy would convey the praise.

Colin even managed to join in the singsong on the bus going home. His head bobbed from side to side during 'Ten Green Bottles'. He even looked dejected when the one green bottle accidentally fell, then cheered again when there was nine left. But he still did not speak. Sometimes Iris thought she wasn't winning at all.

After the buses pulled into Green Cairns, people disappeared into the night. It was too cold to linger. They hugged their coats round them, their cries of departure and thanks ringing through the icy air. The buses, engines grumbling, turned and disappeared back down the road. Iris was left standing on the pavement with Gracie.

'Doesn't look like your mum is coming to take you home.'

Gracie shook her head. 'She's maybe gone to bed and forgotten about me.'

It surprised Iris that Gracie should be so matter-of-fact about not being remembered by her mother. Some children Iris had encountered would stay children all their lives, and some, like Gracie, were six going on forty-two.

'I'll just go home,' said the little girl. And set off at a confident pace.

'I'll come with you,' said Iris.

But Gracie wasn't keen on this. 'I can manage on my own.' She liked the walk down the track. And to make it now, alone, near midnight, was an adventure.

'I know you can,' said Iris. 'But it's been fun tonight. If I walk you home, it'll make the evening last a little longer.'

Gracie stopped walking, turned and looked straight up at her. A piercing gaze. 'No, it won't. You don't want to walk down that track. Not in them shoes.' Pointing at Iris's four-inch heels. 'You just want to make sure I get home safe. Because if anything happens to me, you'll get into trouble.'

'Well, Gracie, you've got me there. It's true that if something happened to you on the way home, I'd be in trouble. So let me take you home.' Iris held out her hand.

Gracie took it, and pointed the way ahead. Iris thought, No, Gracie is forty-two going on six. She doesn't resent or despise or even distrust grown-ups. She just has us all sussed, and, in her young way, has no reservations about telling us. So, Gracie led Iris down the track to the house, confident and unafraid of the dark. Iris quietly wished that when it was time for her to go home again, Gracie would lead her back.

'Are you looking forward to the Christmas party?' she asked.

'Oh, yes,' said Gracie.

'Santa's coming,' Iris enthused.

'Santa Claus?'

'Well, that's the only Santa I know.'

'I don't believe in myth figures,' said Gracie. 'Santa Claus, the

247

Easter Bunny, the tooth fairy . . . they're all inventions to make us suspect to religious dogs. That's what Jake says.'

'Does he now?' said Iris. 'I think you mean susceptible to religious dogma.'

'Yes,' said Gracie. 'Only I don't know what it means.'

'Right,' said Iris. 'Well, I believe in myth figures and mister figures too, like Santa. He's coming down *my* chimney.'

Gracie said she wanted to believe in him, but Jake wouldn't like it if she did. So she believed secretly, especially on Christmas Eve, just in case he didn't come to her. 'Best be safe,' she said.

Emily was in the kitchen when they arrived. She seemed mildly surprised to see Iris, and not in the least concerned that Gracie had been left to come home alone.

'I thought I'd see her safely to her door,' said Iris.

'Oh, Gracie's fine. She knows the way,' said Emily.

Gracie stood looking at her slumbering father, sprawled on the sofa. 'Jake's back, then.'

'Yeah,' said Emily.

Iris said, 'Jake? That's Scott's friend. Has he been away?'

Emily said, 'Yeah,' once again.

Gracie said, 'He's been away for ages and ages.'

Iris detected a certain discomfiture in Emily, but ignored it. 'Only I thought Scott had been coming down here to see him.' She looked round. There were two steaks on the kitchen table, blood seeping through the wrapping. She wanted to say they'd go off if they weren't put away somewhere cool. But really, it was none of her business.

'Scott comes all the time to see Emily. He brought her a hen.' Gracie told her.

Emily said, 'I think it's time for bed, Gracie.'

'And he brought lamb chops, and all sorts of stuff.'

'Bed,' said Emily.

'And he . . .'

'BED,' said Emily.

Gracie gave a dramatic sigh, and went through to her bedroom.

Emily said, 'Thank you for bringing her home.'

Iris said, 'No problem.' Headed for the door. 'Jake is Gracie's father?' she wanted to know.

'Yes,' said Emily. 'He's been away and now he's back.'

Iris nodded. She gave Emily one last, long look and left. The woman was pregnant, Iris noted. Four months, maybe five. How long had Scott been coming here? She made her way across the yard in front of the cottage, past the hens. Scott had brought Emily a hen? What an odd thing to do.

She picked her way up the track, wishing she was home. It was cold, here, and bitterly still. Rustlings in the long grass made her heart freeze. She comforted herself that the small noises she heard were only the movements of tiny night animals, but still she tried to quicken her pace. Not easy in shoes that were fashioned to be worn on dance floors or to the theatre. Lamb chops, she thought, Scott took my lamb chops to Emily Lynne. She stopped as the truth hit home. The baby, she thought. That woman is expecting my son's baby. Oh, my God! She reeled. He's only seventeen, she thought. He's too young. The scandal, she thought. My son with one of my pupil's mother. What am I going to say? He'll have to provide for a child when he's still one himself. Well, we'll just have to manage. She stopped, stood with hand over mouth. I'm going to be a grandmother. The stupid little fool, hasn't he heard of condoms? I'll kill him.

Once home, she stormed up the stairs, shouting, 'Scott, I want a word with you.'

And Scott, who had been watching from his bedroom window as Iris took Gracie's hand and set off for Emily's cottage, moaned and turned over in his bed. He feigned sleep when Iris came into his bedroom.

'The Lynne woman is pregnant,' she said. 'Is it yours?'

Scott gave a light snore.

'Don't pretend to be sleeping,' said Iris. 'You can't fool me. I know when someone's sleeping. Have you been having an affair with Gracie's mother?'

Scott opened his eyes. 'Sort of,' he said.

'Sort of?' said Iris. '*Sort of*? You don't sort of have an affair. You do or you don't.'

'Well, yeah,' said Scott. 'Only it wasn't like an affair. It was sort of like sex 'cos she was lonely.'

'And now she's having a baby.'

'Yeah,' said Scott.

'And you took her my food?'

'Yeah. She was hungry. Jake was away and she'd no money, so I took her some stuff to keep her going.'

'And she slept with you.'

'Yeah,' said Scott.

'What am I to make of that? How could you be so stupid?'

Scott thought of saying it was easy. But looked down at his bedclothes and said nothing.

'Is there anything else you haven't told me?' Iris wanted to know.

Was this the moment to tell her he'd been skipping school rather than face whatever punishment would be dealt him for refusing to cut his hair? Was it best to get all the bad news over in one appalling revelation or serve it up in more acceptable portions? Scott didn't know but shook his head. 'No,' he said.

'Well,' said Iris. 'You are going to have to take responsibility for your child. Obviously, since you are not earning, I'm going to have to help. But you can find a part-time job, and do your bit.' She got up. 'We'll talk about it in the morning.' She crossed to the door. Stopped. 'What was that about you giving Emily Lynne a hen?'

Scott put on his best innocent expression. 'Dunno,' he said. 'You must have picked it up wrong. I never gave a hen to anybody. Where would I get a hen?'

'I have no idea,' said Iris. She scrutinised his face. There was definitely something very odd going on here. She'd get to the bottom of it, she swore to herself she would.

Next day, they all slept in. In the heated rush and bustle of getting out to school, the getting in one another's way, finding shoes which had been kicked off and left where they'd landed, gathering books, there was no time for discussion.

'I'll see you when you get home,' Iris said to Scott.

He said, 'Yeah.'

Sophy sat moving Rice Krispies about her plate.

'Are you going to eat them or play with them?' Iris said.

'Play with them,' said Sophy. 'There's no point in eating. We all just die in the end.'

'Well, that's true,' said Iris. 'But you've got quite a while and quite a few plates of Rice Krispies to go before that happens. So eat up. You don't want to miss the school bus.'

'I don't want to go to school,' said Sophy.

'You have to go.'

'Why?'

'Because it's the law. And if you don't you'll end up stupid.'

'I *am* stupid,' said Sophy. 'What's the point of school if you're stupid?'

'You are not stupid,' said Iris. 'Everyone has to go to school. I went.'

'And you went to college to learn to be a teacher. And you're still stupid.'

'What the hell do you mean by that?'

'I mean, you don't know anything that's going on around you.'

Scott kicked her ankle under the table, and shot her a vicious look. Sophy retaliated with a meaner look. Then relented. If she told on Scott, for she knew he was truanting, then he'd tell on her. She was sure he knew about the silly verse. They held one another in a fierce hostile glare, then looked away.

Guilty secrets.

'Well,' said Iris, 'I'm beginning to find out.'

Gracie was not at school. Iris supposed the child was tired after her late night. At lunchtime she would go to the cottage to find out if Emily was all right. She was, Iris was sure, expecting her first grandchild. And Iris had found to her surprise that she was warming to the idea of having a new person in her life. She wasn't hugely keen on babies, but children she loved. She could take her grandchild on walks, they'd chat, read stories, play games. It would be a fine child, strong, healthy. She'd make sure it didn't develop television eyes. Little snapshots of the relationship ahead formed in her mind. She thought she might enjoy this. She pictured herself holding the first of a new generation in her arms, and was strangely moved.

'Em's not here, sorry,' said Jake when she got there.

'When will she be back?' Iris asked.

Hens moved, crooning softly, round her feet. Dead sunflowers hung their seed-filled heads. From inside the cottage Bob Dylan sang 'Love Minus Zero', a song Iris liked.

Jake shrugged. 'Woke up and she was gone. Taken Gracie. I don't know when she'll be back. She left a note. She's gone to her mother's.'

'Where's that?'

'Somewhere in Liverpool.'

'What do you mean? She's your wife. You must know where she came from.'

He shook his head. 'Not married. I met her folks but I never went to their house.'

'But you've been with her for years. She had your daughter, you *must* know where she lived.'

He shook his head. 'We didn't talk about those things.' He turned and walked back into the cottage. 'We wanted to be free. No past. No hangups.'

'But . . .' Iris said.

'It's our way. We wanted to be together as we are now, not as we were before we met. We wanted just to be us, no rules, nothing like that. The places we came from were behind us and full of people who had houses, cars, things. We don't need any of that. It's all so materialistic. We live our own life. Love and no jealousy.'

'And no myth figures,' said Iris. 'I think it's dreadful you don't let Gracie believe in Santa. She's a child. She has a right to some magic. Remember being a child yourself? When you looked into a puddle, and made believe it was an ocean. When you jumped a small fence, and believed you'd leapt to the moon. When you ran about with arms spread and believed you were a pilot, and you were secretly mighty. You could do anything. And,' getting carried away, 'come Christmas, you stared up at the sky and you'd convince yourself you could hear sleigh bells. The world was alive with wishes and hopes and you couldn't wait for morning. You left out cake and sherry and a little something for the reindeer. The world was bursting with promise and everything glistened. Don't you remember that? Shame on you for denying little Gracie. She deserves a few years of wonder. She'll be a long time grown up.' Her own outburst took her by surprise. She sniffed, and was about to apologise. What people chose to tell their children was none of her business.

Jake looked down at his feet. 'I know. I'm sorry. I just got carried away. And she's so bright, she soaks everything up. Everything.'

'And what about the baby? When is it due?' Iris asked.

Jake said, 'What baby?'

'The woman's pregnant, you must have noticed?'

He shook his head. 'No. She didn't tell me.' Then he said, 'Christ.' And sat down on the sofa, running his fingers through his hair, shaking his head. 'I don't know when she's coming back.'

In the early morning a car had slipped carefully down the track, stopping at the cottage door. Emily's parents had come for her. After her phone call last night, they'd driven six hours through the night to find the daughter they'd thought was lost to them. Emily had sat in the kitchen, waiting. When they arrived the greetings were swift and tearful. Emily had put her few belongings in the back of the car, lifted up the sleeping Gracie, wrapped in blankets from her bed, climbed into the back seat with her and gone home. She needed comfort.

That night Iris told Scott that Emily had gone. 'She's somewhere in Liverpool. I don't know where.'

He said nothing.

'We could try to trace her,' Iris suggested. 'What's her last name if it isn't Lynne?'

Scott shrugged. 'Dunno. I don't do last names.'

Iris said they'd have to wait and hope Emily returned, they'd sort out something then. What, she wondered, would Jake say? She wondered if he was as free thinking about his relationship with Emily as he said he was. Love and no jealousy? She doubted that.

Christmas Parties

Both Sophy and Scott were looking forward to Christmas. Two weeks free from the trials of school or the trials of dodging it. Scott planned to stay in bed for hours every morning and spend the rest of the time watching old movies on television. Sophy planned to play her French horn and read about death, something she'd been thinking about a lot.

A few days ago, the headmaster had issued every pupil with a sheet of blank paper. He'd demanded that anybody who knew the name of the writer of the rude verse that had appeared on the school wall, and had now of course been scrubbed off, should write it down. Nobody was to put their own name on the paper. The person who revealed the secret graffiti artist would remain anonymous.

Sophy had stared at her blank sheet, then written 'ME'. She had folded the paper, and put it in the sack in the main foyer where all the other papers had been put. Forty-seven other people had also written 'ME'. Seventeen had said it was Elvis. Forty-four had said it had been John and Yoko. One had said it was Jack the Ripper. Dennis the Menace got several votes, along with Ghandi, Chuck Berry and Ho Chi Min. The headmaster had said, 'Pah!' flung the papers in his waste basket, and announced that in the new term he personally would interview every single person in the school. 'I will,' he said, jabbing his desk with his finger, 'get to the bottom of this.'

Sophy had gone for several days in a state of deep dread, and had almost wept with relief when the results of the paper poll were announced. But the interview now loomed. She considered death an option, but didn't really want to die. Still, it fascinated

255

her. She wondered what it felt like. What her father had experienced. Her own death experiments had moved from holding her breath while lying under the water in the bath, hair floating about her face as she gazed upward into the steamed room, to putting a plastic bag over her head, feeling it stick hotly to her cheeks, nose, mouth, until she was caught in a tiny tight airless bubble, wide-eyed. Always, gasping, she'd pull it off, and think: Nearly. She'd nearly touched the deep blackness. Stepped close to the abyss.

James, too, was jubilant at the thought of two school-free weeks. No late lie-ins for him, he had to help on the farm. But he relished the thought of fourteen whole days with no visits to the swimming pool. He loathed going with the class. Girls giggling, Mrs Chisholm shouting encouragement, clapping at every small advance her pupils made. The way she shouted, 'Well done.' He'd imitate her, bobbing his head from side to side: 'Oooh, well done, Lorna.' And raise his eyes heaven wards.

The worst thing was Colin.

Colin could swim. It was his joy. Ploughing through water, blood, muscles, heart, lungs, everything pounding. And that fleeting moment of glory when he touched the far edge of the pool, before flipping round and pounding back up the pool again. James hated that. He wanted to be the one doing it. But, being denied that triumph, sat at the edge of the pool, watching, refusing even to enter the water.

He would look at Colin and think, 'Fat boy.' Only he knew this wasn't really fair. Colin wasn't fat any more. He'd grown, and the swimming had streamlined his body. Shoulders squaring, waist thinning, muscles in his thighs and arms. No longer rotund, Colin was now boy-shaped.

James felt churlish, sulky, brooding, and enjoyed it, in a way. Seven of the class could swim easily up and down the pool and the rest of them were nearly there. He was the only failure, a matter in which he took a deal of pride. The Missie wasn't interested in him, after all, she only wanted to win some damn silly competition. Bring a little glory on herself.

'Come on, James,' she'd call. 'Get yourself wet. Jump in. Not scared, are you?' Goading him.

He'd shake his head. 'Not scared. Just can't swim is all.'

It went round and round. The more Iris cajoled, the more James sulked, and quite enjoyed sulking. The more Iris goaded, pleaded, bullied, the more James sank into himself and found some deep inner comfort in being the black sheep, the bad boy. It was very satisfying. Chas bothered him, though. The man would look at him, and smile softly, and leave him alone. James found this oddly upsetting.

Several times a week Chas would go, in the late-afternoon, to tend his vegetable patch in Iris's garden. There was no real need for this, the soil was soft, black and not a weed grew on it. Winter, and nothing much was doing in the ground, everything lying deep, deep under the earth, waiting for spring. But he liked being there. He liked hearing Iris's voice ringing from the school, and the sounds of children at play. He liked the sound of hoe on black loam, evening geese clattering across the sky, keening to their roosting places. The neat, fat cat sitting at the edge of the lawn, watching him. The thin song of chaffinch and robin in the hedges. The smells of coal and logs burning in houses nearby. The feel of winter on his face.

He'd muse. Unearthing a worm, he'd considered its lifestyle. An invertebrate and self-reproducing. Handy, he thought. But is it fun? 'Do you enjoy yourself, worm?' he asked. Considering his own empty sex life, his lonely bed, he thought it might be some relief. But what would it be like to mate with yourself, and produce only replicas? Lots of little Chases. He didn't like the thought. Children should be a little bit of you, a little bit of her, and little bits of other people, ancestors long-gone that you knew nothing about. And you'd wonder where your infant got this or that trait. That was their delight.

And sex with yourself wasn't the same as sex with someone else. A brief moment of release, was all. But someone in your bed was a weight beside you, a breathing warmth. Softness to hold, smell, touch. To spoon into, in the dark, under the blankets, when outside the cold wind blew.

He chipped the ground and wondered why he grew vegetables. There was a thrill in seeing them fatten and turn ripe but, truth be told, he didn't like vegetables. 'Potatoes are fine. I like a plate of new potatoes, fresh from the ground, hot and white, waxy and running with butter. But cabbage you can keep. And sprouts. Waste of space, sprouts.' He didn't know why he grew them. Fruit was another thing he hated. He didn't know why he bought it. Apples, bananas, pears, rotted in his fruit bowl or at the bottom of his fridge. Then he'd throw them out, and buy another lot. 'Why do I do that?' he asked. 'I hate fruit.'

Chip. Chip. The hoe on the loam.

By now Iris had left the school, was walking briskly across to her garden, arms full of books, jotters, bag swinging at her side. She saw Chas and waved. As as she passed him heard his lament, 'I hate fruit.' Not stopping on her way to the heat of her kitchen and a cup of tea, she said, 'Oh, I love it.' Then pausing, turning, 'Especially pears when they're fat and ripe, and you bite into them, and the juices run down your chin. I love that.'

She went indoors, made a mug of tea for herself and coffee for him. He was, as he'd told her often now, a coffee man. She took it out to him. He stood, hands clasped round the mug, warming himself, and said it was grand. Meaning everything, the coffee, the heat of it, Iris's company, and this spot with the geese honking overhead, and the evening closing in. The darkness deepening on the copse on the hill, turning grainy, then velvet. He sometimes thought he could reach out and touch it, but it would only envelop him.

Iris agreed it was indeed grand, meaning a cup of tea at the end of the day. 'Why won't James swim?' she asked. 'Why does he just sit and look sour?'

'Because he can,' said Chas. 'He probably wanted to do what Colin did. Take off swimming. But he didn't. See, Colin swims because nobody told him he couldn't. I expect he's always been told he couldn't do this, couldn't do that. So there he was in the pool, nobody looking at him, telling him he was useless, and off he went. Since James can't do that, he does what he can do: sit and look dour and broody. Leave him be.'

'I need my hundred percent to win the prize,' said Iris. 'They all have to swim.'

'I don't think the other bairns will allow him to let you down. Leave it to them. They're cruel, conniving little sods sometimes, children. Then they surprise the hell out of you by being wonderful.'

Iris sighed and agreed. Sipped her tea, and said it was grand. But this time she meant the crisp air, the encroaching velvet dark, the keening geese, and the smell of pine logs burning nearby.

Iris had always found Green Cairns hall alluring. It was a small wooden building with long eaves that reached nearly to the ground, set against a small copse at the far end of the village. The ground in front of it was unkempt, but had once been carefully tended. Now the roses had turned wild, but in summer lupins still shoved through the undergrowth. Ivy crawled over the hall. At Christmas that ivy was strung with sturdy, weatherproof, multicoloured lights. It was here every year that the Christmas party was held.

This party was one of the big events of the glen calendar. It was usually held a fortnight before Christmas to give people, so the joke went, a chance to recover before the twenty-fifth. Then they had another week to recover from that before New Year. At any rate, if the nods and winks were anything to go by, Green Cairns Christmas Party was a full-bodied, booze-raddled, lusty affair.

Iris was going with Michael. Chas had asked her but too late, she'd already accepted Michael. 'I'll dance with you,' she offered. He told her it would have to do.

She had ordered a new dress – a plain, red sleeveless shift – from her catalogue. At the same time she'd chosen gifts for Ruby, Sophy and Scott. She would have to pay all this off weekly, over the next fifty-two weeks. It would be next Christmas before she finished forking out for this Christmas. Then the whole business would start all over again. This way, she thought, she'd be sitting at her kitchen table every Friday night writing a payment slip for one Christmas or another for the rest of her life.

It would be a difficult time for them all. Their first Christmas without Harry. She'd bought Sophy a pair of long leather boots and a purple silk caftan. Scott was getting Jimi Hendrix's *Electric Ladyland* and a leather jacket. Iris had spent some time gazing at the cover of *Electric Ladyland*, a gathering of nudes staring back at her. They don't look at all well, she thought. She wondered if any of them had caught a chill. Then cursed herself, thinking such things on seeing a group of naked women, she must be getting old. That was the sort of thing her grandmother would think. She wondered what would be the collective noun for such a group. A shiver of nudes? A wobble of nudes? A nestle, perhaps? It was good displacement activity, though. Pursuing such thoughts kept her mind off the fact that this year's presents would not be paid off till sometime after next Christmas.

Scott, at Iris's insistence, was going to the party. He was in disgrace, and had more disgrace to come when she discovered the full extent of his troubles. He wore jeans and a white shirt, a compromise outfit he'd settled on himself. Fearing Iris might object to his Frank Zappa T-shirt, he'd settled for the shirt. In fact, Iris didn't care what he wore, just wanted him to be there.

She wanted them both to be there. 'We should make a show as a family,' she told Sophy.

But Sophy was adamant. 'I hate parties. They're so false. Everyone is all smiley and happy, then next day they're all ordinary again.'

'It's a party,' said Iris. 'Everyone is happy at a party. That's why they have them.'

'I hate them. I'm not going.'

Iris said that she could do whatever she wanted. But she and Scott would be there if Sophy wanted to come along later. The girl shook her head. She was planning to stay in her room, lie on her bed and listen to her Joan Baez record. Sad songs. '*Plaisir D'Amour*', 'There But For Fortune', 'It's All Over Now, Baby Blue'. She'd play them over and over, till the sadness filled her and the room. She had two cigarettes she'd smoke, and would steal a glass of Iris's vodka. She'd read her Sylvia Plath book, and the sadness she'd feel would be huge. Death, she thought, holding her breath. I will die one day. There is nothing ahead, only oblivion. I will sink into the black mire, and there will be nothing left of me, and nobody will remember me.

She had tried playing 'We Shall Overcome' on the French horn, but the song wasn't suited to the instrument. In fact, it did not seem like any sort of protest at all when she played it, but sounded almost jolly. She hated that. In her head, and from where she was, behind the instrument, she could hear the passion, the beautiful call for freedom. But looking out at those listening, seeing, pained faces, she knew she wasn't getting her message across. And so gave up.

But tonight she'd have the house to herself. She could wallow, be profoundly sad without anyone telling her to snap out of it. She would have a bath, and lie under the water till her lungs ached, her hair floating about her face. There was something about all this gloom, this pursuit of depression, that excited her. It gave her a tingle of anticipation in the secret places she touched at night, in bed, alone in the dark.

Iris left to meet Michael at the village hall. Green Cairns was busy. Cars were parked the length of the street and people, dressed up in party clothes, and clutching Tupperware containers with their contributions to the evening, were moving along the pavement. The food had over the years become more and more exotic. Michael blamed television cooks. Once it had been salmon sandwiches, with maybe a slice or two of cucumber to add a dash of sophistication, and sausage rolls. But now Fanny Craddock had opened their eyes, 'And their stomachs,' he said, to the wonder of food.

A groaning table stretched the length of the far wall. There were four six-pound roasts of beef, a huge platter of paella, six fondues, ten pasta or rice salads, sixteen assorted chicken dishes, and a curry that Michael scorned. 'It's got apples and raisins in. That's never a curry! You don't put fruit in a curry. That's women for you, trying to get you to eat fruit by sneaky methods. I'm not eating that.'

There were cheese straws, crisps and nuts, prawn cocktails, potted shrimps, cocktail sticks laced with squares of cheese and pineapple, and more cocktail sticks with sausages and tiny pickled onions. Plus eight cheesecakes, various, four lemon meringue pies, five Pavlovas and several Black Forest gâteaux, honey and walnut cakes, chocolate cakes and mousses.

'It's the decoration gets you,' said Michael, considering a Black Forest gâteau. It was layered and heaped with whipped cream, adorned with sugared fruits and flowers sculpted from marzipan. 'Somewhere underneath all that is a cake. The rest is all frippery and fluff. I don't want that. When you eat a cake, you want cake.'

Iris wondered if there was anything he did not expound on. 'It all looks very tempting,' she said, feeling sorry she had not contributed anything. 'I should have brought something, I didn't know it was expected.'

'It isn't expected of you,' said Michael. 'You're the Missie. Missies don't bring food. They bring themselves and look at the display with approval. They'll be watching to see whose food you eat. You're going to have to fill your plate diplomatically. You'll have to sample everything.'

'I'd be ill,' said Iris.

'No matter,' said Michael, 'you have to try. And anyway, you don't want to bring something. You don't want to get embroiled in the food war. It's fierce. The competition here is worse than the county fair where people lie and cheat and almost kill to win the Biggest Onion rosette. The women here are marathon cooks, the conflict bitter and bitchy. Look at the forearms on them, muscled beyond belief, all that beating and whipping of eggs and sugar and butter.'

On the stage a four-accordion band played a rugged version of 'Please, Please Me', and people danced, or lingered, at the side of the hall, chatting, drinking. Iris had trouble recognising the mothers who turned up outside the school in hurried morning outfits, anoraks, jeans, with pale, sleep-raddled faces, now that they were made up and styled in their good-time clothes.

She saw Scott across the room, and waved. And that was all she saw of him. She decided he'd got lost in the throng. There must have been over three hundred people there. Iris hadn't realised the glen was so populated. She danced and drank and tried to fill her plate diplomatically when the time came to eat. She waltzed with Chas. He held her close, and manoeuvred her across the floor, and said very little. Every now and then he would look down at her, and smile.

But the heat, the noise, the wild swirl of the four-accordion band, several eightsome reels and two plates of diplomatic food took their toll. Iris went outside, to heave some clean winter air into her lungs and to stand with the non-dancers and smokers who lingered at the door, exchanging the crack. She was there when the raffle was announced. The high spot of the evening.

Iris had bought two books of tickets, since the money was going to charity. The prizes started at a case of single malt whisky and ended with a quarter of a pound of milk chocolates. The laird won the case of whisky, the factor who ran his estate won a haunch of venison, Binnie the local landowner and farmer won a gift set of two bottles of malt with two crystal glasses, Michael a bottle of fifteen-year-old malt, the minister and doctor likewise. Iris was next and won a two-pound box of Belgian chocolates. The minister's wife got a bottle of sherry. Binnie's wife a bottle of champagne. Someone Iris didn't know got a bottle of white wine – she supposed this woman must have been of minor importance. And down the local pecking order the prizes went, till the daughter of one of the estate workers, lowest in the scheme of things, got a quarter of Milk Tray.

Iris accepted her winnings with grace, smiled and thanked everybody. Moved through the crowd to find Michael and tell him she was leaving.

'Already?' he said. 'But the night is just beginning. This will go on for hours yet.'

'I'm tired,' she said.

Chas watched. Saw Iris's dismay, and nodded. He knew, he'd been right about her. She'd no understanding of the way of things round here, and, he suspected, never would. Michael walked Iris back to the schoolhouse, hands in pockets, enjoying the stroll, the rush of air that made him feel wildly drunk. He liked feeling out of control.

'That was a fix,' said Iris.

'The most fixed raffle in the world. It's great. They do it every year. People expect it.'

'The laird wins a case of malt? He doesn't need it. There are other people who'd love to win that.'

'He provided all the drink. It's how we thank him. The factor provided the haunch of venison, so he gets it back. Why are you complaining? You got chocolates.'

'*This* is my place in the community, a large box of chocolates?'

'You're doing well. Other Missies got smaller boxes. You came before the minister's wife. They all must be impressed by your panto and swimming efforts,' Michael told her.

She snorted.

'Ach,' he said, 'you're such a townie and city slicker. You'll never understand the ways of country folk.' He gave her a peck on the cheek and ambled off back to the party.

Iris watched him go, and thought that perhaps he was right. Hell, it was only a raffle, nothing to get upset about. It was how things were.

Scott had gone to the party, made a show of waving to Iris, and left. The noise, the crowd, the overpowering smell of alcohol and the four-accordion band playing Beatles songs, were too much for him. People came up to him in the five minutes he was there, slapped him on the back and told him he was the Missie's boy, and that was grand. He didn't know what to say.

He went to see Jake. Perhaps he could find out where Emily was, which bit of Liverpool. But Jake wasn't there, he'd gone to the pub in Forham. The hens were wandering about in the dark, pecking and scraping the ground, looking for food. So Scott went home, took Iris's giant pack of museli, and returned to the cottage. He rounded up the hens, and put them in their coop for the night. He gave them fresh water, and emptied the museli into their trough. Then he sat on the floor of the henhouse, listening to them settle for the night. It was a gentle sound. Contented. He liked it. He thought about Emily, and knew he'd never lie with her again, hold her. He was sure she was having his baby, and was filled with terror and pride. His baby, his and Emily's. But babies terrified him. So little, and noisy, and milky, and they shat in their nappies. Also he'd be a dad, and he really didn't like that thought at all.

After a while, sitting in such a small space started to hurt. He clambered out of the henhouse, and saw his jeans and shirt were covered with muck. He went home, stripped in the kitchen and dumped his clothes in the washing machine. Upstairs, he went into Sophy's room to tell her to switch off the horrible dreary folk music she was playing, and found her lying rigid on the floor, arms crossed over her chest, a penny over each eye. She was surrounded by assorted candles flickering in the gloom. At her head was a vase of plastic daffodils (she couldn't afford fresh lilies), by her side a bottle of Irn Bru she'd been drinking.

'What the hell are you doing?'

'I'm practising for when I'm dead,' she said, not moving. Keeping the pennies in place.

'Jesus, you're weird.'

'I just want to know what it feels like,' said Sophy.

'You won't know what it feels like,' said Scott. 'You'll be dead.'

'This is what Dad felt like,' she said.

'You don't know that. He didn't know that. He was dead.'

'I know he's dead,' wailed Sophy. 'I don't want him to be dead, I want him to come back.'

'He's not coming back,' said Scott. 'And you'll be dead soon enough when they find out it was you wrote that stupid verse on the wall.'

'You know it was me?' said Sophy.

'It was your writing. It was Mum's school paint. I'd hardly have to be Sherlock Holmes.'

'You're not going to tell?'

Scott saw an opportunity. He wouldn't tell if Sophy did his share of the dishes for a month.

'If you tell,' said Sophy, 'I'll tell on you. You've been skipping school.'

At this Scott said, 'Christ!' And went to his room, shouting, 'Turn down that rubbish music.'

265

He heard Iris come in, slam the front door, switch off all the lights and stamp up the stairs, muttering to herself.

'What's up with you?' he called, not moving from his bed.

'I just won a two-pound box of bloody Belgian chocolates,' she said to his door. 'That's what.'

And Scott said 'Christ' again, and did not pursue the matter. He thought that he was the only sane person in the house. After all, what had he done that was so bad? Had sex, that was all – people did worse than that every day.

Three days later, Iris had her own Christmas party for the children at school. This she considered a proper party, with jellies, ice cream, tooters, streamers and games. Chas was Santa. He wore a hired red suit, and Iris had made him a white beard and provided a pillow for him to stuff under the jacket. 'Ho! Ho! Ho!' he said, and patted his new paunch. 'Excellent,' said Iris. 'You were born for the part.'

One by one, pupils sat on his knee and whispered their Christmas wishes. When it was Colin's turn he put his lips close to Chas's ear, opened his lips . . . Iris's heart rose. At last he was going to break his silence. But no. Colin changed his mind, turned to Lucy, and whispered to her. She whispered to Santa.

Chas said, 'Oh, my, that's a tricky one. We'll have to see about that.' And gave Colin a present from his sack.

When the children had gone home, Iris asked what Colin wanted.

'I don't think I can tell you that. Wishes are privileged information. Santa never gives away a secret.'

Iris gave him a mock punch on the arm. 'Stop that. What did Colin ask for?'

'A motorbike,' said Chas. 'I don't see it happening, though.'

Iris shook her head. She didn't either. They sat.

'God,' she said, 'children's parties are knackering.'

Chas nodded. 'You can only be glad they don't drink.'

'Talking of which,' said Iris, 'would you like one? Now. You could come to the schoolhouse.'

Chas thought that a fine idea. He looked round the school room, and asked what would happen to the Christmas tree.

'I'll take down all the decorations during the holidays,' Iris told him. 'I'll take that down too.' It was almost six foot, and stood in a huge pot.

'I'll plant it in the garden,' she said. 'The children can see it grow during the year.'

'You're not putting that thing in my vegetable plot. Take it up the glen. Plant it in the forest, back where it came from with its pals.'

And Iris said she would.

Passion, and the Lack of Passion

On Christmas Eve, late in the afternoon as the sun dipped low and thousands of geese spread across the sky, their clattering cries breaking through the chill and the thin winter silence, Iris looked out of her upstairs window, and sighed. Skies, she thought, beautiful. This one was turning pink. Indigo and pink. It had rained earlier, the earth would be damp. Perfect for planting a tree, she decided.

A drive up the glen into all that indigo and pink would be a peaceful and soothing way to ease her spirits. First Christmas in this house, first Christmas without Harry. She was looking forward to it, she was dreading it. So into the pink I'll go and take a Christmas tree home, she said to herself.

She phoned Stella Vernon and asked if she would help.

Stella said, 'Fine.' She was knee-deep in visiting relatives and cooking and the twins were so high there was bound to be tears before bedtime, so any excuse to escape for an hour was a joy. She'd come rightaway.

They loaded the tree and Iris's dog in the back of the Land Rover and drove up the glen looking for suitable spots. 'Where it will be happy,' said Iris. 'We want it to have a good view.'

'It's a tree,' said Stella.

'So?' said Iris. 'It'll be standing still for a hell of a time. A good view is a must.'

They stopped not far past the track that led down to Stella's house. There was a steep heathered bank, above that a wide empty area of soft mossy grass, lichened boulders, damp and browning bracken, and beyond that a fence. On the far side trees spread in greens and soft greys and browns, all the way up the hill. On the other side of the road, stretching far away below them, lay the valley with the river running through it, constant, shining. 'It will be happy here,' said Iris.

She got out of the car. It always surprised her, every time she stepped outside in that green and mountainous place, how calm she felt. The very air was amazing. Softly scented, gentle on the face yet lively, like good wine. Enveloping. For a few seconds, she shut her eyes and breathed.

A six-foot tree in a huge plastic pot is a large and cumbersome thing. The two women held it between them and started their lumbering climb to the treeline. Iris also carried a spade. It wasn't easy going. The dog spurted ahead, coursing the ground.

'This is the way to spend Christmas Eve,' said Iris. 'Goodwill to trees.'

'I'm not fit,' said Stella. A slow sweat was seeping down her spine. 'I should take more exercise. I keep meaning to, but time slips away. I suppose this almost beats making mince pies and assorted puddings and a couple of stuffings for the turkey. Almost.'

They sweated, heaved and stumbled forward, scratched and pricked by needles. Giggled at the absurdity of what they were doing. They'd started moving forward upright, but the further they went, the more the weight of the tree bowed them down. Soon they were mincing in swift tiny steps, bent double. They'd stop, put the tree on the ground, lean into their pain, palms on the small of their backs, considering how far they'd come and how far they still had to go.

Eventually they reached the fence, heaved the tree over, and found a spot just in front of the treeline where they could dig. The earth was thick and wet, softly fragrant. When Iris stopped, stood up and looked round, dark was closing in.

Stella, wrestling the tree from its pot, said, 'So it's just you, Sophy and Scott for Christmas?'

'Yes,' said Iris. Sweat gathered beneath her thick layer of clothes: jeans, a T-shirt and two jumpers. It ran down her scalp on to her cheeks. Her face was cold, misty breath fanning into the cold air.

'Usually Ruby comes. I asked her, but she says she's going to her sister's. I don't think she's really speaking to me.'

'Well, good for you, you've got your priorities right, falling out with your relatives *before* Christmas. We do it during, but only after I've stood in the kitchen cooking vast amounts, and changed beds, and cleaned, and made more cups of coffee and tea than any human being should make in a lifetime, never mind a few days. Then there's the drink you go through. I think it's called entertaining. God knows why. It isn't the least bit entertaining.' She snorted, thinking of the days ahead, her hours in the kitchen. Then shouted, pointing, her arm rigid, 'There's the boys! They're on the road. I'll kill them.'

Iris stood up. Her nose was running, she wiped it on her sleeve. Through the grainy dark she saw two figures cycling up the road. They were weaving in and out in figures of eight. Then, they'd ride side by side, put their arms on each other's shoulders and surge forwards.

Stella started down the hill. 'Wait till I get my hands on them. I've told them and told them not to go on that road . . .'

'There's nothing about,' Iris shouted at her. 'I'm sure they'll be all right.'

'All right? Cars come up here at all sorts of speed. Hurtling out of the blue. And it's Christmas Eve, there's not a sober person in the glen.' Stella started running, faster than she could cope with. The steep downward incline carried her out of control. She started screaming, and hurtling, and reached the road in seconds. Turned and shouted to Iris, 'That was great!'

Iris saw her get into the Land Rover and take off after her sons. Then she realised she was alone, in the dark, beside a forest with no way to get home. Stella would come back, surely? She resumed digging, panting and grunting. When she had the hole big enough she stood up, put the tree into it, started to pack round the roots with earth. She heard a click, a movement behind her, and slowly turned.

He was standing a few feet away from her. He was old, his face beaten by weather, time and whisky. He wore moleskin

271

trousers tucked into wellington boots, a thick padded sleeveless gilet over a fraying jumper. On his head was a cap that looked older than he was. Iris would have given her attention to the eyebrows that spilled over his eyes and reached towards the top of his brow in long greying tufts, but the gun he was pointing at her took her mind off them. 'What do you think you are doing?' he asked.

'I could ask you the same thing,' she said. 'Would you mind pointing that thing somewhere else?'

'No, I will not. Not while you're stealin' my tree.'

'I'm not stealing a tree. It must be obvious that I'm putting one back.'

'Oh, aye. That'll be right. This time of year we get people coming here special to take a tree.'

'I'm not one of them. Please put that gun away.'

'You've got a shovel. You've got a pot to put it in. You're takin' a tree. You can come with me while I phone the police.'

'I will do nothing of the sort.'

'And you've got a gun dog with you. You're probably after a bit of game and all.' Iris looked across at the dog who was sitting watching with interest, her tongue hanging out of the side of her mouth. She looked insane.

'Gun dog?' Iris said. 'That,' pointing with disdain at Lulu, 'a gun dog? That dog's as likely to catch a rabbit or a pheasant with her teeth as I am. She has the efficiency of a pyjama case.'

'I see a dog. I see you lifting a tree.'

'It's the school tree. The school will be shut for the next two weeks. It might survive out here. Anyway, it'll be happier here than all alone in the classroom. Look, for heaven's sake, it's still got a couple of baubles on it.'

He peered across at the tree. Which worried Iris. Being held at gunpoint by a gamekeeper was scary; being held at gunpoint by a shortsighted gamekeeper was scary indeed.

'Please put that gun down. You're making me nervous.'

He reached into his inside pocket, withdrew a pair of wire-rimmed spectacles, and wedged them on his face. 'Right enough.'

He looked at her. 'And I know you now. You're the Missie. You won a big box of chocolates at the raffle. I had my eye on them.'

'That's me. And this is my tree. And that was my box of chocolates,' said Iris.

He lowered the gun. Iris thanked him. He stood looking at her, wondering if he should demand she ask permission to plant a tree on his land or if he should give her a hand. Instead he asked how she'd got here.

'Stella Vernon drove me. She ran off when she saw the twins cycling on the road.'

He nodded. 'Well, if you're wanting a lift back . . .' And nodded again. Iris supposed this meant he was offering her one. 'Then again, your friend Michael lives in that house over there.'

Iris looked. Standing back from the road, at the end of the line of trees, was a large house surrounded by beech hedges. She said she would see if Michael would oblige. And thanked the gamekeeper.

He nodded again, then at the tree. 'Nice. I like that, putting a tree back. I'll see it all right.'

Iris finished her planting, stamped the ground round the roots, and walked towards Michael's house. By now it was dark and the shock of being held at gunpoint had taken its toll. The effort of digging and lugging a tree uphill had caused her to sweat, and the prickle of fear afterwards had turned it cold. She shivered. At the edge of the trees something moved. Deer walked slowly past, a few yards from where she stood. One, at the end of the line, stopped and stared at her, deep-eyed, nose twitching. Iris froze, stared back. For a few moments they gazed at one another. Then it moved on.

'Well, at least someone thinks I'm harmless,' she said.

Ten minutes later, she rang Michael's bell.

He let her in. 'This is a surprise.'

'To both of us,' she said. And told him of her adventures.

He led her into his living room, and sat her by the fire. She took off her mud-encrusted shoes and held her damp feet before the flames. The room was comfortable. Not untidy, just lived-in and slightly messy. He had a desk at the window covered with papers. A sofa, and matching armchairs either side of the fire. One wall was completely covered with bookshelves, the others hung with pictures. She felt warmth seeping through her, and knew if she sat here for too long, she'd fall asleep. Michael brought her a glass of whisky and sat in the armchair opposite. The dog settled by the fire, and slept.

He spoke about his work, and how he was going to spend Christmas with an aunt who lived further up the glen, his mother's sister who was over eighty and fit as a fiddle. 'She'll outlive me,' he said. 'I'd better phone Stella and tell her I've got you.'

He and Iris sat to either side of the fire. Michael thought this house, this chair, suited her. 'Have you got over your wee scare, then?' he asked.

'It was hardly wee,' said Iris. 'That man held a gun at me. That's not a wee scare.'

'Yes, but,' for he could not just agree, 'I mean, wee doesn't mean small. It means everything you want it to mean. Have a *wee* drink is a beckoning, a luring into sweet alcoholic mists, then have another wee drink, then a wee bit chat and a wee bite to eat and another wee drink. And you'll be a wee bit late getting home tonight.' He looked at Iris who was sitting on the chair, politely listening to him. He thought, What a lovely person she is. 'And a wee cuddle,' he went on, moving across the room to embrace her, 'is a lot more than taking someone in your arms. A whole lot more.'

He sat on the arm of her chair, and kissed her. And when he'd done that he kissed her again. He took her hand, said, 'C'mon.' Led her upstairs to his bedroom. Lulu, watched them go. Sighed. Heaved herself to her feet. Shook herself violently, and followed.

In the bedroom, Michael kissed Iris; and helped her remove a jumper. Then kissed her and helped her with her next jumper. Another kiss. 'Christ, you wear a lot of clothes. How many layers do I have to get through till I get to you?'

She told him she was next, after the T-shirt. Off it came. Iris wasn't sure about this. Taking off her clothes in front of a man who wasn't Harry didn't feel right. Still, she wanted him. So off came her socks and jeans. And he looked her, told her she was lovely. He took off his shirt, then his trousers. And then they were down to their underwear. Lulu sat on the rug in front of the dresser, watching with interest. Michael unhooked Iris's bra, kissed her breasts. Then they both slipped into bed. He pulled her to him, kissing her. She was warm, and the bed was lovely after the icy cold and dark outside.

It was all going wonderfully, this seduction. Iris was willing, Michael was more than willing. He'd been planning this for some time, and couldn't believe his luck when she'd turned up on his doorstep. This was magic. Then Lulu judged it the right moment to leap on the bed and join them.

It would have been fine if she'd just snuck up to lie near them at the far end, where their feet were becoming entwined. But she didn't. She stood staring down at them, wagging her tail with boundless enthusiasm. Then, because it was so available, she started to lick Iris's face.

'Get off,' she said, brushing the dog aside.

It all just happened. As Iris pushed Lulu aside, the dog slipped under her arm, lay beside her, and licked her face, as she had done when she was a puppy. And Iris remembered her doing that, how she'd howled that first night in the house. The old house. The one she'd shared with Harry. It had been Harry who'd brought her home, he'd got her from a friend whose dog had given birth to six pups. Lulu was the pick of the litter. She'd come in his arms, kept warm inside his coat, her little head peeking out at the collar.

Harry. And that was that. Iris thought about him, and he was in the room with her, somewhere, watching. 'Iris? What are you doing with this man?' She was embarrassed at Harry watching her make love to someone else. 'I can't do this,' she said. 'I'm sorry. It's too soon after my husband's death. I can't do it.'

'It's all right,' said Michael, believing a little tender persuasion would do the trick. 'Just relax. There's got to be a first time. A new first time. You have to move on, explore new relationships.'

'I know,' said Iris, 'I know. But not here. Not now.' She was going to say, Not with Harry watching. But didn't. 'I have to go home. Sophy and Scott don't know where I am. I'm always ticking them off for disappearing without telling me where they're going. I can't do the same.'

'They'll be fine. It's not as if they're little.'

'I know. But I've got to get home. It's Christmas Eve, I should be there. Sophy's gone all depressed and into herself. I think she's obsessed with death. And Scott . . . don't ask me about Scott.'

'What about Scott?'

'He's only been having an affair with Emily Lynne, that's all.'

'Jake's wife?'

'Yes. And I think he's got her pregnant. She's gone off home for the moment. I don't know what we're going to do when she gets back.'

And that was really that. Iris's mind was full of Sophy and the slow grief that had been welling within her for months, and now was beginning to swamp her. And of Scott. And of babies. And of how she was going to find the money to help towards the upkeep of a new infant when she could barely make ends meet now, what with the remortgage to pay off. Then there was Ruby, sulking alone in her bungalow, and this being Christmas and all. The passion was gone. Over. It had been lovely for a while back there, a few moments ago. Lovely. But now she was wound up and awash with angst. 'I have to go home,' she said, jumping out of bed and reaching for her socks.

Michael sighed. Oh, well, nearly there, he thought. Next time. But Scott and Emily Lynne? There was a bit of gossip he hadn't known, and he usually prided himself on knowing all the gossip. For a second he envied Scott. At least the lad was getting some. Tonight, clearly, Michael wasn't.

He drove Iris home. Said he'd be in touch after Christmas, and watched her go up the path into the house, the dog at her heels.

Sophy and Scott were waiting for her. Demanding to know where she'd been. They'd been worried, thought she'd had an accident.

'You said you were going out to plant that tree hours ago,' said Sophy.

Iris told them how she'd ended up at Michael's. That she was sorry, she should have phoned. Was this what she was like, quizzing people on their whereabouts? Where have you been? What have you been up to?

'What were you doing at Michael's house?' asked Scott.

'What do you think? Chatting about this and that.' She brushed past him, so he wouldn't see her lying face, and deflected any further questions by asking if they'd made anything to eat. Shifting the guilt.

They both looked innocent. They hadn't known what to make.

'You might have peeled some potatoes,' she said.

She escaped to the kitchen, to cook, noisily, and to think about Michael and his bed. How warm it had been, soft, inviting. For a fleeting moment, she'd been willing, then it had all gone wrong. She cursed herself, wished she had the moment back so she could brush the invasive dog away and turn again to Michael. To do what she longed to do, and ease the swirling lust of the last few months.

She thought about the deer. The silence of them moving through the woods and the dark, and the one that had noticed her and stood watching her, a long contemplative look, and her amidst the over-hanging boughs of pine and larch, stars coming out far above, the scents of peat and soft earth and green. She knew she'd remember that moment for the rest of her life. That, and the fact that she'd jumped out of bed and yanked on her socks first. Michael had seen her naked, except for a pair of bright red woollen socks, and from behind. She really wished she hadn't done that.

Turning

Christmas passed slowly. Iris, Scott and Sophy exchanged presents in the morning. Then Scott had gone to feed Emily's hens. He feared Jake would neglect them. He swept out the henhouse and lingered, watching them fuss and peck. Jake was not there. Had no doubt driven to be with friends in Aberdeen or Edinburgh rather than face the day alone in the cottage. In the evening Scott would come back and herd the hens into their coop for the night. Tomorrow he'd do it all again. it was not much, but it was at least something he could do for Emily. He gathered some eggs to take home with him.

He stopped on his way back up the track, listened. The quiet of a special day. Everything about him was exactly as it had been yesterday, last week. He felt it should be different. That was what Christmas was like, it was special, but everything in the outside world, stayed the same. All the houses in the village had a Christmas tree in the window. And in all of them people would be preparing dinner, playing with toys, doing Christmas things. This year, though, he didn't welcome the season of goodwill. He didn't want it to be Christmas.

At home, preparing the meal, Iris felt the same. She stuffed the turkey, put it in the oven, peeled potatoes and Brussels sprouts – why she didn't know, nobody liked them. She had a glass of sherry and stared out of the window. A thin mist hung over the garden. Somewhere above it a pale winter sun feebly filtered through. It was damp and miserably chill. Doesn't look like Christmas, she thought. Doesn't feel like Christmas. She put on the radio and listened to some disc jockey's absurd incessant merriment, hoping it might cheer her up. In the room above, Sophy was playing 'It's All

Over Now, Baby Blue' on the French horn, badly. Gloom, thought Iris.

Only Sophy voiced what they all were feeling. She toyed with her food, and eventually said, 'This isn't like Christmas. We should be at home. Dad should be here.'

Iris pointed out that this was home, and her father couldn't be here. Never again. 'I miss him, too,' she said. 'But we've all got to get used to it. We have to get on with our lives.'

Sophy said she had no intention of getting on with hers and left the table, leaving her pudding untouched.

'She used to love trifle,' said Iris, pouring herself another glass of wine.

Sophy went out to sit in her favourite place just beyond the garden, where she could not be seen. The mist had turned it magical. It hung on the hedge behind her, and soft droplets clung to spider's webs, turned silver. There were, she noticed, thousands of them. She traced their tender threads with her finger, then leaned against a fence post to smoke.

'What's up with her?' Iris asked Scott. 'She doesn't speak to me any more.'

'She didn't get into the school orchestra,' he said. 'Jean, her best pal, did. She plays the violin. Sophy hasn't got a boyfriend. Jean has. And is too busy seeing him to bother with her now. And Jean has a dad.'

'I would have thought Sophy would have got into the orchestra,' said Iris, doubtfully.

Scott looked at her. 'You're kidding? She's awful. You know she's awful.'

'Yes,' said Iris. 'But I keep hoping someone will see something in her enthusiasm and encourage her.'

'She doesn't need encouraging,' said Scott, 'she needs stopping.'

'OK, she's awful,' said Iris. 'But I can't tell her that.'

Scott said he wasn't going to either, and poured himself a glass of wine.

'I always thought you preferred orange juice to alcohol?'

'Well, I don't.'

They sat. Behind them the disc jockey chattered amiably and played 'Satisfaction'.

Sophy, numbed with cold, stubbed out her cigarette, rolled her tongue round her mouth. She hated the taste and thought she'd never get used to it. Perhaps she ought to give up. Hands in her pockets, she kicked at a stone. She decided she hated Christmas. Hated everything really. And at the school dance she'd only been asked up twice, while Jean had been in the arms of Bobby Reilly all night and had hardly spoken to her. I suppose, Sophy thought, I'm just not very important.

'So when did you start to drink?' Iris asked her son.

'When you weren't looking,' he told her.

'That's not all you did when I wasn't looking.'

He snorted. 'Yeah.'

Two deer, come down from higher ground, walked slowly past Sophy. She held her breath and watched. Sensing her presence, they stopped, ears twitching. She reached out. They were close enough to touch. Alarmed by the movement they took off, starting up other deer close by. Sophy heard their hooves on soft ground, and felt the rush of air as they thundered by. Thousands of them. Well, hundreds. Probably fifty, at least. Ghostly movements in the mist.

'I hope your vices end at a little wine and . . .' Iris's voice trailed off.

'Sex?' said Scott.

'Yes. And I hope you aren't, well, doing it all over the place? I mean, there are diseases.'

'Mother, don't you think it's a little late for the parental sex chat?'

'Don't call me Mother, I hate that. And, yes, it is a bit late for the standard parental sex chat now that you've . . .' she stopped, looked down into her glass '. . . done it.'

Scott burst out laughing. 'You've gone all coy! There's only been Emily.'

'Good,' said Iris. 'Just be careful. You know, use a condom. I don't want a whole brood of grandchildren. And I don't want to have to drive you to the VD clinic. *And* you've got your studies.'

281

Scott drank his wine. Studies he didn't want to think about. 'Yeah.'

Sophy ran after the deer, plunging through the mist. She saw the last of them sail over the far fence, effortlessly. Then on across the next field till the curling damp air enfolded them. She thought it lovely. Swooned to herself at the sight, and stood staring after them. A figure loomed out of the thick icy distance, moving swiftly towards her. She was staring fixedly at Sophy, looking demented. Today she was not wearing her green anorak but a raincoat, fiercely belted at the waist. On her head a beret, not adjusted to a jaunty angle but jammed over her forehead, stopping short of her eyebrows, the little stem on top sticking vertically upwards. Sophy started to walk backwards away from her, the ground sucking at her feet. The Mad Woman kept on her strict path, moving relentlessly, her look, piercing, terrifying. All the horror movies Sophy had even seen flashed before her. Axe murderers, frenzied knifemen, stranglers. She screamed and turned, started walking away. The Mad Woman kept coming, nearer and nearer. Sophy ran, stumbling, towards the house, her breath hot in her throat. The Mad Woman caught up with her, strode past, inches away. Sophy saw her wildly made-up face, lips streaked crimson, eyelids caked blue. Heard her harsh breathing. Smelt the cheap floral perfume. Then watched her melt into the soft fog. Long after she had faded from view, Sophy could hear her steady marching steps, plodding inexorably onwards. Sophy put her hand over her pounding heart, and tried to breathe.

When she got back into the kitchen, Iris and Scott were still sitting finishing the wine. Sophy was pink-faced, her fright still etched on her face.

'What's up with you?' Iris said. 'You look like you've seen a ghost.'

'I saw the Mad Woman,' said Sophy. 'I thought she was going to murder me. She just came out of the mist walking right at me.'

Iris explained about the farmer's wife from Blawcotts, the constant wind, the failed crops, the burning bull, the dead baby. 'She comes by every day.'

'She is seriously scary,' said Sophy. 'I was terrified. She just keeps coming at you, staring.' She put her head on the table, wrapped her arms over it.

Iris put an arm around her. 'She's harmless.'

Sophy was crying. 'I thought I was going to die! I thought it was death coming for me.'

'You're not going to die,' said Iris. 'Not for a long, long time. I won't let you. Anyway, death isn't a demented and sad woman in pearls.'

Sophy turned and clung to her, sobbing. 'I hate death! I hate that Mad Woman. I hate everything.' It was good here in Iris's arms. She had the special smell, the mother smell. Her cheeks were soft. After the cold, the loneliness and the dread Mad Woman coming at her, Sophy found comfort.

Iris stroked her head and said, 'I know. So do I.' Then, 'Not everything. I don't hate everything. I don't hate the Mad Woman. I feel sad for her. And so should you.' She held her daughter, knowing that she hadn't been here, in her arms, for a long, long time. Too long. Considering the things the girl had been through, Iris knew, she should have reached out months ago.

'Hens,' said Scott. 'I like hens.'

Sophy emerged from the comfort of Iris's shoulder. 'Hens?'

'Yeah. They're all different. And they've got their own little society. There's big boss hens, and little meek hens, and fussy hens.'

Sophy looked round, her face drained and wan from crying. Her nose red, eyes swollen. She sniffed. 'I like things, too. I like . . . I like . . . I don't know what I like any more. Anyway, what's the point in liking anything? I'm just going to die.'

'Sophy,' said Iris, 'we are all going to die. Some of us sooner than you. But it's best to pack in as much of what you like before it happens.'

Scott drained the last of the wine into his glass. 'In which case, I'll have more wine.'

Iris reached over and smacked his wrist. 'That's enough of that.'

Sophy wiped her nose on the back of her hand. Pulled her hair out of her eyes. 'I'll have some trifle, then.'

Iris told her to go wash her face, and take off her muddy shoes. Then come back and have some.

When she was out of the room, Scott said, 'She's such a girl. What a state to get in.' He held up the wine bottle to examine its emptiness.

Iris said he might have left her some because right now she really could do with it.

On Boxing Day the freeze began. Icicles hung from gutters, smoke rose straight from chimneys into chilled winter air. Everything was still, waiting.

'Do you think it'll snow?' Sophy asked.

'Too cold for snow,' said Iris. She had never known such cold. It seeped into her bones. It crept through ill-fitting windows, under doors. The three of them huddled close to keep warm. Clutched jerseys to them as they went from room to room. Windows frosted over, intricate patterns on the pane. Iris kept adding black coals to the fire in the living room, and dreaded bedtime when they would have to face the glacial temperature in the hall and bedrooms. Sophy had mastered the art of taking off her clothes after she got into bed. Iris slept with a pair of Harry's old socks on her feet. Mornings when she woke, bitter air chilled her lungs. It hurt to breathe.

Colin, so completely wrapped up he was almost unrecognisable, played in the garden opposite. There was only a small slice of face visible between the top of his scarf and the bottom of his green woolly hat. He ran his new toy motorbike up and down the path.

Iris noted the lack of motorbike noises as he did so. 'New bike?' she said.

He looked at it, then at her, and back at it again.

She thought that somewhere beneath the scarf was a smile.

Ella bustled out, throwing salt before her. 'You could break your leg on ice like this.' And seeing Iris admire the bike: 'A present from Santa. A real present from Santa. It was on the doorstep Christmas morning, all wrapped up in silver paper with a blue bow. Lovely. Don't know who left it, but Colin loves it. Takes it to bed with him every night.'

'So there is a Santa after all,' said Iris. 'Knew it.'

'Must be,' said Ella. 'He certainly knew Colin wanted a motor-bike.'

As far as Iris was aware there was only one person besides herself who knew Colin wanted a motorbike: Chas Harper.

Every day, Scott went to the cottage down the track to feed and tend the hens. Colin watched. Once, when Scott had gone to the dammit shop before his self-imposed hen duty, he stopped to admire Colin's new acquisition. 'New bike, Colin?'

The child looked at him, then handed it over for closer examination.

Scott took it, turned it over in his hand. 'Harley-Davidson, cool. I always wanted one like that. Want to come and feed the hens?'

Colin nodded, and followed him, and after that was Scott's companion and helper. Whenever Scott left the house, Colin was across the road, in his secret spot behind the redcurrant bush, watching, waiting.

Scott spoke to him. There was something about the child's silence that encouraged people to open up.

'See,' said Scott, 'Dylan's the man. People turned against him when he went electric, but I thought it was great.' Then, putting his arm round Colin, 'He writes lyrics that are about more than love. Not that he doesn't write great love songs. "Love Minus Zero", that's probably a masterpiece. Don't you think?'

No, Colin didn't know what to think. And who exactly was Dylan? But for once, speaking, or not exactly speaking, more listening, to Scott, he didn't feel ignorant. He felt part of what Scott was saying, and something deep within him stirred.

Often Scott would take him home, 'Want to come in and hang out, Colin?'

Colin was puzzled by this. He didn't know what people did when they hung out. They seemed to just sit. His gran often just sat, but she plainly wasn't hanging out. Hanging out must be sitting about in a trendy way, on the floor, maybe, with your legs crossed. His gran never did that. He followed Scott anyway. He'd sit at the

285

kitchen table while Scott made him tea. He held his mug with both hands, gingerly moving it up to his lips. Scott let him put three teaspoons of sugar in and watched him stir it, and said he liked it sweet, didn't he? He spoke about revolution and anarchy. Told him about John Lennon and a book he was reading called *Silent Spring*. He gave Colin some of his old toys – a set of Dinky cars, a model aeroplane, a space hopper. 'See,' he said, 'you sit on it and bounce along. Cool or what?'

Soon Sophy was drawn into Colin's absorbed silence, sitting at the kitchen table with him when Scott was out of the room looking for his luminous yo-yo to show Colin how it shone in the dark as it went up and down.

'See, Colin,' she said, 'it's not that I'm afraid of death. Well, I am. But I want to experience it. I want to know what my dad felt. I want to be ready for it when it comes, 'cos we're all going to die, y'know?'

Colin stared. Death. He didn't like that thought very much.

'I try to die. I hold my breath, but then I always start breathing again. It just sort of bursts upon me. I open my mouth, and there I go. Breathing.'

Colin wished Lucy was here so he could tell her to tell Sophy not to die. It only made everyone cry.

Then Iris would breeze in and say, 'Hello, Colin. You here again? Look at all those dirty dishes. I'll have to wash them, nobody else will. You finished with that cup? Can I wash it? Or do you want more tea? OK, I'll just get you some.' She always answered his questions for him. 'So,' she said, sitting close, leaning towards him, 'I was thinking about the school trip. What do you think? Edinburgh or the seaside? The seaside's fun. You could swim in the sea, you being our prize swimmer. Build sandcastles. All sorts of things. But, really, you need the weather. So I was thinking Edinburgh. We could go on a train. Have you ever been on a train?'

Colin's mouth slowly opened. But no sound came out.

'Thought not,' said Iris. 'Then we could go to the zoo.'

'Oooh,' said Sophy, 'the zoo's good. They've got lions and tigers and elephants and penguins, masses of things.'

'Yeah,' said Scott, coming into the room with his yo-yo and his football, 'the zoo's great. Want a kick about in the garden?'

Colin slipped from his chair and followed him outside. Scott didn't mind the boy at all. After all, not only did Colin never argue, he idolised him. Scott had never been a hero before.

Iris was touched at her children's interest in Colin. She hadn't known they could be so considerate and interested in someone so much younger than they were.

In the end, she had to admit the boy was as good for her children as they were for him. They were concerned for him, cared about him, and told him their troubles. He drew them out with his listening. She had to hand it to Colin, he could listen like nobody she'd ever met before. He was the king of listeners. Not that she didn't listen to her children. It was just that she could not do what Colin did, listen in silence. She was always full of opinions, theories, solutions to problems, encouragement, disparagement. She never could keep her mouth shut.

The year turned. It snowed. Iris watched the white ceaseless tumbling. She had been invited to a party at the Vernons', but would not go. The ever-deepening layer of white on the road made it unlikely she would get there, and if she did, she knew she wouldn't get back. She stayed in with Sophy and Scott. The evening passed quietly. At about nine o'clock it stopped snowing and the three of them went out for a walk. The soft groaning crunch of fresh snow underfoot, and everything about them transformed, glistening. Their voices ringing in the crystal air. They looked for deer tracks in the field behind the house. The night was bitter, nipped their faces, numbed their fingers. They stamped their feet at the door, welcomed the hug of warmth in the living room. But they were pink with cold and excitement. It was, Iris realised with some shame, the first time they had all gone out together since they'd arrived in the village. At midnight they all wished each other Happy New Year, and shortly afterwards went to bed. To Iris's relief, neither child complained about how dull it was.

She looked out of her bedroom window. Snow lay thick, white, untouched. The little village hushed. Things were getting better.

Scott had not teased Sophy, had not disappeared to his room to hide himself behind a wall of guitar noise. Sophy had not mentioned death. In fact, as New Years go, this had been quite a success – quiet, homely. Maybe they were all getting better. Turning from old sorrows, making a new life, moving on. Then again, maybe this was the calm before the storm.

A Life Affirming Fruitgum

The village was cut off for three days. Children played in the snow, their cries echoing across the white. Snowmen with carrot noses stood in gardens and there was the scraping sound of paths being cleared. But Iris's school term started on time, with only a few pupils missing because the small farm roads would stay blocked until the thaw set in.

The blocked road was a huge relief to Sophy. During the grilling about who had written the verse on the school wall she was absent, cut off from the world in a sea of icy white. She prayed that the thaw would never come, and she would never again have to enter the dread doors of Forham High.

Iris would stand at her kitchen door in the evenings, staring out over snowy wastes. White everywhere. Icicles dripping from her broken guttering. Evenings the world turned indigo, the first stars glistening, freezing air on her face. Behind her, from the depths of the house, came the jangle of the Grateful Dead and the perfect songs of Joan Baez. She would wonder then what she was doing here, so far from everything she loved. Cities, noise. An itch would start within her then, a longing for the movement and bustle of busy streets. She wanted to be part of crowds once more, to come pouring into the night after the cinema or a meal in a restaurant, or a night pubbing with her old friends. She missed the gossip in the staffroom. Then she'd sigh and tell herself to get over it.

She phoned Ruby who was grumpy and distant. She phoned Morag who was hungover but told her not to worry about Ruby. 'She'll come round. She can only disapprove of you from afar for so long. She'll need to visit eventually to keep track of all the things you're doing wrong. Also, she'll be missing her grandchildren. Give it time.'

Iris said that she would. Meantime she had other worries that she did not confess to Morag or anybody. There was Sophy's depression, and Scott's affair with Emily, and the child on the way. That perhaps the child was not his didn't cross her mind. She just fretted, a constant nagging hum of anxiety that went on day after day as she busied herself, coming and going to and from the school. And, Michael hadn't phoned.

She'd been a fool to run away. And chastised herself for it. But there it was, an absurdity. She'd gone for months missing sex, thinking about it in idle moments, longing to be touched, held and so much more. Then, when the opportunity came along, she'd scarpered. Leapt from bed, dressed in a panic and demanded to be taken home. She didn't just think she'd been foolish, she decided she'd been rude, leading a man on, then when the mood was sweet, the moment ripe, saying no. She writhed with embarrassment every time she thought about it.

Still, the road to Forham was open, a thick icy grey broth of slush running at its edges. The swimming lessons went on. By the end of January nearly everyone could do a length of the pool. Iris ticked them off one by one as they struggled, small bright faces in blue water, from one end of the pool to the other.

James still refused to enter the water. No gentle persuasion, fiendish coaxing or even bullying worked. Iris thought, Oh, well, you can't just force people to do things they don't want to do. Swimming after all was not a stipulated necessity on the school curriculum. They wouldn't win the prize, but the children were closer as a group, less inhibited with one another, and it had been fun.

Sometimes she took a few pupils to the pool in the evening. She would join them in the water, swimming with them, playing games, and afterwards they'd all go for fish and chips. Sit in the back of Stella's Land Rover eating, all of them shiny from the exercise and the cold night. The air thick with the tang of salt and vinegar, and the chatter of children. Iris and Stella would sit, aglow from the snug warmth – too many huddled bodies in too tight a space – smiling, laughing at feeble children's jokes.

'What's the difference between a fish sandwich and a madman?' someone would say.

'Wait, don't tell me, I want to guess.'

Stella would smile. She couldn't afford this fish and chips for herself and the twins. But it was such fun, sitting here in the back of the Land Rover with all these children and Iris. And, hey, they were so overdrawn anyway, what difference did another few shillings make?

'Dunno,' Iris said.

'One's a tuna lick, the other's a lunatic. Ha! Ha!'

And Iris and Stella would groan.

Once Iris's car wouldn't start, so Stella took all the kids home while Iris tried to find someone who would come and fix it at this time in the evening.

Chas came across her outside the phone box, rummaging in her handbag for change. Was something wrong? he asked.

'Globally? Or for me personally?' said Iris.

'I was thinking of you personally,' he said. 'I'm not a man with time to put the world to right.'

'My car isn't speaking to me,' she said. 'It won't start. I always knew that car hated me. Awkward bugger.'

'Maybe it just needs to know you love it. A little tenderness might help. Has it got petrol in it?'

'Of course it has.'

'Well, this weather, like as not it's the plugs. Let's have a look.'

She led him to where she'd parked. He lifted the bonnet, peered inside, and asked her to start the engine.

'If I could start the engine, I'd have started the engine and driven home.' said Iris.

'Well, give it a go. Let's hear what it sounds like.'

It sounded like a clunk. Chas decreed it was definitely the plugs. He would come by and fix it in the morning since she wouldn't need the car to get to work. 'I'll bring it up to you. I'm not standing here this time of night changing spark plugs, and I doubt you'll find anyone round here who would.'

He leaned into the car. 'This is filthy.'

'Yes,' Iris agreed. 'I've never been keen on car-cleaning. Any cleaning, really.'

'Is that bird shit on the seat?'

Iris looked at it. 'I wondered about that. It appeared a few months ago. But it couldn't possibly be bird shit. Could it? It must be a stain left by the kids after swimming. I can't bring myself to imagine what.'

'I'll take you home,' he said. He didn't want to speculate about the stain either.

He started down the road, and Iris pointed out his car parked nearby.

'I'm going for a bite to eat first. Coming? Or do you want to wait here till I get back.'

She went. He took her to the local Chinese. Though Iris didn't think he was taking her anywhere, really, since this was where he'd been going anyway. But she found his gentle company easy. He told her about his travels, his ex-wife, his children, his work. She spoke about her work, her lack of travel, her dead husband, her children. He asked her why she was always so mocking when she spoke to him.

'Mocking?' she said, a forkful of duck in black bean sauce on its way to her mouth.

Piped Eastern music writhed and snaked against the clatter of crockery and the din of other eaters chatting.

'Yes, mocking. Kind of cynical. Tart but quite funny, really. Why are you like that?'

'I'm not like that with children, only with adults. I don't think I trust them. It's a form of defence. Insult me and I'll insult you back. Only I'll win. My insult will be the best insult.'

'I thought that.' He returned to his king prawns with cashew nuts. Contemplatively swigged some lager. 'Would you like to come out with me sometime?'

'Where?' she said.

'That's not very gracious – where?'

'I never pretended to be gracious,' said Iris.

'I thought you might like to go dancing. They have supper dances at the Royal Hotel Saturday nights. I thought you'd enjoy it. A bite to eat, a little wine and a dance.'

'I would,' she said. 'Thank you very much.'

'My pleasure.'

Iris, remembering her embarrassment with Michael, thought to put matters on a proper footing before they went out together. It would save any humiliating moments, for her and him, she decided. 'I want you to know, I'll dance with you, but I won't sleep with you. No sex. I'm all right for sex right now.' Though she wasn't. However, if he thought there might be a chance, he'd try. 'I won't have sex with you. But I'll dance with you.'

'Suits me,' said Chas. 'What makes you think I want to sleep with you anyway? Maybe I'm all right for sex myself.' He wasn't.

'In which case you shouldn't be asking other women out,' said Iris.

'And if your love life's so fulfilling, you shouldn't be accepting invitations from other men.'

She looked down at the table. True, she shouldn't. 'I was just establishing the boundaries of our relationship.'

'Fine, boundaries established. I'll pick you up Saturday night, round about eight.'

They danced that Saturday night. And the next and the next. Every Saturday night after that. And not once did Chas attempt to overstep her boundary, which in time disappointed Iris.

The school trip was to be in April, just before they broke up for Easter. Iris wanted to keep the last term free from anything but the swimming test, which was in early May, so she could concentrate on her summer panto. She would write it herself, there would be a part for every child in the school. It would be a glorious end to her first year as Missie.

In February Michael asked her to go out for a curry again. She accepted. And again the next week. Smoky pub, spicy food, Michael's chat one night a week, and Chas to dance with on Saturday nights. So this was what a social life was like. She'd forgotten. The village gossiped, and some took bets on which man she'd choose. To anyone who asked, Iris said she was having fun.

In March tractors crawled the field behind the house, trailing lines of seagulls squealing across the sky after them. Winds howled down from the hills, whipping the very breath from Iris's throat, pushing beneath her coat, sending it billowing behind her, shoving her hair round her face. Children arrived at school, flushed, high on the thrill of wild rushing air. The Mad Woman stamped by, windswept, crazy-haired, more deranged than ever. The goat ate the first of Iris's crocuses, and was chased by Sophy round the garden for pulling her favourite shirt from the washing line and slowly chewing it. Daffodils shoved through the earth, nubs of blossom appeared on trees. From upstairs music thrummed out: Joan Baez slowly, achingly, sang of love and death, and Bob Dylan cried 'It's Alright, Ma, I'm Only Bleedin', a song that pierced Iris's heart with guilt.

Lucy stopped stammering completely. Colin still didn't speak. James refused to enter the water at the pool till Fiona Wilkinson pushed him in and called him chicken. Humiliating enough, then Colin jumped in and pulled him to the side. Yanked from the claws of death by the class wimp, James slunk off to the changing rooms and sulked. The class was struck by a minor flu epidemic, and one day there were only three pupils present. Stella, at last, let her boys cycle to school. They'd arrive at speed, hair blown vertical by the wind in their pink and vibrant faces. Iris overheard Stella say, 'Oh, I just let them come to school on their bikes. It's important they get their independence. I never worry about them,' knowing that she stood every afternoon at the end of the track with binoculars, watching their uphill progress home. For weeks, she had phoned Iris every morning, checking they'd arrived safely.

James, against school rules, for Iris was tired of children coming into school with soaked feet, played every lunchtime ·under the bridge, throwing stones into the river. One day, when school lunches had included a particularly glutinous and lumpy custard that not even prayers could save, Effie, not knowing what to do with it, had slipped out and tossed an urnful over the parapet of the bridge, dousing James. Iris had to take him home and give him a bath. 'And wash your hair!' she'd shouted from behind the door. She'd given him some clothes Scott had outgrown, and shoved the yellow-encrusted ones into a plastic bag. Teacher, nurse, librarian she may be. Laundress, never.

In Iris's garden, hellebores grew green and lovely. Iris marvelled, 'Who planted these?' Chas had. She ate curries with Michael, and danced with Chas. The betting as to who would win their way into Iris's bed hotted up. Most fancied was Michael: charming, witty, rich, and he drove an expensive car. Fiona and Lucy thought Chas, though they didn't speak of Iris's bed. They wondered who would win her heart. Michael, they thought, wore a super jacket and his car was lovely. But Chas was brave and gentle and true. They wrote Chas's life in their school jotter, making him a World War Two pilot who'd saved a French village from doom with his brave deeds. Chas would have blushed. When the Second World War raged, he'd been twelve. James complained to his father that he'd been bullied in the swimming pool. His father called him a jessie for not being able to swim. James sulked. Scott fed the hens. And Colin followed him down the track, and silently helped. Life went on.

At the beginning of April, Iris got a letter from Emily Lynne saying she wouldn't be returning to the area and therefore Gracie would not be back at school. She thanked Iris profusely for the help she'd given Gracie with her education. '*She's way ahead of the others in her new school*,' she wrote. '*I have you to thank for that.*' There was an address. Iris would write soon and ask about the baby. Only, she didn't know quite what to say.

In the second week of April a coach stopped at the school gates, brakes sighing. At eight in the morning, the children stood gathered and ready. This was their first school trip, they were going to the zoo. Lucy's mother, Fiona's mother and Carol, mother of the Hay sisters, had agreed to come along and help keep an eye on the outing.

'We don't want to come home with one child missing. Or worse,' said Iris, 'we don't want to return with one extra that we don't know.'

Everyone laughed. And shuddered. To lose a child would be awful, just awful. To return with one nobody knew would be unimaginably dreadful. They all knew what Iris meant. They would be vigilant.

The coach left the village, streamers and balloons dangling from its windows, the voices of singing children ringing from within, singing the theme from *The Flintstones*.

Iris thought, This is going to be jolly. At nine they boarded the train to Edinburgh. She noted that the Hay mother and the Wilkinson mother were sitting together lost in chatter while children raced up and down the aisle past them. Whenever a child approached and disturbed their flow of laughter, small confessions, intimacies, quick recipes and grouses, he or she would be swatted away like a small annoying fly. These two hadn't come along to help look after the children, they were having a day out. The children were spoiling their fun. Dread settled in Iris's stomach. She had a feeling that things were going to go awry, and it would have nothing to do with her pupils. But they reached Edinburgh and boarded the number twelve bus heading for the zoo.

At lunchtime, Iris found a spot where the children could eat their packed lunches, while the Hay mother and the Wilkinson mother disappeared in to the zoo restaurant. Through the window, Iris noted that they were drinking. Not good, she thought. She exchanged a look with Lucy's mother who nodded agreement. Not good.

Still, at three o'clock they headed back to town. The laughter of the naughty mums was growing louder, more raucous. Their jokes were getting dirtier. Iris took the group to a huge department store for afternoon tea. She'd been dreading this, children running amok amongst the lingerie and cosmetics. But no, her pupils formed a line and walked behind her to the lift. The naughty mums, however, were in heaven. Iris could almost see their pupils widen, and their blink rate slow. They passed on afternoon tea. They'd shop.

The lift was a wonder. A silent shifting sanctum. Doors slid shut, a powerful upmarket hum, doors slid open and they were in a world of white tablecloths, uniformed waitresses, the polite clatter of crockery and the buzz and murmur of ladies taking afternoon tea. Iris saw the wonder in her children's eyes. Pressed the button, and took them all down again.

It hadn't occurred to her that none of her pupils had been in a lift before. There were none in Forham. It had one department store that sold hats and ladies' coats upstairs, but no lift to get you there. The one supermarket spread for aisles and aisles over the same gleaming level. Oh, the wonder of this mobile compartment. They all hurtled to the ground floor again. Doors slid open on to lights, busy shoppers, displays, and above all that the drunken cackle of the naughty mums playing with the tester lipsticks at the Max Factor counter. Iris apologised to the converging horde as the lift doors opened. 'We're country bumpkins. We've never been in a lift before.' Pressed the up button, and they all slid back to the tearoom.

So, the children behaved immaculately. The naughty mothers became naughtier. By the time afternoon tea had been drunk and cakes eaten, Iris had lost them.

She led her party along Princes Street to look at the shops and the Castle, towering floodlit above them, but saw their faces. Little country people who were not wise to busy street culture, they tried to look into every passing face, watched every bus and every car. It exhausted them. She led them into the gardens where they could watch the squirrels and play on the swings. Sat, down herself, with a long sigh, on a bench. Wriggled her feet from her shoes, and held them into the breeze to cool.

Lucy's mother said she was off to buy presents to take home. She wouldn't be welcome if she arrived empty-handed, and could Iris hold the fort?

'Fort-holding is my forte,' said Iris.

Colin sat beside her, putting his foot between himself and Iris, looking to her to tie his lace.

'Colin, can't you tie your laces yet? How can you grow up and marry me, when I won't marry a man who can't tie a knot?'

He smiled. Then, lace tied, sat beside her.

'Have you had a lovely time?' asked Iris. 'I have.' Because she had to provide answers, since Colin never spoke. 'What was your favourite thing? I liked the tigers. Tigers are my favourite.'

He nodded. Well, she thought, it's communication.

Iris smiled. He slipped his hand into hers and sat next to her, swinging his legs.

'Isn't the Castle wonderful?' she said to him. 'It's hundreds of years old. Mary Queen of Scots lived there.'

He looked at her, eyebrows raised. His 'Oh, really?' expression. Then, to make the moment complete, he pulled out his packet of fruit gums. Took the last one and put it in his mouth.

'Oh, Colin!' said Iris. 'Haven't you got one for me? I love fruit gums. Was that the last one? I like the black ones best. I don't know if I can marry a man who doesn't give me a fruit gum.'

Colin took his hand from hers, reached deep into his pocket. Iris could tell from the way he rummaged about there was a lot of stuff in there. He finally withdrew a fruit gum. It looked as if it had been in that pocket for some time. It may even have been sucked a little, then put away for more sucking at a later date. It was covered in fluff, pocket fluff. The kind of greyish-purple matting that lines the bottom of pockets, and is never seen anywhere else. This fruit gum was not a pretty sight. He handed it to Iris.

'For me?' she said. 'Colin, that's very kind of you.' She took it, turned it over, wondering how to get out of actually eating it. Perhaps she could pretend to put it into her mouth, palm it, and sneak it into a litter bin. But Colin watched intently.

'And it's a black one. I love black fruit gums.'

His face shone with pride. 'It's my best one,' he said. 'I've been keeping it for ages. Ages and ages.'

What could she say? If she made a fuss, commented on the fact that he had, at long, long last, uttered a word, she might put him off speaking again. If she refused the proffered sweet, threw it aside, saying, 'Yuck!' which was what she was thinking, he might associate starting to speak with a negative response, a rejection of his gift. So, thinking it was a far, far better thing she was doing now than she had ever done, she put the fluff-encrusted fruit gum into her mouth.

Sucked it and said, 'Yes. This is very good. I can see why you were saving it. Thank you very much.'

Colin shrugged. Looked proudly benevolent. 'That's OK.' As if there had never been years of silence. As if he'd always been speaking.

And in his head, Iris thought, he probably had.

Going into the station she spotted the naughty mums heading into a pub. 'Train leaves in ten minutes,' she shouted.

They waved, pointed to the pub, and swigged from pretend glasses. In the short time they'd been let loose on the shops, they'd accumulated a huge number of bags that banged against their legs as they struggled to open the heavy wooden door. They giggled.

Iris herded her party on to the train. Colin pushed through the crowd moving up the aisles and sat next to a window. He put his small duffel bag and collection of goodies on the seat next to him. He was saving it for Iris.

'Ooh,' she said. 'A seat next to Colin. Excellent.'

The children took their places on the train. Soon, Iris knew, when movement lulled them, they'd sleep. She looked round, watching for the arrival of the naughty mums. But the train doors slammed shut. The whistle blew. And as they pulled out of the station, she saw the two of them running up the platform, hands full of the spoils of their shopping spree. She heard their shrieks as they saw the back of the train pull slowly away from them. She leaned across Colin to the window, and saw the two of them double up with drunken laughter. Fools, she thought. But it had been a good day. She'd been given a life-affirming fruit gum.

It Never Rains

It was after seven when the group got back. Children dispersed into the evening, leaving Fiona Wilkinson, Lorna Hay and her younger sister, Julie. They stood looking at Iris. The moment they had been worrying about all the way home had come. Iris took them into the house and phoned Fiona's father who arrived ten minutes later to collect his daughter. 'Bloody woman can't be trusted near shops,' he said. 'I mean, you'd expect one of the kids to be trouble, not a bloody mother.'

Iris didn't tell him it was more than the shops had distracted his wife. The pubs also had a certain allure. She figured he'd discover that for himself when his wife got home. Now she was left with the two Hay children. There was no reply when she phoned. She asked if their dad was likely to be home. They shrugged.

She fed them, since she had to feed her own two, then drove them home, hoping their father was there if not answering the phone. Or perhaps their mother had arrived by now. She hadn't. The house was empty. Unwashed dishes were piled in the sink. There was a row of empty bottles on the drainer. The place was filthy. Though it was not dirt that Iris saw so much as loneliness, depression. This was the quiet despair that happened when all you saw was empty fields about you, silent hills in the distance. When the phone never rang and nobody ever dropped by to say hello. Every day was as hollow and empty as the one before, and the next one would be the same.

Iris told Lorna and Julie to get ready for bed, she would wait for their mother. She sat. It was cold here. Ashes in a fire that had not been lit in weeks. She kept her coat on. Looking round at layers of dust, piles of newspapers, a carpet stained and covered in cat hairs, she thought that, but for fortune, this could be her home. If Miss Moffat hadn't come to her rescue, got her a job, she might have ended up in a rented flat she hated and hadn't the heart to clean. She could have sunk into despond. It happens, she thought. She could have tumbled down a different road.

Carol Hay arrived after eleven. A late train, a bus to Forham then a taxi to the glen. She knew Iris was there, had seen her car at the door. And by now she was sober. She smiled, a wan and guilty flicker of the lips. Iris was a teacher, and teachers were people who stood in front of you and ticked you off for all sorts of reasons. Carol was expecting a serious scolding for missing the train, getting drunk, and having a dirty house. Five hundred lines. I must try at all times to be on time, to catch the train and not linger in pubs drinking alcohol. And I must do the dishes, dust and vacuum the house every day and keep it immaculate. It would take her ages. She looked feebly around, and said she hadn't had time to clean up before she left.

'Who does?' said Iris. 'Well, I must be going. Getting late. The girls are fed and in bed, sound asleep. Been a big day.'

Carol said that indeed it had.

'Is your husband around?' Iris asked.

'He works on the oil rigs in Aberdeen. He'll be home next week.'

'You don't have anyone to talk to when he's away?' Iris said.

Carol shook her head.

'Well, mums are always welcome at the school. They drop in all the time, help in class. And we have dancing once a week, we're always looking for people to make up the numbers. You should come along and join in. It's fun, you know.'

Carol said she would. She didn't actually know if she wanted to, she just didn't know how to say no to a teacher.

Iris said, 'Lovely, we'll look forward to seeing you then. I'll tell the class you're coming.'

Carol nodded. There was no getting out of it now. And Iris went home, smiling. She knew she was a terrible bully. But sometimes bullying worked.

It was time, she decided, to get in touch with Emily Lynne. The new baby would be due, might even be in the world. She should let

Emily know that they were prepared to take responsibility for the child. Since Emily was now living in the south, Iris would offer money. Not a lump sum, for she had no lump sum, but perhaps a small monthly allowance. She would chip in a little and Scott could get a part-time job. She wished Emily well, said they would love to see the child, and could they have photos if Emily wasn't up to coming to see them? They hoped she was well.

'Did you tell her I was looking after the hens?' Scott asked when Iris told him she'd sent the letter.

'No. I'm sure she'll know that anyway.'

At school, Colin had reverted to his old ways, whispering answers in Lucy's ear rather than talking directly. Iris thought of challenging him, but didn't. She wanted the decision to start communicating again to be his. No goading. After a few days, he started to speak, and for a while would sometimes address her through Lucy, and sometimes by himself. He's on the way, Iris thought. Meantime his grandmother had taken him to the doctor, and his lazy eye had been declared cured. The mono-glasses had been removed. The child was beginning to look normal.

Lucy's stammer had cleared up, and there were no strange nervous rashes in the class as there had been when Iris had arrived. Apart from the minor flu epidemic earlier in the year, there had been very few absences. She felt proud of this. Pretty damn good, Iris. And if her son hadn't got one of her pupils' mother pregnant, and her daughter wasn't playing death games, things would be wonderful.

At four in the morning, John Vernon sat at the kitchen table, in front of him a glass of whisky and a bottle. He'd woken, as he woke every night now, half an hour ago, and lain staring into blackness, worrying. He'd left Stella sleeping and come here where he could worry some more, with the light on, and a glass to swig from, and the night outside.

Stella worried, he knew. But not constructively. She presented herself with a set of dire 'what ifs', scared herself witless, then put everything out of her mind because all her imaginings were too hard to bear. She tidied bills into neat piles, and thought that was them under control. She spent money they didn't have. 'Oh, John, we're so deep in debt what will another few pounds matter?' Not a lot, he supposed. But there seemed hardly a week passed when Stella did not say that. The twins wanted football strips, they got them because, 'Oh, John, we're so deep in debt . . .'

It was time, he decided, to do something before something was done. Sell up before they were declared bankrupt, and while they might still make something from the sale. If they let things go on, the bank would take the lot. Best emerge from the mire with something, a little to put down as a deposit on a new house.

Stella woke, reached for John, found herself sleeping in an empty bed, and got up to go find him. 'What are you doing through here alone in the middle of the night?' She took his glass from his hand and sipped.

'Worrying,' John said.

'You shouldn't do that. It'll only give you ulcers.'

'I won't get ulcers. I've decided to put this place on the market. Quit before we lose everything.'

'You can't quit. A Vernon never quits.'

'A Vernon is now. We'll sell up. Go live where we can both get jobs.'

'We can't do that. The twins love it here. I love it here.'

John shook his head. 'The twins will love it wherever we go. We have four bookings for this year, Stella. We're bust. It'll take a miracle.'

She filled their mutual glass. 'Miracles happen,' she said. 'I'm banking on one.'

Iris danced with Chas. Round and round the ballroom of the Royal Hotel they'd go, whirling together to the polite stomp of the Wilma Mackilvoy Jazz Quartet. They could play 'Basin Street Blues' and 'Alexander's Ragtime Band' as if they were bland lullabies, stripping them of all their joy and frenzy. Iris marvelled. It must have taken years of musical apathy to master such soulless musicianship. Still, she had fun. Chas would hold her, look into her eyes, and dance. All her life, she'd loved to dance. Sometimes he'd leave her at their table and take some other woman to the floor. She'd sit twirling her wine glass, watching. She could tell, from the way they moved, the way he looked at the woman, the way he made her laugh, that at one time they'd been more than just a couple who did a swift tango or waltz. She came to the conclusion that at some time Chas had been in all their beds, but now he was just some kind of flirtatious friend. He was, she could see, a fabulous flirt. He enjoyed the game, the meeting of eyes, the silent approval, the unspoken hankering for what might happen. Only with all his other dancing partners, Iris knew, nothing would happen. He was with her now.

Round about midnight, they'd leave. Hot from the crowded, noisy room, heady from wine, they'd step into the bitten, frosted air, him with his arm round her and her leaning slightly into his shoulder. They'd drive up the glen, stopping sometimes if the night was fabulous to watch the moon through the stark branches of the rowan trees at the sides of the road. She always invited him in.

They'd sit by the fire, drinking coffee, talking. They'd talk and talk and talk. Wasn't it strange how some people came into your life, and you could talk to them endlessly and never run out of things to say? Still, after her intense introverted silence on their first evening together, when Iris had been too lost in her own private musings to chat to him, this flow of conversation surprised Chas. He'd watch her face. It had changed since they first met, softened, relaxed. Maybe this place was good for her. Maybe it was the air. Or, perhaps, dancing was good for her, exercise was good for easing stress. He knew that over the past months she'd had plenty of that. Then again, she probably just needed someone to talk to. Yes, he decided, that would be it. Everybody needed someone to talk to. At three or four in the morning, Chas would slap his hands on the arms of his chair and declare he should get some sleep. He'd lean over, gently kiss Iris's cheek and tell her goodnight. That was the deal. She would dance with him, but nothing more. 'Sex,' she'd told him. 'I'm doing all right for sex right now.' He assumed she was sleeping with Michael.

Michael assumed she was sleeping with Chas. He had said their dinners together were not a date. Had told her he just wanted some crack, the chat, the exchange of notions, whimsy, fantasy, outrageous and bizarre doings – though, of course, he'd wanted more than that. Thinking that Chas had won her and been invited to her bed, he stopped even kissing her at the end of their evenings together. Instead, he'd touch her cheek and say, 'Are you up for it again next week?'

Iris would tell him of course she was, and thank him for the evening they'd just had. It had been lovely.

She started to watch the post, waiting for Emily's reply. It didn't come. What she did get was a letter from Scott's school saying that as he hadn't attended classes for several months, and as letters enquiring if he had decided to leave had not been answered, his name had been removed from the register. She put the letter in her dressing-gown pocket and went to the kitchen where Scott, in school uniform, was eating Cornflakes.

She sat opposite him. 'What are you doing?'

'Eating breakfast.'

'And why are you in school uniform when you are not going to school?'

He didn't answer. Just turned pale.

'What have you been doing when you were meant to be there?' Iris asked.

'Wandering around. They wouldn't let me go to school with my hair long, and I wouldn't have it cut. The more they went on about it, the more I let it grow. It was sort of war, and I couldn't face it, so I skipped.'

'What happened to all the letters the school sent? Where have you been wandering around to? And why didn't you tell me?'

'I got to the letters before you so you wouldn't see them. I've been wandering around Forham. And, dunno, really.'

She stood up stiffly. 'Well, that's that, then. I'm not going to say anything. Because I think if I did say something it would be so awful we'd never speak to each other again. I'm going to get dressed. And you are going to take off that uniform, and stay home and clean the house. Do something useful.'

She went upstairs. Dressed. And left for school without speaking to him. She thought perhaps, yes, she might never speak to him again.

It was a swimming day and, sensing her mood, the children were behaving. There were no fart jokes on the way to the pool, and no complaints about everyone being squeezed together in her car. At the pool, they dived in and swam their length. Except James, who sat at the edge, feet dangling in the water.

'James,' said Iris, 'I have had enough. Today is not a day to muck around and act all adolescent and moody. You are letting the school down, and letting down all those who have worked hard here to learn to swim. I will count to ten and if you are not in that water, swimming, I will throw you in.'

'You can't do that . . .'

'I can and I will.'

He stood up. In the months since Iris had arrived, he'd grown and now was not that much smaller than her.

'Don't think that because you've grown I won't throw you into the pool. What sort of achievement is that? Growing? Anybody can grow.'

'You didn't.'

She had to give him that. 'No, I didn't need to. There's enough of me as it is.'

Chas agreed with that. 'Any more of her would be just too much person.'

She glared. The full-on furious glare. And James shuffled to the end of the pool, jumped in, and stood looking at her. Well, glaring, really.

Iris glared back. Now she'd got him into the water, she didn't quite know what to do next. She knew he wouldn't swim, but didn't want to lose face. 'Excellent,' she said.

He stood looking moody, defiant.

'You could make an attempt at swimming,' Iris suggested.

He bent into the water, feet on the bottom, and did a feeble breast stroke.

Iris said, 'Excellent,' again. And walked away.

When the lesson was over, she said that while she was in bullying mood, would Stella and Chas please take the children back to school? She had to see someone.

She drove to the High School and demanded to see the head-master. She stood in the reception area, looking about. She'd forgotten what big schools were like. The noise, the jostling pupils, heaving bags of books. If you weren't in the swing of it, it could be scary. The headmaster refused to see her.

'In my school no parent is refused a meeting, ever. The doors are open. I'm available at any time. And in a country school that often means eight o'clock in the evening. Tell him I insist,' Iris argued.

He kept her waiting for half an hour, then said he'd give her ten minutes. His office was large with huge windows overlooking the playing fields. He sat behind a large oak desk, covered with papers. He was an untidy man. Unruly hair; an old Viyella shirt, the collar of which refused to lie flat and curled up at the corners over his lapels. His twill trousers were fraying at the bottom, and his shoes had never, ever been polished. Who was this man to criticise Scott?

'I believe you banned my son from coming to school till he got his hair cut. Why?'

'I did not ban him. I said if he did not cut his hair, there would be repercussions.'

'What,' said Iris, 'has the length of someone's hair got to do with their ability to perform at school?'

'As I told you, Mrs Chisholm, we have standards. If one child got away with it, they'd all start doing it.'

'And I suppose the world would end,' said Iris. 'Who gives you the right to decide what length of hair is acceptable?'

'The education authority.'

'Do they?' She hadn't known that.

'If I do not think a certain person conforms to the standards we set in this school, I am within my rights to insist they should do so. Scott refused to meet those standards.'

'Well, good for him.'

'He was also drinking at lunchtimes.'

'Ah.'

The bell rang for the end of the day. There was uproar outside. Children escaping.

'Scott is a kind and considerate boy whose father died and who . . .' She stopped. Who has got an older woman pregnant, drinks, and goodness know what else. This wasn't going to be easy. '. . . wants to continue his studies.'

'He may come back if he accepts the usual punishment for what he did wrong.'

'And what is that?'

'Six of the belt.'

'I don't agree with corporal punishment.'

'Perhaps if you did you wouldn't have such problems with your son.'

'Perhaps if you didn't you wouldn't have such problems with your pupils. Look at you, telling other people to look smart! Your hair's a mess. You've got a soup stain on your tie. Your shoes are filthy. Your trousers have seen better days, and quite frankly your shirt could do with an iron. So who are you to make judgments?'

'The headmaster of this school.'

He had her there.

'So, what am I to do with my son?'

'I'd recommend an adult education college. There's a very good one in Edinburgh. They won't object to his clothes or his hair, though I suspect his drinking won't go down all that well. I'll write him a reference. Mention his father's death, and the problems of moving to a rural area where he had no friends, and his grades before he stopped coming to school, which, by the way, were excellent. We had high hopes for Scott. As we did for Sophy.'

Iris thanked him, and left. Driving home, thinking about the confrontation, she gave herself nothing out of ten. She had been rude and aggressive. The head got eight. He'd been calm, had made his points clearly and, yes, he'd won.

At home she told Scott.

309

'An adult education college in Edinburgh.' He nodded.

'You can pass your exams there and move on to university. If you want.'

He nodded again.

'But I'm still not speaking to you. I'm still angry. You should have told me. Do you know, you did just what your father did?'

'What?'

'You left this house every morning on the pretence you were going to school. But you weren't, you were wandering about. Going to the pub. Your dad lost his job, was made redundant, but left the house every morning carrying his briefcase, saying he was going to work. He wasn't, he was going to the bookie's and then to the race track. He gambled away all our money and never told me.'

'He *what*?'

'He lost everything. Our house. His pension. His life insurance. I had to sell the house to pay off his debts. That's why we came here, a job with a home attached. And you lied to me.'

He said nothing. They sat in stiff silence.

Then Scott said, 'You lied to me, too, in a way. You never told me.'

She had to give him that. So they stared for a while. And forgave one another, slightly.

'Why didn't you tell me?' Iris asked eventually. She needed to know.

'Because you're my mum. You don't tell your mother these things.'

'Why not?' said Iris.

'You just don't. Did you?'

She thought about this, dredging up naughty moments from her youth – and there were a few – and had to admit that, no, she hadn't. They resumed the silent, contemplative staring till something crossed Iris's mind. 'Sophy,' she said. 'The headmaster said he'd had high hopes for you, and for Sophy. What did he mean by that?'

Scott shrugged. 'Dunno.'

'Scott,' Iris insisted, 'what did he mean by that? What has Sophy been up to?'

He sighed. 'There was this verse painted on the school wall and the headmaster went ballistic. The way teachers do, you know?'

'No,' said Iris. 'But tell me – the verse?'

'Sophy did it. He's probably found out. He was grilling everyone in the school. Someone will have grassed.'

'How do you know she did it?'

'It was the same paint as Chas used on your school. And it was Sophy's writing.'

'My paint? And what was the verse?'

Scott sighed again, and chanted: ' "Poor Virgin Kramer's out of luck, nobody's going to give her a fuck". Except she ran out paint and didn't finish the last word.'

'Sophy wrote *that*? Our Sophy?'

Scott nodded.

Iris let this all sink in. ' "Poor Virgin Kramer's out of luck, nobody's going to give her a fuck". Sophy? It doesn't even scan.'

'Yeah,' agreed Scott.

'And who is Virgin Kramer?'

'A teacher.'

'Poor soul,' said Iris. 'Not because nobody's going to . . . you know. But having that verse written about her.'

'Yeah,' said Scott. 'She was pretty upset, I think. And she's married with three kids so someone must have . . . you know. Sophy's been in hell, really, imagining what they're going do to her when they find out.'

Iris nodded. 'Poor soul,' she said, meaning Sophy this time.

'She only did it for a laugh,' said Scott. 'She thought the other girls would think it funny. But they thought she'd gone too far and still won't talk to her.'

'Poor soul,' said Iris again.

She went upstairs to find Sophy who was sitting alone in her room, in the gathering dark.

'What are you doing in here without the light on?' said Iris.

'Sitting. I like the dark.'

'Yes,' said Iris. 'It's comforting sometimes.' She crossed the room, sat on the bed. 'Especially when you're worrying yourself sick about some daft verse you've written on the school wall.'

Sophy looked at her, eyes wide in horror. The truth was out. 'You know?'

'I know,' said Iris, 'and I'm not at all impressed. That verse didn't even scan. You could do better, Sophy.'

'You think?'

'I know. Why did you do it, anyway?'

'For a laugh.' Nobody had ever sounded so glum.

'Ah, the mistakes we make when pursuing popularity,' Iris said. She was quite pleased with this, it sounded wise.

'Is that all you're going to say?' said Sophy.

'Yep,' said Iris. 'That and Virgin Kramer has three children, apparently, so not only does your verse not scan, it's inaccurate.'

The girl started to sob. Not cry. Her shoulders shook, a deep bawling came from her throat, she gasped for breath. Iris went to her, stroked her hair. 'It's all right.'

'It's *not* all right. What are they going to do to me? They'll beat me then report me to the police. I'll be sent to a home for young offenders . . .'

'No, you won't. I won't let anything happen to you. Now stop worrying. Everything will be fine.'

'Will it?' said Sophy.

'I promise,' Iris said.

Then she sighed. She'd another meeting with the headmaster looming. 'Poor soul,' she repeated. Meaning herself. Thinking about the verse, her day, and her own somewhat celibate love life, she thought, all in all, the verse would be a lot more accurate if it read, 'Poor Iris Chisholm's out of luck . . .'

...But it Pours

Two weeks later, the children took their elementary swimming certificate. They drove to the pool in nervous silence. Their first test. There would be more, Iris knew. Tests and tests, a young lifetime full of them. And an old one too, now she thought about it. Only in some of them you didn't get As or Bs, you just got dumped by someone you loved, scowled at by your husband over the dinner table, your soufflés fell, your tights laddered, your children shamed you, your dog jumped on the bed and ruined your love life. In the face of all that, Iris thought, who was she to chastise James for not being able to swim?

'Never mind, James,' she said.

He replied with a jerk of the head and a sniff.

Iris responded in a similar way. She thought they understood one another.

There is something about an empty pool, shimmering, enticing. Iris longed to jump in and move through still and empty waters alone. Only she wouldn't really be alone, there was a couple of hundred children, from all the schools in the district, gathered in assorted swimming costumes and caps around the edge, waiting their turn to do a length and gain their first certificate. They were all goading each other to new heights of nervousness and fear. A rising hush of skittish whispers echoed through the cavernous damp, till they were whispers no more but squeals, jeers, titters. From the depth of the crowd a shrill, sharp voice shouted, 'QUIET!' And the whispers returned.

At the far end, at a small, shaky wooden table, sat a neat man in a slightly shiny suit. Spread before him were the lists of schools and pupils about to undergo the trial – the swimming of the single

313

length. He held a pen in one hand, a stopwatch in the other. They were to be timed.

Iris hadn't known this. 'I didn't know about the timing thing.'

Chas, at her side, said, 'Trust you not to read the small print. It's fine. They'll be fine.'

James walked slowly from the dressing room and joined the Green Cairns queue.

'What's he doing there?' said Iris. 'He can't swim. I've never seen him, anyway.'

'You've never seen me dive from the top board, doesn't mean I can't do it. I'll bet you've never seen the Aurora Borealis dancing in the hills, doesn't mean it doesn't happen.'

'You've been giving him secret lessons,' said Iris.

'A couple, Friday nights.'

'You sneaky bum.'

'I told you, he wanted to be a hero, wanted to be the best, and Colin beat him to it. Now he can be what he wanted. He's the one going to give you your hundred per cent. None of the other schools here have that.'

'Excellent,' said Iris, swiping the air with joy.

'And when James does his length, you let him be a hero. You go up to him and say, "Thank you, James."'

'I will not!'

'You will, too. And you could try, "Thank you, Chas," while you're at it.'

'Thank you, Chas.'

'No bother. I tell you, that boy's just like you, stubborn and self-willed. You're two of a kind. You both want to be heroes.'

'I do nothing of the sort. I simply want to get my kids some decent sports equipment.'

'And be a hero in the doing of it,' said Chas.

Iris said nothing. Chewed her lower lip, considering this. 'I hate being understood. It's so belittling. Having someone look into the depths of me and see the truth. I could hate you for that, Charles Harper.'

'No doubt you could, but you don't.'

She looked at him. But he didn't return her gaze, he was watching James swim easily from one end of the pool to the other. And as the boy pulled himself from the water, and stood wiping the wet from his eyes and face, he told Iris to go thank him. 'That's all. Just thanks. Let him have his moment.'

So she did. A quiet touch of his arm, and a gentle thank you.

James shrugged, and nodded. Iris nodded back. They understood one another. And, considering his muted reaction, she hoped when it came to big moments he had many more, and learned, on his journey to them, how to throw his arms in the air and whoop with triumph.

Like she did after the celebration in the pool canteen – hot chocolate and cakes – when alone in the car, driving to a meeting with Sophy's headmaster. Dreaming of trampolines and footballs, she parked. Heels clicking on tarmac, a little song of triumph. As she crossed the playground, and climbed the steps to the reception area, she clenched her fists in glee. No other school could possibly get one hundred per cent. It was in the bag.

The headmaster was behind his desk, smiling as she came in. Already high, Iris felt that nothing could go wrong today. It was that sort of day – sunny, fluffy clouds near as dammit bouncing in the sky, the air warm with promise.

'So, Mrs Chisholm,' he said. 'What can I do for you today?'

She noted his shirt was ironed, and his tie stain-free, and decided she must have struck a chord at their last meeting. She decided he'd deemed her a worthy opponent and had cleaned himself up, ready to meet his match. 'I've come about Sophy.'

'A bit withdrawn, disruptive in class, sometimes. But considering her circumstances, I think we can all understand that. She's a very bright girl – lively mind. You must be proud.'

'I am,' said Iris, 'very proud of both my children.'

A stiff moment's silence while they both thought about, but did not mention, Scott.

'So,' he said, 'what about Sophy?' He thought this was going to be about her horn-playing, her failure to meet the standards required by the school orchestra, and was searching for a tactful

315

way of saying that Sophy's musicianship was atrocious, the worst the music master had ever heard. But no.

'She's in a state of nerves about the verse,' said Iris.

'Verse?' He was, for the briefest second, puzzled. But the bewilderment didn't last long. '*Sophy* wrote the verse?'

'Yes. I thought you knew?' said Iris.

He shook his head. 'I never did find out. Not for want of trying, mind you. So, Sophy.'

Iris let this sink in. Here comes Big Mouth, she cursed herself. Damn. 'Sophy is worried you'll report the matter to the police. I think she has nightmare visions of herself in the dock.'

'No. We'll deal with it here. No police.' He smiled.

Iris chilled inside. 'I hope you're not planning to hit her? I won't have that.'

'The belt would be my usual manner of dealing with something like this. Pupils prefer it. It's quick, painful. But once over, it's over.'

Iris shook her head. 'You're not hitting my daughter.'

'Well,' he said, standing up, moving towards the door, 'I'll have to think about this. I'll let you, and of course Sophy, know.' He stopped halfway across the room. 'Sophy? She's the last person I'd have suspected.'

'I think she had some sort of mental aberration while seeking popularity,' said Iris.

'I appreciate why she did it. What to do with her is the problem. Well, thank you for coming in, Mrs Chisholm.' He shook her hand, ushered her out.

Iris drove back to the swimming pool party. The meeting hadn't gone as she'd planned. She'd thought the headmaster would think Sophy had suffered enough, and would let it go at that. But then, she'd thought he already knew that Sophy had written the verse on the school wall. Damn, if I'd known he didn't know, I'd have kept my mouth shut she told herself. But Iris had never been one to keep her mouth shut.

Sophy got home shortly after four in the afternoon. Iris was in the kitchen, waiting for her. The door slammed, a schoolbag was thrown furiously to the floor. Sophy shouted, 'Mother!' Iris now knew that Sophy knew the headmaster knew. And Sophy knew, too, who had told tales.

'You told!' She pointed an accusing finger at Iris. 'You went in and told on me. I can't believe you did that.'

Iris tried to look righteous, 'I thought he knew. Scott said he did.'

'How would Scott know that? He's not at school any more.'

'Good point.' Iris turned to her son.

He shrugged. 'I just assumed somebody would tell.'

'Somebody *did* tell,' wailed Sophy. And the rigid finger pointed once more. 'She did.'

'Well,' said Iris, 'all this screaming and accusing isn't going to get us anywhere. What did the headmaster say he was going to do with you?'

'He's thinking of expelling me from school. He has to make an example of me, since you won't let him belt me. This is all your fault. You've ruined my life.'

'No. You wrote the verse.' And to Scott, 'And you skipped school and got that woman pregnant. You'll both take some responsibility for your actions. It is not all my fault.' She took a deep breath, and said, 'Well. This is not good. Not good at all. What are we to do?' She looked at Sophy and at Scott. 'You're not happy here, are you?'

They shook their heads. 'Hate it.'

'I rather like it, now. But I moved you both too soon after your dad died. Much too soon. What are we to do now?'

They looked at her. What to do? Neither of them knew.

'Well,' said Iris, 'I know one thing we're all going to do. Start communicating. There hasn't been a lot of that recently.'

Three days before the end of term the twins were cycling home. It was a balmy spring afternoon. Lambs in the fields. Jenny at the dammit shop swore she'd seen the first swallow. 'Daft bird,' she'd said. 'Frosts aren't over yet. You have to wait till May is out. It'll never make it to summer.'

The twins always raced one another up the road. Or they'd cycle in figures of eight, weaving in and out, crossing one another's path. Or they'd ride side by side, arms on each other's shoulders. They'd

317

whistle 'Please, Please Me' as they went. They heard the car coming, and stopped their side-by-side riding.

Stella was outside in the courtyard taking in her sheets. She had the first visitors of the season arriving tomorrow and had scrubbed out Lupin Cottage. Clean sheets, a vase of flowers as a welcome. She even had a few new gourmet meals in her freezer. The bookings were coming in for summer, and she was almost allowing herself to hope that things would work out. They wouldn't have to sell up, they'd make a go of this. She stopped, looked round. She thought she'd heard something.

Stephen had fallen back behind Simon, but hadn't made it quickly enough into the side of the road. The driver, seeing a long straight stretch ahead, put his foot down. All Simon heard was the roar of gunned engine, the clunk of bike being hit. The thick thud of Stephen hitting tarmac, head first. The soft groan as Stephen's breath left him. He looked back and saw his brother lying on the ground, and the spill of blackened blood oozing on to the road. That and a crumpled bike, back wheel still spinning. He turned as he saw the car disappear into the distance. He did not get the number, did not even see what make it was. He screamed.

It was the scream Stella heard. She did not stop to get the keys of the Land Rover. She just ran.

The Hush

A hush fell on the glen. A shocked silence. People spoke of the death of Stephen in whispers. A child, they said, just a child. There were hoarse enraged cries at the speed of cars, and the folly of drivers who saw a long straight road and just put their foot down. And if you were not safe on the road here, where were you safe?

Stella had sat at the roadside with her son for an hour and a half, waiting for an ambulance. She had sent Simon home to find his father and make the emergency call. The ambulance had finally wailed up the glen, siren reverberating through the hills. Everyone knew something had happened.

On Sunday they prayed for the Vernons in church. Iris went to the service and sat, hands folded in her lap, a hanky crushed in her left palm. In the face of tragedy, she could do nothing but cry. Three days later they buried Stephen in the churchyard.

Stella stood by the grave, drawn and white and pale. John held her arm, as if he feared she was going to jump into the ground to join her son. She looked up at the gathered mourners, and seemed to be trying to thank them for coming and to express her grief. Her lips moved, but no sound emerged. What could she say? What she was feeling was beyond words. But then, her face torn and wretched, said it all. Iris's heart went out to her.

They held a mournful wake in the village hall afterwards. Nobody laughed, everyone spoke in muted voices and left as soon as they could. This was too painful.

Next day Iris went up to see Stella and John. They sat with nothing to say. Stella looked at Iris. And Iris said, 'I know.'

Stella said, 'I know you know.'

'How's Simon?' asked Iris.

'In shock. He's hardly opened his mouth since it happened.'

'Takes time,' said Iris.

Stella said she knew, but didn't think she had as much time as it would take left in her life. Iris looked at John. 'Time,' she said again.

He said he knew. But some things never healed. 'They just become slightly less painful.' They sat, saying nothing. Iris felt her face tighten as if it had only one expression, that gaunt, grim look of worry and grief that had been hers for months and months after Harry died.

'We were thinking of selling up,' said John. Stella said they couldn't possibly go on. They couldn't leave this place. 'Stephen's here.'

Iris thought to say she was thinking of leaving Green Cairns. Her children were miserable here. Teenagers needed more than a fabulous view and cheery voices saying, 'Hello,' in the morning. But no, she would not mention this now. She hadn't come to unload her own problems. So she reached out, took John's hand, and Stella's, and said that if there was anything she could do. Though she knew there wasn't.

When she got home, Chas was there. It was Saturday, and they had a dancing date.

'I don't feel like it,' said Iris.

'Didn't think you would. Don't feel like it either.'

They agreed to go for a walk instead. And Iris went upstairs to tell Sophy where she was going. It was oddly quiet. No music pouring out. Scott had gone to round up the hens, but there was usually a dirge humming in Sophy's room. Iris went in.

It was dark, curtains drawn. Sophy was lying on the floor surrounded by candles, arms folded across her chest, pennies on her eyes.

Her stillness alarmed Iris. 'What the hell are you doing?'

'Death,' said Sophy, 'I'm waiting for death.'

'Well, let's hope you've got a long wait. Be thankful you're alive. This is terrible, Sophy.'

'I want to know what it's like to die. One day it will happen to me.'

'One day,' said Iris, 'it will happen to me. But for the moment, I don't know what it's like. And I don't think I want to know.'

'You don't know anything,' said Sophy. She still lay rigid.

Iris went over and removed the pennies from her daughter's eyes. 'You're right, I don't know anything. The older I get, the more I don't know. But at least I know that there's a lot I don't know. The difference with you is, you're so young you don't even know what it is you're ignorant about.'

Sophy said, 'Eh?'

Iris said that she knew what was meant. 'You'll never know about death,' she said. 'Because one of the things you learn is that there is more to everything than you think. Once when I was little we went out on a boat. My mother told me to put on a warm jersey because it would be cold. It was more than cold. It numbed me to the bone being on that boat. I hadn't known cold could do that.

'I used to think giving birth was painful. Then I gave birth. It was more than painful, it was excruciating. But I forgot all about it when I saw you. I was filled with wonder and joy.

'I used to think that when someone died, you grieved. But it's more than grief. Everything changes. You live in a hollow and numb yourself because you know you can take no more. Thing is, you get by. Because you have to, you're alive. You're alive, Sophy. Be glad.

'I used to think I could protect you and Scott from life. But I can't. I can only help. Or at least, I like to think I can. Now, put those candles out, pull the curtains, put on happy music and start trying to be happy. I am going out for a walk with Chas.'

They walked down the track to the Lynnes' cottage. Iris told Chas that she didn't know what she was going to do about her children.

'They're fine,' said Chas.

'Fine? Sophy's up in her room playing at being dead and Scott got kicked out of school. He hasn't sat any of his exams. *And* he got the Lynne woman pregnant. That is hardly fine.'

'Scott and the Lynne woman? I don't think so. She was down at the doctor's getting tests before you even arrived. He may have slept with her, but he didn't put her in the family way. Her man did that himself.'

'How do you know that?'

'Small place, people talk. My sister is receptionist at the surgery.'

Iris said, 'Oh, my God, I've been a fool! I wrote to Emily offering to help with the upkeep of the baby.'

'That was very kind of you. No need, I'm sure.'

'The relief,' she said, putting her hand on her heart. 'Oh, the relief.' They walked on a few slow paces and Iris said, 'Damn, I was quite looking forward to having a little one about the house.'

At the cottage, Scott was putting the hens into their coop. Chas saw the cockerel, and knew where it had come from. He thought that Iris's problems with her son were not quite over yet but didn't mention it.

Home Again, Home Again, Jiggedy Jig

At the start of the summer term, Simon was back in class. He sat quietly at his desk, did his work diligently, joined in discussions. But there was no denying there was a new quietness about him. If he wanted to sit alone in the reading corner, Iris let him. Still, she admired the resilience of children. He still cycled to school. In fact, had taken a tantrum when Stella had refused to let him. At first, she had crawled behind him in the Land Rover, keeping him in sight all the way. But, in time, she let him go. The boy seemed to need to be on that road. This puzzled Stella. She'd have thought it would have scared him, that he would have avoided the scene of his loss. There was no doubt his missed his brother.

Stella would sometimes see him standing alone outside, hands in pockets, looking dejected. She would try to pull him into doing something, anything. 'Do you want to go to the pictures in Forham, Simon?' Or, 'Do you want a game of ping-pong, Simon?'

The child would shake his head, say, 'Nah,' and disappear into himself again. Stella never knew if she should bully him out of his withdrawal, help him forget his loss. Or let him be, let him come to himself. Sometimes she did one thing, sometimes the other.

What she couldn't understand was Simon's eagerness to cycle alone down the road. The only times he seemed really alive, like his old self, were when he was setting off in the morning, and in the afternoon immediately after he returned home. Stella had thought he would find the ride to school without his brother upsetting. Instead, he seemed to find it almost exhilarating.

Iris decided to end her first year at Green Cairns school with a panto. A summer panto, she thought, and every child will have a part. She set about writing one in the evenings, chipping slowly at an old Olivetti with two determined fingers. She called it *Swimderella: A Water Panto On Dry Land*. She thought this very clever. There would be three ugly mersisters, a merprince, and Colin would play Buttons.

Scott had been accepted at his adult education college, and was due to start in September. He seemed cheered by the news. Sophy, meantime, as far as Iris knew, had stopped playing her death game. In the end, she wasn't expelled from school but was, instead, doomed to pick up litter for a term. Litter in the morning, litter at lunchtime, and litter at three-thirty, after school broke up. Chocolate wrappers, drinks cans, chewing gum, crisp bags, sneaky cigarette ends, and once, last week, to her horror, a used condom. It had been dropped in the playground, just outside the lavatories, by the sixth-year boys, who hung around to smirk as with two disdainful fingers, enclosed in the rubber glove Iris had provided, Sophy picked it up.

'Do you know what I had to pick up, today?' she demanded of Iris. Iris shook her head.

'A thing,' said Sophy. 'A bloody thing.'

'I imagine you have to pick up many things,' said Iris.

'No,' said Sophy. 'This was a *thing*. You know, that men use.'

'Good heavens,' said Iris. 'A condom? Surely not. It hadn't been used, had it?'

'As it turns out, no, it hadn't. But it was still disgusting. I hate it. And I hate people, the whole human race is revolting.'

Sensing an outburst coming on, and feeling unable to cope, Iris agreed. 'I expect it is.'

Sophy, feeling that her observation about the vileness of humanity was being dismissed, drove her point home. 'It is.'

Once she was unveiled as the author of the verse on the school wall, Sophy had experienced a surge in popularity. For months the only people at school who knew Sophy had written the verse were a few girls in her immediate circle of friends, and they had shunned her. But now everyone knew. Sophie became a hero, a rebel – a celebrity. But this attention was not the attention she sought. A small group of gossipy and boy-orientated girls seemed keen for her to join their ranks. Senior girls gazed at her, some with scorn, some in awe. Sophy found all this interest tiresome and embarrassing. She craved what she would never have, the respect of the members of the school orchestra.

Then more verses appeared. Ruder than Sophy's. The headmaster cursed, and knew he should have been more severe, he should have expelled the girl. Made an example of her. Now it was known that the only punishment for scrawling filth on the school wall was a spell of picking up litter. The Chisholm girl was a pest, her mother more than that. 'Damn them both,' he said.

Sophy relieved her tensions by playing her French horn. An abominable sound resounded through the house; Iris wrote her panto, trying to block it out. Saturdays she danced. Occasionally she ate curries with Michael, for their evenings together were fewer now.

Having sent off copies of the swimming certificates, Iris waited for her grand prize to arrive. She dreamed of spending the money, the equipment she would buy. After summer three pupils would move on to the high school, and only one would join her school. Numbers were going down. She found she was looking at her group of mums, hoping for a pregnancy. Lucy's mother had given birth to a boy not long after Christmas. That would be one in five years. If things went on like this, the school would close down. Evenings, sitting at her kitchen table writing her summer panto, Iris thought about this. And worried about Scott going off to Edinburgh on his own. And she worried about Sophy. The girl needs to get out more, Iris thought. But in a place like Green Cairns the only bright light was the telephone box. And she worried about Ruby. Months and months and they hadn't been in touch. Really, she should phone and ask her mother-in-law how she was getting on.

In the end, though, it was Ruby who turned up on Iris's doorstep one Saturday morning. She said she'd just thought she'd drop by. She was missing her grandchildren.

'How are they?' she asked.

Iris said they were fine.

'Been behaving themselves?'

Iris said, 'Of course.' And looked away. 'Scott is going to adult education college next year to top up his exam results. Get a better university place.'

'Good idea,' said Ruby.

'We think so. In fact, I was thinking of going with him.'

'To college? Surely you don't need to do that?'

'To Edinburgh. I was thinking of getting a job there, so he could live with us just until he's ready for university. I think a couple more years at home would be good for him. He'd be ready to strike out on his own after that. And there'd be more for Sophy to do, things are a bit limited here. I've been thinking about it.'

Ruby looked round and clenched her fists. She would like to set about this place with a cloth and a bottle of bleach, she thought. Get it scrubbed up. Ah, well, people had their own standards, not for her to interfere. 'Where will you live?'

'I'll have to find somewhere. I can't afford very much. In fact, I can hardly afford anything.'

'You'll be saying that it's Harry's fault.'

'I said nothing of the sort.' Though it was.

'I've been thinking, though. You're right, Harry did gamble away all that money. He always liked a flutter. And when I went to my Italian cookery classes, I used to see him, three o'clock in the afternoon, coming away from the bookie's. He never saw me. I never thought much about it. But then I did. And . . . he used to take money from my purse.'

'Good,' said Iris. 'Well, not good that he took money. That's awful. But good that you've been thinking about it.'

They sat, drank their coffee and said nothing.

'Your kitchen's needing a bit of a wipe,' said Ruby.

Iris laughed. 'So it does. I'll get to it.'

Chas passed the window on his way to his vegetable patch, knocked and waved to Iris.

'You'll miss him if you go,' said Ruby.

'I expect I will. He's good company. I will miss my school. I will miss a lot of people. I might even miss this dreadful, draughty old house. But I think Scott and Sophy are city kids.'

'Nice man, that gardener chap.' Ruby nodded to Chas, hoeing between his lines of cabbage and beetroot. 'Steady.'

Iris nodded.

'You'll not get your fresh vegetables if you go.' Ruby sounded aggrieved for her.

Iris laughed again. 'No, I don't expect I will.'

'Only . . .' said Ruby. She straightened her cup and saucer, put her palms on the table to either side of them. 'I've got money put by. It was for Scott and Sophy after I'm gone but you'll be needing it now. If I gave it to you, you could buy a house. Not a very big house. Maybe even a flat.' In Ruby's opinion a flat was not a proper place to live. A house should be a bungalow, on one floor, surrounded by garden and with a proper drive where a person could leave their car. 'But I've been thinking, you wouldn't tell me all that about Harry if it wasn't true. And you wouldn't have brought the children away out here if you hadn't had to.'

Iris nodded.

Ruby fished in her bag, pushed a cheque across the table, noticing the crumbs as she did so. 'Here then. I think the Chisholms owe you.'

Iris looked at it, and looked at Ruby. And said nothing.

Ruby squirmed. 'You can tear it up if you want to. But there it is. The offer's there.'

Iris looked at her again. She knew, given the amount of money she was being offered, she should be the embarrassed one. But she wasn't. It was Ruby who was hot under the collar. Iris took the cheque. She wanted to hug Ruby, but knew Ruby never did like any kind of heated response to anything. She said, 'Thank you.'

That night she wrote a letter of resignation. She didn't have another job, and she had nowhere to live in Edinburgh. But it would take time to find someone to replace her. It was done. She was leaving.

It was May. Swallows returned to nest in the eaves of the schoolhouse. Mornings, Iris could hear their teasing chatter. The deer that all winter had slowly roamed the field behind the house moved back into the hills. The world turned green. The vegetable patch flourished. And Iris got a letter from Emily Lynne.

Dear Mrs Chisholm,

I know I ought to call you Iris, but it doesn't seem right. You were Gracie's teacher after all. I am deeply touched by your offer to help with the new baby. It's a boy. But it isn't Scott's, it's Jake's.

I know, thought Iris. Still relieved. And still a little disappointed, a little one would have been lovely.

Jake has been to see him. He wanted to call him Rimbaud, but I put my foot down. He is Jason Scott Lynne. I thought to give him the middle name after your Scott, who was so kind to me.

I am returning to my studies as soon as the baby is old enough. My mother is going to help look after him. I hope to become a teacher like you. And if my son turns out to be as considerate and loving as yours, I'll know I've been a good mother to him.

Yours, Emily Lynne.

Iris showed the letter to Scott. 'Somebody thinks well of you,' she said.

'She called her boy after me, cool,' said Scott, thinking of the food he'd taken to her, and of trials undergone while stealing a cockerel. Thank God Emily hadn't mentioned it. 'That's for all I did for her.'

'What did you do for her?' Iris wanted to know. 'Apart from giving her my food.'

Scott shrugged. 'Nothing.' He left the room. Some things you didn't tell your mother. In fact, a great many things you didn't tell your mother.

A week later, when Scott went down to feed the hens, and gather the eggs that were keeping the Chisholm household in omelettes, Jake emerged from the cottage, blinking in the sunlight.

'Hey, man,' he said.

Scott said, 'Hey.' And offered Jake some eggs.

He nodded and took them. 'Cool.' He stood watching Scott sweep out the hen coop. 'Want to hit Forham tonight?'

'Nah,' said Scott. 'Given up all that.'

'C'mon,' said Jake. 'It'll be fine. We'll go to the pub. Drink a little. Hang out.'

He was so relaxed, so friendly, Scott thought that perhaps he knew about him and Emily. Perhaps he really did believe in peace and love and no jealousy. So he agreed to go. They would do the Forham run. They would start at the far end of town, having a drink in every pub till they reached the other end, then back again.

They left just after seven. Jake had a pile of spliffs made up and ready for the evening. They smoked. Listened to Radio One. The world was theirs tonight. They walked slowly, only slightly stoned, into the first pub, the West End Bar, but found it hard to get served.

'Girls shouldn't go into pubs alone,' said someone, flicking Scott's hair. Someone else called them filthy hippies. It wasn't turning into a fun night.

Jake said, 'Fuck this. Let's go to the Deer and Thistle. They'll serve us there.'

'Yeah,' said Scott. 'Let's go where people know the people beneath the hair.'

Jake thought that a cool thing to say. So that's where they went. Michael was there, in his seat, eating a curry. And when he saw Jake and Scott, he waved them to join him.

It was a Wednesday, the pub was quiet. Not smoky, boozy and humming as it usually was. But music was playing, and there were enough drinkers to make what Michael called a mingling.

'A mingling of party people,' he said to Jake. 'Enough for a bit of the crack.'

Jake agreed, introduced Scott. Though he'd introduced him before, only this time he mentioned who Scott was.

'So, you're Iris's boy.' Michael looked from Scott to Jake, beaming approval. 'This is nice, the two of you together. I like that sort of thing. Very liberal. Is this your hippy way, then? Sharing your women. No jealousy. Peace and love, as they say.' He'd had a little too much to drink. Not enough to slur his words, but enough to mar his judgment.

Jake asked what the hell Michael was talking about. Scott felt his stomach crawl with nerves. He froze, drink halfway to his lips.

'I mean, there's you and Scott getting along so well. And him being the father of your lady-friend's baby.'

And then the night went black.

All heads in the room turned. Scott put down his drink, raised his hands in apology and to protect himself from any onslaught. 'I'm not, I'm not. It's your kid.'

Michael looked at them and said, 'I thought you knew.'

The words filtered into Jake's consciousness. Most of the evening he'd been floating. There'd been the beer, and he'd been smoking dope all day. He'd been on a very dreamy cloud all evening; even the jibes in the pubs – girls, filthy hippy scum – had wafted past him. This didn't. The words seemed to hit him in the middle of his forehead, then they worked their way through layers of chemicals and eventually reached his brain. It took a few minutes for he wasn't quite able to absorb the shock at first, wasn't quite able to come out of his dream-state.

Then his face twisted with pain, rage, grief. He looked at Scott who saw murder in his eyes, and scraped his own chair back several feet. The room seemed to slip into slow motion. Jake lifted a chair and held it high, ready to smash it on to Scott. He put his hands over his head. Michael took a step towards Jake to stop him. Others started to move in on him. And Jake, unable to bring this heavy wooden weapon down on Scott, hurled it through the window, and stormed out of the pub.

Scott ran after him. 'It isn't true! It isn't mine, it's yours. We found out.'

From behind the bar, the publican shouted, 'Hey, you'll pay for that.'

Michael reached into his jacket for his wallet. 'No, I think I should. I've just said one of the stupidest things I've ever said in my life. I assumed Jake knew.'

Scott stumbled up the street after Jake's van, watched it disappear round the corner then started for home on foot. He could not face the shame and embarrassment of going back to the pub. Besides, right now, the mood he was in, a long walk on a soft spring night seemed like a good idea.

He was three miles out of Forham when Michael drew up beside him. 'Get in. I owe you a lift at least.'

Scott got into the car.

Michael drove. 'Did you know, I can do this road with my eyes shut? Did it with your mother once. Scared the wits out of her. Do it all the time now.'

Scott wasn't too pleased about that but said nothing. He sat looking out of the window. It was only when they swung wide round a corner that he looked over and saw Michael had his eyes shut. He started to scream. 'Open your fucking eyes, man!'

'Don't need to,' said Michael. 'I can do this road blindfold. Really, I can.'

Scott took hold of the handbrake, and yanked it up. He had no idea it would have the effect it did. He thought it would just stop the car. But they spun round and round till they were facing in the opposite direction.

Scott had smoked too much and drunk too much to cope with this coolly. He took Michael by the collar and screamed at him, 'Don't fucking play with me! Open your fucking eyes when you have me in the car. You're a fucking idiot, do you know that?' And he got out. 'I'll walk,' he said, slamming the car door shut. And as Michael drove away, shouted, 'And you stay out of my mother's life.'

He walked the rest of the way home. Got in at half-past ten.

'You're early,' said Iris, tapping at her Olivetti.

'Yeah,' said Scott. He put on the kettle. 'How's the play going?'

'Fine,' said Iris. 'Make me a cup, will you?'

'Yeah,' said Scott. He sat opposite her. 'You see that Michael?'

'Yes.'

'I don't want you going out with him again,' said Scott. 'He's screwed up. And I don't like to think of you going in his car.'

Iris stopped typing. 'Why not?'

'He drives with his eyes shut. He's nuts.'

'He just thinks he knows the road so well he doesn't have to look at it.' She returned to her typing. Plick, plick, plick. And looked up. 'How did you know that anyway?'

'He drove me home.'

'I thought you went out with Jake?'

'Yeah. But I came home with Michael.'

Iris sat back, arms folded. 'Tell me about it.'

He told her his evening. She told him he was too young to go into pubs.

He shrugged. 'Everybody does it. Didn't you?'

'That's by the by,' she said crisply.

'Will you go and see Jake and tell him the baby isn't mine?'

Iris thought about this. 'No. I think that's for you to do.'

Next morning at hen-feeding time Scott went in to talk to Jake. The cottage door was open, had been all night, and Jake was sitting in the kitchen staring at the floor, watching the long silver threads that trailed across it. Reminders of their visit from slugs that had crept in while he slept. He was mesmerised. 'Look at them. They're amazing.'

Scott supposed that they were, when you thought about it.

They sat in silence. Till Scott said, 'It's your baby.'

Jake nodded.

'You know that?' said Scott.

Jake nodded again. 'I phoned her last night when I got back and asked if it was yours. She told me no. But you were sleeping with her.'

'She was lonely,' said Scott. 'Why did she just go like that?'

'She didn't want to be here alone again. She didn't want to stay here in this house with no doors. She says it's draughty.'

'Why did you take down all the doors?'

'For the community. We were all going to live here. No doors, nothing shut. Everything open. No secrets. No jealousy.'

'What community?' asked Scott.

'The community that didn't come. Least, some of them came but they went away again. There was only me and Emily and Gracie left.'

Scott nodded.

'Also,' said Jake, 'she wanted a decent hot bath.'

Scott nodded. 'Women like things like that.'

Jake nodded.

'Aren't you jealous, about me and Emily?' Scott wanted to know.

Jake nodded, still watching the silver trails on the floor. 'I'm gutted.'

That was all he said. When Scott went back that night, Jake was gone. Scott never saw him, or Emily, again.

Last Days

For weeks Iris rehearsed her panto, at first in school, then as the big day approached in the village hall. It went well some days, and horribly wrong on others. James had been cast as the Prince, but had in recent months turned truculence into an art form. He would walk on to the stage, wait for several minute before delivering his lines, and when he did, they came out in a long, lifeless monotone. He chewed gum constantly.

Iris asked him if he'd rather help backstage. And when he said he would, recast Billy Ramsay in the part. Billy was several inches smaller than Swimderella, and did have an unfortunate nose which made him not at all prince-like. Then again he could sing and had no problems kissing the heroine, though the heroine had problems kissing him. Fiona Wilkinson played the female lead with such dramatic histrionics, Iris thought the girl would surely end up on the stage professionally. She had already complained to Iris that her leading man wasn't good-looking, and she had tried to wriggle out of a duet with him because Billy was the better singer. At one point, the girl had put her hand on her forehead and declared, 'How can I act when there is so much noise in here? People thundering around moving stuff. I need silence.'

Iris had said, 'She's eleven. God help us all when she gets to thirteen. And let's all be grateful we won't know her when she's thirty.'

It didn't really bother Iris, though. She knew the star of the show would be Colin. Not that he could really act. Indeed, he didn't have many lines and Iris was worried he might dry up, suddenly, decide to go silent again. But he was just delighted to be part of what was going on. So every time he did say something, he'd turn to the audience, and grin, and bow.

The panto was now called *Swimderella and the Glass Flipper*. The flipper was to be made from cake icing by Stella, and eaten in the very last act. Iris was longing for that last act, the last curtain. Then it would be over, her last duty as the Missie. She felt some sorrow at that as well. It was dawning on her that she would really miss these children.

Three days before the big production, she was sitting in the kitchen, feet up on the chair opposite, sipping a gin and tonic. Chas was making soup. Which was, he told her, his speciality. 'Carrot,' he said.

Not that he'd planned to make soup for Iris. He'd been working in the garden, come in to wash his hands. Put some fresh vegetables on to her draining board, and then started peeling them.

Sophy had found him chopping them. 'What are you doing?'

'Making soup for your mother.'

'Men don't do that,' said Sophy. 'Men don't make soup.'

'Really?' said Chas. 'I always thought they did. Some of the finest cooks ever, in fact most of the finest cooks ever, have been men.'

Sophy hadn't replied to this, but had stamped upstairs to the bathroom where Iris was soaking in the bath, banged on the door and said that her gardening chap was in the kitchen making soup.

'Excellent,' said Iris. 'If I stay in here long enough, perhaps he'll do a main course and pudding as well.'

So now she sat, freshly bathed, watching. 'You can make soup *and* tie your laces,' she said. 'Perhaps I shouldn't bother waiting for Colin to grow up, and marry you instead.'

'Anytime,' said Chas. He was joking. And not joking.

'Nah,' said Iris. 'I've done that once. Never again. Actually, Harry and I were very happy for about fifteen or so years.'

'Then what happened?' said Chas.

'Then we met,' said Iris. And laughed at her own pathetic joke. 'That's not bad. Perhaps I'll write it into the show. Actually, we did have quite a few good years, Harry and me.'

The doorbell rang. Neither of them made any move to answer it.

'It's your house,' said Chas. 'I'm making soup. You don't expect me to answer the door as well, do you?'

'Nobody asked you to make soup. I just came downstairs and there you were at the kitchen sink.'

'I had nothing else to do. I worked on the vegetable patch. Came in to wash my hands. Saw all them dirty dishes. Washed them for you. Then I remembered the first of the carrots were ready and thought I'd do you soup. I didn't plan it, it all just happened.'

The bell rang again. Iris went to open the door. The man standing before her was small and thick-necked, wearing a tweed cap, and oddly familiar. Iris was so absorbed in trying to remember where she had seen him before, she forgot to say 'Hello' or 'What can I do for you?' She stared, rummaging through her brain trying to place the red, weathered, and rather angry face that confronted her.

He broke the silence, leaned forward, poked her in the shoulder and said, 'You stole my cockerel.'

It was so absurd, Iris laughed. 'Me? I don't think so.'

'It's down at that empty cottage them hippy people were living in, and your boy is feeding it and taking the eggs. It must be you.'

Iris realised who this was. Months and months ago, she'd met him on the path by the river when she was walking the dog. He'd been walking, too. Had a very small dog on a long lead, and had looked her up and down and accused her of being young. She had said that she'd get over it. Then shouted the afterthought, 'You obviously did.' She had felt at the time she shouldn't have done it, there would be repercussions. 'I didn't steal your cockerel,' she said. 'I have no idea how it got to the Lynnes' cottage.'

'Well, it was either you or your boy,' he said.

Chas came to the door, wiping his hands on a dishtowel that had a recipe for lasagna printed on it. 'What's all this?' he said.

Hugh Stone, of the stolen cockerel, pointed to Iris. 'She stole my cockerel. Her or her boy.'

'I don't think so,' said Chas. 'Look, why don't you just go down to the cottage and take it, and forget all about it?'

'I'm fetching the police. I'm going to get to the bottom of this.'

Chas took him to the garden gate where they could negotiate without Iris interfering. After a few minutes of heated debate they parted, nodding though not smiling. Chas returned to the house, went into the kitchen, and got on with his soup-making.

'Well?' said Iris, coming after him.

'He's agreed not to go to the police. He's decided it was Emily Lynne who stole his cockerel, and he's agreed to take all the hens as compensation. OK?'

'They're not your hens to give away.'

'They're not yours either, though you've been eating the eggs.'

'I know I've been eating the Lynnes' eggs. They're not here, to eat them. Besides, Emily ate my lamb chops – fair exchange!'

'Are you going to take the hens to Edinburgh?' Chas asked.

'No.'

'Well, drink your drink and shut up.'

Iris had a new job to go to: deputy head of a country school just outside Edinburgh. The headmistress was a year from retirement. Iris had her eye on the job. She had also used Ruby's money to buy a ground-floor flat in Portobello. It looked over the sea, and had a small garden at the back. Scott and Sophy had both seen it, and selected their rooms. Sophy was enrolled at a new school.

'I don't want to go now,' said Iris. 'I've come to like it here. I like running my own school, being my own boss, making my own decisions. It suits me.'

'Stay, then,' said Chas.

'I can't. There's a new Missie coming for the next term. Same age as me, younger actually, she's thirty-eight. Got three children and a husband. Her children will go to the school, which will be good for the numbers.'

'Thirty-eight,' said Chas. 'Same age as me.'

'You're younger than me? I didn't know that,' said Iris. 'That's not very nice of you.'

On the day before term ended, the day of the show, Iris received a letter from the Lunan Lemonade Company congratulating her on a splendid effort. Green Cairns had, indeed, been the only school in the country to have a hundred percent of its pupils pass the elementary swimming certificate. However, many other schools had a great many more passes. It was therefore felt fairest that another much bigger school with three hundred children who'd gained the certificate should win. The money was being sent there. Meantime, they hoped she would accept the consolation prize of four cases of fizzy drinks and half a dozen plastic footballs.

'I will not accept that,' said Iris. 'How dare they? I won fair and square.'

Scott told her not to fuss. Her time at Green Cairns was over. 'Let it go,' he said.

Iris snorted about the unfairness of life, and the direness of huge companies. And left. Today was panto day.

It went well. Fiona only took one tantrum, and Iris thought that as leading lady she deserved an outburst. Colin didn't dry up but safely delivered his lines, and turned to grin at the crowd every time. The ugly mermaids sang 'Get Off Of My Cloud'. In one scene, several pupils were dressed as pink flamingoes. Using painted hockey sticks as long necks, they sang 'Pretty Flamingo'. There were jokes about Mental Dental and the dammit shop. At the end, when the glass flipper fitted Swimderella's foot, Billy sang 'I Wanna Hold Your Hand', and stole the show. Fiona flounced. The Reverend Woodman was in the front row. And, when the Prince and Swimderella discovered the glass flipper was made of sugar, they ate it together. The final curtain dropped. It was an old sheet cut in the shape of a huge pair of bloomers.

He presented the swimming certificates, and Lucy presented Iris with an engraved crystal vase. It had a wide fluted rim and a flat bottom. She was tempted to put it on her head, pretending it was a top hat, but demurred. Perhaps not, she thought.

The moon was huge, the air scented with honeysuckle. Child flamingoes, a prince, a princess and Buttons ran out into the night, high on laughter and applause. Iris watched them go. She would always remember them that way.

Colin's grandmother came to her. 'I want to thank you,' she said. 'Nobody in this family has ever got a certificate for anything. It's grand.'

Iris said that it was nothing really.

'Well, when all's said and done we can say one thing: at least you taught them to swim.'

Iris nodded. She thought she'd done a lot more than that. 'It was fun,' she said. In the end, nobody but she minded that they hadn't won the competition. In fact, they all seemed delighted with free fizzy drinks and a few plastic footballs.

Two weeks later they were packed and ready to leave. Iris, with Scott's help, squeezed the goat into the back of her car and drove it up to Michael's house.

'I've brought you a goat,' she said.

'What makes you think I want a goat?'

'You seem to know all about them. Don't let it just eat grass, it'll swell up and explode,' she told him.

'I think I told you that.' He looked at it. 'Nice-looking thing, though. How do you think it'd taste curried?'

'Don't you dare,' she said. Kissed his cheek, and told him she hoped to see him sometime. But doubted she would. He never left this place. He loved it too much. 'And stop driving with your eyes shut. You need to drive carefully. Look what happened to Stephen.'

'It's lovely driving with your eyes shut. All the senses tingling,' he said. 'I hope you're not thinking it was my car hit Stephen. I told you I know this place, every inch of it. Everything that goes on. I wouldn't be driving blind when there were kids about.'

'I know. And thank you for all the curries and the chat. I don't know if I'll see you again. But if I'm ever round this way, and you see me, please wave.'

'Ah, Iris,' he said, 'I'll be thinking of you often. And every time I think of you, I'll wave.'

She smiled. Scott, at her side, snorted. He considered Michael to be too grandiose, over-the-top, a verbal show-off. He didn't like him. In fact, he hated him and the way he drove. He thought it arrogant, crazily careless. It vexed him that his mother had sat beside Michael, in that car, Michael's eyes shut, speeding along narrow, twisting roads. Something could have happened to her. He'd already lost one parent, deep within him was the very private dread he might lose another.

They got back into the car, and drove to see Stella and John.

'Just a quick call to say goodbye,' said Iris.

Stella was in the kitchen, at the table, slowly turning the pages of a newspaper. Glancing at her briefly, through the window, it was plain to Iris that she wasn't reading any of the pages in front of her but gazing at the words while occupying herself with her own thoughts. Her face, in the short time since Stephen died, had grown thin. Her eyes had deepened into pools of sorrow. Always, now, when she and Iris met, there was before the laughter the most fleeting of moments when they looked at each other, exchanged sympathy, mutual knowledge of grief.

'Just dropped in to say goodbye,' said Iris.

Stella switched into bustling, rose from the table, put on the kettle. 'You'll never just drop by, you'll have a cup of something.' She knocked on the window to tell John they had visitors. He joined them round the table.

'Busy?' asked Iris.

'Not bad,' he said. 'Not bad at all. We've got bookings for most of the summer, and old Binnie's not daring to block the track these days. Not after Stephen.'

They fell silent. What to say to that? They drank their tea.

'I just wanted to say goodbye,' said Iris. 'We're off this afternoon.'

'Goodbye?' said Stella. 'This is never goodbye. This is just see-ya-later. Now we've got you in our lives we're not letting go. We'll be down to see you, check out your new house and report back to the dammit shop. They'll be needing to know all about you.'

On the way back down the glen, they saw Simon Vernon out cycling.

'They never did find who drove that car that killed Stephen, did they?' said Scott.

Iris shook her head. She tooted and waved to the boy. But he didn't notice. He was lost in some world of his own. Turning to talk to someone who wasn't there, he cycled figures of eight and reached out as if to touch someone, put his arm on some invisible shoulder. He smiled and grinned to the other person, his hair swept by the wind, his cheeks red. This was what he did, every time he came to this bit of road, he cycled with his brother. 'Oh,' said Iris. 'We all thought he was getting better, but he's dancing with Stephen's ghost.'

'I know,' said Scott. 'He'll probably do that all his life. He'll come here and be with his brother.'

Iris rounded the corner. Stopped the car and cried, 'I thought I could help him. I thought I could make it better.'

Scott said, 'You can't. You can't do everything. Who do you think you are, God?'

Iris sniffed, blew her nose. 'Now you're getting it.'

They were hurtling towards Edinburgh, Sophy in the front of the car beside Iris, Scott sprawled in the back with the dog and the cat basket.

Iris said, 'Weirdest thing happened the other day. That Hugh Stone man came to the door and accused me, or you, Scott, of stealing a cockerel. Bizarre.'

Scott said nothing. Sophy turned and gave him a look.

'I mean,' Iris went on, 'what would I be doing with a cockerel? It was down at the Lynnes' place. It must have been one of them. How on earth would you get all the way down to his farm and back in the middle of the night, Scott? I don't know.'

Scott thought he'd wait to tell her. Maybe when he was twenty-five, when he'd finished university and had a job. Then again, maybe when he was fifty.

They arrived in Edinburgh at two in the afternoon. By five the removal men had left. Iris, Sophy and Scott stood surrounded by packing cases, boxes, plants. The cat ran off to find a safe hiding place where he could recover from the shock of being uprooted from his rural life. The dog sat at Iris's feet. She was in her new kitchen, at the table. In front of her the ancient Olivetti.

'Sophy,' she said, 'make up your bed. Scott, find some cups and the kettle and make some tea.' She rolled a sheet of paper into the machine.

Dear Sirs,
I am writing to convey my utter disgust at your treatment of Green Cairns

School. We were the only people to gain a one hundred percent passrate in the elementary swimming certificate, and on examining the entry form and the invitation to compete I see nothing in the small print that says the number of pupils makes any difference.

I intend to take this matter further. I will write to the press telling them of the unfairness of your decision. One hundred percent, you said. My pupils passed, one hundred percent. My children . . .

She stopped. Her children. They were lovely. She would always remember them: Lucy who stammered, Fiona the drama queen, James the silent and moody one, silent and moody yet, Simon and his lost twin, Billy Ramsay who could sing. They'd be there now, where the hills towered silent, huge, purpling in the distance, and all that green rolling between the tiny cluster of houses and where they started to shove into the sky. The muddy river that tumbled next to the path. The dammit shop where, dammit, everything cost twice as much as in town, but the crack was worth it. And Colin with his shiny face.

Just before she'd left, she'd seen him standing by his front gate, watching. He was wearing new jeans, stiffly new. Rolled up at the bottom because they were too long. She'd gone across to say goodbye.

'I'm off, Colin. You be good now, and look after your new Missie.'

Colin nodded, and Iris noticed his shoelace. He lifted his foot. She leant down to knot it.

'Now Colin, how can I marry you when you grow up, if you can't do your laces?'

He looked at her. 'I don't think I can marry you. When I grow up, you'll be old.'

'Oh, Colin, you've broken my heart.' She bent to whisper in his ear, 'I've taught a lot of boys and you're one of my favourites. You're a lovely person, Colin. Don't let anybody tell you different. Do well for me, promise?'

And Colin nodded. He would. In his new jeans he could go to Hollywood and be a star. He thought he could do anything.

I've Brought Your Veg

August. Harvest time. The days hot. Tractors clunking by. Chas is in the vegetable patch, the earth beneath his feet soft and black, his digging rhythmic.

He lays his crop in wooden boxes, in immaculate rows. Bulbs of garlic, long thick broad beans, onions, beetroot, cauliflowers, potatoes, white and waxy, underneath their papery brown skins. He puts it all into his car,

He will leave this place. Has before, if there was something worth going to. He knows her address, though he doesn't know his way about Edinburgh. Driving through the town, he notes all the houses. There are gutters needing cleared out. Behind those front doors will be rooms to paint, in front of them gardens to be tended. There's work here, he thinks. He imagines a small business, Charles Harper Handyman, no job too big or too small. I could get by, he thinks. I could live here.

He parks opposite her house. Recognises the curtains, and her car parked at the door. He rings her bell. Hears her coming up the hall. For a moment he worries. What if she doesn't want to see him? What if she thinks him foolish? What will he say to her? And what if she looks at him and says dismissively, 'What the hell are you doing here?'

She opens the door, and smiles. 'Chas. What are you doing here?' But this is not dismissive. It's warm. She is delighted. She has missed him – his comfortable face, his easy manner.

Chas says, 'I brought your veg. It was our deal.'